WEAPONIZED

By Neal Asher

Agent Cormac series
Gridlinked • The Line of Polity
Brass Man • Polity Agent • Line War

Spatterjay trilogy
The Skinner
The Voyage of the Sable Keech
Orbus

Standalone Polity novels
Prador Moon • Hilldiggers
Shadow of the Scorpion
The Technician • Jack Four • Weaponized

The Owner series
The Departure • Zero Point • Jupiter War

Transformation trilogy
Dark Intelligence • War Factory
Infinity Engine

Rise of the Jain trilogy
The Soldier • The Warship
The Human

Cowl

Novellas
The Parasite • Mindgames: Fool's Mate

Short-story collections
Runcible Tales • The Engineer
The Gabble

NEAL
ASHER
WEAPONIZED

TOR

First published 2022 by Tor
an imprint of Pan Macmillan
The Smithson, 6 Briset Street, London EC1M 5NR
EU representative: Macmillan Publishers Ireland Ltd, 1st Floor,
The Liffey Trust Centre, 117–126 Sheriff Street Upper,
Dublin 1, D01 YC43
Associated companies throughout the world
www.panmacmillan.com

ISBN 978-1-5290-5003-5

1 3 5 7 9 8 6 4 2

A CIP catalogue record for this book is available from the British Library.

Typeset in Plantin by Palimpsest Book Production Ltd, Falkirk, Stirlingshire
Printed and bound by CPI Group (UK) Ltd, Croydon, CR0 4YY

MIX
Paper from
responsible sources
FSC® C116313

Visit **www.panmacmillan.com** to read more about all our books
and to buy them. You will also find features, author interviews and
news of any author events, and you can sign up for e-newsletters
so that you're always first to hear about our new releases.

In this era of supposedly fake news and 'fact-checking' it's difficult to know where to find the truth. Certainly governments and corporations distort it to their own ends, often hand in hand with each other, while legacy media has become the home of almost laughable bias. It's therefore great the internet has allowed the rise of many independents: the citizen journalists, interviewers, podcasters and bloggers – the curious and the enthusiastic. Whether you believe them or not is immaterial, because nowadays we need to learn to distinguish fact from fiction, and that cannot occur with just one narrative that allows no competition.

I thank them.

Acknowledgements

Thanks to the staff at Pan Macmillan, and elsewhere, who have helped bring this novel to your e-reader, smartphone, computer screen and to that old-fashioned mass of wood pulp called a book. These include Bella Pagan (editor), Georgia Summers (assistant editor), Samantha Fletcher (desk editor), Neil Lang (jacket designer) and the Pan Mac marketing team; also free-lancers Claire Baldwin (editor), Jessica Cuthbert-Smith (copy-editor), Robert Clark (proofreader), Steve Stone (jacket illustrator) and Jamie-Lee Nardone (publicity); and others whose names I simply don't know.

I should further thank those publishing science articles on the internet (after excluding those partisan political articles that masquerade as science), which I read in the morning before getting to work. My reading technique is a bit 'throw it at the wall and see what sticks', but plenty does. This stuff sets my brain buzzing with ideas, while some simply surface later on and unexpectedly. All grist to the writing mill.

Glossary

Augmented: To be 'augmented' is to have taken advantage of one or more of the many available cybernetic devices, mechanical additions and, distinctly, cerebral augmentations. In the last case we have, of course, the ubiquitous 'aug' and such back-formations as 'auged', 'auging-in', and the execrable 'all auged up'. But it does not stop there: the word 'aug' has now become confused with auger and augur – which is understandable considering the way an aug connects and the information that then becomes available. So now you can 'auger' information from the AI net, and a prediction made by an aug prognostic subprogram can be called an augury.
                          – From 'Quince Guide' compiled by humans

First- and second-children: Male prador, chemically maintained in adolescence, enslaved by pheromones emitted by their fathers and acting as crew on their ships or as soldiers. Prador adults also use their surgically removed ganglions (brains) as navigational computers in their ships and to control war machines.

Hardfield: A flat force field capable of stopping missiles and energy beams. The impact or heat energy is transformed and dissipated by the hardfield projector. Overload of that projector usually results in its catastrophic breakdown, at which point it is ejected from the vessel containing it.

Hooders: The devolved descendants of Atheter biomech war machines. Creatures that look like giant centipedes, they retain some of their war machine past in that they are rugged, tough, vicious and very difficult to kill with conventional weapons.

Jain technology: A technology spanning all scientific disciplines, created by one of the dead races – the Jain. Its apparent sum purpose is to spread through civilizations and annihilate them.

Nanosuite: A suite of nanomachines most human beings have inside them. These self-propagating machines act as a secondary immune system, repairing and adjusting the body. Each suite can be altered to suit the individual and his or her circumstances.

Polity: A human/AI dominion extending across many star systems, occupying a spherical space spanning the thickness of the galaxy and centred on Earth. It is ruled over by the AIs who took control of human affairs in what has been called, because of its very low casualty rate, the Quiet War. The top AI is called Earth Central (EC) and resides in a building on the shore of Lake Geneva. Planetary AIs, lower down in the hierarchy, rule over other worlds. The Polity is a highly technical civilization but its weakness is its reliance on travel by 'runcible' – instantaneous matter transmission gates.

Prador: A highly xenophobic race of giant crablike aliens ruled by a king and his family. Hostility is implicit in their biology.

Runcible: Instantaneous matter transmission gates, allowing transportation through underspace.

U-space: Underspace is the continuum spaceships enter (or U-jump into), rather like submarines submerging, to travel faster than light. It is also the continuum that can be crossed by using runcible gates, making travel between worlds linked by such gates all but instantaneous.

1

Present

'No sign of the bastards,' said Callum, as they stood looking at the screen. It gave one of the last remaining views out across their ruined fields and exterior facilities, towards the dusty flats and rocky slabs of the Bled – the desert areas of Threpsis. Callum, Ursula noted, had begun fiddling with his bracelet. They itched underneath sometimes, but had bonded to the skin so the itch was impossible to scratch.

She looked down at her own – the devices were to initiate their 'new upgrade'. Hers seemed to have sunk into her wrist a little way, just as it had on the first recipient of one – the biologist Nursum. Around it the skin had the scaly, hard crystalline look she'd seen on him. Yet when she pressed a finger into the skin, it felt as soft as before, though maybe a little rough.

Ursula shrugged. 'They're smart, they're waiting and they know.'

Her certainty worried her. Sure, by their behaviour she had surmised that the cacoraptors, or simply raptors as they were now called, possessed intelligence, but her assurance went beyond that. It was almost as if she could feel them out there, their purpose and collective will. She shook her head. That made no sense, did it? She glanced at her bracelet again, remembering precisely what Oren had used in the upgrade. She shivered.

Callum glanced at her and said tiredly, 'If that's the case, according to the Polity proscription on colonization of worlds with sentient or pre-sentient life, we shouldn't be here anyway.' He snatched his hand away from his bracelet and shook himself. 'But then, with the danger they represent, we shouldn't be here, despite their intelligence.'

He suddenly didn't look tired any more. It was probably a further sign of the upgrade's effects. Ursula had been seeing subtle changes in those around her since they had all been given the bracelets – quicker movements and thought, fast recovery times, changes to their adaptations. Oren had told her that the changes were kicked off by surges of stress hormones, as had been the case with Nursum. The constant low-grade stress in here was almost acceptance.

She nodded. 'I rather think the Polity has things other than colony regulations to occupy it right now.' She shrugged. 'Anyway, when we came here we were breaking no laws. They weren't intelligent then. It's their most recent adaptation, of course – to get them to the plentiful food supply that we are.'

Callum grimaced then shook his head sharply, sending an iridescent ripple down his neck and across the metallic skin of his bare chest. 'I'll go and check on progress.' He turned away and headed off through the armoured complex of their base.

Ursula watched him go, damning herself for the comment since one item of what she had so casually called 'food supply' had been Callum's brother. They hadn't been close – his brother working on agriculture before their last retreat – but they had stacked up many years, some together, some not. All in the colony, Callum included, were very old and experienced, expert in many disciplines and mature beyond ancient iterations of that state.

Ursula returned her attention to the view, but the screen went out. A raptor had found the camera, even though it'd been the size of a pinhead, and destroyed it. Again this was something she *knew*, just as she knew they were burrowing under the base to try and get around those areas the colonists had blocked off. Another frightening possibility was what preparations the raptors might be making outside, for they knew about the prador assault craft which had landed on this world, and that their prey would try to get to it – she was sure. She closed her eyes for a second, trying to get some sense of it. Shadows seemed to flicker around her for a second, and she could hear a distant chittering – similar to what they heard over the electromagnetic spectrum, the EMR – from the raptors. But when she turned her perception towards this it fled. Damn it, no. This had to be due to the strange physical and mental changes of the upgrade, tiredness and stress, and what seemed to be a steadily growing paranoia. Aural and visual hallucinations weren't unexpected.

She sighed and stood up, weariness in her bones. This annoyed her because she had too much to do. After glancing down at her own bracelet again, she abruptly slapped her hands together hard and *pushed*. The weariness dissolved, as it had before, and she walked out of the viewing room and deeper into the colony's base; more shadows seemed to flicker around her as armoured doors closed behind. In the corridor she paused to view repairs to a wall. A raptor borer had come through here, emitting an acid that turned ceramal armour as frangible as burned bone. It had destroyed two mosquito autoguns before the mobile weapons eventually drove it away. She considered what might have happened had there been people close by, and just what the 'new upgrade' might have turned them into, and she pondered on what new nightmares this world might have in store.

The survey of Threpsis had shown an Earth-like world, its gravity at 1.2, its temperature a little above that of Earth, so apparently good living conditions could be found in the north and south, except when killing summer temperatures arrived, while a band of desert around the equator would cook an unprotected human. A normal human. Standard humanity, or rather the antique kind, would have died here, if not from the temperature changes then from the solar radiation on a world with such a weak magnetosphere. But humans had ceased to be 'normal' some centuries ago.

Ursula and her people, when they'd arrived from the Polity Line world of Kalonan, had prepared themselves. Oren Salazar, whose multiple qualifications sat under the title 'biophysicist', had modified state-of-the-art nanosuites for them – the masses of nanomachines that served as internal doctors and complementary immune systems – far in advance of the usual ones in the Polity. These new suites could respond rapidly to changes in the environment – giving Callum his radiation-resistant skin, giving Ursula kidney and liver organelles throughout her body. Others had different adaptations. All were what her fellow colonist Annette had described as extremophiles, creatures adapting radically to their environment, before something more extreme here had eaten her.

But with this 'new upgrade' they'd been given something more.

She continued along the corridor to where it terminated against another armoured door, palmed the control beside it and walked out onto a gantry over the inner chamber. Their main car sat down below her, along with a small grav-car they had aboard it. The huge vehicle was three hundred feet long and ran on adaptive wheels. The last of their grav-motors were inside the thing, but only capable of lifting it for short hops before they drained the super-capacitors. Two of their base's fusion reactors powered it and topped up the capacitors. These also supplied power for weapons and its new adaptive armour. They'd piled every last erg of power and every scrap of useful technology they could into this car, but it still might not be enough. It was their last chance to escape this place before the cacoraptors found some new way to penetrate. She gazed at the people working around it, her people. Three hundred and twenty of them remained out of the eight hundred who had originally come here. All of them had taken long strides away from standard humanity due to their special nanosuites and the pressures of staying alive here. And now they might be forced to go even further – anything to survive.

Ursula glanced at the bracelet again while remembering the first nightmarish retreat to base, their first encounter with a cacoraptor.

Near Past

Ursula gazed through her small armoured car's chain-glass screen at the land ahead. Yellow surface roots, poisonous to many forms of life here, had first spread from seeds which later produced the blue cycads now occupying the churned-up ground. After days of work clearing and cultivating this land, the infestation had established in less than a day, and the cycads were already putting up flower spikes, like inverted bunches of grapes. She peered over at where many of the cycads had been shredded down to ground level, for now brontopods had arrived.

The colonists had taken the dozer across this twenty-five acres of land, tearing up plants that fought back with mobile vines, poisoned spines, stings that shot out like those of a jellyfish, and sprays of enzyme acid. One plant had even deployed its biological flamethrower, others had tried to retreat into the ground or move out of the dozer's path. Even as the heavy machine had rumbled across, its ceramal armour smoking from acid and fire, other robots had trailed it on insect legs, selectively targeting any new shoots which appeared, hitting them with local toxins, laser, chemical flamer or ionic electrocution. Flying herbivores like pterodactyls, but with four wings and drill-like beaks which they used to suck the plant bodies dry, soon attacked the dozer-heaped debris. The dozer, after using its thermite jet to set an intense fire, fed that with oxygen until only a low heap of embered ash remained. They then sowed the field with further toxins in preparation for a crop of plants, adapted and genetically modified from local flora, they could actually eat, though poison for a 'normal' human of course. But they hadn't been quick enough.

The seeds had swept down in a wind from the mountains. They hit the soil and germinated explosively to spread their poisonous yellow webs to kill any rival flora, slammed down roots that grew with the speed of snakes, and began sucking nutrients to grow the cycads she saw now. Ursula engaged drive and rumbled her car closer, hearing the sounds of things pinging against its armour. Spines landed on the screen and slid down its almost frictionless surface, trailing blue globules. The toxin component of the spines' poison didn't affect humans in the same way it did local herbivores, but it did cause a massive allergic reaction that could kill. Before that its enzyme component would have done the job anyway – eating through human flesh like nitric acid.

'The dozer's got its work cut out,' said Chandar over radio from one of the other three cars accompanying her. 'At least we'll only need that and one toxin to kill this lot off.'

'There is that,' Ursula replied, 'though it'll be two days before Shaben layers new armour on the dozer.' She paused contemplatively. 'We need those brontopods gone. If they destroy enough cycads, other stuff will come in and we'll be back where we started.'

'Best we get on that, then,' Chandar opined.

Ursula checked her satellite feed. Previously, the outer fence, electrified and armed with other intermittent deterrents, had been enough to keep the animals out. But it seemed the new bloom of cycads had been impossible to resist and, hooting and clattering in pain, the brontopods had trampled the fence and broken into colony lands. They had spread out through this bounty of plants that were, in terms of this world, quite a vulnerable food source. But now, infrared showed them all gathered in one place. Ursula drove her car towards them through the cycads, the other three following, spines pinging off them all. Back at base they would have to put the cars through a deactivating wash, and Shaben would have more armour work to do, since the new adaptive armour wasn't ready yet.

Soon she could see them, the brontopods. These huge, heavily armoured herbivores walked on eight legs and sported heads with armoured shields, like those of a triceratops, and beaks that could shear through stone. They had joyfully tucked into the blue cycads while the spines bounced off their hides. Now, instead of steadily grazing, they had huddled with their head shields facing outwards. She checked heat signatures and saw something else moving between the cycads. The brontopods watched intensely, clacking their beaks and stamping clawed feet.

'Chester, I need more imagery on whatever that is.' She touched the screen with a hand gloved in the new biotech armour they were calling 'skin' and highlighted the signature. Glancing over through the small side window, she saw a turret on the top of Chester's car turn and disperse drones like Christmas baubles, which sped away through the air. Imagery immediately began to come in, automatically cleaned and sequenced for viewing. The first still image showed a thing almost like a heron standing ten feet tall. Its long muscular neck terminated in a dark head resembling a bird's skull, with white markings like a Rorschach blot running down its centre. Recognition software struggled with the creature for a moment, eventually coming up with 'unknown'. Video feed kicked in to show it loping, head down, between the cycads and rearing up at intervals to inspect the big herbivores.

'Predator, obviously,' said Chandar. 'But one we haven't seen before. Nasty-looking fucker.'

'You seen anything here that isn't nasty?' enquired Chester.

Annette chose this moment to interject, 'I guess it's a tendency for extremophiles to take on a less pleasing appearance.'

This was a dig at Chandar, whose adaptation to this world had resulted in insect mandibles on his face. He could have had them removed but chose not to. Ursula contemplated the word Annette had used.

All life on this world was extremophile, and that included the human colonists, but via a different course. Bio-archaeologists studying the Polity survey data had ascertained that in the far distant past life had evolved here much as it had on Earth. The planetary water had previously been in oceans and not in underground aquifers as now. Life had obtained sufficient complexity to produce megafauna and flora, but then, about five million years ago, the sun had changed. It had become more active, gradually. It almost seemed like intent, for it did not flood the planet with enough radiation to kill everything, but produced just sufficient to penetrate the weak magnetosphere and drive intense mutation. The evolutionary race had speeded up. Plants that had once just been fodder for herbivores evolved the gamut of defences, evidenced by the spines now sliding down Ursula's front screen. Concurrent with this, the herbivores developed their own defences and methods to access their food supply, but these changes also made them much more difficult prey for the predators, which of course also evolved. In short, everything stepped up a level in lethality, and the place was lacking in the soft and cuddly.

'We watch for now and stay wary,' she told the others. 'We've no idea what this thing can do.'

After studying the brontopods for a minute, the heron-thing probed the ground and found it still loose from cultivation. Stretching upright, it rippled down its length and its legs melded together. Then it looped over like a worm, sprouting paddle-like digging limbs, and speared its head downwards.

'What the fuck?' said Ursula.

'Fast body morphing there,' commented Chandar. No one else said anything.

The creature's course towards the herbivores was visible at first, then it disappeared like a shark diving. A moment later, one of the brontopods shrieked, and the others immediately fled, hurtling away from their stricken fellow.

'Chandar! Move your – damn!'

A brontopod crashed into the side of Chandar's car and tipped it on its side, scrabbling over it. The tons of heavy animal were too much for armour and chassis, always under constant repair, and the car distorted, popping out its front screen. Ursula swore and began to move her car over, but Chandar quickly rolled out through the screen and stood up. He wore their new 'skin' and, carrying a laser carbine, began trotting over to Annette's car, which was closest. He should be okay, she thought. The skin protected him from the poisonous spines, while all but one of the brontopods were heading for the horizon.

'Move it, Chandar,' she said.

'You tried running in this stuff yet?' he enquired.

She returned her attention to the remaining brontopod. Abruptly its screaming ceased and it slumped, puking chewed-up cycad. It looked dead and she was damned sure the movement she could see came from the thing inside it. While she watched, one of the armoured sections in the brontopod's side lifted to expose knotted red muscle, the worm-thing heaving this up as it nosed out of a hole issuing clear fluid. The section fell aside and more of the thing came out. It had gone through further transformations. Its limbs were now jointed hooks, doubtless perfect for tugging it through the flesh of its prey, and its head a nightmare creation of a wide slot mouth surrounded by buzz-saw mandibles, though it still retained the white markings she'd seen earlier.

'Very fast adaptation,' she noted to the others, trying to keep to the practical and the factual while she felt something creeping up her spine. That was scarily fast.

It rose up and paused. The head sprouted a stalk that swelled at the end and opened a double pupil eye, which turned towards Chandar. The creature flowed out of the corpse of its victim, its legs folding in and melding to leave only four, which rapidly grew fat with muscle and acquired feet that could not have been better designed for the loose ground and poisonous cycad web. Its body contracted and fattened too as it hit the churned soil, its tail deflating to a whip-like thing, in which vertebrae appeared visible. It now looked like some kind of nightmare hellhound, as it first began loping towards Chandar, then accelerated. Ursula just gaped, trying to get her mind in motion. They couldn't use the flamers they had mounted on the cars because of the danger of incinerating Chandar.

'Carbines now!' she shouted, hitting her belt release and grabbing up her own weapon. She quickly reached the door of her car and felt the usual reluctance to face what might be out there, but opened it and did step out. She initiated her helmet, its skin covering flowing into place and attaching around the edges of the chain-glass visor.

Chandar shouldered his carbine and opened fire on the creature hurtling towards him. He hit it once behind its head, burning a smoking hole. The thing halted, turning its head from side to side, and Chandar used the opportunity to run. The hole closed rapidly as a shot from Chester hit it again further down its body, but this time causing much less damage. Annette opened the door to her armoured car, stepped out and went down on one knee to fire her carbine. Even as the beam struck, a ripple of iridescence passed down the creature's body, which turned as reflective as mercury.

'Oh hell,' Ursula muttered.

She joined the others in firing at the creature, but the shots simply had no effect.

'Redirect at the ground around its feet!' Ursula bellowed.

The steam explosions and flying debris did slow it some, but Chandar paused before reaching Annette's car and fired again at close range. He should not have. His shots just raised black areas on its body – most of the energy reflected away – and the creature leaped and came down on him hard, slamming him to the ground. He tried to crawl but turned bloody in seconds as, just like a dog, it shook him. Someone was screaming . . . him? No, Ursula saw the thing rip his spine out, which must have killed him instantly. It began to shear away his limbs.

'Get inside, Annette!'

She continued screaming, backing away as the thing sucked in Chandar's limbs like spaghetti and, with its mandibles, began chopping up his torso. But then it dropped Chandar's remains and leaped towards Annette, driving her back in through the open door of the car. The screaming continued for a moment, until it morphed into other sounds. The creature's body rippled and pulsed as it swallowed.

'Back in your cars! Now!' Ursula ordered. 'We head for the base.'

★ ★ ★

Ursula felt sick and angry. The creature had simply not stopped coming after them as they fled in their armoured cars. Returning to the worm form, it had tried repeatedly to penetrate Chester's car in the same way it had the brontopod. After it bounced away with its head reforming, Chester hit it with the turret-mounted flamethrower he had on the roof and sent it writhing to the ground, allowing them to gain some miles on it. But it returned, dog form and asbestos white now, and attacked again, and again. Finally it seemed to find the required approach and, splaying its limbs to hold it in place, it attached its head end to Chester's car like a leech. Later analysis of the damage showed it had been grinding into the vehicle's armour with chains of diamond-hard teeth, lubricated with an acid that ate into the alloy while the teeth ablated the ceramic component. It had got two inches into three-inch thick armour by the time they came in sight of the base. A railgun, swiftly pulled out of storage and running on a hastily-prepared and dangerous program, scoured it from the car. Some projectiles slammed into the armour, breaking apart, and riddled one side of Chester's body with fragments. The railgun hits should have been enough to kill the creature but, even partially dismembered, it had collapsed away, worm-like again, then protruded paddle legs and burrowed into the ground. Ursula grimaced at that. The thing had not been destroyed.

It surfaced some distance from where it had escaped the railgun, and biologists at the base tracked it using the satellite. They saw it return to its earlier brontopod prey but, this being a world where a free lunch wasn't to be ignored, the scavengers and morticians had already arrived. Creatures like armoured hyenas, which bore some resemblance to the dog form the creature had taken, were tearing the corpse apart. Swarms of insects rose in clouds around them as they fed, and the remaining meat crawled with worms, bony hook-tailed nymphs resembling foetuses and the bright green threads of some fungus or plant. The creature reared out of the ground nearby and instantly split open one of the scavengers, feeding on it while the others fled, shrieking and hooting.

The biologists and ecologists, who of course were recording this feed, kept watching the creature – it was the most fascinating thing they'd seen in a while. They gave it the placeholder name 'raptor', then with the addition of a prefix, a cacoraptor. After feeding, and almost tripling its mass, it closed up its paddle legs and lay on the ground shivering and rippling until the shape of new limbs became etched on its surface and folded out. Retaining its birdlike head, its body returned to the earlier dog form, it set out fast. It circled the outer fence, keeping its distance from the deterrents. The satellite lost it when it returned to its worm form and disappeared into the ground.

That was just the beginning. Only days later, two armoured cars, collecting samples beyond the defensive perimeter, had been hit. Because the cars were so far from the base, they didn't have time to get in range of the base railgun. Two more colonists died, screaming in their vehicles, no remains were recovered, and the cars had to be abandoned because they were infested with other Threpsian life. It got worse when the raptors hit one of their outposts shortly after the two cars – there were no survivors. Then another facility was attacked and Ursula made the decision to send four of their grav-cars. They managed to get all except four of the colonists out, but one of the grav-cars crashed, severely injuring the occupants.

Twenty-eight people were now dead.

Ursula marched down the corridor and came to a halt at a door. She needed to be calm and precise. Oren Salazar's laboratory was about the largest research area in the base. Here he had created the rugged crop plants that could grow on Threpsis, and here he had also designed the tweaks to the colonists' nanosuites which enabled them to eat those crops. He constantly wanted samples of anything new found in the wilds of this world. As she entered his storage area to walk through to his laboratory, Ursula studied his collection and tried to shed her anger.

Many samples sat in sealed cylinders with monitoring equipment attached all around them. One wall consisted of hundreds of drawers filled with nanoscope capsules, each containing microscopic life. Another wall with larger drawers contained creatures, or samples of creatures, up to the size of a fist. Some, including plants, he had on display in chain-glass cases of various sizes. She paused by a case containing the head of a brontopod, sliced neatly from front to back with its internals exposed under a glossy film. She remembered a piece of ancient art on Earth, before the Quiet War and domination of the AIs. Another case contained one of the cycads, alive and well but its growth in some manner retarded. Further recognizable plants sat in a series of glass cylinders while a stand of flat glass cases that could be pulled out of a rack contained a huge range of mid-size life forms preserved in some fluid. She noted all the scanners and instruments directed at the cases and often penetrating them. Oren never stopped studying his collection. Like many of the colonists, he had adapted to function without sleep and never stopped working. And the latest sample they'd brought him had occupied his attention for the last two days and nights.

She finally entered the gleaming chaos of his main laboratory. Oren was studying screen views projected from a nanoscope, at present poised over a long glass cylinder, its business end inserted through a hole. Ursula noted the caps at each end of the cylinder, with pipes attached, ready to run oxygen through the bunches of iron nanorods they contained. These were iron-burners which, should they be initiated, would burn to ash the contents of the cylinder. She nodded approval at this precaution. These things were highly aggressive, and the thing in the cylinder was by no means dead.

She studied the cacoraptor in the cylinder – this one in worm form – and became lost in her thoughts for a while, worrying about the future. The things were lethal, unexpected, and why the Polity survey hadn't picked up on them she had no idea. In her less optimistic moments, she wondered if their presence might signal the necessary retreat of humans from Threpsis. She imagined returning to the shuttle, loading up all their gear to head for orbit, and asking for Polity evacuation. But no, she had invested all that she was in making this break from the AI-dominated Polity, and the humiliation of return would be too much. They could deal with this. She turned away from the thing and moved up behind Oren to peer over his shoulder at the screens.

Complex organics were revealed under the nanoscope. She identified molecular helixes, odd outgrowths and surrounding structures that might be some form of RNA, twisted rings and ellipsoids and forked strands. All were moving in a slow dance, everything constantly changing. Even her limited knowledge told her she was seeing something loaded with much more organic data than human DNA, including the modern iterations of it. Other views showed cellular structures that could have come from any Terran animal or xenomorph, though one did draw her attention more than the others. Here she observed a cellular structure in a constant state of change. The cells put out spears to shift positions, continuously rearranging, until every now and again some major change occurred and the whole mass shifted like a kaleidoscope image.

'So what do you have for us?' she asked tightly.

'Fascinating, absolutely fascinating,' Oren replied. He pushed his chair back and stood up, stepped over to the cylinder and peered inside.

After the appearance of further cacoraptors in the lands beyond the colony, and the deaths that had occurred, Ursula had decided they really needed more data. So they'd run out an armoured car to the largest concentration of the creatures, remotely controlled and with a deliberate weakness in its armour. They'd put liquid helium jets inside it, as well as electrostunners and projectile injectors of various toxins they had learned worked against the cacoraptors. This creature had inevitably attacked the car and got inside through the weak point. When they brought the car back, Ursula had taken every precaution possible: sealing the bay they brought the car into, surrounding the car with weapons and further liquid helium. She'd not been surprised to see the thing still mobile when they opened the car, but the second jet of helium froze it solid, and there were no casualties.

'How did I know you would say that,' she said.

Calm, stay calm.

He turned his head right round to her and, as ever, she felt her own neck wince in response to the motion. For Oren was an example of his own interests. He looked nominally human, from a distance, but close up the difference became more evident. Similar to some surgeons who liked to be more at one with their work, he had found two hands a limitation. Unlike many of them, however, he did not have cybernetic arms extending from attachment points on his lower ribcage, but had gone right into his own source code and altered it. Two arms extended from there, double-jointed like his nominally conventional arms, and with long wrists that had a great degree of motion. The hands at the end of these possessed bilateral symmetry with extra thumbs, the tips of each digit narrow and sensitive. Like some of the colonists, he could also extend claws – not for defence but for his work.

Oren walked on wide feet that offered more stability, his spine could flex as far backwards as it could go forwards, while his limbs moved as if on ball joints. He could turn his head right around, while the head itself had its differences too. His eyes were larger and more protuberant, with musculature around them enabling him to focus on things close to microscopic. The extra brain matter needed to control his extra limbs and enhanced senses was contained in a skull that protruded at the back. His ears, mouth and the rest of his physiognomy were the only things apparently normal – although Ursula suspected they were not, and that he only retained this veneer of humanity for the sake of others.

'I still think multidapt is a better name for these creatures,' he said, waving one of his subsidiary limbs, 'but cacoraptor has stuck now.'

'I'm not even sure where the name came from,' said Ursula, containing her irritation. 'Some discussion about demons, then cacodemons.' She had to be patient with Oren. He would go through his discoveries before getting to the meat of the matter, which was how the hell they could kill the things.

'Whatever.' He turned round, his head still facing her, which eased the psychological crick in her neck. 'Millennia of mutation and evolution have produced in these creatures a genetic library more extensive than anything I've ever seen. The constant pressure of survival has enabled them to apply this database with close to immediate effect. Something hits them and they toughen up, something penetrates their skin and they grow armour – this is all on the physiological level. However, there is also a mental component we saw with that raptor that killed Chandar. It wanted to see something that perhaps puzzled it so it grew an eye. And it wanted to move faster to get to this distant prey which, I surmise, it sensed to be loaded with water and other useful nourishment, so it grew longer more muscular legs.'

'Yes, but are there weaknesses in this ability to change? Some point of penetration?'

'As we have seen, the extent of adaptation is phenomenal,' Oren replied. 'I fear that seeking out points of penetration will simply result in a stronger animal.'

'That's not the kind of answer I came here for.'

Oren shrugged – a strange gesture for someone with a body like his.

'Our techniques at present are the best we have available: weapon strikes that destroy the creature before it can adapt. However, even that has its limitations because now they are showing behavioural adaptation alongside their physical ones.'

'They go into the ground,' said Ursula. She felt Oren was deliberately closing down options in order to make, as he had many times before, his casual suggestions. They always went in one direction and she needed to get past them to learn any raptor weaknesses she was sure he'd found, and which she could exploit.

'A dangerous enemy,' she said. And, to lead him to his point, 'It seems we are running out of options.'

'Our grossly material technology gives us advantages outside of our bodies,' he said, 'but as you can see it is steadily being destroyed and we are struggling to maintain and renew it. The cacoraptors have no such disadvantage – in essence their technology is them. We need to do something similar. We need to upgrade ourselves radically to face this threat.'

Ursula nodded: there it was. She'd seen much of Oren's research, his theories and his plans. She had seen schematics of weapons grown from the human body – slug throwers and energy weapons. She had seen humans with capacitance layers in their bones, organic superconductors lacing through their bodies, hard technology meshed with flesh – beings she felt could no longer be classified as human or even extremophile human. This was where he wanted them to go, even further than they had already.

'It's an idea and already we are far beyond what we were when we first came here,' said Ursula carefully. 'However, this would require long-term development and testing, while the threats we face are immediate. Even while we institute something like this, we could be wiped out. You know this. Don't forget that while you are down here deep in your research, people are fighting and dying up there and' – she stabbed a finger at the cacoraptor in the cylinder – 'if we fail, one of those will be in here with you, and not sitting safely between two iron-burners.'

He grimaced, and nodded. 'You have that right, I guess – I sometimes get carried away by my enthusiasm for this.' He then perked up. 'But it's certainly something to think on for the future – the environment here is very hostile.'

'Quite, but right now I need to know how to kill these fuckers.'

Oren stepped past her to a nearby console. He turned his head to face her again while operating a touchpad and bringing up a control hologram with one of his extra hands. The way he worked this while still looking at her seemed to confirm her suspicion that he had some form of vision, or other sense beyond touch, in his fingertips.

'I'm distributing data now,' he said, 'along with methodology.'

'The gist?' Ursula asked.

'Their adaptation, their speed of transformation, is of course energy hungry, on a world where sources of nourishment are hard won. They are very efficient in their use of biological energy sources but still, when transforming, they burn through a lot of what might be described as their fat. I've listed toxins that build up in that fat and can interfere with adaptation, powerful oxidants that inhibit too. We have many new things to try but, basically, they all interfere with that energy process.'

'But do not kill,' said Ursula.

'Some of them might,' Oren allowed.

'Okay, let me know if you come up with anything else.' She made to go.

'There is something else.'

She turned back. 'Go on.'

After hesitating, he said, 'It is dangerous and involves major physical transformations,' he said. 'It's very radical.'

'Back to that again, Oren? Haven't we already been over this, time and time again?'

'You don't understand.' He looked crestfallen.

'Oh I do,' she replied. 'I do.'

She stepped out of the laboratory and looked down at her hands, seeing they were shaking. She just breathed for a moment, then reached up and activated the coms unit on her collar. She had delayed making a decision on their next step for too long in the hope Oren would come up with something *useful*.

'General address,' she said, voice-activating that option. The coms unit beeped readiness and she continued, 'Okay, people, listen up. As of right now, everybody outside the fence is to return inside, bringing as much of their equipment as they can. All sample collecting missions are henceforth cancelled. This will be a temporary measure until we find a solution to the raptor problem.'

She didn't know what else to add, so after a moment tapped her coms unit and activated it again with two names: 'Vrease and Callum.'

'We're listening,' Callum replied.

'Those multiguns you talked about – get on that.'

'Will do,' Callum replied firmly.

Ursula felt a small elevation in her mood. All the colonists had their expertise – she had confirmed that when they'd first gathered everyone – but Callum and Vrease were the best of them. The job would get done. They'd all known it wouldn't be easy when they'd chosen this world and first set out.

Past

When those who had signed up to be colonists began arriving on Kalonan, Ursula met each of them personally. Later, as more and more arrived, she had to focus on organizing things. These people were diverse and uniquely themselves, but all had certain attributes in common. All of them were over a hundred and fifty years old, with some sliding into the start of their third century. They were intelligent, sophisticated and had done much with their lives, and all were experts in a particular discipline, often in many. They had also taken their fill of adventure during their time of ennui – that period of a person's life when the length of their existence started to trigger boredom and dissatisfaction, and they increasingly sought out dangerous novelty. So Ursula knew they were signing up for other reasons.

'What was your poison?' asked Callum Iverson, who she had already assigned to her command staff. They stood together at a viewing window in the space station, gazing through it at an internal space dock. Callum of course was as familiar with such sights as she was – once having been a technician working in such places.

Ursula didn't need to ask him what he meant by his question. 'The usual to begin with: free climbing on Earth, Mars and other worlds with the minimum of survival gear.' She took a coin out of her pocket and smiled down at it. The thing was worn out by the decisions it had made. With a grimace she put it away again and continued, 'Swimming in dangerous oceans, lava surfing and, of course, just about every dangerous drug or body morph I could get my hands on.'

'As all of us.' Callum nodded. 'But usually there's one activity that comes to occupy the most of one's time.'

'Mine was exploring underwater caves on Desander,' said Ursula.

'Right – with just a gill and a harpoon, I'm guessing.'

'Quite. Initially.' Ursula grimaced at the memories. 'I saw some nasty things down there and was lucky to make it out. As soon as I made it back to the surface, I took a trip back to Earth and did some studying. I still wanted dangerous novelty but decided I might as well spend my life doing something useful.'

'That is . . . concerning,' said Callum, frowning at her.

Ursula shook her head. 'When I began putting together plans for this colony, that was my attitude. I now see it as a route to elevating some humans to a higher state, and one that doesn't involve simply sliding into the realm of AI. I have to believe we can be something more.'

'You see adaptation to a hostile environment as the course.' Callum looked at her. 'But it must concern you that there could be a degree of sublimation there?'

'Not really. I seek success and not oblivion, and see it as akin to the occupation of the addict changing the course of her life. It's a chance to make something completely my own . . . our own.'

Callum inclined his head. 'We inspect the intricacies of our minds.'

Ursula wasn't quite sure what to make of that as she gazed at the view. The shuttle before them – a massive thing nearly a mile long – had been opened all down its length. Other colonists were suited up, in the vacuum of the space dock, running loaders and robots and giant hoists to load their supplies. Every day now another load arrived via instantaneous transmission through a runcible to then be transported by slower conventional means up here from the surface of Kalonan. She turned from the inner viewing window and walked over to the one facing out into space. The *Foucault* sat out there in orbit. The Polity cargo hauler was a four-mile-long cylinder with a massive cluster of engines at the back – including the drive nacelles to submerge it in the faster-than-light continuum of U-space. Its diameter was two miles and, at present, it also stood open down one side to expose a cavernous hold, from which much structure had been removed, so their shuttle would fit inside.

'We have everything now,' she said, 'but for one last item. I need to go and meet our biophysicist.'

'Oren Salazar,' said Callum. 'A very smart man – I'm surprised you got him.'

'Just lucky I guess,' Ursula replied with a smile that covered her disquiet.

Ursula accepted Oren's appearance because she had seen other more radical changes and, during her time of ennui, and before, had undergone them herself. But she knew, despite this, she would never get used to the wide degree of his head's motion.

'So, what made you change your mind? Earth Central Security let you go?' she asked, as she entered the apartment she'd rented for him on Kalonan. The place had every luxury, could provide the best food from its fabricator, the best drinks and drugs. It had a bathroom where every conceivable ablution could be performed. Oren sat at a fold-out plastic table away from all this, street-food containers on the floor beside him. He had disassembled something and was working with it. She glanced across the room to the kitchen area and saw that he had taken the fabricator apart, for its components lay strewn on the kitchen counters; it was a portion of them that he was working on at his table, which looked as if it had been retrieved from a dump.

'My equipment has arrived?' he asked.

'It's come through the runcible but at present is still down here. It will be transported up to the shuttle tomorrow and Vrease says she'll have your temporary laboratory installed the day after.'

He grimaced and continued his intricate work.

'Earth Central Security was fine about you doing this?' she rephrased the question. 'ECS is normally quite reluctant to let useful people go and very reluctant to let them go with any of their research . . .'

He turned his head right round to look at her, his four hands still at work. 'Probably eighty per cent of the nanosuite you and your fellow colonists intend to deploy is my work. The adaptogens and other tech, including the agricultural stuff and the xeno techniques . . . I am familiar with them. I see this as an opportunity for research and testing that expands my knowledge base. ECS sees it that way too. I am on a retainer and will return there afterwards.'

Ursula felt some disappointment. She had hoped she could snare him completely for this project – that he would become one of the colonists. 'You'll be leaving once we're established?'

'Yes, though that may take years and, when I am ready, I will train some people to take over. Many of those who are joining you have extensive knowledge of nanosuites and the other technologies and can take the requisite mental uploads.'

Of course there was still a chance that while he was there Oren might change his mind. Yes, others could learn from him but, even in this time of mental uploads, with augmentation both mental and physical, genius was still a nebulous thing. Oren had it in spades.

'That will have to do, then,' she said, taking a seat on a nearby sofa. 'But we have yet to discuss your contract – degrees of responsibility and veto on my part and on yours.'

'We already have the outline of that,' he stated.

'Yes. You will optimize the nanosuite to give us maximum survivability in the new environment: radiation resistance being the main aim, followed by adaptation of the crops and adaptation of us to the crops we can grow.'

'There will be much more than that, as I am sure you are aware. The hostility of the environment indicates that alien biology – ours – will not be a barrier to many parasites and other life forms. A very large degree of immune ruggedness will be required. Also gross physical enhancements, and further requirements we are not yet aware of. I suspect the contract will have to cover a degree of . . . plasticity.'

'Strange choice of word,' Ursula noted.

'Choices will have to be made.'

'Then, as per the contract, we must agree when choices have to be made.'

'Quite. It may be that your adaptations will have to be extreme.'

Ursula accepted the premise but felt uncomfortable with this, especially looking at what Oren had done to himself.

'Many of the colonists have, in their time of ennui, experienced forms radically different from human standard,' she said. 'I too did this. All have returned to that standard and I believe it a psychological anchor. I don't think many will agree to . . . large degrees of change. I won't.'

'I had understood your aim to be an advance in human evolution. Was I wrong?'

'No, you were not, but while remaining human.'

'A definition with wide parameters now . . .' He smiled. 'But all this will be a matter of agreement and negotiation on the ground, so is not an issue. I will head up to the shuttle tomorrow to oversee the work on my laboratory – some of the equipment is delicate.'

'I am glad to have you with us,' said Ursula. Curiosity finally overcame her. 'Was the fabricator malfunctioning?' she asked.

'It was inefficient and not working to its optimum. I am making a few adjustments.'

The fabricator, she later learned just prior to the *Foucault*'s departure, produced a different kind of food after Oren re-installed it. Nutrients and drugs were combined for fast and efficient entry into the human body, raising physical and mental performance to a peak. The hotel removed it because it was too unexpected for their usual guests, but sold it on to a pharmacy concern for study and replication if possible. Much later, on Threpsis, she wished she had thought a bit more about that, just as she wished she'd thought more about the fact that Oren was continuing to work for Earth Central Security, whose aims very much diverged from her own.

2

The colonists glanced up at Ursula from around the car, some with reserve and others with hopeful expectation. They moved quickly and efficiently, she noted, with none of the numb tiredness of a few weeks ago. The upgrade again. Checking medical stats from the two medtechs, Lars and Donnaken, she had learned about sleep. For a long time it'd been medically possible to adjust people to do without it. Many here hadn't chosen that option because either they liked sleep, or had found or heard that the adjustment came with mental side effects. It was a fairly new adjustment to be incorporated but not necessarily used in nano-suites. Now it seemed that those without it were sleeping less and less, while those who had it were occasionally falling into coma-like sleeps, haunted by nightmares. Major physiological changes were occurring and some disruption was to be expected, Oren had explained, but the changes were inexorably leading to greater strength, durability and efficient energy usage. The cost? Ursula wondered, now eyeing someone else down by the car.

Nursum was there. He was wearing the adaptive armour Oren had created, and constantly enhanced, based on the defences of local life forms here. He wore this 'skin' all the time now and it gave him the insectile look it lent everyone who wore it, but on

27

him it seemed emphasized by the way he moved so easily in it, as though it had really become part of him. He did thankfully keep the face covering down, retaining some humanity. He was carrying a heavy crate that would normally have been the territory of one of the handler robots, and went inside the car, out of sight. But still, it wasn't his strength, speed and ability to alter his physical form that really bothered Ursula. Nursum, who'd suffered so much and had needed the upgrade before anyone else, still just wasn't *right* – and, damn, she had seen how he could change. Would they all end up like him?

Ursula gripped the rail ahead of her tightly, plagued by doubts. She was doing her best, wasn't she? She felt responsible but didn't entirely own what had happened to them. The survey had completely failed to identify an apex predator here. Perhaps she had left it too long before making the decision to leave. But she couldn't accept blame for the confounding factors which had all mounted up, the most shattering of which was the attack on their shuttle.

She'd pushed things to the limit in the hope they could still succeed in making a stable life and community here. Even the loss of their shuttle should not have been such a disaster. Just one U-mitter call should have brought in a Polity vessel down to the surface and they could have left. Now their satellite with its U-mitter was gone, and the Polity was now otherwise engaged. Having encountered its first ever sophisticated alien civilization, it was fighting a desperate battle with creatures in nigh-indestructible ships. There would be no rescue sent here.

Ursula went over to the stair and down to the floor of the chamber. Callum and Vrease came over to her. Callum wore the 'skin' too, over his own metallic skin, with the living thing linked into his body underneath. It possessed the toughness and impenetrability of normal Polity body armour, but also defences against local toxins, boring insectoids, the cornucopia of acids and enzymes local life forms had weaponized, as well as a venous system that carried a biological immune system almost as efficient as the nanosuites. On Callum it looked like an addition and not an outgrowth, as it did on Nursum. Presently the covering that could snap up over his head had settled back into muscular slots in the bulging neck ring. His head and face were conventionally human in shape, but seemed spotted with acne – the spots being the orifices where the suit melded with his body. After long enough out of the suit, the orifices would heal. Ursula knew because she had only shed her suit a few days ago, but would need to don it again soon.

Vrease favoured Polity body armour over her almost completely prosthetic body. Her internal organs sat in a Golem chassis, which meant her whole skeleton was joint-motor-powered ceramal, her skull ceramal too, while her skin and flesh were artificial. Her choice of garment reflected the fact she had less to protect, or so she said.

'What is happening with the vessel now?' Ursula asked.

'The usual,' Callum replied.

'Nothing new on the scans?'

'Still the same story: they've got a chemical drive and they've got grav, but little in the way of power. They managed another short hop – just a few miles – but the raptors were back on them in a moment. Perhaps they should just stay inside their ship – that armour . . .' He shook his head.

'You know why,' said Vrease.

'They need organics to burn,' said Ursula, and Vrease nodded. 'And the uranium.'

The vessel, according to the data originally sent to them by the Polity, was a hostile alien assault craft, though it was huge. It had been involved in a battle above Threpsis that had taken out its reactor but left other systems intact. They now needed power to get off the ground. Their previous hops on grav were on a course to a dried-out seabed where colony scans had found a huge, almost fissile, concentration of uranium. Ursula surmised they must have the means of making a fission reactor aboard, or they simply had one and no fuel. But they needed to power those hops somehow, and had clearly been leaving their craft to gather up organics. Judging by the smoke that occasionally belched from ports in that impenetrable armour, they were burning this to drive some primitive generator, in turn topping up capacitor or laminar storage.

Walking with Vrease and Callum, Ursula came to the yet-to-be-closed cargo ramp in the side of the car. Inside rested the fusion reactor they'd managed to retrieve from their shuttle. The cacoraptors' shrewd destruction of the shuttle's engines had luckily not included this. It had cost them a lot to recover it, Vrease especially, but it would be able to power the alien assault craft and was therefore vital to their plans for escape. All they needed to do was get to that craft, deal with its current inhabitants and fit this reactor to the alien technology. While fighting off the cacoraptors . . . Ursula shook her head. It was a plan, at least, and better than sitting underground in increasingly permeable armour, waiting to die.

'What about linking it to the car?' Ursula asked, gesturing to the reactor.

Vrease shook her head, but Callum replied, 'Connection is okay but if we power up we then need to run the power-down cycle before moving it to the other ship. That would take days.'

'Connect it anyway,' Ursula instructed, 'and prepare it to be powered up quickly.'

They nodded understanding. Should their aims to take over the assault craft be defeated, the big reactor could be used in the car instead to take them away from the concentration of cacoraptors there. It would mean survival, at least for a little while longer.

Ursula went over to the monitor console and checked progress on preparations to leave, then headed out of the chamber towards her apartment. She started thinking back again on the arrival of that first raptor, and wishing she'd ordered the colonists' departure straight after that. When the damned things attacked the shuttle she should have known for certain humans had no place on this world. Sitting in her chair, she called up an old file and played it. The view it gave was from out beyond the edge of the land they'd developed.

She watched footage of a brontopod, shrieking and clattering, as it had come towards the colony. But, before it was in range of any of their border deterrents, a cacoraptor had swept in along the ground and slammed its bird-skull head into the brontopod's side, between its armoured plates. It went right for the creature's primary organ – a combination of heart and liver with lung organelles scattered throughout. Tearing this apart brought the creature down, and ripping out its secondary organs killed it.

At the time, being informed about this by the biologists and intent on other matters, Ursula had thought the brontopod had run into the raptor by accident. But no, watching the entire recording now, she saw that the raptor had driven the creature towards the colony. And, closely studying this raptor, she noted the white Rorschach pattern on its bird-skull head. Cross comparison with older recordings gave her a match. All raptors bore similar markings but they were as unique as fingerprints and this one's markings identified it as the first raptor they had encountered.

She played the next piece through quickly, seeing the brontopod deflating as raptor nymphs ate out its insides. The creatures that emerged from the 'pod carcass were wormish but with heads like mosquitoes, bearing heavy mandible arms underneath. Nearly a hundred of them moved back through the vegetation to a slab on the Bled, and there they unfolded two sets of wings to dry and toughen in the heat. It had all been of great interest to the biologists – some part of the cacoraptor life cycle. That was, until those same flying creatures had attacked the shuttle. She was sure now that this parthenogenesis had happened before, because hadn't the number of raptors suddenly ramped up after they'd lost sight of the first raptor? It seemed likely all, or most of them, were its offspring.

Switching back to the recording from a drone that had remained at the brontopod, she saw the original raptor depart it. In worm form, it seemed weary at first from its efforts, but it paused to rear up, one eye sprouting from its head just as it had to watch Chandar in their first encounter. She was damned sure it was looking at the drone this time. It next sprouted paddle limbs and burrowed into the ground.

Know your enemy, she thought.

The various implications frightened her; it was after this incident that Ursula had instructed that all cacoraptor activity must be reported to command staff. It appeared that this larger transformation they'd gone through required an incubator – the brontopod. The way the raptor had herded it to their boundary, then used it to produce these young which would attack the shuttle, definitely showed intelligent planning. But something else was evident here too. The transformations the raptors had gone through relied on source data in the creatures' genome. The fact they'd become intelligent indicated that intelligence was something they had deployed before and, looking at the heavy mandible arms the things had used to destroy the shuttle's drive, perhaps manipulation of technology had been part of their genetic

32

heritage too? But most frightening of all was the question of how they knew to target the drive and how to destroy it so precisely. Some kind of technical knowledge stored in their genome? Inherited knowledge?

She sighed and turned off the screen. The flying raptors had not been the worst of it. Sitting back, she grimaced at remembered disasters and her own feeling about the injustice of it all. It wasn't just the raptors. It was as if the entire universe had turned against humanity in general, and their problems here were a pale reflection of that.

Near Past

When she heard the knock on her door Ursula felt a surge of panic. Not again, please not again. It seemed that every time she got that knock, or someone unexpectedly contacted her via comlink, another person had died. Even though all the colonists were now within the perimeter, cacoraptor breaches of it had become more frequent. She felt some relief upon opening her door and seeing Gurda standing there.

Gurda wore her long rough blonde hair in plaits and was a heavyset woman who liked to wear tight, revealing tops. Her current adaptation to the radiation lay halfway between Ursula's and Callum's, and had made Ursula wonder to what extent the mentality of the person influenced their adaptation, for her skin had taken on a sheen, and her breasts an alluring glitter. Some of the colonists called her 'Brunhild', which she didn't seem to mind, and she was highly sexually active among them. In another age and with different people, Gurda might have borne watching, since her proclivities could lead to tension, but the colonists were old, mature and experienced. Gurda's apparent enjoyment of her activities sometimes led Ursula to wonder why she herself had so swiftly asked Oren to tweak the new nanosuite to shut down her own libido. Sexuality never seemed to interfere with Gurda's professionalism.

Gurda was in charge of their U-com with the Polity. She also kept their science database updated, ran searches on recent studies, kept channels open for private coms and provided a selection of media and entertainment links. As had been a proviso when the Polity allowed their colonization, Gurda kept the Kalonan runcible AI updated on their activities too. Now she was looking agitated, a little sweat appearing on her brow.

'It might affect us here,' she said. 'Some might want to return because of this. I thought it best to run it past you first.'

'Really?' said Ursula tightly, having no idea what the woman was on about.

'The ramifications are huge. Some of our xeno-biologists specialized in xeno-archaeology and ethnology. Nursum . . .' She paused, looked speculatively at the ceiling for a moment, and continued, obviously deciding to discount Nursum from wherever she was going with this. 'Others too will maybe want to activate and access past research, so you'll need to decide. It's for situations such as this that we have a command structure, with you at the top.'

Ursula stepped out of her apartment and closed the door behind her.

'You have yet to tell me what "this" is,' she noted.

'Oh, well, it's confirmed: a huge volume of space.'

They began walking towards the new control centre.

'Think about what you have told me and what I know, then try again, Gurda.'

The woman was silent for a moment then said, 'I've been babbling.'

'Quite.'

'The Polity has encountered a huge extant alien civilization.'

Ursula just kept on walking, the words floating in her skull and failing to connect to anything she knew. She had to suppress a rising inner turmoil and maintain her outward appearance of calm as she finally comprehended what that really meant.

This was a first. Polity exploration had, over the last few centuries, only turned up the archaeological remains of defunct civilizations. There were the Atheter who had apparently died out about two million years ago, the Csorians whose terminal date remained vague, and then there were the Jain whose artefacts were dated at five million years ago. Those same artefacts which still contained a technology the Polity AIs had designated as highly dangerous. But during all those years, and massive expansion of the Polity, with probes shot off into every corner of the galaxy, no living alien civilization had been found. Now, it seemed, one had been. She wanted to shoot questions at Gurda but obviously the woman wasn't operating with her usual efficiency. Ursula needed to look at all the data that had been sent. Then, yes, she had some decisions to make. Gurda was right: some people here might want to return to the Polity on the strength of this development. As she speeded up her pace towards the control centre, an aberrant thought occurred. Gurda had said the civilization was huge. How, with all those probes and the reception of out-Polity signals, had this been missed?

The control centre was abuzz with the news but, adhering to Ursula's protocols, it had not yet been generally distributed until she'd made her assessment. The mood surprised her, considering all they had been going through, but she supposed they'd taken the news as something positive at last. Callum was euphoric.

'This is stunning,' he said. 'It changes everything.'

Vrease was speculative. 'The technological exchange with a

new civilization could drive new lines of research in science. In a way the Polity has been moribund, which was part of the reason why I came here. There will be new directions.'

Everyone had something to say about it and were on the whole optimistic. Ursula began to realize that this major news had come as a welcome distraction from the escalating threat they faced here. She also understood Vrease's perspective. Though the Polity was huge, it had begun to feel too cloistered and controlled. There were not enough new directions, or fresh thought. She sat down and put in an earpiece, initiated the three screens in front of her and then, breathing evenly and using mental techniques learned long ago, she readied her mind to absorb data from multiple sources. She began reading, listening, running image files, synergetically taking them in and integrating them.

The prador . . .

The name itself, chosen by the AIs, immediately rang alarm bells in her skull. The AIs did not name things randomly and lightly, and 'prador' had too much of the ring of predator to it. Probes had returned data on a highly technical society. This was based on worlds with oceans, strange organic dwellings as much in the sea as on land, and large shoreline enclosures holding herds of creatures like giant mudskippers which they'd identified as livestock. The probes had not lasted very long, due to the, perhaps understandable, paranoia of these prador. The ships that destroyed them were huge, heavily armoured and loaded with weapons.

Communications had been opened and were difficult at first. It seemed the prador didn't have the Polity type of AI but something organic – the speculation being that their computers, as such, were some form of themselves. The creatures were terse and tended not to release information easily, only doing so when it might gain them some information about the Polity in return.

This made Ursula realize that though the prador might be recent news here, ECS had clearly been talking to them for some time.

Reading on, she found that researchers had managed to divine a great deal from the probe and communication data. The prador were creatures at home both on land and in the sea. The design of their ships, and some nuances of their language, indicated they might be exoskeletal, maybe insectile. They had not developed sophisticated AI, so it seemed likely they were highly individualistic, highly capable as individuals, and definitely somewhat paranoid in outlook. They communicated using sound, and the larger components of their sensorium were compatible with those of humans: their main senses probably being sight and hearing. Scanning of their ships' hulls indicated that their ability to see might stray into the infrared, with some loss at the other end of the spectrum, however. And analysis of communications revealed that their hearing moved into the infrasonic. Their language, just by usage, also indicated a sense of smell as a strong characteristic. AIs claimed, with a certainty above ninety per cent, that the prador were carnivores, hence the corruption of the word 'predator' to create their name.

And now it seemed that humanity was about to meet these creatures. They were advanced, they had created, without the aid of AI, a spacefaring civilization, a workable U-space drive, and it seemed, by some quirk of their development, their metallurgical science sat some way ahead of the Polity's. They didn't have runcibles which, being based on a technology completely at odds with the straight-line thinking of evolved creatures, required AI. Apparently a human ambassador was set to meet them on Outlink Station Avalon. Ursula sat back and mulled all this over.

The news that the human race had encountered an extant alien civilization travelled through the colony within a day. In any

Polity society it would have travelled much quicker but, like Ursula, many colonists had got rid of augs and other enhancements which enabled mental access to computing. She still wasn't sure how she felt about that. They had made the step away from AI because all agreed with her own thesis that it would have a deadening effect on their colony. The AI would act as a buffer between them and their world, slowing their adaptation, and it would end up functioning as just another outpost of the Polity. But why sacrifice the hardware that allowed mental linkage to computing which wasn't AI? Her only answer to that, still, was that it felt right.

Instead, the news travelled by word of mouth, whether by comlink or otherwise, or people finding it on the colony computer message board, or through the media news and Polity update channels that Gurda ran. Ursula watched the discussions onscreen and listened to them in the few colony bars and canteens, but kept her opinion to herself for now. Everyone seemed excited about the prador and in a sense it had come at a good time. Oren's new poisons seemed to have driven many cacoraptors into the ground or made them less active, and no 'incidents' occurred while the colonists were absorbing the news. Ursula didn't see people wanting to leave, as Gurda had feared. But then, after the railguns brought down a cacoraptor within just half a mile of the base itself, comments began to lean in a new direction. Perhaps this encounter with an intelligent alien race would drive the kind of new changes in the Polity they were looking for? And since this new civilization didn't possess AI, humans would need to be the conduit to them, and in turn gain stronger influence on the governance of the Polity? Maybe this was actually the wrong time to leave the Polity behind to start a new colony? The hostility of this world would eventually drive them away anyway? Ursula called a meeting.

First she invited all the heads of the various departments – Biology, Agriculture, Construction, Survey, Communications and many others besides. She next announced the meeting and asked for representatives of interested groups. It would be informal, she said, broadcast to everyone, and no final decisions would be made during it. She wanted a limitation on the number attending so it wouldn't get out of hand. At the appointed time, she sat waiting behind a row of tables with Vrease, Callum, Gurda and other command staff on either side of her. First to come in was Oren, taking a seat near the back. He was nominally one of the command staff but had demurred from taking a seat at the front.

'I can sit up there and give my opinion,' he told Ursula, 'but it is known that I'm still attached to ECS and intend to return to the Polity. I am not, in fact, a colonist here. Best I keep a low profile.'

Ursula felt his physiology also had an influence: people did not interact with him in quite the same way as they did with other colonists. Despite their adaptations and visible changes, he still didn't look like one of them, still did not look quite human.

Those she had invited and others filed in and took seats. The atmosphere was jovial, though some were wrapped in intense conversations. Whether about the prador or colony business – perhaps that raptor that had got so close – she did not know. She counted forty-five of them: many fewer than expected. She stood up.

'We have all seen the news with its decided lack of detail,' she said, looking round.

Many nodded agreement and she heard muttered comments about 'controlled news' and the 'AI drip-feed of information'.

'More news and more detail will be forthcoming, I have no doubt, and we will make decisions later based on that. However, since there has been so much discussion and speculation on the matter, we need to talk about how this affects our colony.' She looked around again. 'Since we seem to have lapsed into primitivism—' That got a laugh. '—and many of us have abandoned our augs, I will take comments and questions from the floor. Raise your hand if you have something to say and I'll try to ensure everyone gets to speak.'

A number of hands went up and she pointed. 'Trakken, Agriculture.'

The man stood up. He was a thin, acerbic-looking individual who she remembered spent most of his time in the greenhouses, raising modified crop plants for trial. Only a few of these had succeeded outside the chain-glass protection.

'I want to get this out there straight away,' he said. 'We have eight hundred . . .' Trakken paused, looking grim, then continued, 'We have fewer than eight hundred people here, a gene bank and artificial wombs in storage, but that is still a low figure on the stats for colony expansion and success. It seems likely to me that if a large enough number return to the Polity because of these events, the colony will fail.' He sat down.

'And I should add, in that respect,' said the woman Elene who worked in Medical, 'that post-ennui humans do not make good breeders. Out of the entire colony, I have only had two come to me who want children in vivo, and only four who want to use those artificial wombs.'

Ursula saw that Oren had his hand up and pointed to him.

'It's early yet for population increase.' Oren remained in his seat as he spoke. 'I've also advised holding off on it until your nanosuites have incorporated more data on the environment.' Ursula noted how everyone in the room was looking round at him intently. He added, 'But this is getting away from Trakken's original point: if too many people leave, the colony might fail.'

'Too many people die and it will fail too,' someone said.

Ursula glanced at the individual, and couldn't remember his name. Before she could reply to that, the biologist Nursum spoke up.

'I personally didn't sign up to do something easy. We knew the risks when we came,' he said.

'We didn't know about these fucking raptors,' said the other.

'Let's stay on track,' Ursula interrupted. 'This is about the Polity and the prador.' But even as she said it, she knew talk about the raptors was valid. This world had become a much more dangerous place than they had planned for. It did not, however, fit her agenda.

'But this changes things,' another said. This was a woman working in Communications under Gurda. 'I mean the prador.'

Ursula glanced around at the man who had mentioned the cacoraptors. He sat back, a sour look on his face, and folded his arms. He obviously had more to say. Ursula noted Gurda frowning at the woman, who continued: 'We have to analyse properly our reasons for being here. We've all had the sense that the Polity was set upon one course – a non-human course – and came out here to find our own way. But this is big and could change the Polity paradigm. Shouldn't we be there to influence that?'

Another said, 'I disagree with the phrase "non-human". AIs may be intelligences running in crystal, or some other substrate, but they follow the line of our evolution and should be defined as post-human, not non-human.'

A lively discussion then erupted on definitions, but there was no anger yet. The man who had mentioned cacoraptors just got up and left. Ursula sat down and let it run, nodding to herself and thankful for the maturity here. She didn't need to select speakers often because when someone had a point to make others politely allowed it. She just oversaw everything. All the issues were raised and covered, just as she had expected them to be, and in time fewer and fewer people had anything to say. Finally it was Trakken who gave her what she wanted.

'Ursula, you're our leader here. You initiated this colony expedition and worked to get it running. We have all financed this too and are effectively shareholders, but we agreed on your leadership under certain provisos, none of which are in breach due to recent events. What is your opinion? What is your leadership decision?'

Ursula stood again. Absently, she put her hand in her pocket, but had lost her coin when she arrived here on Threpsis. Not that she needed it to make any decisions about what she had to say next.

'There can be no doubt the discovery of an alien civilization is paradigm shifting for the Polity.' She shrugged. 'However, how much change this will bring about in the Polity as a whole is debatable. The desire of some to be amidst this is understandable, but laced with a degree of arrogance about their own effectiveness, their own influence on the course of events in the Polity. We are seven hundred and seventy-two people. The Polity is trillions. There are more AIs in one Polity city than there are people here.'

The admonition raised not a single comment. A couple of people who had been advocating for a return looked a bit shame-faced.

She continued, 'Our overall purpose in coming here is still not completely clear to all of us, even me. It's part logic and part feeling based on the experiences of long lives. It's my opinion that these events do not change this purpose, so we must continue as we are. But I must also raise another issue that you all seem to have neglected, but which relates to Trakken's point: colony finances.'

She paused and looked round at her command staff. They all knew this was coming and all wore bland expressions.

She continued, 'Whether we like it or not, we started this colony under Polity auspices and we adhere to their rules. We have a colony account on Kalonan that covers some resupply but mainly covers rescue. Resupply would be by robot ship and orbital insertion, so there is no option for people to leave by that route. If a few colonists wanted to leave, we could perhaps buy in a transport ship but that would kill our resupply. If more than a hundred wanted to leave, that would kill our rescue. Either of these would have to be by agreement of the entire colony.' She grimaced and waited for comment. There was none.

'I don't see that happening, do you?' she added.

She noted mostly agreement in their expressions, though also a large element of doubt. Maybe, having experienced the dangers of this world, some would rather return to the Polity, with its controlling AIs, and the set destiny they'd laid out for humanity.

She did not.

Past

The audience chamber resembled the interior of a small Mediterranean church. Noting the icons on the walls, the stained glass and the altar, Ursula searched memories of some cultural research she had done when only decades old and remembered: Greek Orthodox. Apparently the Kalonan planetary AI had taken great interest in ancient Catholicism and the schisms of that religion, Byzantium and the like. Of course its studies went deeper than those of human historians from previous ages – it researched everything that related to it, such as the technology and art of the time and how they blended. It was rumoured it had even been making an effort to reconstruct the minds of people from that age through the data available on them, even down to the pressure of a single stroke of a quill. Ursula didn't like this church. The fact the AI had chosen to shape its audience chamber like this hinted at arrogance and perhaps some inclination towards godhead.

She walked in and sat down on one of the pews. Another aspect of this she didn't like was that the AI actually had an 'audience chamber'. On other worlds you could gain the full attention of one of the big AIs at any location, having gone through the correct channels first. But perhaps she was being a bit simplistic. This AI probably used its little church as a means to study the person who wanted the larger part of its attention for a while.

'Eight hundred people have signed up,' she said. 'I have personally checked the profiles of every one of them. The submind of Acanth Station also vetted them, as well as your submind too, and found nothing anomalous. All of them are past the worst of ennui so are not a risk – just seeking something meaningful to do with their lives.'

A figure materialized on the pew beside her and she felt it sink a little. Nice touch that, since the figure was a hologram – an Orthodox priest in a long black robe, with a long black beard. He peered at her for a moment, then back towards the altar.

'The technology you have acquired, and propose, requires expert oversight, yet you don't want an AI to accompany you. Perhaps you could explain that?'

'It is about our search for meaning,' Ursula replied. 'The people on that list would not want that kind of oversight.'

'Nor you,' Kalonan observed.

Ursula considered the kind of conventional explanations she gave to humans she discussed all this with, and dismissed them.

'I had a friend on Earth who liked to renovate chairs. He

would find something old and falling apart, usually antique, and repair it with hand tools and materials found locally. He could, if he wished, image the chair and stick it in a cheap renovating manufactory and it would be done, perfect, in a matter of minutes. He didn't want to.'

'Hands on,' said Kalonan. 'The presence of an AI takes away the satisfaction of achievement.'

'Exactly.'

'You have your list and you have chosen a world beyond the Line here. I note that this world is extremely harsh and will require technological barriers and/or extreme adaptation. I have to ask, why this choice?'

'My options were limited.'

'No, they were not.'

Ursula grimaced. 'My options of extremely harsh worlds were limited. Many were outside the range of human adaptation available, or affordable. Many required subsurface dwellings and enclosed hydroponics, or other methods of food production.' She paused for a second then added, 'Many also had strictures on what could be done there – they were supposedly designated as having potential for terraforming.'

'That still does not explain the "extremely harsh", does it?'

'Achievement,' Ursula stated, but knew it would not be that easy.

'Try again,' said the AI.

'Human evolution,' she conceded.

'Better. Do continue.'

'The human race lags far behind its creations. You. I am old now and aware that this is a state of affairs the AIs would like to change but, since time is of little relevance to them, they drive change slowly and come up against the barrier of human complacency. I would like to do something about that.'

45

'You could upgrade to crystal – you could be an AI yourself.'

'But I would not be human.'

'Ah, that old shibboleth.'

'On a hostile world, with the requirement for adaptation, both physical and technological, the drivers for change would be purely that world and us. We'd become something more and take on a shape uniquely our own. Something still human, not AI.' She studied his profile. 'Surely in the interests of diverse growth, the AIs would find this intriguing and useful?'

The priest nodded, and the AI looked at her with black eyes. 'You have made preparations . . .'

'My personal wealth, and that of those who've signed up fully, has been put to good use. We have the equipment and, as you are probably aware, a shuttle that will be able to take us down to the surface of Threpsis. We still have money left to buy our transport across the Line, as well as an invested sum to cover any possible future rescue. I've included everything and can do this at no cost to the Polity, though I am baffled by the requirement when this is something they could easily cover since we are centuries into post-scarcity.' She grimaced at the term.

'It discourages the inept and those who are not fully committed.'

Ursula nodded, having expected that. 'I am, however, struggling to find a Polity ship that will take us, and when I tried Outlink traders I found myself subtly blocked – problems with money transfers, or with them coming here to collect the shuttle, or equipment delayed in runcible transport – things of that nature.'

The AI gave no reply to that, instead saying, 'You have acquired a team of experts covering many necessary fields. You do not, however, have someone to apply, monitor, tweak and upgrade the advanced nanosuites you intend to use.'

'I have new candidates to approach,' she replied. 'Someone will turn up.'

'Oren Salazar,' the AI stated.

'I approached him first, but though he showed a great deal of interest he finally rejected my proposal. Apparently Earth Central Security employs him and the work it gives him is of more interest to him.'

'Ask him again.'

'Something has changed?'

'Yes, something has changed. And a great deal more is about to.'

'What do you mean by—'

But she was talking to empty air.

3

Present

Ursula hit the palm reader beside her locker and its door slid aside. The rack at the back stood empty because her personal weapons were already in her cubby aboard the main car. Other useful equipment she owned was also aboard, but personal items not relevant to this mission had to be limited. Colonists were only allowed pieces weighing less than a total of ten pounds and no larger than would fill a one-foot cube. All that remained here now was her suit, her 'skin'.

It stood in a frame linked to nutrient and power feeds. These feeds were all but dead now, since the cacoraptors had destroyed the solar panels the colonists had fixed on top of the massif – the rock about which they had built the base. The skin looked like medieval armour fashioned out of sections of insect carapace, but there the resemblance ended. Even as Ursula stepped closer, the thing quivered and shifted, as if tired of standing. She closed a hand around one wrist and it shuddered eagerly, with plates that initially appeared rigid folding back like flower petals to open up arm coverings and gauntlets, the torso and the legs. Ursula stripped off her overall and her underwear, discarding them on the floor. Turning her back to the skin, she slipped her feet into the open boot sections, then eased back against the inner layer of slightly warm muscle and other organics, and it began to wrap its armour about her.

She had thought she would never get used to this, or wear it other than over clothing or combat armour, especially the rather disconcerting moment when it engaged its catheter arrangement to her vagina and inserted a tube into her arsehole. Now she felt it enclosing her in protective comfort. She was beginning to understand how for other colonists the skin had rapidly become their preferred clothing. They did everything in it, even sex.

As the skin closed around her it engaged with her nerves, enabling her to feel through it. She took a breath, senses displacing and then stabilizing. A tight panic suddenly arose in her torso as she seemed to sense even more of that *other* beyond the base. But suppressing this took only a small effort of will, and again she dismissed it as illusion. She left and was soon walking onto the gantry above the car.

'So that's it, people – we're sealing the inner doors,' she announced, speaking into her skin microphone and her voice broadcast by the PA system. She looked down at the colonists queuing to board, as on some antediluvian commercial flight, waiting for the less able to get on first. Medical personnel ran up the ramp and into the cargo section of the car with two regrowth tanks, their human contents floating in amniote, surrounded by masses of tubes and wires. Walking wounded went in next to take their places in a cramped hospital area. No one was on gurneys, since either skin or powered armour moved those who couldn't otherwise walk, and the new upgrade had been speeding up healing. Oren had wanted to use it on the two in regrowth tanks but, still very suspicious about the changes Nursum had undergone, Ursula had scotched the idea. She felt sure he couldn't predict what it would do with someone severely injured and already wound through with medical support tech.

49

She turned her attention to where the biophysicist was supervising the loading of his remaining equipment. Oren had commandeered a section inside the car larger than the hospital even and, though she'd objected, had managed to get his cacoraptor aboard. He twisted his head round to look up at her for just a moment, then flicked it back to studying those all around him. Perhaps, with his enhanced senses, he saw more changes in the colonists than she did. She grimaced, utterly sure now Oren had achieved what he wanted, and transferred her attention to Vrease, who peered up at her from beside a weapons turret on top of the car. Ursula nodded. Vrease pulled her tablet from her belt and stabbed a finger down on it. All around the chamber entry doors swung shut. A moment later, with a thump and hiss, each of them engaged heavier locking mechanisms and sank down on their seals.

Ursula scanned the area. The place looked gutted, as did the rest of the base. A few minutes earlier she'd received warnings of cacoraptor incursions over in the North Quadrant, and cursorily dismissed the feeling that she'd already known this. Now there was nothing to stop the creatures flooding into the rest of the base. She had considered mining the place, to kill those that would soon swarm in, but that seemed like a burned bridge. This place could be made more secure than anywhere outside and might again become a place of retreat. She nodded once, briefly, and headed for the stairs.

By the time she reached the floor the uninjured colonists where finally filing in to take their places. Those driving the car and operating manual weapons, as well as adaptive armour systems, had already boarded. She heard something rumble and clatter distantly and had a brief hallucination of bat-like shadows flickering around her. Detritus in her eyes perhaps – from the changes she'd gone through? The raptors were almost certainly in the base. She felt the urge to get aboard and into the control room but worried that might look too much like running for cover. As leader of this now all but defunct colony, she felt she should be the last to board.

Hissing and clattering drew closer, and then something thumped against one of the armoured doors sealing the chamber. Another door thumped, lifting on its seal. A chittering sound impinged and she felt that clench of panic again. She tried to convince herself she had heard the sound and it had not arisen in her mind.

'Speed it up there,' she said, as calmly as she could.

An odour, like burned pasta, permeated the air, and she recognized the enzyme acid that ate into ceramal. A shriek and steady thrumming made her jerk round, but the sound issued from the car's closing ramp. She observed it rising. The thing lay two feet thick and consisted of multiple layers, with sockets and plugs all around its edges to engage with the surrounding armour of the car. She transferred her attention to the personnel entry doors. One of these began to close too – swinging into position before running into the hole on hydraulics, more like a wine cork than a door. Four people remained by the final door, ducking down so their heavy packs wouldn't catch on the frame. She walked over, noting fluid had started to pour out round the rim of one of the chamber's armoured doors, and then a hard clawed finger poked through, traversing down, stripping out the seal. She stepped up behind the last colonist as he boarded the car, not so much because she felt herself in danger – the raptors would not have time to get to her – but because she didn't want to see what came through that door. It seemed, in the end, that the grotesquely familiar could be more terrifying than the wholly alien.

Near Past

With what had become a familiar hollow dread inside her, Ursula headed out into the corridors of the base, finally making her way to an elevator that led up into the massif. Here she walked into the control room. Ten personnel sat at consoles, including Vrease and Callum, who ran defences from here. Though the guns were automatic, and their programs highly sophisticated, Vrease often had to make adjustments for some new technique the cacoraptors were employing. Only a day ago the raptor borers had somehow worked out what level of movement the seismic detectors would ignore and had inched their way underneath a multigun to attack it. Fortunately, the gun had responded fast enough to destroy them before they destroyed it. Callum meanwhile kept the minelayers running, gathered what data he could with their remaining drones and decided when to use one of their, also limited, supply of missiles to hit something suspicious outside the perimeter.

'It all just gets better and better,' said Callum.

Gurda's report over com had been brief, but even with so little information, Ursula could see the implications – especially now they no longer had their shuttle to get them off planet. She moved over to stand behind Gurda at her console.

'Tell me what you have – I'll look at a more-detailed report later.'

Gurda looked up, her eyes glazed. She was wearing twinned augs either side of her skull, one of them running an optic to the console. She was one of the few colonists having less trouble with augmentations than others, though she admitted the nano-suite they'd all been given was beginning to interfere with them, resulting in their safety protocols steadily detaching them from her brain. Her screen showed an eye-aching representation of local U-space on one side and a star system map, with shifting numbers, on the other. She nodded.

'It's bad,' Gurda replied.

'I'm aware of that. Give me the highlights.'

'We've got data up to the eyeballs.' Looking lost, Gurda hesitated, then continued, 'The aliens, the prador, sent representatives to Outlink Station Avalon, where an Earth ambassador went to meet them.' She swallowed with a dry clicking, shrugged herself and her expression blanked. 'They simply came aboard and slaughtered their way through the population there. And that seemed to be the signal to attack elsewhere. Their ships swept in and just started hitting everything. Their weapons are fairly conventional but nothing seems to get through their armour. Exotic metals involved, apparently. I have data on their weapons, tactics and lots besides, though not much that will be of use to us here. The Polity defensive line is now back beyond Erista.'

Ursula stared at her, trying to understand precisely what that meant. So many worlds and stations lay in the volume of space between where the original Line had been and Erista. The likelihood of being rescued from here had just plummeted. She felt a further sinking sensation.

'Kalonan?' she asked.

'Kalonan is out of contact and disconnected from the runcible network, as are all worlds in that volume of space,' said Gurda emotionlessly. She closed her eyes, shook her head. 'It went out of contact when the prador started bombing it.'

Ursula continued staring at her. 'Traskal?'

'One of the first cities to be destroyed. Completely destroyed.' Gurda now did show some emotion, her eyes tearing up. She swept the liquid away with an irritated gesture, glanced at her screen and changed the image feed.

It looked like something from a war-game virtuality. A

monstrous, many-legged creature the size of a grav-car, and much like some by-blow of a wolf spider and a fiddler crab, scrambled up onto a dais in what looked like a space station park. Though she assumed by its shape it was naturally armoured, it also wore armour. Attached along one claw was a weapon like a Gatling cannon, only bigger, with looped feeds running to a large case on its underside. The tip of one claw folded down and issued the searing blue white of a particle cannon beam. Then it fired its Gatling cannon too. The view pulled back to show people running as the beam swept across, turning them into screaming torches. Gatling slugs tore into others, shattered trees and ripped up the ground.

'These recordings are from Avalon, and I have plenty of others too,' Gurda told her.

Ursula shook her head. 'I really don't need to see any more.'

'General distribution?' Gurda enquired.

'I'll have to think on that.' Ursula walked over to the window and looked outside.

Vehicles were on the move out there and people too. Though they were under constant attack, or threat of attack, from the raptors, the necessities of survival had to be attended to. The spraying of the new crops must continue, agricultural bots had to be maintained, crops harvested, treated and stored and new ones planted. Those machines laying mines were also still at work just beyond the multiguns, and new guns were being put up on the base and elsewhere. The first six guns, efficient as they were, could not be expected to stop everything. Of course all of it now no longer looked like a colony foothold, but some last-ditch fort, such as the Alamo. It was an analogy that was too troublingly true.

Ursula grimaced. So, the Polity was now at war with the prador. Most of the people here weren't actually from Kalonan since it had merely been a staging point in their preparations to come here. Nearly everyone had cut their ties back in the Polity too – a key condition of their choice to come here. But they had all spent almost a year on Kalonan, forming attachments there, and no matter their aims to start afresh, they still felt something for their home worlds. Would the colonists feel the same way she did? That the whole war out there was unreal – almost a footnote to what they were facing? No, she couldn't assume that. She turned back to Gurda.

'Just give them the gist of it and leave out Kalonan,' she instructed. 'And you also understand what I mean when I say leave out the gory details?'

Gurda nodded.

Ursula continued, 'Full distribution to command staff only.' She shrugged. 'The data might give us something useful.'

She scanned around those sitting at the other consoles. Callum nodded agreement, others just seemed tired and annoyed, though in some she detected a lost look, like despair.

Night time gave them an aubergine sky. It was never completely dark because of the density of stars in this part of the galaxy, and usually one or two of the planet's moons was up there too. Tonight one of those moons, Trisk, rolled around the world – a misshapen nugget a thousand miles across that sometimes looked like the cartoon face of an old man. Another, Brant, sat on the horizon, perfectly spherical and dotted with the glints of sulphur volcanoes which reflected the sunlight. As she stepped out onto the surface of the massif, amidst the solar panels, sensors and dishes, and other spectators, Ursula saw that tonight was brighter still.

A strew of light stretched from horizon to horizon, even putting Trisk into partial silhouette. It glittered with flashes and streaks of light. Ursula felt cold running down her spine. It might have all seemed a little unreal, with the intermittent U-com updates from the Polity being their only knowledge of the war, but this . . . She walked over to where Callum and Vrease had brought a mobile console with hologram projector.

'Do you have anything?' she asked.

'They're fighting,' said Vrease.

Ursula nodded to herself. That Vrease had said 'they're fighting' rather than something more like 'our forces are fighting the prador' brought home how much the colonists now felt themselves to be separate from the Polity. Good, because it seemed unlikely they would be returning to it any time soon.

'I'm getting some feeds,' Vrease continued. 'Intermittent and quite degraded – some heavy EMR out there. Not getting much on U-com even though they're close – just light hours away.'

'Gurda?' Ursula asked.

'She's working on it.'

Ursula tapped her coms unit. 'Gurda,' she said, activating the link with the name, 'there must be more we can pick up on U-com.'

'I know,' Gurda replied, 'but since the Polity is at war they're encoding stuff now. I sent a request for an update on the codes and it should come through any time now . . . I hope.'

'You sound doubtful.'

'We don't have a direct feed any more – just packet transmissions, and they're getting more intermittent. I've been warned that since they don't know the extent of prador code-breaking and U-space tech we may lose even that.'

'Really?'

'Really. For our own protection, apparently. We're effectively in prador-controlled space now and if they find out about us . . .'

'Okay.' Ursula didn't like how that news made her feel. They were an independent colony, yet losing this last link to the Polity felt . . . bad.

'Phew, we're okay,' said Gurda. 'I have the coding and am sending the feed to Vrease.'

Ursula looked to Vrease, who nodded and began working her console. Stepping back, Ursula just watched, but became aware of someone else standing behind her and felt her spine prickling. She glanced round. Of course, it was Nursum. His eyes had changed again – some reaction to the dark. His pupils were now big and black while the iris was gold, seemingly formed of petal-like plates reaching to the edges of his eyes. He raised one hand in a jerky, unnatural motion and gestured ahead. Ursula looked to where he was pointing and saw an area clear of spectators, hazed now by a holographic projection from the equipment. Out of this grew blackness, as if a hole was forming in the air. It shimmered again and filled with specks of light which the view closed in on. Ursula found herself gazing upon a giant brass-coloured ship that bore some resemblance to a prador carapace but with manta wing-like sides. It bristled with weapons and sensor devices, spitting out a particle beam that speared away into darkness, royal blue in vacuum.

'This doesn't give us much of an overview since the ships are so far apart and most weapons fire is invisible,' said Callum, moving up to the console beside Vrease, 'but we can collapse distances by orders of magnitude to . . . well, bring it down to a perceivable scale.'

He made some alterations and the image distorted then grew brighter. Now a tightly curved line of prador ships appeared, spewing out particle beams, lasers and streams of projectiles artificially made visible. Their targets were presumably the Polity ships. She recognized some of their forms – big lozenge-shaped dreadnoughts that had been knocking around for ages – but others of a sleeker design were new to her. Still, they seemed to be getting the worst of it. They were surrounded by the bright spears of hardfield projector ejections as ships rid themselves of melting and exploding force-field generators, shedding burning armour, and some just disappeared in immense explosions. The prador vessels meanwhile were taking impacts on their hulls and coming out of the fireballs seemingly undamaged.

'They're burning the fig,' said Nursum, uncomfortably close.

It was one of the apparently nonsense phrases he often came out with now which, on closer examination, might not be nonsense at all.

'The Polity is losing,' Callum noted needlessly.

The prador weren't completely without casualties. They saw smaller ships amidst them explode or tumble away. Callum and Vrease kept picking up other feeds and showing new scenes. In one of them a big prador vessel hurtled back through vacuum from some immense explosion, its hull utterly out of shape.

'Bloody hell,' said Vrease.

'What was that?' Ursula asked.

Vrease sorted through images and came up with something strange. A large hexagonal frame was sitting in vacuum, being towed on all sides by Polity ships. The gap within the framework seemed to shimmer and flash, then darkened again.

'A runcible,' Ursula stated. This instantly brought to mind her time in the military and her friend Manseur, who had test fired such a weapon.

'Yes,' Vrease replied, as multiple impacts on the object broke it apart and any surviving tow-ships detached and sped away. 'They gated something through it unbuffered, and it came out very fast . . . and even that wasn't enough to break the prador's armour.'

Throughout the rest of the night they watched the battle, until the surviving Polity ships finally fled, U-jumping away from the battlefield. Ursula considered all the lives lost and ships destroyed. She had no doubt that the AIs running the Polity had known from the start this was a battle they couldn't win, but had expended resources to test their mobile runcible gate. Ursula was again baffled by the fact the prador didn't have AIs. Finally, with dawn fingering over the horizon and most of the other colonists back inside, she decided it was time to return to her quarters in the massif.

'Burning the fig,' Nursum repeated.

He startled her and she looked round, watching him move off, allowing herself a shiver in the dawn chill.

On the second night the only thing visible, beyond what was normally there, was a loose spread of red cirrus cloud – presumably the still-glowing embers of the battle. A week later their satellite gave them views of meteors burning up through the atmospheres of other worlds in the system. On the ensuing day, one streak cut across their own sky, breaking up above them and hurtling on behind the horizon. That night, the colonists gathered on top of the massif again to observe the spectacular meteor shower of battle debris coming down.

As Ursula watched with them, she still felt strangely detached from any worries about the war out there. It was their own particular battle here that preoccupied her. The cacoraptors seemed to have paused, as if they too were interested in these outside events. But what really spooked her were images from the various cams and other sensors on the perimeter of the base, as well as those surviving beyond it. The cacoraptors out there had grown eyes, like the first one they'd seen, as well as other sensors too. And they were watching the damned sky.

She left the display and went to find Oren to get his take on this.

'Asteroid and meteor impacts are probably a feature of the past here,' he opined. 'This system doesn't have a sweeper like Jupiter and when the sun grew more active, that likely disturbed things and increased their frequency.'

'So it's their evolved response to threat? Survival instinct or something?'

'Evolved, yes, but also part of their rapid adaptation. If this gets heavier, it wouldn't surprise me to see them start to burrow and encyst in the ground or something.'

'I see,' she said, for some reason feeling he was being parsimonious with the truth.

The following night, the beeping of the emergency channel from her coms unit, sitting on her bedside table, woke Ursula. She sleepily inserted it in her ear, but felt a tightness in her stomach. That beeping never brought good news.

'Something big is heading towards us.'

It took a moment for her to decipher what Gurda was talking about. Had the cacoraptors undergone some other change and begun attacking in a new way? No, Occam's razor suggested this was likely related to the debris falling on their world.

'Something?' she repeated.

'Looks like one of the prador ships.'

Now she really woke up. 'With that armour, we could be in for a dangerous impact if it hits down here,' she said, thinking 'extinction event, extinction event'.

'I don't know that there will be an impact,' Gurda replied. 'The satellite telescope shows it's heavily damaged, but it did a slingshot around the ice world Chomar and I'm pretty sure we recorded a drive flash. There was also some grav activity from the ship.'

'What are you saying?' Ursula was already pulling on her overall.

'Looks to me like something is guiding it here, aiming for us as the nearest inhabitable world on which to make repairs.'

Oh hell.

As if cacoraptors weren't bad enough, they were now about to be visited by armed hostile aliens. Why the hell couldn't it have been a disabled Polity ship heading here? But even as she thought this she felt bad. She shouldn't wish cacoraptors on anyone . . . then again, heavily armed Polity marines? She headed out of the door.

In the control room Gurda, Vrease and Callum were analysing image, vector and scan data.

'We thought at first that active scan from the satellite might be a bad idea,' said Gurda. 'But sure as shit the thing is going to see the satellite on the way in anyway, and likely our colon-ization, so why not use active scan while we still can?'

Ursula looked at her. She couldn't find fault in the reasoning but resented that Gurda had taken this decision without consulting her. Stupid really, they could not afford any kind of infighting.

'While we still can?'

Gurda replied, 'They'll identify us as human at least and likely as Polity. And if they have any active weapons they'll probably take out the satellite . . . if not us.'

Ursula absorbed this and turned to Vrease. 'Order all personnel back here and under the massif.' Even as she said it, other thoughts impinged. If the ship had active weapons, for example a nuke or a CTD, a contra-terrene device, they might survive here but would be in a whole world of trouble. The prador could be a problem, but a worse one would be a weapons strike that knocked out their defences against the cacoraptors.

'Should I give them detail?' Vrease enquired.

'No reason why not.'

Vrease left, speaking: 'General address to all coms units. Emergency protocol.'

'Speak to me, Callum,' Ursula said to the man.

He swiped a hand over his console. A black hole appeared in the air, which then filled to show a ship. This vessel didn't resemble a prador carapace. It was a blunt, lumpy cylinder with a teardrop drive protruding from the back end at the top, as well as recognizable fusion ports at the back and stubby forward-slanting wings deployed towards the nose.

'Any Polity data on it?' Ursula asked.

'A small assault craft is the vague description,' Callum replied. 'Kinda equivalent to a Polity attack ship – used to target and breach larger ships or space stations, when they're not simply blown to pieces.'

'Small,' Ursula repeated, looking at the size of the thing. 'How many aboard?'

Callum shrugged. 'Little data on that. AI extrapolation gives anywhere between ten and a hundred.'

Ursula found she had run out of questions.

'Note the wings,' Callum continued.

'I'm noting them.'

'They're either some sort of effecter or to take the brunt of atmospheric entry. They tell us something.'

'Do elaborate,' said Ursula sarcastically.

'Okay. We know now that this ship has grav, and likely fusion. These items tend to either work well or fail catastrophically – there's no in between – yet the ship has deployed its wings. This tells us that their problem is most likely power supply, else they would have used grav or fusion to land here. Also, as far as I can judge by their profile and recent measurements, those wings are not fully opened yet – they're coming out very slowly, probably because of the aforesaid power supply.'

'Good news for us, then,' said Ursula. 'They at least won't be able to use energy weapons.'

Callum shrugged. 'But a nuke or CTD will have its own drive.'

'You're a bundle of joy,' remarked Vrease as she returned. To Ursula she said, 'Most likely its armoury is empty since it's obviously been in the thick of it.'

Ursula could see that now. The vessel had been distorted by impacts and deep scars ran across its hull.

'But no guarantees, of course . . . They're coming in?'

'Yes, and fast.'

'Good.'

They watched for hours as Callum's assessment proved true and the wings eventually deployed fully. In the final hours, the assault craft fired thrusters and turned, releasing a long fusion blast towards the world. When the drive flame went out, it did so like a candle snuffing, not the usual wind-down of such engines. The vessel then continued its long fall, with thrusters stuttering and only just turning it nose on to atmosphere in time. Once into atmosphere, the wings took the brunt, but the whole thing still heated up till it was glowing like iron out of a forge. The wings fragmented, whether by design or failure Ursula couldn't know. Lower down, it deployed parachutes, which slowed it a little until they too tore away. In the end it went in hard, ploughing a long furrow through the landscape over a thousand miles from their base. Ursula noted that despite the crash-landing, the thing had hardly been damaged any further. The craft lifted out of the furrow on a surge of grav and deposited itself on a nearby slab.

'Keep the satellite on it,' she said generally. 'We need as much information on that thing as possible.'

The prador assault craft just sat on its slab for five days with nothing happening. Ursula assessed the situation. If the thing had a missile to sling at them, surely it would have done so by now? She cancelled the emergency protocol and colonists returned to work in the fields, as well as the remaining greenhouses and hydroponics units. She could think of no other response as yet. Sitting inside the massif, hoping it would protect them from a nuke whose yield they couldn't be sure of, seemed ridiculous. On the eighth day, while she looked through the chain-glass window of the control centre to those at work out there, noting again that the cacoraptors seemed suspiciously inactive, Callum spoke up.

'Something happening,' he said.

'What?'

'Changes in EMR – something's powering up.'

Ursula turned her attention to the screen wall. The satellite feed gave good imagery in daylight of the prador assault craft. Ursula stared at the thing, sure it looked a little less damaged than it had when it came down. Perhaps its armour was memory metal of some kind? A misshapen ramp dropped down from the side of the ship onto the rocky slab and six prador came down. All were loaded with equipment and all had their Gatling cannons along one claw. Remembering imagery from the Polity, Ursula supposed they might also have particle cannons inside their other claws – just a matter of folding down one claw tip and incinerating anything nearby.

They trooped down from the slab with the ramp closing behind them, towing a couple of grav-sleds. Nearby stood what might be described as a copse on this world. It consisted of a variety of lethal plants which she had become all too familiar with. The first species the prador came upon was a cycad, which instantly sprayed them with poisoned spines. One of the creatures responded with a blast of Gatling fire, blowing the thing to shreds, then turned the weapon towards another of the plants. The larger prador next to it banged a claw on its carapace and side-swiped its legs to throw it to the ground. Ursula suspected some admonition about wasting ammunition.

'I think the big one is what is called a first-child, the others are second-children,' said Callum.

Ursula trawled her memory for Polity data. Those terms were translations from the prador language. The AIs had judged that the prador soldiers were their children in various stages of growth, usually commanded by a father-captain. Ursula felt there was rather too much in the way of anthropomorphism going on with the translations.

'Close on that armour they're wearing – I want to see what the acid is doing,' she said.

Callum opened another frame in the screen wall and brought up a close view. Here they saw the glutinous acid and poison of the spines oozing groundwards, but it seemed to be leaving merely gleaming lines down the armour. As the prador moved into the copse, a variety of other toxins and acids hit them, but again just seemed to polish rather than eat away their armour.

'Exotic metal component,' said Callum. 'Though I'm not precisely sure what the data from the Polity meant about that.'

'Generally it's just a metal not on the common elementary table – has unnatural proton, neutron and electron counts, and balance is only maintained by the molecular lattice, or alloying, or other factors,' said Vrease. 'However, the Polity data referred to the ships. Apparently their body armour is something similar to our ceramal.'

'Right,' said Callum dismissively.

Ursula nodded to herself. It made sense. Their own ceramal armour only ceased to be effective when other factors came into play, like grinding teeth, adaptive enzymes and strange fungal fibres that sought out weaknesses.

Amidst the plants, two of the smaller prador, the second-children, started wielding devices that looked like long bow saws, but with shimmering wires where the blade should be. Under a toxic rain of plant defences, they used these to cut, and then slung the plant matter onto the sled. When one plant tried to escape, the first-child scuttled over and grabbed it, bashed it on the ground a few times, tossing it onto the sled too. Ursula felt a chuckle rising, and suppressed it as inappropriate, though the prador did seem almost comedic.

Once the sled was spilling over, they towed it back to the ship.

'What the hell do they want that stuff for?' Callum wondered. 'From everything I've seen, the fuckers aren't exactly vegetarian.'

Over the ensuing weeks, they continued to watch the prador and saw smoke vented from a port in the upper hull of their ship. Analysis revealed it to be from burning plant matter. So, it seemed they were burning the stuff for energy, and whenever they had accumulated enough power, they jumped the ship on grav for eight miles, bringing it down again near more vegetation. They made multiple forays out to collect plant matter and multiple jumps, and Ursula was thankful to see they were heading away from the colony base. But she became curious to know where they were going.

'They're on a straight line course for an ancient seabed marked on the geological survey,' Callum told her. 'Uranium.'

'If they power up fully, that probably won't be good for us,' said Ursula. 'What's happening now?'

On the surface of the ship, a ball-shaped device, almost like an eyeball, shifted and then opened an irised port at its centre.

'Another vent—' Callum began, just as a bright light flashed in the hole. 'Gurda!' he said urgently.

'On it,' she replied.

Three image feeds came up on the screen wall at varying

distances from the assault craft. The first one missed it while the second briefly showed a fiery streak; the third picked up and began to track it.

'Fuck,' said Callum.

The feed showed a classically dart-shaped missile hurtling up into the sky sitting on a glare. Ursula stared at it, her mind blank for a moment, then hit her coms unit. 'General address,' she said. 'Listen up, everyone. The assault craft has just fired a missile. If you're near the massif, clear away from it. If you're inside, head to the lower levels. Find what cover you can.' She was about to order the control room crew to head down, but her tactical integration and logistics training kicked in. 'This is a precaution only. It is highly unlikely they are trying to hit us here.'

'What makes you say that?' asked Vrease, looking up from her console.

Ursula studied the frightened faces. 'They almost certainly scanned us when they came in. They'll know the extent of our base and that a large portion of it is inside the massif. To destroy us they would need a thermonuclear warhead or a CTD. If they had either radioactives or antimatter missiles we would be gone by now. If they have a limited supply, they would use it to power their ship to that uranium. I calculate this is a chemical warhead and, through their foraging, they just reached the point of being able to load and fire it.' She hoped she was right, she really hoped.

'So what is the target?' Vrease asked.

Ursula looked at Callum. She already knew, or thought she knew, but waited for confirmation.

'It's heading up out of atmosphere. Calculating its vector.' He worked his console for a moment, then sat back. 'Fuck.' He looked up at her. 'They're going for the satellite.'

Ursula just nodded.

The satellite tracked its own doom. The missile sped up out of atmosphere and disappeared from its view around Threpsis. It reappeared from the other side with its drive now out, hurtling along a course as inevitable as fate. The final close view was of a shiny nose cone, then the satellite feed dropped out, all screen wall images turning to fuzz.

'Send drones – lots of drones,' said Ursula. 'With any luck they'll be too much of a small irritant to destroy.' She said next, 'General address: we weren't the target. They just took out our satellite.'

Ursula wiped her face and let out a slow breath of relief but noted Vrease's rigid posture.

'Vrease?' she asked.

Vrease just sat there for a long moment staring at her screen, baffled, then looked up. 'We've got some of our people, survivors, trying to get back from beyond the old fence.'

It made no sense. After the depredations of the raptors out there she had pulled everyone inside the multigun defences.

'What? Show me!' Ursula turned away from the window.

4

Present

The massive car's cockpit-cum-control room sat fifty feet above the ground, with a wrap-around chain-glass screen to the fore. The cacoraptors had not yet found a way to break or burn through chain-glass but Ursula had still ensured that adaptive armour shutters were installed to close across it. She'd gone beyond surprise as far as these creatures were concerned, and could imagine them at some point creating the molecular decoder that would unravel chain-glass to dust, as Oren had warned.

She took the seat in the middle of the room and swung a console across her lap, a film screen rising out of the top of it. All around the walls, other consoles gave direct control of weapons and armour in different sections of the car, while Vrease and Callum took an overview and integrated them all. Vrease concentrated on the armour and the more technical aspects, including damage and repair, while Callum focused on the weapons and ran the – they hoped unnecessary – in-car defence. Above these stations, a screen-painted wall ran frames showing views across the different sections and Ursula was able to revolve her chair to get a good view of them all.

'Status,' she asked.

'We're up to full capacitance,' Vrease replied. 'Reactors are running as smoothly as ever and the shuttle reactor is ready to go online in minutes, should we need it.'

'Okay.' Ursula pulled up the joysticks from the console. 'You all know what you have to do but I'll go over it again because this is it – no more training. We blow the outer doors and upper wall of the chamber. The inner doors will open on air-blast hydraulics and then we head out. Nose guns should be on automatic scouring. Everyone else stays hard on this – I want nothing hanging onto us when we make our jump on grav.' She paused before continuing, 'Vrease, grav is good?'

'It's good. I have them all perfectly aligned and they should stay that way.'

They had scavenged the grav-engines for the car from their stored supply of grav-cars, since it was too difficult to salvage the grav-engines from the shuttle.

'Blow the doors now!'

Ahead lay a garage that had been opened out so the car could pass through it. The original doors had been too small, so they'd built larger ones inside, first installing charges against the original doors and the walls above and to either side. The whole base thrummed and ahead the big doors shook down dust. Immediately afterwards, the hydraulic door rams gave an almighty shove, sweeping away debris and opening the base to daylight. With the light came a sense of a presence out there. Ursula again dismissed it as hallucination, but wearily now.

She quickly took in the scene. Wreckage still strewed the landscape and, in the time since they had closed the base, plants had reoccupied the area. As she'd noted before, these were mostly the cactus things with their organic flamethrowers. She now wondered: *deliberately planted by the cacoraptors?* She thrust the joysticks forwards and the giant armoured car rumbled out into the new day, wheels twenty feet across crushing both wreckage and plants. Fire bloomed all around as the plants tried to defend themselves, flaring on the screens. Ursula spun her chair to check the rear view, then back again. She flicked a control and this gave her a graphic of the car's movement in relation to the base. It would not do to engage grav too early and smash the back end of the car into the structure behind.

Now something else flared out there.

'Hits on the armour,' Vrease stated. 'Both sides and tracking from nose to tail.'

'Hits?' Ursula asked.

'They're firing at us with our own perimeter guns.'

Ursula felt a familiar sinking sensation. The bastards were using technology and had never done so before. There was absolutely no doubting their intelligence now – those guns had been all but scrap just a week ago. She felt a surge of adrenaline and anger. Her grip tightened and, looking down at the skin suit on her arms, she saw it raising diamond patterns. This confused her for a second, but the anger gained ascendance.

'Take the fuckers out!' she commanded.

She surveyed the screens as her order was carried out with manual fire, seeing crosshairs appear. In one case, she could actually see the target. Realizing it lay off a forward quadrant, she turned her chair again to look out of one side of the chain-glass front screen. Beyond a group of cycads sat one of the plasticrete pads with the gun mounted upon it. The raptors had obviously moved the entire thing miles to get it here. It fired its minigun and she heard the hail against the armour, then a series of thwacks against the chain-glass. The slugs impacted but the glass held and they soon peeled off and fell away. Next the weapon fired its particle beam, the thing sizzling low down along on the car, doubtless going for the wheels.

'Where the hell are they getting the energy?' she asked.

'From the raptor itself,' Vrease replied.

The creature wrapped around the gun mountings bore some resemblance to the worm form, though thicker. She called a view up on her own screen and focused in, seeing power cables running into the thing. She was thinking *electric eel* just as the car's weapons replied. A missile streaked in and struck the plasticrete pad just ahead of the gun. The explosion threw chunks of plasticrete in every direction and tossed the gun up into the air, the raptor still wrapped around it. As it came down and bounced, the raptor detached, chunks missing from its body, but it still managed to produce paddle limbs and burrow into the ground.

'We're clear of the base now,' Callum observed.

Ursula checked the graphic. She wanted to stay and destroy all the guns and all the cacoraptors she could – there was a tight ball of anger inside her. But with shaking hands she grabbed the joysticks and pulled them both up. As she did this, she noticed her skin armour again. The diamond scales had firmed and taken on an iridescent glint, and was it her imagination or did her hands look bigger, her fingers longer? The car heaved into the sky, still taking fire from the guns. She turned it – grav-planing operating now, but when she needed to manoeuvre faster, thrusters fired up on its surface. Lining the car up on a new positional graphic with the distant prador ship, she thrust the joysticks forward. The car slid through the sky on grav, accelerating as the thrusters kicked in.

She glanced at Gurda. 'Drop some drones.'

'Already done,' Gurda replied.

'What are they doing?'

A small frame opened in the corner of her screen and, using a ball control on top of one joystick, she selected and opened it. The guns, scattered about the base, were still firing, but raptors were coming out of the ground now and on the move. Of course they were following, and in all their different forms. But it was only then that she noted this made no sense in terms of simple survival and the acquisition of nutrients. And that could also be applied to their previous behaviour. She surveyed the people in the control room. All those wearing skin had acquired diamond scales too, as well as odd protrusions sprouting from their suits. In Callum's case, a series of these had grown from his arm, and he didn't seem to notice some had entered the console he was working on.

She checked telemetry. The raptors' current pace would bring them to the car when it landed again and she had no way of avoiding that. Whether she simply stopped the car to charge the capacitors more quickly or ran on the ground at full speed, with slower recharge of the capacitors, they would still reach it.

'Gurda,' she said. 'Take over here.'

Since Gurda's tasks were limited to running their coms and drones, and she'd once been a shuttle pilot in her distant past, she got the job of co-driver.

'When you bring us down, run on fifty per cent,' Ursula added.

This would be optimum, she calculated, her mind snapping through the sums with surprising ease. She put the lock on the joysticks, swung the console aside and stepped out of the chair. They had been reacting all the time with new weapons, new techniques and then the upgrade, but now she needed to know what had driven them to where they were now. The time had come, she felt, for some explanations. She would speak to Oren.

Near Past

Ursula looked round at the smoking ruination of their land. Two more missiles streaked across the sky, their courses parting. One explosion raised a cloud of fire to her right while another lit the horizon to her left. These were to drive raptors back from where fence repairs were being made. She was all too aware that their missile supply was now down to the dregs, until they could produce more. It had taken nearly their whole stock to drive the cacoraptors beyond the fence, and she doubted the hasty repairs there would last. Heading in the direction of the last blast, she could see Shaben's new armoured car. Other cars were out here too, most of them gathered around the steadily advancing plasticrete platform on which they had mounted the multigun. Standing on this platform, Ursula shifted her footing, feeling the thing's caterpillar treads rumbling underneath. She wondered if she'd made the right choice in putting her confidence in the weapon in front of her, or whether she should have stayed in one of the armoured cars.

The weapon consisted of a variety of barrels or other firing mechanisms, weighed in at a few tons and had to be aimed with hydraulics. A further five of these weapons were ready to be positioned to give coverage on the new inner perimeter they'd made. Ursula tried to feel some satisfaction at the deployment of this weapon since the test in the base had been a success – especially the minigun with its dense ceramic bead ammunition – but it still marked a stage of their retreat. Oren's poisons had worked for a while, but the cacoraptors had adapted like bacteria to an antibiotic, and the perimeter fence could only slow rather than stop them now. She'd wanted to save the equipment and weapons they still had out there, but that would have required either colonists or machines retrieving them. And in so doing, they would have weakened the perimeter, leading to the fence failing catastrophically. She would lose more people and she'd lost too many already. The same applied to any machines she sent, which they could ill afford to lose either.

The platform finally arrived at its designated position, sank down over its treads and, with four loud thumps, drove anchors into the ground. Ursula looked around. Things had gone surprisingly well thus far and she'd not seen one raptor. Vrease, on the platform too, stood with her at the back, studying her tablet. Armoured cars parked behind, on a gravel road cutting through an area of the Bled – an area of desert where even the plants struggled to establish. They had intended to clear this for planting and to irrigate it. Now it formed part of a ring which lay inside the failing perimeter fence. Other parts of the ring had been croplands but Ursula had ordered the irrigation there turned off. The theory was that such an area could be another barrier to the cacoraptors – that lack of food for them might drive them to seek prey elsewhere. But Ursula doubted they would lose their taste for human flesh.

'Run the test,' she instructed Vrease.

Vrease smiled at her confidently and jabbed a finger down on her tablet.

The weapon's hydraulics shifted the mass of disparate barrels and emitters so fast they made a snapping sound. It then ran through ranges of fire, at one point aiming straight back at them, before halting. Vrease stabbed down again and the weapon centred ahead. Though the Bled lay behind them, and ahead they had turned off irrigation, a crop of adapted maize was still clinging to life. It bore a slight resemblance to the original. It had the reed-like stems and fat cobs of corn, but each plant stood ten feet tall, stems as thick as a man's thigh. The plants were a deep blue, the leaves razor-edged with the added facility of delivering nasty poisonous spores into any cut they made, and from which grew a flesh-eating fungus. The fungus died in human flesh but not in that of the local animals. Yet another barrier against the cacoraptors, but one they had adapted to in just a day. The cobs were the size of marrows and showed purple corn, with each seed the size of a grape. If 'normal' humans had tried to eat this stuff, it would have burned the lining of their mouths and cut holes through their stomachs. The colonists ate it now with butter and salt, or turned it into flour for other foods.

But this crop, now without irrigation and without being tended to, had been invaded. Blue cycads had grown, and white nodular plants perambulated slowly through, tearing down the maize plants and macerating them with saw-toothed leaves to feed their mobile roots. Red-leaved bushes pushed thorns into stems and sucked nutrients, infecting the crop with a virus, while other parasitic vines and epiphytes caused damage too. And in one area, a plant like a big fat cactus with a wide multicoloured flower on top could open splits in its sides and ignite a jet of methane to incinerate the surrounding plants.

Eyeing the vegetation, Vrease said, 'On your mark.' She'd scanned this area and based a fire test on what was here, though she did have other tests to run, should raptors put in an appearance.

'Run the program,' Ursula instructed.

Vrease thrust her finger down once more.

The weapon fired lasers, burning down the nodular white plants. Another beam lashed out, blue white and visible in the air. As this ionic beam hit the red-leaved plants, they shuddered and retracted their thorns, whereupon the lasers set them burning. Another barrel clattered a wide spray of projectiles, while hydraulics snapped the weapon around. In the smoke, green lasers became visible, eating up epiphytes, tracking the course of vines. Another thump released a small missile. This looped up and over on its own bright drive and came down on top of the cactus-thing, blowing it apart in a spectacular explosion fed by the plant's own gas supply. Ursula stepped back, her helmet snapping up and visor rising to protect her face. Cinders and other debris rolled past in a hot wind. By the time it was over not a single invading plant survived. After a moment Ursula touched a soft control on her wrist to open the head covering again.

'Our crop is not looking so healthy,' she observed.

Vrease shrugged. 'We couldn't use it, anyway.'

'Quite.'

'A successful test?' Vrease enquired.

'A successful test that—'

Ursula's radio in her ear beeped the emergency tone. Callum spoke, panic in his voice, 'They're attacking the shuttle – they're inside!'

Ursula tried to remain calm as she glanced at Vrease, who would be hearing this too. 'They're through the outer fence again?' As far as she could recollect, the fence over there was still upright and undamaged.

'Not through it, fucking over it! The bastards have grown wings!'

'Who is in the shuttle?' she asked.

'No one.'

'What?'

'There's no one in there!'

Ursula tapped the coms unit off as she digested this, feeling the sinking dread in her guts. The implications of this only confirmed what she had been suspecting for a long time. Initially the cacoraptors had attacked like animals. Even though they tried to adapt to the weapons used against them, they still threw themselves against the defences without intelligence. But she had seen behavioural changes, much more sneaking about using cover, and raptors adopting the defences or physical changes others of their kind used, as if they were learning. The things seemed to be becoming intelligent. Now this attack on the shuttle . . . She swallowed dryly and looked to Vrease, feeling cold sweat under her skin suit.

'Range of fire? Coverage?'

Vrease nodded and worked her tablet for a second. The weapon tilted to point up into the sky then right back over towards the base. Ursula nodded as if she had expected this, but in reality she'd been frightened the hydraulics would only allow the weapon to operate at ground level.

'Why the shuttle?' Vrease asked. 'It doesn't make any sense – there's no food in there.'

'Understandably, they make no distinction between the food – us – and our defences. It's probably like an Earth mammal biting off a scorpion's sting before eating the scorpion.' Again she expressed a confidence she didn't feel. She held up her hand to still Vrease. 'Callum,' she said, name activating the coms unit again, 'get the rest of the mosquitoes out of storage – I want that shuttle clear. Immediately.'

'I've anticipated you,' Callum replied. 'We're loading them into a remote-controlled car right now.'

'Good.' Ursula nodded – all business.

When she finally returned to the base, she watched the recorded feed of the mosquitoes going into the shuttle. Resistance had not been as strong as expected. She watched worm-like creatures being shredded under their concentrated pulse fire. Analysis revealed that to become light enough to fly, the raptors had sacrificed much of their ability to change and adapt. This group of them was almost like a suicide squad. And when Ursula later learned the creatures had simply destroyed the shuttle's drive and little else, her dread seemed to turn into a singular beast.

The gun tipped back with a crack to point up into the sky. It stuttered, tracking the flying cacoraptor, shredding the thing's body and shattering its wings. As it fell, the weapon targeted it with a laser whose red beam only became visible in the smoke trail of the creature, which finally hit the ground and broke apart into red-hot embers. The gun then spun to the left, tracking something picked up by the seismic detectors and ground scan. It spat a single missile whose slow flight Ursula could see. The thing ploughed into the earth, flipped upright like a post and drilled down. A moment later, a deep detonation lifted a bubble of earth which collapsed, issuing smoke and flames.

'We are fucking winning!' Callum exclaimed, punching a fist into the air.

Ursula nodded and tried to feel at least some agreement. As they'd hoped, the guns were stopping the cacoraptors dead. For now. The eighty-seven colonists who had been in the infirmary or regrowth tanks had, by dint of their advanced nanosuites, recovered quickly and were now back at work. But one hundred and fifty-four colonists had died during the incursions through the fences. They had lost factories, greenhouses, bioreactors, roads and dwellings, and tons of their equipment, including the shuttle's drive. Energy wasn't yet a problem, with the fusion plants, super-capacitors and laminar storage within the perimeter, but Shaben was struggling to keep up the supply of some of the specialized missiles and projectiles like the mole mine. And out here?

Ursula looked around. Fields were appearing again, craters being filled in and new planting beginning, but how long could this last? The cacoraptors had meanwhile brought in a whole herd of brontopods and slaughtered the creatures in a copse of fern trees, whose dense and highly reflective leaves the scanning of their drones and satellite had failed to penetrate. And she felt sure the creatures had planted those things themselves.

She turned her attention to a machine working round beyond the perimeter, laying mines. The heavy vehicle ran on caterpillar treads and sported layered reactive armour. This was the first iteration of the adaptive armour they were aiming for. It brandished a cornucopia of weapons to keep the local wildlife away as it drilled into the ground to deposit its load. Yet they had still lost four of these minelayers, while the production of mines was also on the brink of failing to keep up with demand.

Her radio beeped the emergency channel and Vrease spoke: 'There's someone out there, with cacoraptors closing on whoever it is.'

'Your location?' Ursula asked.

'Gun Three.'

'The gun is keeping them back?'

'For the present.'

'Is rescue feasible?' As she said it, Ursula felt slightly sick that they had to make such calculations.

'We'd lose cars.'

Ursula glanced back to her own vehicle. She now used a grav-car for brief surveys like this one. They couldn't carry much armour or weapons, so landing them anywhere wild usually resulted in a lot of damage. Encounters with the rare large fliers often ended in fatal damage too, and now the cacoraptors had taken to the air, Ursula had confined their use to within the new perimeter. She abruptly came to a decision and ran over to her grav-car, climbed inside and threw it into the air.

The car lifted raggedly – another machine Shaben had been struggling to maintain. She sent it back over the scattered buildings and new crop fields within the perimeter. Dust rose from channels made through the base buildings to the massif. They were cutting new shafts into the stone, and piles of flaked stone had been heaped out beyond these. The steady enlargement of the chambers underneath the massif, to take equipment, manufacturing and accommodation, was a sensible move. But it was a further retreat.

Rounding the massif, she brought her grav-car down towards Gun Three. The guns weren't always attended since they didn't have the spare personnel, and the weapons could function perfectly well by themselves. Vrease was just climbing out of her car when Ursula brought hers to a hover there, so she could view the scene ahead. Beyond Gun Three, local plants had burgeoned across fields surrounding a collapsed warehouse. Since the colonists had disconnected the irrigation out there, the plants had closed down into a waiting state to conserve moisture. Spread bushes had closed up into knotted lumps, cycads had closed their leaves and looked like smooth-skinned cacti, while tree ferns were standing spikes, their leaves wrapped close to their trunks.

Amidst all this she could see cacoraptors chasing a human clad in skin. The multigun was blasting the raptors all around him as he ran, shredding plants too, and rising up occasionally to incinerate the flying ones which tried to drop on him like hawks. Ursula dismissed her initial idea of flying in to perform a quick, morale-boosting rescue. The flying raptors would tear her car apart before she even got close. Instead she descended to land by the other vehicle, climbed out and trotted after Vrease, who was climbing the steps onto the plasticrete platform. By the time Ursula reached her, Vrease had raised a control and diagnostics column out of the plasticrete and opened a screen to give a better view of what was going on.

'Who the hell is this?' Vrease gestured at the screen.

'We've recovered a few bodies after the attacks,' said Ursula, peering at the screen. 'Maybe their life signs monitor was knocked out – it's happened a few times.'

The colonist was running fast for someone wearing skin. He'd nearly reached the collapsed warehouse when a borer broke from the ground, its head a mass of revolving tooth belts, spraying soil in every direction. He swerved as it lunged for him, then a missile thumped into the creature's head and blew it apart. The shock wave sent the colonist tumbling but he was up in a moment and running towards the warehouse wall.

'Fuck,' said Vrease. 'Don't go there – stay in the open.'

'Have you tried com with him?'

Vrease shook her head. 'No response.'

Ursula's stomach steadily tightened. She felt herself dipping forward as if she might be able to impart some energy, some impetus to the figure's flight. Raptors came in from one side – the kind that penetrated brontopods – but it wasn't their attack that drove him closer to the wall, it was the heat and explosions destroying them. Ursula found herself growing cold, almost certain what would happen next. She considered future options. Perhaps something should be changed in the weapons' base programming? It prevented them firing on humans, but maybe something should be added that adjusted for the overall effects of the weapons, and in turn the reach of blast waves or heat? She then realized this wouldn't work. If the weapon had limited itself in such a way, the runner would be dead by now.

The figure had nearly reached the end of the warehouse wall when this wall simply fell apart as a mass of raptors came through. The multigun did its best to hit them with everything it had, but the great tangle of wormish forms, even exploding and burning, still fell upon the colonist. Even from this distance, Ursula heard brief screams, glimpsing sprays of red and body parts sliding away into the mass. She turned her attention from the screen and looked out as the multigun shut down.

'We'll do a search,' she said tightly, 'and try to find out who that was.'

But of course they never identified the runner, because no humans had survived beyond the perimeter.

★　　★　　★

Oren, besides being their resident expert on nanosuites, and alien life, and especially cacoraptors, also acted as their coroner and forensic examiner. So he was the one to compile all the details of the deaths. After checking through the files once more, he turned his head right round to look up at Ursula.

'All I can give you are potentials, and too many of them to really make any sense of,' he said. 'I looked at the video feed and ascertained that the subject was male. The appearance of the skin suit he wore could fit that of at least fifty casualties. It was heavily scarred and, as you know, the suits can heal and change as required.'

'Do you have any that are most likely?' she asked.

'Only by circumstance,' he replied. 'Seven colonists were in an agricultural station the raptors hit.'

'Outpost 32 – they called it the Stink Cellar.'

He nodded. 'You remember.'

Of course she did. She remembered each one of them and wished she could edit them from her mind. But she hadn't. Apart from the fact that editing might lose her vital knowledge, she felt she should bear the guilt.

He continued, 'We never saw what happened inside and found only scraps from which we could identify two women and two men. Of three other men there, we found genetic traces but nothing to definitively say they had died.' He shrugged. 'That's often been the case.'

'Thank you for trying anyway,' she said, and turned to head away from his work station. On the way, she paused by the window into the morgue. Only two of the body compartments were occupied – by two decapitated corpses. In their case the raptors had been driven back by autoguns before claiming their prizes. Oren had resorted to other storage for most of the remains – containers ranging from the size of a teacup to a bucket.

Standing there, she remembered when she'd cried, and then there being a time in her life when she'd been incapable of that, and was glad of it. Now her eyes were utterly dry, but she felt no fear of this. She grimaced and moved on, her mind straying back to when her emotions had started to die, and when her old life ended.

Past

It had once been mooted that landing sites on the Earth's moon should be preserved for posterity and, in the decades before the Quiet War, when the AIs took over, many of them had been protected under glassy domes. But even then no one could decide where the cut-off point should be between 'history' and the less interesting near past. Meanwhile, arguments raged about who owned which artefacts and what territory on the moon, and had been getting messy, while protecting the numerous scattered sites wasn't easy. Items went missing, or were relocated if they obstructed the path of lunar developments, and some were destroyed. When the AIs seized power from the corporate entities and governments of the Solar system, they had built the upper levels of the Viking Museum in the centre of Mare Tranquillitatis, diligently recording every detail of the landing sites, then moved all the artefacts into their new home. Historians were apoplectic, of course, but a lot of people were angry at that time about a lot of things. But while the AIs might listen to human concerns, generally they went on to ignore them and did things in their own much better and more efficient manner.

Ursula Ossect Treloon did enjoy the displays of antiquated technology in the upper levels, but the regimented viewing necessary to accommodate millions of visitors every year annoyed her intensely. She passed quickly along the moving pedway which ran through the centre of the museum, while thousands of people swirled around the giant display cases on either side, looking at the artefacts and carefully transplanted areas of regolith, as well as moon dust with centuries-old footprints in it. She had of course been here before, both physically and in virtuality, and seen much of it. But today was special. She had finally been granted permission to see artefacts which few, in terms of the Polity as a whole, got to see. She had applied for permission to view them nearly fifty years ago. That this permission had been granted upon her first return to Earth in decades was passing strange, but she'd lived long enough to know that coincidences were more common than supposed, though in this case it wasn't an aspect of the human mind's propensity to look for patterns.

As she approached the edge of the lunar history display, an area of twenty square miles, she moved out to the slower lanes of the pedway before reaching the angled padded barriers. She then crossed a floor of polished moon rock slabs – surprisingly colourful considering the usual impression of the moon from its exterior grey and silver appearance. Finally she came to a wall of chain-glass that stretched up to the glass ceiling, and she moved along it to find one of the doors. It looked like a piece of rectangular cut slate in a silver frame and no handles or locking mechanisms were visible. Via her augmentation, she sent the code they'd provided her with – an n-dimensional construct she could neither transfer, copy nor access, and which changed as time passed. The door swung open silently and admitted her to the outer ring.

No displays occupied this area and the glass ceiling had been displaced by one loaded with scanners and security drones that could drop down at any moment. Rumour had it that there was more here than just them. This might have been true, but seemed a pointless addition, considering the security of her destination. She turned left and began walking. On her right, in the outer wall, heavy circular doors gave access into tubes running across the surface. At the ends of these were large spherical display capsules that contained dangerous, rare or highly valuable items. Personally, Ursula thought that the way these capsules were dotted regularly in a ring around the main museum had more to do with AI OCD than any necessity for these items to be stored separately. In reality only one of the capsules needed to be isolated – the one she was heading to.

Finally, she came to the circular door she'd been looking for and walked over to stand before it. She sent the code once more and, as it went, its base format in her aug dissolved. She would never be able to use it again. As she stood there, she felt suddenly hot – a wave passing from the top of her head down through her body. She'd just received a highly active scan and now her enhanced immune system and nanosuite would be repairing or destroying damaged cells that might otherwise turn cancerous.

'Shut down your aug,' murmured a voice seemingly out of the air beside her.

She reached up to the slug of grey metal anchored to her skull behind her ear and pressed the, positively retro, off button. A gulf seemed to open in her mind and, as the door ahead thumped open, she felt slightly more stupid than she had a moment before. She stepped through into the long transparent tunnel running over the regolith. Ahead she could see the upper hemisphere of the spherical storage and display capsule. The lower half, below the ground, was apparently filled with security systems, weapons and a collection of CTDs that if detonated would probably break the moon in half, while below that was a massive fuser engine. She strolled towards it, coming to another security door, where she was subjected to yet another scan before being admitted.

'Do you want the narrative?' the same voice asked her.

'No need really, unless you have something new to say,' she replied.

'Another artefact is on display . . .'

'Well, tell me about that while I look around.'

She walked in. Display cases were evenly positioned across the floor while, around the edges, further cases had been inset in the walls. She walked up to the first on the floor and peered inside. Lying on a small plinth was a chunk of something that looked as if it had been dug out of one of the landfill excavations on Earth. A mess of metals and ceramics bound together with rust. Not impressive at all.

'The new artefact was found on a moon of the Demeter gas giant in the system of Eradni Four. It was discovered during a mining operation – that moon is laden with cantaloupe diamonds with rare metals doping.'

'Manufactured diamonds?' Ursula enquired.

'Natural,' the Viking Museum AI replied. 'After the discovery of the artefact the mining operation was of course cancelled while further investigations were made.'

'Same date as the others?'

'Within a hundred thousand years, yes – the rock the artefact was found in was formed five million years ago.'

'Raises some interesting questions, like: was the moon created by a natural event or not?'

'That question may get an answer when the xenologists have finished taking apart the moon.'

'I bet the miners were pissed off.'

The AI just grunted an acknowledgement.

Ursula reached out to touch the glass of the display case and it opened a frame for her with touch controls along the bottom. The first magnification showed her something that looked like a crushed mess of ancient electronics. She went down as far as the microscopy could take her, revealing further regular complexity with each magnification. Nanoscopic magnification gave her the same, right down to its limit. The stuff was fractal, with that same regularity and deliberate structure that was supposedly picoscopic and maybe even femtoscopic. But she knew all this and had already studied these objects in virtuality.

'Where's the new artefact?' she asked.

A line appeared on the floor and she followed it to a case set into the wall. Inside this rested a block of what looked like translucent blue glass. However, as she peered closer, she saw it seemed to contain, again, ancient electronics.

'Laminar densified sapphire,' said the AI. 'Speculated to be a foundation piece of some Jain structure, maybe a house.'

'That seems far too prosaic. What's that inside it?'

'The same as you saw in the other item you looked at.'

'So you've no real idea?'

'We have ideas,' was all the AI said.

Yes, she had studied all this. The scraps of technology they'd found contained computing, and the ability to grow and become more complex when in the appropriate environment. The conclusions were that this stuff was capable of, well . . . anything. Rumours had it that the AIs had experimented with some artefacts before classifying Jain technology as dangerous and illegal to possess. The questions she had asked were just rote since all the available information could be accessed anywhere with an aug. The reason for visiting in person was the frisson of accessing a part of the museum that could be ejected at any moment by the fuser drive, and then vaporized by the CTDs under her feet on its course towards the sun. But she wasn't really feeling it.

Ursula spent her allotted hour in the capsule looking at all the objects, moving to the door when it was all over.

'Was your experience satisfactory?' the AI asked.

She shrugged. 'I would have preferred to see the stuff you don't have on display.'

'There is nothing more than what you see here.'

Ursula nodded. The AIs had been telling that lie for a long time but, as many had pointed out, why was every Jain artefact just the right size for the display cases here? Where were the larger items, and the stuff the AIs were undoubtedly studying? She headed out, through the tunnel and back into the main museum. She considered going to look at some of the other exhibits but the idea bored her. She carried on towards the exit which would take her to the runcible back to Earth. As the pedway swept her along, she realized she had just ticked off one of the last major items on her bucket list. She needed a new list now – she needed something to do to alleviate a growing numbness inside that she was too frightened to name.

5

Present

After a brief visit to her cubby to confirm something she'd suspected, Ursula went to find Oren. His new laboratory on the car was obviously smaller than at the base. The cacoraptor's chain-glass tube stood upright, half sunk into one wall. Glancing at it, she noticed changes – spines protruding along its length. Her thoughts about the chain-glass screen of the car replayed; she wondered if the damned thing was trying to escape, and worried it would be here that a raptor learned how to decode chain-glass.

Equipment was neatly arrayed around the walls, other items kept up in the ceiling to be lowered when required. Despite it being cramped, Oren seemed happy enough studying various nanoscope views while, without looking, he also worked on one of the colonists' upgrade bracelets that was suspended in a small frame and surrounded by arrays of micromanipulators. His head turned right round to track her. She peered down at his wrist and saw he was wearing an upgrade bracelet himself, but that meant nothing – he might have deactivated it.

'I've had some thoughts,' Ursula began. 'These were things that bothered me on a subliminal level before, but now I seem to be thinking about them very clearly.'

'Really?' He smiled. 'Mental pressure is a pressure nevertheless. The cacoraptors enhanced their minds to achieve sentience to face us – they became intelligent – and the same option is available to us: mental enhancement.'

'To face us,' Ursula repeated. 'Which begs the question: why are they facing us?'

'We are a bounteous source of nutrients and water.' He paused thoughtfully for a second, then added, 'Water is the main attraction, I believe, since the human body contains more even than a brontopod.'

An interesting fact, but Ursula saw it for what it was: distraction, diversion.

'That won't do, Oren. The cacoraptors have very little problem bringing down their conventional prey, like the brontopods, and are not suffering any lack. Our more accessible nutrients might have explained the initial attacks upon us, but do not account for the later ones. We've killed many of them and they passed the point long ago where the energy, nutrients and water they expend in hunting us can be replaced by . . . us. Their hostility goes beyond mere predatory instinct.'

He shrugged. 'Intelligence.'

'Yes, they grew brains and reason, yet still the same thesis applies. Why do they keep hunting us beyond any gain for themselves? Why the hostility?'

This time he didn't shrug, but repeated himself: 'Intelligence.'

Of course: intelligence. He could keep going back to that and had all of human history to back up his claim. But it didn't get to the heart of the matter which, despite her clearer thinking, was still nebulous.

'And another thing: they're outside of the usual predator–prey cycle. There is no balance. Predators with such an advantage would annihilate their prey and end up dying out from starvation.'

'No,' said Oren. 'On some worlds there are predators with an extreme advantage over their prey. The droons of Cull and the hooders of Masada, for example. They achieve continuance in the first case by hibernation when prey numbers drop, and in the second because of the sheer profligacy of prey. The hooders also have a super-efficient metabolism and a slow breeding rate.'

Ursula didn't know this and realized she'd been basing her contention on Terran life forms, and she wasn't sure that was entirely the case there. But she wasn't about to let this distract her.

'Then there's the genetics of these creatures. You opined that they transform themselves – adapt – on the basis of their genetic library, and that they can copy and utilize alien genomes.' She felt a surge of something, some excitement. She was getting closer to some truth now. 'But how is it they can respond to things which simply couldn't be part of their environment? How can they grow defences against energy and projectile weapons and, like one we just saw operating one of our guns, create their own system to supply bio-electricity to technology?' She paused and added, 'Do not say "intelligence" again because that first raptor we encountered grew laser reflective skin way before the fuckers grew brains.'

Oren watched her in silence for a long moment, then said, 'I could offer explanations. The reflective skin might have been a development in the past arising due to high solar output. All the abilities to resist projectile weapons are simply explainable in terms of a hostile environment and hostile prey, some of which do in fact fire projectiles. Bio-electricity is a defence Earth creatures use, but combine that with growing intelligence and, of course, their powering up of the weapon is explainable.' He smiled a bleak smile. 'But we are past that now, aren't we? The upgrade is in you all and cannot be removed and soon enough you'll work it all out for yourselves.'

'What do you mean?'

'Think again on what you said a moment ago: "they can copy and utilize alien genomes". Ponder on this fact.'

Ursula stepped back as if she had been struck. Her mind went into overdrive. Disparate facts and data points seemed to orbit some inner self before collapsing back to a shape that made logical sense.

'They can copy and utilize alien genomes but, of course, they retain useful survival traits.' She felt suddenly hot as she got it. 'They copy alien genomes to their genetic library and use them again. The traits we have seen, the resistance to weapons, comes from an alien source . . . as does the intelligence.'

As she now thought about where next to take this, Oren added, 'As does the hostility too.' He winced a smile.

'Explain,' she said.

He reached out and tapped a finger against her bracelet. 'The connection is there and it took me a little while to recognize it. The few examples of Jain tech are locked away in the Viking Museum on Earth's moon, though the Four Seasons Changer is proof that some of it escaped the AIs hunting down every scrap of it. As I told you before, it's dangerous because all of it can replicate. But it can also become more complex, and it is hostile – it always tries to sequester any machine with which it comes into contact. From this we can suppose that its creators were hostile too.'

'One could suppose that from a Polity weapon. That doesn't make all humans killers,' she replied.

'You misunderstand. The hostility is at the root of this technology. Most Polity weapons are inert until an activating mind uses them. This is like a gun that immediately opens fire on any target. The AI analysis goes even deeper than this, to the very shape of the thing. They have extrapolated it will not stop at mere machines but transfer to a controlling mind and distort it to its purpose, which seems to be the subsumption or destruction of just about anything it encounters.'

'You're saying the Jain were here on this world? And that the raptors took on their genome?'

'Those strange crystal formations on the shore of the dried-out seabed the prador are heading to. They were assessed as natural. They are not. They are the hard crystal foundations of something the Jain built. Maybe homes, though the very idea of home seems prosaic when it concerns them.'

Ursula rolled this all over in her mind and inspected it from every angle. She remembered in the Viking Museum herself feeling 'house' was too prosaic when it came to the Jain. It all had the ring of truth but she knew there was more Oren hadn't told her. She thought back to her brief visit to her cubby.

'I'm not able to remove my skin suit,' she said.

He nodded. 'I used some elements of the cacoraptor genome when I made those suits. The integration is likely to be total.'

'Something you neglected to mention,' said Ursula, at last finding a point to be angry about.

'We agreed, when I manipulated our crops to grow here, and ourselves so we could eat them, I would have carte blanche on my use of genetic matter on this world if it was to our advantage.'

'Outside of the human body, I believe we agreed.'

'The skin suits were effectively outside the human body, and that agreement is somewhat out of date now . . .' Oren held up his wrist with the bracelet around it.

Still Ursula felt she must be missing something, further nebulous knowledge just out of her grasp. She gazed at Oren as she tried to nail it down, but the beeping of her communicator interfered.

'What is it?' she asked snappily.

'We've got fliers approaching,' said Callum.

'Well deal with them.'

'And they're armed,' he added.

'What?' Ursula was already on her way towards the door. She paused there and turned back. 'This is not over, Oren.'

He blinked at her and returned his attention to his nanoscope screens.

Only when she was halfway to the control room did she realize something. The fact that the full Polity survey of this world had missed the cacoraptors raised some serious questions, but Jain technology too? It was one of the most dangerous things the AIs were always on the lookout for, so how could they have missed Jain ruins? Hating the necessity, she shelved her thoughts on that. Survival came first and she would not allow this distraction to result in any more of her people dying.

Near Past

No, just no, thought Ursula as she drove her car out. Since the most recent deaths, she'd become even more determined not to lose another colonist. On hearing that one more had gone missing she headed out with the search teams. It wasn't her job, but she damned well wanted to find him and bring him home.

'Nursum?' she enquired, using an emergency channel direct to the biologist's radio. No reply again.

She peered down at the screen in the armoured car. His locator implant signal was absent. They'd been having problems with implanted devices for some time now. Right from the start, the intense solar radiation here had been causing interference with delicate electronics in devices with extreme miniaturization. Subsequently, nanosuite updates and the recent digestive upgrades had resulted in their bodies becoming a much more hostile environment for anything foreign. It seemed the synergy between nanosuite and immune system had resulted in one or the other attacking any of the colonists' implanted technology. Those who'd remained still using augs had now mostly removed them, and the list of other devices heading into recycling kept increasing. She was, however, getting something from Nursum's suit, though oddly dispersed and intermittent.

'Found something,' said Vrease over radio.

'I'm coming over,' Ursula replied. 'The rest of you keep searching your areas.'

She located Vrease's car on the screen, also seeing the other cars in the search grid. She pulled up the joystick and turned her car, tempted to head directly to Vrease, but that would have meant crossing the field ahead. She eyed the neat rows of purple sprouts stabbing out of the ground, an agribot perambulating alongside them. Its laser occasionally flashed as it located some local spore, seed or fungal growth. These plants were sweetcorn – extremely rugged and capable of chemically fending off all sorts of pests.

Her screen map generated the shortest route to Vrease's car via the tracks running between fields. She turned right and accelerated, kicking up flaked stone and mud, then slowed to turn alongside a channel recently dug up to take an irrigation pipe. Soon she motored past a field where green-red bushes sprouted from long low mounds. Lime-green sensory flowers tracked her progress, as they did any nearby movement. If anything drew close, the bushes thrashed out stalks covered with sharp poisonous hooks. These weren't the actual crop because that lay below. Ursula shook her head. Never in her previous speculations about this place had she imagined driving past a field of aggressive potatoes.

Further turnings took her past wheat with poisonous spines, a kind of cabbage that retreated into the ground when anything came close, a field necessarily fenced to prevent the pepper plants there from wandering away, burrowing carrots and whip-lash celery. Again she found herself shaking her head. Those working in agriculture were finding much amusement in all this, but if the crops weren't successful they would have to spend off-world colony funds on a shipment of food. They couldn't afford to do that more than once and, if the food supply wasn't sorted by the time *that* ran out, they would have to abandon this place.

Vrease's car was parked by two silos, built to take a crop of barley which had failed just before harvesting. They'd found that every grain contained the nymph of a parasite whose genetics had originally been employed for the barley's defences. This alone might not have been a problem, but the nymphs had stripped the grains of any nutrition that the adapted colonists could digest. As she always felt it necessary to dampen down Oren's eagerness for change, Ursula had cited this as proof of how risky it was to introduce xenogenetics to their food. Oren grudgingly agreed, to her surprise. Later he came back to her with evidence that the infestation had actually arisen from an easily correctible mistake. She still had her qualms, but by then the colonists were eating the first crop of sweetcorn, and euphoric about its success. She decided to let it go.

After parking her car, she walked out to where Vrease was standing in a field of carrots. As Ursula walked into it the greenery of the carrots nearby, sprouting from bright red tops, closed up as the bashful vegetables slid into the ground. This occurred within a circle twenty feet across around her – this travelling with her as those behind rose up again while those ahead went down. A similar empty circle surrounded Vrease. Ursula came up to stand beside Vrease as she pointed at the ground ahead. A shoulder section of a combat suit lay in the dirt.

'I don't know if it's his,' she said, 'but it seems likely.'

Ursula inspected the ground, noting that something had churned up the earth here. A trail of this led from one side of the field to the other, with no indication which direction the source of those marks had travelled. There would be forensic evidence here, which was why Vrease had not yet picked up the piece of armour. Ursula studied the marks further to assure herself they'd not been caused by adaptive wheels, treads or anything else from one of the colonists' vehicles, before stepping forward and lifting the piece of armour.

Some of the underlying fabric had been torn, which would have taken the kind of power found in an industrial machine. But the plants and animals here had long demonstrated such traits in one form or another. Inspecting the edge of the piece, she found a barcode. After making a few brief changes to the lasers, which raised the control hologram from her wristcom, she ran the code over it. A quick crosscheck showed it to be the serial number of Nursum's suit.

'Cacoraptor got him?' Vrease suggested.

'If so, how did it get through the fence without us knowing?'

Vrease shrugged, but looked worried.

Ursula stared at the marks in the ground for a while longer. She couldn't keep a check on everything happening in the colony but did still try to take a general overview. Nursum's expertise mainly fell on agricultural biology and genetics so he, among others, had been working with the new modifications to the crops under Oren. But Nursum also had another interest in something. When she'd first seen it wandering back towards the base all those months ago, it had interested Ursula too.

'We learn never, ever to take anything for granted here,' she said. 'Get back to your car – we'll know shortly where to go next.'

As soon as she was back in her car with the piece of armour lying beside her, Ursula checked her map. One locator had been placed on a local life form and she saw that it was not far away.

'Follow me,' she told Vrease, and sent over their course, this time heading straight across the fields to their destination.

Vrease quickly understood what that destination must be.

'Oh hell,' she said.

Carrots quickly ducked for cover as she drove across the field, diverging from the track marks already there. Whatever had made them had obviously turned down the side road by the field for a while, then onto a swathe of land where the agronomists had been growing a form of fungus that attacked local wildlife and might help with land clearance. Even as she drove onto this, she saw a tangled mass that looked like fabric from a combat suit. After a moment she saw her target in the distance, lurching along like a tall arthritic old man: the mobile strangler fig.

'Zodac,' she said over radio – another colonist and the erstwhile pilot of their shuttle, he now worked out here in the fields. He was parked back at the agricultural complex where they kept a lot of equipment. 'I want a disposal car with the full complement of cutting gear to my location.'

'Problem?' Zodac asked.

'I think we might have found Nursum.' She sent the same target location she'd sent to Vrease.

'Oh, I see,' Zodac replied. 'I'll get a med team out from the base to you too.'

'Yes, do that.'

The fig had first been seen wandering around the base and around the fields being prepared for trial crops. Callum's brother Hale had deemed it safe while Nursum had confirmed this and taken a special interest in it. The poor mobile tree was looking for its preferred prey, either the blue cycads that threw poisoned spines, the flamer cactus or any of a number of fat scaly trees that resembled palms. Those working in agriculture out here had kind of adopted it as a pet. They often left treats for it in the form of the seared remains of cycad sprouts, which it gobbled up eagerly. These also guided it away from trampling on new plantings or prevented it wandering onto newly tilled and sterilized soil.

She drew her car to a halt fifty feet back from the thing and climbed out just as Vrease pulled up beside her. Vrease stepped out of her car carrying a pulse rifle. Sensible. Ursula ducked back into her car and pulled out her own laser carbine. As they began walking over, she noted that the trail the strangler fig had left was pretty much what she'd seen in the carrot field. Perhaps it'd be better to hold back and await reinforcements? No. Despite the fact that Nursum had lost his suit, he still might be alive.

As they drew closer, the fig ceased its perambulation and Ursula got the weird sense it was now turning its attention towards them. She studied it closely. The tangle of main woody trunks bore the same shape as when she had first seen the thing. These branched at the top into what looked like asparagus spikes, which occasionally opened out flares of petals, bristles and photosynthesizing leaves. Apparently the whole body of the thing, whose colour was a grey green with dull red stripes, had layers of photosynthesizing cells. External branches lower down were slowly mobile, as was the flare of roots that led to its 'feet'. The 'twigs' of these lower branches were its main feeding apparatus. When it closed itself around another plant, these pressed into the surface and slowly stabbed in feeding tubes that injected acid to dissolve the victim's insides. Right now only a few of these were visible, while many of the branches had folded in. The fig was holding something and feeding on it.

'I don't hold out much hope for his recovery,' said Vrease, displaying a black humour Ursula had never noticed before.

As she had feared, the fig had Nursum. And he had been reduced to a shrivelled mummy, skin and muscle shrunk to his bones, teeth exposed in a horrible grin. The lower parts of his legs, she noticed, hung like empty socks. The thing was dissolving him from the inside while somehow not burning holes out through his skin. And now it seemed to be eating his bones. She wondered just how long it had taken him to die, since the nanosuite would have been fighting to keep him alive. Then he turned his head towards them and opened one remaining eye, followed by his mouth, as if he was trying to scream.

'We have to get him out of there!' Ursula moved forwards, not sure what she was going to do. A branch lashed out, much faster than she had seen this fig ever move, and its twig fingers closed around her wrist. Steam rose from the 'skin' covering there, bubbling with acid. She tried to pull away as another branch began to unwind from the central body of the plant. Light flared beside her as Vrease fired, hitting the branch – the thing juddered and wrenched at Ursula's arm. Vrease moved closer and concentrated fire just out from Ursula's wrist, the woody material of the branch flaking and curling as it burned. Finally it broke and she and Vrease ducked away as further branches lashed out at them. Ursula tried to peel the woody fingers from her wrist but they were tough. So she took out a vibro-knife and cut, having to peel every bit away from the underlying armour. The 'skin' there had been burned through, but it quickly began to grow back to fill the hole.

'What the hell do we do now?' Vrease asked.

Ursula picked up her carbine. The tools they required were on their way and the medical team shortly behind them, but both would take some time to get here. Meanwhile Nursum was still looking at them. And was that some movement of his one shrivelled hand? Yes.

'We hit the branches holding him,' she said. 'The nanosuite has kept him alive this long and once he's free of this thing, it should keep sustaining him till the med team gets here.'

Vrease nodded, walked in until she stood just out of range of the groping branches and began firing with cold precision. Ursula didn't trust her own aim as she moved closer, so she made a link with her weapon to bring up a crosshairs in her visor. She began shooting too, and flinched when a branch flared and burned right next to Nursum. But really, could she hurt him any more? Branches flaked and curled, dropping to the ground burning, all of them leaving 'hands' attached to the biologist's body. The fig began to back away and they advanced as it did so. It seemed to get the idea and Ursula wondered about its degree of intelligence as it started to detach branches from its prey. They were winning, it was going to release him. But she then wondered about the degree of viciousness in that intelligence when, with the remaining branches, it tore Nursum in half at the waist and threw him towards them.

Vrease kept on the fig, driving it to retreat further. Smoking and burning, it continued its slow perambulation away from them. Ursula stooped by the top half of Nursum. He turned his head towards her, blinked, and shifted his jaw as if trying to chew something. She reached out and took hold of one withered hand and felt it move slightly – some pressure of his fingers against hers.

'What do you want us to do with it?'

She looked around. She hadn't noticed the other vehicle – an armoured truck loaded with equipment – arrive. She looked up at Callum's brother Hale. He was staring down at Nursum in horror, but then met her gaze, his expression hardening, and pointed to the retreating fig.

'Burn it,' she replied. 'Burn it until there is nothing left.'

He nodded smartly and headed away.

What could Nursum be thinking now, what would he say if he could speak? She knew the answer to that just as she'd known it when he looked at her from the strangler fig: kill me, kill me now. But she'd thought that in the past herself too. Pain, no matter how intense, would pass, and if there was mental damage there was always memory editing.

She continued to hold his hand as she heard the whoosh of a flame unit, felt the wash of heat and heard the clattering and snapping of the fig's branches. Soon other people were next to her. She looked up and saw someone bagging the lower half of Nursum's body. Those beside her shifted him onto a grav-gurney and she released his hand. They inserted tubes and wires from a collection of cylinders, and fluids began running into Nursum under pressure. She saw one of the medics nodding as he worked, issuing instructions to another. She only later learned that Oren had been telling them what to do. Soon Nursum was sliding away towards the armoured ambulance, which in turn pulled away.

Ursula stood, looked across to the burning fig, then wearily returned to her car.

The new covering Oren had created for the combat suit seemed to have subsumed more of the suit itself. The armour plates were now integral and included a substance like chitin copied from one of the local herbivores. It also connected to the computing of the suit, and through that to the nanosuite within whichever body it was protecting.

'Do you think that link is entirely necessary?' Ursula asked.

Oren nodded. Of course he did. 'The suit is the first line of defence but there are things here we know could get through it eventually. I want that first line providing information to the second line of defence, which is the person's nanosuite.'

'I see.' Ursula nodded.

'I would even prefer a more direct connection between them,' Oren added.

Ursula decided not to respond to that, instead reaching out to tap the visor of the new suit. 'Chain-glass still. Perhaps we could make suits entirely of this?'

He shook his head, its range of movement again giving her a crick in her neck. 'Very risky. Chain-glass is tough but, once you have the decoder molecule, it's powder. And it's nowhere near as complex as some of the . . . defences life forms here can get through. We should not rely on such a singular barrier.' He pondered that for a moment, then added, 'I'm working on a solution to that.'

'I never said we should,' she pointed out. 'But an outer layer of chain-glass might be a good idea, don't you think?'

'It's a thought, but still doesn't get round the decoding issue. If something cracks that, it will be through the visor and straight into the most vulnerable part of the human body.' He paused, introspectively. 'And I don't think we've yet seen anywhere near what the cacoraptors might be capable of.'

'Okay. I'll accept that for now. So this will now be resistant to that acid the fig used?'

'A catalytic acid,' he said. 'I've never seen anything like it outside of an ECS laboratory. But even that wasn't the main problem – it was the boring tubules that delivered it. This new covering is more resistant to the acid than Polity materials and will react to the tubules with a shifting grid that either snips them off or crushes them before they can deliver their load.'

Ursula studied the suit again. She saw that the covering didn't spread across the suit once it was donned but sat permanently in place. This had required redesigning the way it was put on, with the thing opening out like space armour so the wearer could step inside it. She wondered at what point they would cease calling it Polity combat armour.

'Okay,' she said. 'Start recalling the other suits and altering them.' She went over to the door, pushing it open. She wanted to go straight back to the control room or her quarters, but felt she had a duty to perform here first. Oren crowded up behind her, no doubt anxious to get to work on the suits. She turned to him. 'Let's go to the infirmary.'

'You want to see him,' said Oren. 'There's not much to see.'

'Nevertheless.' She stepped through and gestured him ahead along the corridor.

Oren set out at a fast walk. As she followed, she pondered on the fact he'd never yet left the base and appeared perfectly content with the data, imagery and samples others provided. It seemed to her almost as if he occupied a Polity cyst at the centre of her colony . . . or rather an ECS cyst. Again she had qualms, despite the fact he had pushed for the changes she herself had initially felt would be necessary. The biotech covering of the combat suit worried her. It was almost as if the life of this world had begun eating into their technology by a more subtle route, and Oren was assisting it. This feature that enabled a computer link between the organic tech of the suit and each nanosuite was a case in point, especially with Oren saying he wanted a more *direct* connection. And something else concerned her: Oren's suggestion that the cacoraptors could get worse than they were already. It wasn't a particularly unusual observation to make, but still, something about it wasn't right.

Oren turned through the door into the infirmary. A woman Ursula had seen who'd been in there growing new bones had left long ago, apparently delighted that she was now unbreakable.

Ursula had since learned that, as she had the new bones to handle it, the woman had asked for a special muscular-boosting upgrade too. Oren's reply that she should go and lift some weights would have been amusing, if he'd not been deadly serious. All the woman had to do was continue to put heavy stress on her muscles, and the new nanosuite Oren had fashioned for them would provide . . . and swiftly.

Two beds were occupied. A man had opened his visor for a breath of air, but too near a blue cycad. He'd lost his eyes and part of his face to the poisonous acidic spines. Now he was wearing a grotesque mask, as underlying flesh and new eyes grew in his head. In the other bed lay a woman, drip fed and covered in a plastic suit filled with an emollient to keep her comfortable and hydrated, while her nanosuite and boosted immune system fought a flesh-eating amoeba parasite. Ursula raised a hand to the two of them, only receiving a response from the man. The mask gave him vision by induction through to the optic nerve. The woman was either asleep or unconscious.

They carried on through another door at the end of the small ward into the original room for regrowth tanks. Six tanks were in this room and all were occupied, while beyond them she could see doorways open into new areas where further tanks and a larger infirmary were being built. Two tanks contained survivors from cacoraptor attacks before they'd started using Oren's chemical warfare against the creatures. Both had been in there for a long time, regrowing lost limbs and severely damaged organs, and looked almost ready to come out. They were the only two to have survived a close encounter with a cacoraptor. Ursula walked over to peer inside. Three other tanks contained people who'd lost limbs and chosen tank regrowth to speed up the process of regeneration. The occupant of the remaining tank did not look so good.

Nursum, or rather what remained of him, floated in the thick fluid in such a dense mass of tubes and wires it looked as if he'd been a victim of some explosive parasitic epiphyte – a life form of which this world had no shortage. What she could see of him was a grotesque sculpture of human flesh and bone. His ribs had been splayed like wings, internal organs raised partially clear so she could see his spine down to the point where the fig had severed it. His skull had been stripped down to muscle, as had the rest of him, because they'd needed to scrap his skin to get rid of the 'glue' which the fig had used to hold him together while it fed on the rest of him. However, she could see patches of new skin already appearing. A large ribbed tube, not normally part of the tank complement, was attached to the top of his skull. This contained a skein of nanotubules and neurochem feeds run by a computer which matched the growing brain matter to his last body scan. Below the attachment of this, Nursum's remaining eye survived, still open.

'We're trying to upload the academic stuff he'd saved to his brain throughout his life,' Oren stated. 'This might help shape the rest, by elucidating scraps of cerebral and body memory, and experience.' He shrugged.

'I didn't think it possible for him to survive,' Ursula stated.

Oren looked at her for a long moment. 'I won't pretend the optimism of others. It is highly likely he will die in there. I give him perhaps a twenty per cent chance of survival. And if he does survive' – Oren gave the word a doubtful emphasis – 'what will come out of the tank will perhaps be ten per cent of the man who came to this world.' He turned back to look into the tank, and frowned. 'In the Polity, ECS and others have been working on full mental recording of the human mind.'

'Soul Bank,' said Ursula distractedly, 'I've heard of it.' She stared at Nursum. So he was likely to die and there was nothing she could do. She felt responsible.

'We have two forms of mental editing: erasure of memories and uploads that are shaped by the receiving mind. Memcording has advanced, but what is recorded is without the context of the organ from which it came; the recordings are made and sold illegally but never really establish properly in different minds.'

'I thought memories could be extracted and then put back.'

'They can, but only in the mind concerned. This all works with some heavy computing and aug-related wiring but is no use if the brain concerned has been heavily damaged or destroyed. Context is required: such as the function of the organ and how it grew, the balance of neurochem and many other complicated issues.'

'So no good here for all of us . . .'

'We would need a vast amount of storage to record all the data of the people here and still we'd be without that context. There is, however, some interesting work being done privately in the Polity. Sylac, a rather brilliant man, is working on a memplant: a crystal unit with quantum processing he claims may be able to record context too. If he's right, then in future it will be possible for people to have a cerebral implant that records the whole person. That is sadly not the case just yet.' He turned and looked at her again. 'He uses rubies.'

That seemed an odd thing to say, but Ursula acknowledged it with a nod.

Oren continued, waving one of his subhands at the tank, 'We may, if we are very, very lucky, get a person back, but he won't have the breadth of knowledge and experience of the original Nursum – there will be large holes in his mind.'

Ursula stared at the remains in the tank. Even while they'd been standing here the ribs had begun to close up – their movement hardly perceptible. For over a century now scientists and philosophers had been debating the line between life and death, as it was possible to recover people like Nursum from the most extreme injuries. The consensus had it that the line was death of the mind, but here she could see even that as a matter of degree.

'So there is nothing more that can be done?' she asked.

Oren didn't reply immediately, then he turned to her and shrugged again. 'You have been reluctant to take things further – to allow me to use more radical options.'

'There *is* something more?'

'The nanosuite as it stands is limited by its source material and by the extent of the repairs it can make. Something radical I've been working on would, I am sure, save a great deal more of Nursum's mind and increase his chances of survival to above fifty per cent.'

She stared at him, not liking where this was going. But should she sacrifice Nursum's life to her doubts about Oren's work, his intentions, his *agenda*? This was a moment of decision and – remembering a time in her past, before her new purpose of creating a colony had found her – there had been another tank, with her inside. A decision had been made at the time based on the flip of a coin, but she had lost that coin. She made the decision without it.

'So what are you waiting for? Do it.'

She turned away, duty done, but again feeling Nursum's eye watching her all the way.

When she visited the next time, the tank room was uncomfortably warm and Ursula could hear and feel the air conditioning labouring to bring the temperature down. She walked over to the glass and put her hand against it, felt the warmth there and saw bubbles rising up the glass. She couldn't see Nursum, though, because the murk concealed him. Maybe with what had happened here she didn't want to.

'Either of you have any idea what the hell is going on?' she asked.

The two medtechs – Lars and Donnaken – were as highly experienced in their field as all the colonists. They'd served in Polity Medical for many years before transferring to the military research wing of the same. They'd been on rescue missions to failed colonies and disaster zones all across the Polity, including one in which Separatists had apparently blown up a runcible buffer and caused thousands of deaths. She wondered now, with everything she'd learned, whether Separatists had had anything to do with that at all.

Both the medtechs looked just a little angry. Lars – a woman with a heavyworlder physique and emerald eyes – shook her head and looked to Donnaken. The thin acerbic man shook his head as well and pursed his lips. 'We were going to dump the amniote but Oren told us that would kill him. We disagreed. We kept the temperature down as low as we could but it's still too damned high.'

'Let us drain the tank,' said Lars. 'He still has a chance.'

Ursula clamped down on her urge to tell them to do it at once. Nursum's chances of survival had been minimal without Oren's *radical* option and it had thus far provided an astounding recovery. She had to assume Oren knew what he was doing, despite the disagreement of the two here.

'Did Oren bother to explain anything this time?' she asked.

'Fast and violent regrowth generating heat, he said.' He glanced behind him. 'Oren is on his way, doubtless with further . . . information.'

The two techs had both agreed not to divulge to anyone else that something more radical was being used to save Nursum's life. Much pursing of lips and frowning had ensued when no detail on that was forthcoming, but they'd stuck to their word, and even now followed his instructions. No one else in the colony seemed aware of what was going on here.

'Tuned to stress reactions,' said Donnaken. 'Everything was going fine while we kept him unconscious but then somehow the drugs stopped working and this happened.'

'Scanning?'

'Yes.'

'Nursum is still alive?'

Donnaken shrugged. 'I don't know. We've got plenty of data, but limited access to it as it goes into Oren's private database,' said Lars. 'From what I've glimpsed, Nursum has his limbs back and they all seem to be the right shape. I can only guess at lots of organ reconfiguring inside.' She stared directly at Ursula. 'Given full access to the data I should be able to . . .'

'We do not drain the tank. We'll leave it to Oren for now,' said Ursula. 'He's the expert on this and I don't want any procedures you might think necessary but which could interrupt the process.'

Whatever that is, she thought to herself.

'I've been studying the data,' Oren announced, entering the tank room.

He looked a little hyped, his head twitching from side to side as he took in the readouts of monitors, peered at other equipment and stared momentarily at the cloudy tank. With almost laughable surreptitiousness, he studied the three standing before him.

'We can detach all monitoring now and drain the tank,' he added.

'Are you sure about that?' asked Donnaken, but he might as well not have spoken.

In a moment, Oren was over by a console, all four arms working the touch screen and tessellated keys at frenetic speed. Monitors blanked, while leads and tubes entering the steaming fluid at the top of the tank began to withdraw. A gurgling sound ensued as the fluid began to drain.

'Straight to flush?' Lars enquired, looking mildly suspicious.

Oren looked at her. 'The amniote cannot be cleaned up – it's too laden with nanomachines, most of which are defunct, and toxic by-products. Flushing it is best.'

Ursula understood. Often an amniote could be filtered, scrubbed and sterilized for further use. Flush would take it straight into a hard boiler and EM scrambler – the resultant inert mess would then be discharged into a vessel that extracted water only. It made sense to do this when dealing with a large quantity of nanites that had survived high temperatures. But she was also very aware this meant none of the amniote would be available for analysis either.

'You're saying he survived this?' She gestured to the tank.

'Of course,' Oren replied.

Ursula turned to Lars. 'What temperature?'

'Enough to cook a joint of ham,' Lars replied.

Ursula looked back to Oren for an explanation but he ignored her and kept his gaze focused on the steadily dropping fluid level. She decided she'd catch him later when others weren't present.

The fluid dropped down and down, finally revealing a naked human form. Nursum lay coated in a grey layer almost like river mud. Oren worked the controls again and the tank began spray cleaning him. The layer over Nursum fell away in rubbery pieces, washed down the same drain that had taken the amniote. His exposed skin looked healthy enough, though with a rich golden brown tan as if he had just wandered back from some holiday world in the Polity. He even had a full head of hair, Ursula noted, though previously it had been dark brown and was now pure white. He turned his head to one side and coughed out something black and glutinous, shoving himself up on one elbow to vomit copiously.

'Nursum?' she called.

He opened his eyes and looked at her. For a moment they appeared black, as if the irises had opened right across them, but then they shrank, returning them to a more conventional look.

'The end seal,' Oren pointed. 'I don't see any point in using the hoist.'

Lars and Donnaken headed over to undo the hatch at the end and swing it open. Nursum looked towards the opening and heaved himself towards it. Ursula noted how he moved quite quickly and without the expected weakness of someone who'd spent so long in the tank . . . and who had previously lost most of his body. Lars and Donnaken helped him out and kept a steadying hold on him, though that didn't seem required. Lars finally stepped away and returned with a towel for him. Nursum stood holding it as if he didn't know what to do, then his brain seemed to kick into gear and he started drying himself. Lars returned, unwrapping a disposerall.

Ursula turned towards Oren and raised an eyebrow. The man was still studying something on the console but swiped it aside, doubtless into his private database. He came round the console and stood beside her.

'He seems in very good condition,' Ursula commented.

'The fast regrowth was unexpected,' said Oren. 'It seems that with this procedure the nanosuite decided the constant drugged unconsciousness was hindering his survival and, of course, as he woke his cortisol rose and then he went straight into panic.'

Ursula nodded, again noting a concerning choice of words. The nanosuite 'decided' he should wake up. But perhaps she was being overly paranoid and the word choice was simply an aberration of someone used to dealing with AI. Sub-AI and simple computing could make 'decisions' based on input data and set programs. She went over to Nursum, who was now pulling on the disposerall.

'Nursum, how are you feeling?' she asked.

He finished closing up the stick seam down the front of the garment and focused on her. His expression seemed almost childlike and she wondered just how much of his brain had been recovered – how much of the original Nursum.

'They burned the fig,' he said.

'Yes, yes they did,' she replied, before realizing it had not been a question.

She noted his eyes again. The irises seemed to have golden scales in them when before they had been brown. There was something odd about his skin too and his hair, as if something hard and crystalline might be in or on both.

'The fig made me,' he said.

Ursula just stared at him.

Finally he added, 'I feel surprisingly good, considering what happened to me.' He smiled, childlike again.

Ursula nodded. 'Good, we need you back at work.' She clapped him on the shoulder expecting it to feel clammy, but it was hot. 'Busy busy,' she said, heading for the door, anxious to be gone.

6

Present

Angels, was her first thought, but then she remembered the pictures displayed in the Kalonan AI's reproduction churches and she added, *the fallen kind.* When Callum had told her fliers were approaching, she'd assumed they would be like the raptor fliers that had attacked the shuttle – worm-like creatures with wings. No way had she expected this.

These creatures had human forms but with large bat wings sprouting from their backs, and wing skins that connected to jointed spines protruding from their bodies and running down the sides of their legs. Their coloration was red-brown, their feet bird claws and their hands clawed too. The heads sported large pointed ears, faces pushed into pit-bull muzzles, fanged mouths and yellow slotted eyes. Only the addition of horns could have made them more demonic.

'Our weapons,' said Ursula, as she took the seat Gurda had just abandoned.

The things were carrying laser carbines, pulse rifles and an assortment of projectile weapons, some of which were antique or copies of the same. All were personal armaments of the colonists – doubtless colonists who had died outside the base.

'One wonders what they hope to achieve,' said Vrease.

True enough. The strictures of weight applied as much to the cacoraptors as they did to the grav-cars, which the colonists had put away after a number of disastrous crashes. These creatures couldn't easily carry armour, or transform, or flee into the ground, and were therefore much more vulnerable to the main car's weapons. Hundreds of them filled the sky behind, trailing them. They were in range of the weapons but no one had opened fire yet since the raptors themselves hadn't fired on them. She stared at the image feeds, but also felt sure she could sense the creatures behind, impelled by one will. She just accepted it this time and didn't try to explain it away. Her control room staff awaited her orders.

'We must follow the prador's example,' Ursula said, 'and only use our ammo and energy if absolutely necessary. Ignore them unless they draw closer and try to attack.'

The flying demon cacoraptors continued to trail them for an hour, by which time the car's energy reserves were bottoming out. Ursula started to bring it down, expecting the flying creatures to attack now, but they carried on flying and passed overhead, disappearing from sight even as the car landed.

It settled with a crunching rumble, sinking slightly into soft ground. Ursula checked the status readouts on her screen before engaging the drive, the wheels biting and pulling the car up and out of the hollow it had made. As she'd instructed Gurda, she took it up to fifty per cent speed, then let it run. Bled wasteland surrounded them, scattered with tilted slabs that acted as moisture collectors, with strews of growth in the shade they provided. Ursula rounded these rather than go over them. The car was quite capable but she saw no point in testing it just yet. In the distance she saw a small herd of brontopods fleeing across the iron-coloured sands – obviously spooked by something. One of the rare large fliers appeared overhead, four short wings propelling its gas-filled body through the sky. With its long neck and head like that of a hippopotamus, it quested through the air to snap up smaller flying morsels.

After a couple of hours of travel, the cacoraptors pursuing them on the ground arrived earlier than Ursula had expected. She studied their strange forms. At some point they'd shifted the joints in their legs, with their body now weighted forwards, and extended their necks. They slightly resembled ostriches, though they had retained their arms to hold the weapons they'd brought, and their human heads had sprouted numerous sensors. They diverted slightly to run alongside the car. Ursula felt her adrenaline spike and with that came tactical calculations. How would they attack? Their hand weapons were all but useless unless they actually got inside the vehicle. The process of transforming to enable their attack on the car's adaptive armour would take time. Maybe a new generation of raptor would need engendering in the carcass of a brontopod or some other life form here. Either of these options would leave them far behind the car.

'They won't attack,' she stated.

'Your reasoning?' Vrease enquired.

'Tactical considerations,' Ursula replied, even though she felt sure she'd actually sensed their intent. 'They stand little chance of success while attacking the car in motion and they know where we're going. They will await their opportunity there.' She paused for a second, then added, 'I'm certain our drones will see those fliers arrive at the prador assault ship to await our arrival too.'

Even as she spoke the raptors accelerated and moved ahead of the car, kicking up dust as they sped into the distance.

'It makes sense,' said Callum. 'I've worked it through too.'

Ursula turned her attention to him. He was no longer working on his console with his fingers but still had the organic attachments to it. Surveying the others, she noted again the spiky growths from their 'skin', the appearance of nodules and other formations. Gurda, she noticed, was running multiple screen images very fast, and when the woman turned it took a moment for her eyes to align again – she had been watching different scenes with each eye.

'We're changing,' Ursula said. 'Callum . . . your adaptation?'

'It's similar to aug linkage into the computer systems,' he replied. 'I wanted a larger overview, including ground radar and seismic sensors, because I was worried about an attack on the car's undercarriage. A short while later I found myself collating that data and only then noticed this.' He raised an arm to show the connections more clearly.

Ursula looked at Vrease and the woman shrugged. She, of course, had not changed at all because she had no upgrade other than the grossly technological. The others detailed their adaptations and all of them involved better use of the equipment in front of them. After she'd assessed them all, Ursula called up Oren on her screen and told him what had happened to them.

'Circumstances and adrenaline,' he told her. 'In other situations their adaptations will be different. I suggest that none of you neglect nutrients and fluids, because you will be burning energy fast.'

Now he said it, she did suddenly feel very hungry. She'd deal with that later, though.

'We need to talk some more,' she said.

'Concerning?'

'The Polity survey and what it apparently missed.'

'Oh that,' he replied. 'You know where to find me.'

When his image clicked off she noted his use of 'none of you neglect nutrients'. She was now pretty damned sure, despite him wearing a bracelet, that he hadn't used the 'new upgrade' or any of the previous forms of the nanosuite he'd given them. This made her suspicious, but she had to respect the fact that he wasn't actually one of the colonists and supposedly only here temporarily.

'Take turns on breaks,' she told her crew. 'We need to feed ourselves up – the changes we're going through burn energy.'

They ran along the ground for another two hours before the capacitors reached full charge again, then Ursula took them up into the sky. Their flight was without event, but even when they landed again, Vrease noted, 'The fliers should have arrived in the vicinity of the prador assault craft by now, but there's no sign of them.'

As they set out along the ground once more, Ursula felt a leaden sensation growing inside her. A certainty of intent, lying ahead. She started to think tactically again, and realized she'd made an error. Sure, there were good reasons why the cacoraptors might wait until they reached the assault ship, but there were also very good reasons for them to stop them reaching it. She wondered why Callum had agreed with her initial assessment and not seen it too. She closed her eyes. The fliers? No. They were flimsy and wouldn't have time to transform into something more capable. And, of course, with their speed of parthenogenesis, it didn't need to be anything she had seen before.

'There'll be a trap,' she said.

She spun her chair and took in the screen images. There. The collapsed remains of a brontopod lay out on the Bled. The cacoraptors which had almost certainly been engendered in its carcass, and then fed on it, had already departed. Even as she surmised what this might mean, the ground gave way under the car and dropped it into a pit trap. And the cacoraptors attacked. As she responded, Ursula felt a stab of gratitude that at least, this time, they didn't wear human form. She'd never forget when they'd first attacked that way.

Near Past

Vrease swept a hand across her screen to one wall of the control centre in the base. Multiple frames opened over fizzing ones which had previously been feeds from the satellite the prador had destroyed. Cacoraptors were converging on points all around the perimeter where groups of humans were running in. Some of the humans wore skin, some conventional armour and others simple clothing. Ursula saw weapons fire and three in skin firing laser carbines at an approaching raptor. It turned mirror bright to reflect the fire, then tore one of them in half while the others retreated. Another figure deployed a flamer, shooting chemical fire into a tangled mass of raptors – a useless weapon again, as the things turned asbestos white and came on. But now people started to reach within firing range of the multiguns, and these hit the attacking raptors with superior firepower.

Ursula stared at the scene in bafflement. She felt utterly over-loaded and this new furore just seemed to blend into what had occurred before. Her integrating facility locked and for a moment she didn't know what to do, didn't know how to think. But lives were in danger and from some deep reserve she found a way to push her mind into action again. What had Oren said about those missing colonists: 'only traces' and no definitive way to prove death? How had these people survived? Had the raptors captured them to keep as a future food supply and now they'd escaped? Or perhaps something else had happened out there – had refugees from the war with the prador landed here?

'What do we do?' asked Vrease.

Ursula felt numb as she groped for answers and alternatives to one she felt reluctant to face. She riffled through a hundred possibilities: strange quirks of biology, a rebel group within the colonists falsifying their own deaths. Was this whole colonization just some AI war game or test, and maybe she was in a virtuality and didn't realize it? But these explanations rolled away to leave the one incontrovertible truth.

'They're not human,' she said.

Everyone in the control centre gaped at her.

'We've seen how the raptors can alter their bodies,' she said leadenly. 'We've seen them developing intelligence and finding ways around our weapons. This is just the next logical step.'

'I have to change the settings . . . the guns . . .' Vrease looked at her controls, then at her hands as if they were alien to her.

The guns wouldn't fire on these apparent humans. Altering the program so they would do so meant going through all sorts of safety locks, while the multiguns could point inwards. They might end up turning their own weapons against themselves. And, in the end, time had run out.

In one feed, the apparent humans diverted from their inward course and suddenly increased their speed. Even as they reached the nearest multigun they started to change, fingers extending into hard scythes, other limbs sprouting from their sides, heads opening out and extruding iterations of raptor mouthparts, like red cactus flowers. They were all over the weapon in a moment, some tearing into the plasticrete platform below. The gun did begin firing, shredding or incinerating some whose form had diverged far enough from its definition of 'human', but most were too close.

'General address! All personnel out there get back to base!' Ursula yelled, her mind at last accepting the words she'd just spoken, as the human-form raptors pulled apart the multigun she was watching, as well as attacking others elsewhere on the perimeter. 'Cacoraptors have taken on human form and are swarming in!'

She turned to Vrease, 'The base guns?'

'As good as the perimeter ones,' Vrease replied. 'They'll start firing soon . . . at those that are losing human form, but only them.'

The colonists still out there moved fast, piling into armoured cars, simply dropping whatever they were doing and running. It passed through her mind to send out more cars, maybe the grav-cars, but in horror realized this was happening too fast for that kind of organization. She saw armoured cars coming in, stopping to pick up others, with many clinging to the outsides. The killing started. Colonists were simply torn apart with no attempt made at feeding. The cacoraptors seemed only intent on wiping colonists out. Two perimeter guns, still functional, opened fire, pointing inwards and hitting cacoraptors that had diverged from human form. The base guns began firing too at those raptors which came in range. Maybe they had a chance of rescuing this . . .

'How many people out there?' she asked.

Gurda replied, 'Just under four hundred.'

Ursula nodded. Armoured cars were now entering the garages, with colonists on foot going in through those and other entrances. But the raptors were drawing closer and closer, and then she saw another change: raptors reverting to human form, running faster than any human could and passing through the trailing colonists to head straight for the base.

'Target those moving fast,' she stated flatly, knowing she would soon have to make a horrible decision. No coin to flip for this – an immaturity she had left far behind her.

'That's vague,' said Vrease.

'Do what you can or hundreds will die.'

Vrease worked it, and fast. The raptors were now out of range of the remaining perimeter guns but the base guns opened fire again. She saw raptors exploding under minigun fire, trying to reform themselves to withstand it, only to be hit by lasers and particle beams. But she also saw three figures in Polity armour running on suit assist, flying apart in bloody explosions. Human blood.

'Garages closing,' Callum stated, adding, 'We cannot let any of those fuckers in here.'

He'd said it, and she knew what he was implying. She watched more raptors transforming and going into the ground, while others slowed, having recognized too quickly the new setting of the guns, and running in at the same pace as the colonists. Using one of the touch screens, she got a distance reading on those she knew were cacoraptors and then chopped off fifty yards for safety.

She gave Vrease the order to fire.

'Close the doors when everyone within that range is inside,' she added, even as death and destruction spread out from the base.

Ursula leaned against the wall outside the control centre. She wanted to throw up, but her toughened body wouldn't allow it. She held out a hand and watched it quiver for a moment before it grew still. All the advantages of her nanosuite and the changes it had made to her didn't allow her even the weakness of an adverse physical reaction to horror. She moved on, the screams still echoing in her mind.

'Target everything beyond a hundred yards,' she had said. 'And open fire.' The line she'd drawn meant life for some and death for others. She would probably have to make further decisions like that, if the raptors continued to outmatch them. They needed something more. The time had come, she felt, to use every advantage they could, even the dangerous ones.

'Locate Oren for me,' she said.

The sub-AI voice of the system replied, 'Laboratory A2.'

Oren had not yet gone to assist with the wounded. Was that because he didn't care, or because he'd coldly calculated that the colony's survival would be better served if he focused on some other duty? As she headed to his laboratory, her rescue of Nursum played in her mind. Oren had harped on about the advantages of extreme adaptation along the lines of his research from the beginning, and in Nursum he had proved it. They needed that survival now, all of them. They needed his *radical* option.

She found him in his laboratory studying the cacoraptor in its chain-glass cylinder. He looked round with one of his disconcerting head-turns, then adjusted his body to match and stepped towards her.

'Human-shaped cacoraptors,' she stated, her teeth clenched.

'Mimicry is a common biological trait, but in this case the methodology is unusual.' He gestured with one of his subsidiary hands to the raptor. 'It turns out that they can read the genome of other creatures internally and use it, up to and including copying the forms of those creatures. A very useful ability for a predator, as you can imagine.'

'But we're alien life forms here. Our genome is only vaguely comparable to theirs!'

'Quite – they are very adept.'

Ursula shook her head. She needed to clear her mind, stop protesting about impossibilities that had already occurred and face this. They needed something. They needed advantages.

'You have always talked about major physical transformation – something more radical,' she said. 'You did it with Nursum and it worked. It's got to the point now that we all need to get radical, but time is a factor. We need fast results.'

'Yes, we are at that point,' he said. 'In fact, it's time to do what they do.' He gestured to the raptor again.

'What do you mean?'

'We've been using the nanosuites to repair the forms we already have, as well as to evolve what we have to fit the changing circumstances,' he said, pointing over to the far side of his laboratory and heading there. 'Because you were attacked by a pretty nasty alien virus, your suite adapted to that and then changed you to deal with it, hence your scattered liver and kidney organelles. We've also extracted information from other Earth organisms, and that's in the nanosuites too. Chandar ate some food with bad enzymes in it that started to destroy his mouth, oesophagus and stomach. So the suite in him used something from the insect world to combat this and that's why he ended up with mandibles. And there were larger changes inside him too.'

Ursula nodded as she followed. 'Fuck it, Oren. I'm aware of all this, of course, but Nursum has more than we already have – we need whatever the fuck that is!'

Control, must control.

Ursula halted and closed her eyes, her fists clenched. Getting angry with Oren would lead her nowhere. They needed him and they needed what he could do for them – what he had done for Nursum. The time for raging and doubts was over.

When she opened her eyes, Oren pointed over to a glass bell jar Ursula had often noticed here. Underneath it rested a ceramal bracelet with stones inset all around, each a different colour. 'That's a Four Seasons Changer,' he said.

Ursula snorted. 'Really, you're serious?'

Oren smiled. 'Oh it's deeply rooted in the fictional world and often dismissed as a myth.' He shrugged. 'But many of the intelligent weapons Algin Tenkian made were dismissed as myths, until they surfaced again in private collections.'

'Okay, let's say that's a Four Seasons Changer,' said Ursula. She thought about humouring him for a while, and perhaps easing away some of Oren's responsibilities. The man was very old, rumoured to be over two hundred, and maybe well into his time of ennui. He could be looking for dangerous novelty and here that might kill them all. But then the hard cold horror of what had just happened around the base sledgehammered back into her and dispelled that train of thought.

He smiled a little tiredly at her and she abruptly came back to something she'd discovered about people his age, and her own: having had many decades of human interaction, one tended to intuit what others were thinking. She nodded an acknowledgement of her doubts and he tipped his head in return. Without speaking, they stepped past such immature aberration.

'It's dangerous technology and in the fictions we have seen it turn people into monstrous by-blows of the human and the alien, usually resulting in a lot of the "good" humans getting killed before the hero kills the monster. An old story.' He lifted the bell jar and put it to one side, taking out the bracelet and staring down at it. 'As with Algin Tenkian and his weapons, this was created by someone brilliant. It's an antique, in fact, just after the first diaspora from Earth.'

'So what does it really do?'

'Oh, the fictions aren't completely wrong. It can combine alien genomes with human DNA to enable the recipient to survive in a harsh alien environment. A lot of the science of adaptogenics stems from this device, though those who have studied it have never quite understood it completely. The one who made it used alien technology . . . Jain technology, in it.'

'What the fuck?' said Ursula.

'Quite.' Oren put the device back and replaced the bell jar. 'I've found that with the correct inputs and materials, this tech copies itself, while the rest of the device is easy enough to design and put into a nanofactory.' He stepped over to a nearby wall and palmed a lock. A drawer slid out and inside, like jewellery in a box, rested four bracelets. They weren't as fancy as the original changer band, being just plain polished ceramal with inset displays.

'So you've used an alien genome?' asked Ursula, taking everything in properly now, and integrating it.

'I used the cacoraptor genome,' Oren replied.

The fact bedded into her mind with an almost audible *thunk*: Nursum's changes, his abilities. It was one of those realizations which had an undercurrent of, *You knew this all along*. It was good, she supposed, that she'd previously limited her understanding of Nursum's *radical* option and not allowed herself to comprehend that he was actually part cacoraptor now.

Oren picked up a bracelet and gestured to an inset touch screen. 'The device will link to our nanosuites, creating a synergy between them and the alien genome.'

Ursula just stared, the weight of all the deaths on her mind balanced against this. Jain technology was hugely dangerous and she really didn't feel great about the idea of taking their enemy's genome into her body.

She just said, 'Nursum,' and shook her head.

'Yes. It went very well, didn't it?'

Finally she answered, 'Yes, I've seen, but detail it for me.'

'Rapid adaptation,' he said. 'You grew your organelles over some weeks while on medical support, as Chandar grew his mandibles. With this, changes will happen as fast as those we've seen in the raptors. Your bodies will adopt their rapid energy and nutrient usage, along with their genetic libraries, combined and working in synergy with our own. The changes you, Chandar and others underwent would have been much better than they are at present and a lot, lot faster.'

'And Nursum?' she asked.

'It preserved and repaired areas of his brain tissue the previous iteration of the suite would have discarded – other body tissue too. It kept him alive beyond where cellular collapse should have occurred, adapting him to lethal poisons and acids floating round in his system, and removed stuff the previous suite would have failed to clear.'

It all seemed unbelievably good and that was the problem: Ursula didn't quite believe it. She hovered on the edge of giving a flat 'no', but such a decision seemed impossible, with the bodies outside still haunting her. Well, the bodies that had been outside but were now being digested inside cacoraptors.

'Tell everyone it's a new upgrade only. I think it might be a good idea to leave out any mention of the genome you're using, as well as the Jain tech,' she said and picked up one of the bracelets, looking at Oren questioningly.

'The cacoraptor genome is already in place,' he said. 'You just put it on and it will do the rest.'

She opened a simple catch and studied the inside of the bracelet. Complex quadrate patterns were there and seemed to be shifting slowly. She snapped the thing around her wrist, felt it tighten and grow hot. A moment of panic ensued, but this was probably just psychological.

'What will happen?' she asked.

'Some increase in efficiency, and you'll probably notice other steady changes, but nothing "radical" until you are under survival pressure – I've made damage, cortisol and adrenaline the prime activators for adaptation.' He turned to the drawer. 'I need to get some more made.'

'How long will it take you?'

'I have rather fewer to make than before,' he said, and she winced. 'Maybe four days to produce all we'll require.' He gestured to the drawer with a main hand and to his laboratory with an additional one. 'I can distribute them as I make them – the most essential personnel first.'

'No,' she said at once. 'Only once you have them all ready.' She assured herself that she would use those days to find out if there were any problems with the bracelet, but then acknowledged her response was just a weak version of her first instinct to say no.

He nodded mildly, as if it was of no consequence.

She turned away. She needed to get back to the control centre and see to their defences. As she headed away, something about his subdued and offhand attitude impinged upon her. It had seemed like an act. She felt sure Oren now had what he wanted – what he had always wanted.

Past

Oren Salazar's laboratory aboard the shuttle they would take to Threpsis was crammed with gear – most of it still in packing cases.

'Everyone on here has a nanosuite,' he stated. 'You have to go beyond the Line to some of the first diaspora worlds to find a human who doesn't have one.' He grimaced. 'At one time, there was a sect called the Originals on one world inside the Polity. They had decided to rid themselves of all humanity's additions and return to some pure original state. I think they had some connection with Separatism.' As he spoke, Oren was both programming a small fluid autofact and preparing a belt running into it air-blast injectors with two drug cylinders.

'What happened to them?' Ursula asked from the stool she was sitting on, pushed back out of his way.

'They returned themselves to what the human state was before the Quiet War, and in fact before the first diaspora, but failed to account for evolution.'

129

'I don't think we've evolved much, unless you include the genetic alterations we've made to ourselves in the centuries since then.'

'No, we haven't, but our diseases have. In the past, our repeated attempts to wipe out diseases with vaccination sometimes worked but often just did the evolutionary thing and created stronger diseases. Most of these now fall foul of our current boosted immune systems or nanosuites. But given fertile ground, they will proliferate. The Originals got themselves a modern iteration of chicken pox, refused assistance and were all dead in a month.'

Ursula absorbed that, then said, 'Back to your original point: everyone aboard already has nanosuites . . .'

'Yes, everyone. And they are all different. Some interfere with the new suite and need to be completely shut down; others can be reprogrammed and incorporated, with some work. I could spend time analysing each suite to that end, but it's quicker and easier just to shut them all down and let the new suite establish.' He gestured to the double syringes. 'The first injection is essentially an off switch. I will give that here. The second injection, which everyone will take away with them, must be administered three hours later – the injector will signal when it's time.'

'So I'm presuming for a short time we'll be like those Originals?'

'Yes, but not long enough for anything to kill you. The new suite will begin working very quickly and wipe out any nasty colonies that might have established in the intervening hours. This process also doesn't interfere with boosted immune systems, which most have too . . . There, it's ready.'

He waved a hand at the machines and the first double injector slid into the autofact on a belt like a bandolier. It disappeared out of sight for a moment, reappearing shortly with its two cylinders filled. One contained a clear fluid flecked with gold while the other gleamed like liquid emerald.

'Pretty,' said Ursula to cover her sudden nervousness, as Oren held the injector up. 'Why a pressure injector? I expected a patch, pill or at least an ultrasound injector.'

'Ease of use and ease of manufacture.' He stood up, his body swivelling round to match the position of his head, and walked over, holding the injector.

He waited and finally Ursula tilted her head to one side and leaned forwards, as if waiting for a kiss there. The nose of the injector felt warm. It hissed and out the corner of her eye, she saw the cylinder of green fluid emptying. He finally pulled the thing away and held it out for her. She inspected it briefly and put it in her pocket.

'Will there be ill effects?'

'You'll get the mild symptoms of a cold,' he said, then, after an amused smile, 'but of course like most Polity humans you won't know what cold symptoms are. You'll get a bit of a sore throat and allergy symptoms, which you must have experienced at some point.'

'Unavoidable on most alien worlds. That's all?'

'That's in the first three hours until the second injection. Symptoms vary, as the suite establishes to different physiologies. I can say no more than that. Different for different people but probably nothing that will interfere with functionality.'

As Ursula left his room, she walked past a line of nervous-looking colonists. Callum nodded to her and asked, 'All good?'

'I'll let you know in a day or so,' she replied.

Vrease, who had recently joined the command staff and seemed ever at Callum's side, said, 'Probably allergy symptoms and adjustment changes. Most of what people will feel will be psychological – nocebo and placebo effects.'

Vrease was clearly highly technically minded – a useful addition to the group.

'No more, I suspect, than people suffered from vaccinations in ancient times,' Ursula stated, and then moved on because she felt slightly sick.

She left the shuttle and returned to her cabin aboard the Polity cargo hauler they were on – the *Foucault* – aware she was more vulnerable to invisible death in the air than ever before. In three hours, after the next injection, the new suite would establish micro-factories that attached to the walls of her veins and elsewhere throughout her body. These made nanomachines to repair cellular damage constantly, even to the genetic level. They boosted immune systems and hunted down and destroyed alien hostile microbes or viruses. The suites Oren had made for them also possessed a great deal of quantum processing and memory space. They could be programmed to make changes to a human body, from the genetic level up to gross physical changes – it would be their way of surviving more than just hostile microbes. When Ursula left her cabin half an hour later, the back of her throat felt sore and her eyes were streaming. Later she developed a cough and started producing yellow snot. Her body felt as if it had been beaten and her temperature regularly ricocheted between hot and cold, while she seemed to be sweating all the time.

Symptoms of a cold, she thought, and felt pity for all those billions who'd suffered this throughout the ages before the modern era. And this was the least of the maladies they'd gone through back then. Thinking on that, she gritted her teeth and bore it until the syringe buzzed and rattled in her pocket like a cicada to tell her it was time for the next injection. She later learned that many had returned to Oren, sure that something'd gone wrong and they were dying. When the new nanosuite began establishing, she felt sometimes euphoric, ridiculously strong and full of energy, but this slowly settled until she felt no different from before. Other colonists talked of the wonderful effects of the new nanosuite on the strength of those feelings. When she heard this again in the presence of Vrease, the woman rolled her eyes and shook her head before walking away.

7

Their car's guns opened fire where they could – mostly on the upper armour and down in the space below the undercarriage. But the walls of the trap hole they'd fallen into had collapsed against the sides of the car.

'Do we have movement on the guns?' Ursula asked. She was out of her seat and fizzing with the need to do something physical. All around she could feel *them* and *it* – one will pushing, driving and needing. It almost overwhelmed her but, after a second, she stepped back and pulled out the laser carbine holstered at the side of her chair.

'Some movement but the earth is restricting them.' Callum slammed a hand down on his console, but raised it in puzzlement before peering down at the shattered composite. It didn't matter because his connection now ran through the tendrils inside the thing.

Vrease turned her chair around, studied Callum for a second, then focused on Ursula. 'Depth of penetration of our shots is minimal and detection too. We need to get out of here and fast.'

'The armour?' Ursula asked, noting in passing that Callum's head seemed to have become slightly bigger, and was it lopsided too?

134

'It's holding at the moment and the—'

The crump of an explosion shuddered the car. Ursula scanned the screen wall quickly, sorting images in her mind. New ones appeared in one section and they were of narrow corridors, people there, smoke rolling through.

'Explosives?' said Vrease disbelievingly. 'They've used explosives?'

Ursula felt no surprise at all. Hadn't it been obvious? Then, undermining that: why had it been obvious? She gestured to her chair. 'Gurda. Take over. Callum?'

'Trakken is moving the internal defence squad there.'

'Vrease?'

The woman looked round, obviously still stunned and then angry. She seemed slow to Ursula and there could be only one reason for that. Vrease did not have the upgrade. She might be mostly machine but she was still, inside, conventionally human.

'Put the big reactor online,' Ursula instructed, turning to Gurda, who had taken her seat. 'Get us out.'

'But the reactor—' Vrease began.

Ursula cut her off. 'We use it now; we'll put it in shutdown once we're clear.'

Vrease nodded and quickly worked her controls. When she was done, the details came up on the wall above her as the reactor came online. She nodded to Gurda, but the woman was halfway out of the control chair. Others were swinging their chairs around, while Callum was staring with irritation at his tendrils, which Ursula watched detach and then curl up into his arm. Everyone was reaching for hand weapons, provided in the event of any raptors getting this far inside.

She sensed it: their concerted urge to attack the intruders. It seemed to lace them all together into a whole and felt unstoppable. She could also feel it as a response to an amorphous presence all around outside – the intruders being an extension

135

of that presence reaching in. Ursula tried to shake this all from her mind, to stop it driving any irrationality.

'You will all remain at your stations!' she said.

'You're going,' said Callum, mildly accusing, and muttered agreement rumbled around the control room and through this other substratum, this *connection*. No. She could not allow it. These people were needed at their controls. It was tactical madness to abandon their stations. Yet it was also wrong for her to do so. She felt a surge of resentment. She would go and they would stay. She pushed for dominance and a way to assert her will. On a more intellectual level, she knew what was happening and could feel its chattering and wittering in her mind. Under pressure for survival, they had just taken another adaptation step and started utilizing the cacoraptor manner of communication. She now acknowledged that her odd visual and aural hallucinations had been precisely that: she'd been *hearing* the enemy.

She felt herself spreading, infiltrating. Callum's degrading data connection opened to her, as did Gurda's multiple vision and ability to process audio and other com in parallel. The focus of the others, with their sections of the car and almost complete mental modelling of the same, had at first combined together but was now degrading because they wanted to fight. Her own expertise, her ability for tactical integration, reared up and with that she clawed a hold on the visceral communication. She *was* the best leader here, but she also acknowledged that her dominance arose from her having taken the upgrade before them.

'You will all remain at your stations,' she said again and asserted herself through that other stratum. They pushed back and then crumbled under her will and logic. Callum sat back down abruptly and looked puzzled, and others followed. Weapons went back into chair holsters, and Gurda pulled across the controls, looking around her somewhat fearfully. Ursula turned to the door but caught Vrease's eye before heading there.

'There must be a dominant raptor,' the woman said.

Ursula jerked as if she had been slapped.

'How?' she asked.

'How did I know what just happened?' Vrease asked. 'I am not changing as much as all of you but my prosthetics enable more than just human senses. I modelled the EMR emissions, the connection and the burst from you that just swamped other signals. It's not only EMR either. I can smell the complex compounds in the air.'

Ursula stared at her, feeling an irritation swirling up into something more dangerous. Vrease was not one of them. She imagined what might be needed to take down a person in a Golem body and felt the structure of her own body shifting. She clamped down on it. She had to stay in control. She couldn't let what felt like an extreme xenophobic impulse control her. Or the others. She reached back and quelled the same surge against Vrease growing within them. Then, as she stepped through the door, Gurda initiated grav, powered by the big reactor, and began hauling their vessel out of the hole. Ursula winced at an analogy which flashed over her: they were in another deeper metaphorical hole the raptors had been digging for some time.

Near Past

Ursula felt horribly calm. Perhaps that was due to her original nanosuite, or the new upgrade, or to a firm inevitability she had that if they stayed on Threpsis they would become one of those failed colonies she'd read about – the ones where Polity marines found nothing left to rescue.

She scratched at the skin around her new bracelet as she studied the feeds in the massif base control room. The drones they'd sent out floated like bubbles – their material as light as air and micro-aerofans keeping them buoyed. But Ursula doubted very much they were invisible to the prador, and she didn't know if it was a good or bad thing they hadn't destroyed these little watchers as they had the satellite. On the one hand they might not have the resources to expend in shooting at so many small targets, on the other, they might already have assessed the colonists and their base and dismissed them as being of minimal danger, and something to be dealt with later. She felt sure they'd only knocked out the satellite because of the U-com there, and the possibility that Polity forces could be summoned.

Another thought occurred. Perhaps the prador had taken out the satellite because that was all they could do. They didn't have anything powerful enough to destroy the massif and the human colony here. Integrating and assessing more data, she saw other scenarios. The prador clearly needed energy so, if they were confident of killing off her and her people, why not come here rather than take the long, halting journey to that dry seabed and its uranium salts? They would surely know this colony had its own power supplies . . .

On another jump with their ship, and a mission to collect plant matter, the prador came down near the edge of what might be called a forest. There they encountered a herd of brontopods. One of these charged, knocked a prador onto its back, then rushed back to its fellows and gathered together with them in a belligerent huddle. The prador flipped back onto its legs – the one now identified as their commanding first-child – folded down a claw tip and fired once. The particle beam struck the attacking brontopod's head and turned it into a burning red explosion. As it dropped, the rest broke and ran, crashing off through the forest.

The prador moved in and began cutting again, but it seemed the furore had attracted other attention.

A cacoraptor appeared and started to circle the prador in the forest. It checked out the dead brontopod, but didn't linger to use this ready supply of nutrients, instead closing in on its new prey, appearing in the same form as the first raptor Ursula had seen. Its narrow bird-skull head split and receded and in its place sprouted a ring of tentacles with a grinding mouth at the centre. It wormed its way close and lunged up at one of the prador. Sticking to the armour just above the legs, it tried to chew its way in, acid dripping and smoking on the ground.

'That's different,' said Callum flatly.

Ursula felt the tightness in her stomach again. It was almost as if this raptor, though nearly a thousand miles away, knew about the latest adaptations of the other raptors here, for it had changed straight into a form that could attack armour. No, it wasn't possible. She mustn't get paranoid about this.

'And it's the same,' Callum added.

The words were like a key, opening up a morass of previous speculation. Raptors could move incredibly fast on the ground and, of course, they could fly. There had easily been enough time for one of them from here to get to the location of that assault craft which, she was sure, they had observed coming down. *Military, intelligent*, she thought yet again. She felt a momentary relief with the consideration that a military response would have been to send a squad, a number of *soldiers*. But the relief swiftly died with the realization that, as they had also seen, one raptor could engender many others as required. She grimaced, shutting down this line of thought which just seemed to become an endless descent into nightmare – they had enough to deal with right now.

Everyone in the control centre was subdued and precise today.

The latest numbers of the dead were in and now they knew Threpsis had taken over four hundred colonists. They also knew just how much equipment had been destroyed, how low their supplies were, and only had to look through the chain-glass window to see the devastation outside. If that wasn't enough, the occasional vibrations through the floor told them the base guns were firing at the cacoraptors, which were drawing ever closer.

Ursula turned her mind back to the scene on their feed. The prador reached back with one claw, grabbed the attacking raptor and pulled it off, then inspected it for a moment before closing its claw with a click. Two halves of the raptor dropped to the ground, but immediately writhed back together, extruding strands to rejoin. The prador pointed its Gatling cannon at the thing, but when the clattering and bubbling of prador speech issued from the first-child commander, the other prador grabbed the raptor again and threw it over the nearby trees.

Ursula gritted her teeth. The prador should have killed the thing, blown it to pieces and incinerated it all with a particle beam. She noted how much she hated the raptors more than this new dangerous alien civilization.

The cacoraptor returned with a new tentacle head, which stuck to the prador commander's armour and spread its tentacles over a wide area. This time the prador struggled to prise it off and when it finally did Ursula saw that many of the tentacles remained, writhing across the armour's surface, exploring. The prador tried to snip it in half again but this time failed to cut through and, tossing it aside, hit the thing with Gatling fire. The raptor bounced and twisted along the ground in explosions of debris but did not die. Instead it folded out paddle legs and, in a blur of motion, buried itself. The commander studied the point where it had gone into the ground, the other three turning to watch too. They discussed the matter and then, with room still left on the sled for more plant matter, went back to their ship. The raptor attacked once more as they reached the vessel and this time a folded-down claw tip and particle beam fire sent it burning into the ground, turning into what looked like a vertebrate's spine issuing oily smoke.

'They're not stupid, are they,' Vrease observed tightly.

Quite. The prador had realized they faced something dangerous and decided their better course for the moment was simply to avoid it. But from what she'd seen of the Polity reports, this would only be because they lacked resources, rather than any lack of aggression, which confirmed earlier thoughts on this matter.

As they observed the assault craft again make a jump, Ursula said, 'Keep some drones on that raptor.'

The creature eventually came out of the ground again, back to its original form. Had it also decided avoidance was a better option? It streaked along the ground to the dead brontopod, scattering circling hyena creatures, and burrowed inside the thing. Over the next hour it fed, and in this time the corpse began to collapse as other cacoraptors issued from it. Their skin was mirrored and ribbed in black, with heads wielding four pincers and an array of other manipulators in between. These creatures hooked up from the ground, heads questioning the air, then headed off, directly towards where the prador assault craft had gone.

And there's the squad of soldiers, thought Ursula.

The first prador to be attacked at their next landing site was a second-child. The raptor clamped its pincers around the leg socket of the armour and coiled its body around the leg, while its tail went into the ground. The prador tried to pull the thing off and move its leg, which now seemed stuck in place on the ground. It next activated a weapon that rose up from the equipment on its back and targeted the raptor, burning it with a laser. But this was just reflected away. One of the other prador joined in, folding down a claw tip, and fired a narrow-focus particle beam. The ribs on the raptor's surface glowed and the ground all around it smoked.

'Jesus!' said Vrease. 'It has some kind of conductor and a heat sink in the ground!'

Suddenly the prador's leg came away and the raptor drilled into the socket hole, with gristly debris, green blood and other matter spraying out. Now freed from the ground, the prador made a run for it, crashing into a tree and bouncing away. It started firing its Gatling cannon and then the particle beam, sending the others rushing for cover. Eventually it skidded to a halt, shuddering. Other raptors began to appear and the three remaining prador retreated, firing every weapon at their disposal and turning their surroundings into a fire storm. One of them had the perspicacity to take the half-loaded sled with it. They made it to the ship and, as the ramp lowered, managed to keep the raptors back while they clambered inside to safety. Ursula watched the raptors next attack the ship's armour, seemingly unable to get a grip on it or mark it in any way. Armour with an exotic metal component, she thought, and filed that away for later inspection. Suddenly intensely weary, she turned from the screens and left the control centre, to try and get some sleep.

Ursula expected sleep to evade her but she was dead to the world for the next eight hours. This seemed to be the only physical change she'd experienced since putting on Oren's bracelet – she was normally a light sleeper, for an average of only four hours. Once she was awake and up again, she made her rounds of the base, receiving reports on supplies and defence activities.

She saw the walking wounded and those still in the tanks, and people seemed to be working robotically, with nothing else to do. Most had lost someone close to them and were in a mental haze of grief. She tried to instil some optimism but failed. There was no hope to offer them and she was glad that no one asked, 'What next?' The summons to the control centre came finally as a relief.

After the prador's next jump in their ship, eight of them came out, and Ursula wondered just how many more were inside the vessel. They worked hard and fast and were back inside their ship with two sled-loads of plant matter before the raptors arrived. But the creatures were not to be put off. They appeared more quickly at the prador's following landing site, long-limbed and dog form, just as the prador were returning to their ship, and another of the second-children met the same fate as the one before. The raptors attacked the assault craft, new versions of them issuing from the hollowed-out prador armour. But again it seemed nothing they did could penetrate that exotic armour, and the craft jumped away.

'It has grav and fusion engines,' Vrease observed, turning to Ursula. 'And we have a fusion reactor that should be able to power them.'

'But it's all the way out there.' Ursula gestured beyond the base towards where the assault craft lay. 'And I don't think its owners would welcome us.'

Vrease simply nodded.

Ursula thought about what they were up against: creatures almost impossible to destroy, which could grow defences resistant to prador particle beams and Gatling cannons. Creatures that also developed intelligence when needed. Then she considered that prador assault craft, clad in armour these things could not penetrate. The people of the base needed something, some prospect of a future. All they had been doing was retreating and surviving, and if they stayed on this world they would die. Here fate had offered them a chance of escape.

'We retrieve the reactor from the shuttle,' she said.

Ursula found herself struggling to surface from her deep sleep into some state of urgency. It reminded her of her time hunting spearpigs in the underwater caves of Desander, as if a blue hole to the surface lay far above her and she hadn't inflated the buoyancy ribs in her suit, and the weights were still dragging her down. Slowly the illusion faded until she finally opened her eyes.

'Lights,' she said with a mouth that felt coated with dried slime.

The lights came on and she blinked. Her vision was blurred and that instituted a moment of panic. Her eyes watered and it felt as if they were reshaping themselves, then everything became abruptly clear. What had been the urgency? Another knock on her apartment door reminded her and she slid quickly from the bed, grabbing her robe and pulling it on. Panic roiled inside her because knocks on her door now seemed only to signal disaster. For a moment she felt sick, but this dispersed and she was shaky, until that faded away too and she just stared at the door in anger, as if she wanted to attack it. It was as if her body was searching through its repertoire of responses, trying to find the correct one. All of this just wasn't right and she glanced down at the band around her wrist, utterly sure these strange sensations had something to do with Oren's upgrade. All it seemed to be doing was making her feel out of sorts. She stared at the door some more, as if trying to see through it and predict what disaster had befallen. Oddly, when she stepped over to open it, she knew who would be standing there.

'How are you feeling?' Oren asked, inspecting her closely and, she sensed, probably with more than just simple vision.

'Crappy,' she replied, turning away and going to fetch herself coffee as he stepped inside and closed the door behind him. 'What do you want, Oren?'

Her fabricator quickly produced a cup of coffee. Its taste was slightly off, but she didn't know whether that was due to the local additives now used to keep their digestive systems working properly or the changes she was undergoing, whatever they were.

'I just wanted to see how you are doing,' he said innocently.

'That's a lie,' she stated flatly, utterly sure. 'Get to your point.'

'Okay.' He nodded his head loosely. 'You need to delay this mission to retrieve the reactor from the shuttle.'

'Why?' she asked, her mind's integrating faculty kicking in fast and finding the answer even as he spoke it.

'One more day and I will have all the upgrade bracelets done. Anyone who goes out there is almost certainly going to come up against cacoraptors. With the upgrade, they stand a greater chance of not ending up dead . . . a much greater chance.'

'You said the same to me three days ago and still you don't have the bracelets ready. Is there something you're not telling me?' She held up her wrist, displaying the bracelet. 'Is there something I should know about this second version of what you used on Nursum?'

'Just hardware problems,' said Oren smoothly. 'Since the tech can increase in complexity as it grows, it requires constant monitoring and adjustment to keep it at the base format. This has turned out to be just a little bit more difficult than I thought for mass production. I have to take care.'

Jain tech. He was talking about Jain tech. *It can increase in complexity as it grows.*

'The mission is planned for today.' She realized as she said it that she didn't need to check the time. 'In six hours.'

'My contention still applies.'

'Have you seen how everyone has responded to this plan?' she asked. 'They finally have some hope and focus, preparations have been made, they're ready. If I delay it for what is supposedly just an advanced upgrade, that will arouse suspicions. They'll think I'm delaying because the mission is a pointless one, or they'll wonder why this upgrade is so important. These are not stupid people, Oren. I can't wait until you've finished them.'

'I have enough changers to supply those who are going on the mission,' he said. He didn't sound very convinced, as if he'd known he wouldn't be able to change her mind.

'And what will they do? Will they work as you promised or will they do the same thing to these people that this' – she waved her wrist at him again – 'has been doing to me? I feel exhausted, out of sorts, not right at all. Sometimes I feel stupidly strong, other times I just want to lie down and sleep. I need my people sharp for this. Sharp.'

'A period of adjustment is required.'

'It's been over a week now. How much longer?' She shook her head. 'We can't wait that long. Those raptors haven't managed to get into the base yet but they keep trying new methods. One reached the base wall yesterday before the guns could destroy it. They're not just animals, they're an army forcing us into siege.'

'More reason to have to . . .' He seemed to lose the thread.

'More reason to be like them, I think you were trying to say.' Ursula grimaced. 'Don't get me wrong, we will use this upgrade, but we retrieve the reactor first.'

She gulped the coffee and put the cup down. After a moment of consideration she stripped off her robe because, really, she did not see Oren as a man and doubted he saw her as anything more than an interesting experiment. Stepping over to her shower booth, she jerked the door open. 'I have work to do, Oren, and so do you.'

He didn't take the hint and replied, 'And then what? When you have the reactor, then what? Yes, it can probably be installed in that prador assault craft, giving us a way out of here. But there are prador aboard that thing . . .'

She turned back towards him, now feeling uncomfortably vulnerable in her nakedness. This was a question she dreaded and one everyone had been circumventing because, in reality, they were happy simply to be doing something positive. To have a focus.

'One step at a time,' she said.

'The upgrade is that step. It is the first step – the most import-ant step.'

'Will it make us more capable of stealing a ship from heavily armed aliens? Even the cacoraptors aren't faring that well against them and haven't been able to get into the ship.'

'Unlike the cacoraptors, we have technology exterior to ourselves. We also have years of experience and intelligence to call upon.' He tilted his head as if pondering on something, but only added, 'The upgrade is essential.'

Ursula felt her mind able to snap onto minutiae and slot them into integration. The words came out of her seemingly without conscious intercession: 'Are you sure the raptors don't have experience and intelligence to call upon? And as for technology exterior to themselves . . . They took up human form, so how long before they can do what humans do?' He seemed to have no answer for her, so she continued, 'Their behaviour is becoming more and more complex . . .' She stopped, not knowing where to take this.

He looked thoughtful again for a long moment before, without comment, turning and leaving. She stared at the closed door, then stepped into the shower, which gurgled before coming on – problems with water supply, apparently. As it washed over her and she soaped herself, she didn't feel as if she was cleaning anything off, as though she was covered in some barrier. And drying herself afterwards, she noticed glinting flakes of skin on the towel, almost like flecks of brass. She tried not to take this as some sign that Oren might be right about the importance of the upgrade, but she also couldn't put out of her mind the way Nursum's skin now sometimes looked. She thought about all the irreversible changes – changes that had been happening to them all from the moment they set foot on this world . . .

Ursula slid into consciousness without seeming transition. That was probably because of the drugs and the feeling of weightlessness. Opening her eyes, she had the momentary illusion of being in a deep pool surrounded by strands of water weed but, having experienced a regrowth tank before, she recognized her surroundings through the close-fitting goggles. Inspecting herself in the murky green fluid, she saw first her nakedness and second all the tubes and wires entering her body – some in her arms and legs, others into her mouth, but most converging around her waist.

'Can you hear me?' a voice asked.

Being incapable of speech, she nodded at the vague figure beyond the glass. It moved in a way she recognized and belatedly she realized the voice was Oren's. She moved closer to the glass, and he became clearer now.

'The parasite,' he said, 'penetrated your right kidney, then burned and chewed its way up through your liver and into your lungs. Quick thinking on Callum's part saved your life. He realized what had happened and opened you up with a vibro-knife and pulled the thing out. Apparently it even damaged his Polity gauntlet and the sole of his boot when he stamped it to slurry.'

Ursula had so many questions. She would think about her

injuries another time and, doubtless, they didn't concern her now because she was as high as a kite. Other people had chosen simple envirosuits too, so were there further casualties? How was the work to establish the base going?

Oren continued relentlessly, 'Unfortunately, in having to cut open your envirosuit and then you, Callum exposed you to the local micro-fauna and flora and this is why we couldn't just repair the damage and send you on your way. Your nanosuite has responded admirably but what with the damage and the concerted attack on your system, it requires support. I printed in kidney, liver and lung material as a replacement but it seems these are not enough. Your suite is growing organelles of these throughout your body.'

All that came to Ursula's mind was: how could it grow lung organelles? Surely it needed some method of getting air to them? She puzzled further about how to ask questions. If she'd retained her aug it wouldn't have been a problem. After a moment, her military training kicked in with a solution and she began making hand signals.

'Oh that's an old method,' Oren responded, 'for vacuum combat when EMR is too high for com. Give me a moment . . . Right, got it – memories accessed.'

Ursula paused in her signing, for Oren didn't wear an aug to access information either. As far as she could see, all his augmentations were organic, so he must have some organic cerebral equivalent . . . or did he have one of the new gridlinks etched inside his skull? It wasn't unfeasible since he worked for Earth Central. She shrugged the thought off, the drugs draining away the concern, and continued signing.

'No, no other casualties like yours,' Oren replied to her question. 'The parasites attacked your car, mistaking it for one of their usual hosts. Three other cars went down, resulting in some broken bones and two concussions, but all the people involved wore Polity armour so were unharmed.'

She signed again.

'The cars were completely trashed,' he replied. 'The parasites ate their way through everything organic, and plenty that wasn't. They even chewed into the laminar power storage and it didn't kill them, and they dropped egg sacs throughout. Vrease ran a scanner over one of the cars and declared it unsalvageable. We moved all of them away from the base and burned them.'

More signing.

'Yes, other casualties. An armoured creature survived the flaming in a crevice in the massif. It attacked two colonists and they suffered much internal damage despite their suits. Fortunately the ovipositor it used to try and inject its nymphs inside them couldn't penetrate the fabric.'

Ursula signed frantically.

'Your envirosuit? Burned along with the car,' said Oren. 'I have others to attend to. You should be out of there in a little while.'

Ursula felt a surge of frustration as he moved away. She hadn't wanted her envirosuit back, but a coin she had acquired long ago on another world. But it seemed apposite that – having acquired the coin on that world after coming out of a regrowth tank – on this one she had lost it. Perhaps it signified that she had moved beyond the immaturity of making decisions based on a coin-flip. The loss bothered her, but it quickly faded. As she slid into unthinking somnolence, she realized he had increased the hypnotics dosage.

Ursula woke again feeling battered and sore with a warm surface below her. Under her hand she recognized the slight give of a surgical slab's rubberized self-cleaning meta-material. Her memory blurred with hundreds of other occasions like this and she recalled being in a regrowth tank just before, but specifics evaded her. She opened her eyes to see a mass of concentric rings, lenses and needle emitters directly above her head and recognized a medical scanner. Looking down, she saw she was completely naked, lying on the slab.

'Please keep still,' said a voice. 'The scanner is more than able to compensate but still gets a better read if you remain motionless.'

Oren. Memory returned in a flood. She was about to reply, but her throat felt dry and tight and now the scanning head began humming and traversing in a slow zigzag down towards her feet. She waited impatiently as the thing ran its course. Occasionally she felt flushes of heat as its scanning became more active to resolve one point or another. When it finally finished and folded away, she turned to look for Oren, and found him sitting beyond a viewing window, studying screens on the console before him. Something about this puzzled her, but her thoughts moved with the alacrity of slugs. After a moment he swiped a hand across the screens and stood up, staring through the glass at her. It was odd how, with any other man such an inspection of her body still raised some sort of reaction, after all these years, yet with Oren there was none. She guessed he diverged sufficiently from her perception of the human male to be discounted on some deep level.

She next wondered why she was thinking about this at all and realized the root of it: though aching and damaged, she also felt horny. Other thoughts tumbled together, but only giving her a partial picture. She had set up her previous nanosuite to suppress her libido but it seemed likely the new suite, which Oren had given them all aboard the ship bringing them to Threpsis, had removed or otherwise interfered with that setting. She would have to do something about that.

Sex had its uses as an energetic driver and was of course pleasurable, but as an authority figure, and while establishing a colony on a new world, it could become a major hindrance.

'So what do you have to tell me?' she asked – her voice catching as she sat up and swung her legs over the side of the slab. Dizziness assailed her for a second, but quickly passed.

'Liver and kidney organelles are spread throughout your body, along with other related additions.' His words opened up further memory. 'Your defence against the radiation is subdermal with a high turnover of outer cells – your immune system there is driving intense autophagy and apoptosis. Others have the same. You'll find you're shedding a lot of skin.'

High solar radiation, she remembered. Memory keyed to memory, further opening her mind to the present.

'Lung organelles?' she asked, remembering some of their exchange while she was in the regrowth tank. She stood up, feeling a bit shaky but not as if she was about to keel over.

'The nanosuite started to grow air channels from them to your lungs. It then changed its mind and got rid of both them and the lung organelles.' Oren shook his head. 'The other organelles work well to boost the function of those organs and as a backup should they be destroyed. But should your lungs be destroyed, the scattered organelles would likely lose their oxygen supply. Any boost of function is better served by lung expansion.'

She took that in, but mostly mulled over that 'changed its mind'. Though she remembered their arrival here and being injured, it still seemed she had yet to grasp her situation fully.

He looked contemplative for a moment, then adding, 'Of course, secondary lungs are an option, but would require some substantial alterations of physical structure that would have to be discussed.'

He said it casually, but was definitely putting it out there. She at least knew that, and now remembered other things about Oren.

'Yes – that would have to be discussed.'

During the journey here to Threpsis, Ursula had been studying much of the man's work, including his detailed proposals for radically upgrading the human form. As she recollected, the form with extra lungs had a long segmented body with new sets of arms, just like his, at every join. Each segment held extra organs, including lungs, with ribs and musculature wrapped around them and tubular additional air intakes protruding from the joins too. The thing also had extra arseholes to complement the convoluted digestive system.

'The benefits would be quite extensive,' he added.

She nodded vaguely and turned to inspect her surroundings properly. The format of examination rooms like this was pretty similar across the Polity, but now she noticed differences. The scanning gear was nonstandard, biohazard vents and spray heads were mounted in the ceiling, walls and floor. Ultraviolet lights were also scattered all around and surrounded by rings of micro-lasers for the identification of, or to zap, anything from the size of a bug down to a bacterium. The door was also biohazard proofed and the inner one of a clean lock.

'We're not in the shuttle,' she said and then, because her mind had begun to wake up properly, 'How long was I in the tank?'

'Eighteen of your days,' Oren replied.

Eighteen Threpsian days about equalled twenty-two days solstan. That seemed like an awfully long time to have spent in a regrowth tank. This concerned her. She also noted Oren's use of 'your'. Would he ever consider himself one of the colonists?

'So I'm clear to get back to work?' she asked.

'You're clear,' Oren replied. 'And I'm clear to get back to my work. The auto-analysers and the biologists are providing a great deal of data and I'm constantly updating the suites.' He shrugged, smiled. 'Soon we'll be able to breathe the air here without something eating our lungs.'

Now he used 'our'.

'You have one of the nanosuites yourself?' she asked.

'I've had one for some years. They have programming and memory capacity far beyond that required to deal with the maladies and dangers of just one world. I see no reason not to take advantage of the things they are learning here.'

Again he gave her pause. Learning here? She was about to pursue that but Callum came in behind Oren. They spoke, but Oren had obviously shut off the speaker for a moment. Callum nodded, then looked in at her. Now she did feel something she hadn't done with Oren. She walked over to a dispenser in the wall to remove a disposerall and pull it on.

'I've brought your new protective suit if you're ready,' said Callum. 'Time for your people to see you're okay, and for you to begin an inspection.'

Yes, she really wanted that. Obviously this examination room was part of the new base and, if everything had been going to plan, eighteen Threpsian days should have seen the work substantially advanced.

'We need to have a further talk about these nanosuites,' she said to Oren, closing up the overall and heading for the door. 'Specifically about their degree of intelligence,' she said, and thought to herself she also needed to get that libido block back in.

Oren nodded mildly. He operated some controls, stood and walked away. The clean lock inner door whoomphed away from its seals and swung open. The whole lock protocol was unnecessary this time, and it just flashed ultraviolet, rapidly exchanging its atmosphere before opening the next door. She stepped out into the viewing room and now properly looked at Callum.

First she noted his skin. It had taken on a metallic sheen that spread to his eyes and was probably all over his body. Next she noticed the Polity combat suit he was wearing. It had additions, such as extra ribbing for structural strength, and a new layer put over the armour segments and the stretchable sections between them. It looked vaguely organic – white with a bruised tone made by capillaries and veins running just below the surface. But it also had more mechanistic structures, like tessellations of quadrate scales.

'Tell me about this.' She waved her hand over the suit.

Callum pointed towards the single door. 'While you've been recovering, Oren has been perpetually upgrading our nanosuites to deal with local toxins, acids and micro-biota, but some of that stuff is vicious and can survive the usual washes and clean lock routines. This' – he gestured at the new covering – 'is biomech stuff. He's been incorporating defences that plants and animals have here to deal with the more common forms of attack, so an astringent wash can deal with the rest. Says there's much more to learn and this might be a step towards something far more suited to this environment.'

'That's good,' she replied, thinking *eighteen days?* Oren was certainly demonstrating his genius, and that gladdened her. But then her more cynical side noted how Oren would probably have preferred to incorporate this new layer into the colonists themselves. 'And your skin?' she asked.

He smiled and touched his fingers self-consciously to his face. 'My particular adaptation to the solar radiation. My brother has the same, as do about a quarter of all the colonists. It not only reflects a lot of radiation but incorporates a meta-material layer, similar to that in spaceship hulls. It reacts to bombardment by throwing up electrostatic and magnetic fields. Doesn't stop everything, but the nanites deal with the rest of the damage. Apparently it's not fully grown yet – I'll be like a mirror soon.'

He seemed happy enough about it, so Ursula nodded and smiled along with him. She couldn't help but feel a familiar disquiet, though. Yes, they needed to adapt to this world, but this was just an early change. How much more would there be? As Callum turned and headed for the door, Ursula shook her head, annoyed with herself. She'd felt from the beginning they could explore a new course for humanity here, and that they would undergo change. As she had told the Kalonan AI, evolution had been one of her aims in selecting such a hostile world. She shouldn't now be having doubts about the adaptations. And in the end, perhaps Oren had the correct approach: should she let go of her aversion to changes in the basic human form?

Beyond the door was a hospital area. Only one bed was occupied, by a woman with high-tech casts on her arms, legs and torso, as well as one on the side of her head, like a half-helmet augmentation. She was sitting upright and looked up from her tablet to smile at Ursula. What was her name? Talfennon.

'I'm surprised to see someone still here,' Ursula said, walking over.

Talfennon shrugged. 'Since that fucking thing in the massif broke just about every bone in my body, it seems my nanosuite decided I needed stronger bones. The thing is even putting alloy layers in there but that takes some time. Oren says I'm likely to end up with a skeleton like a Golem chassis.'

'Well I hope it gets it done soon,' said Ursula. 'We can't be doing with this kind of indolence.' She waved a hand at the bed. Talfennon laughed as she moved on. The woman also seemed happy about her changes, but again Ursula wondered about word choices. Her nanosuite had 'decided' she needed stronger bones?

8

Present

'You're still going.'

In their new form of communicating, Callum's thought followed her out into the corridor, then down the spiral stairs into the lower section.

'*You have your orders,*' she replied perfunctorily, but felt glad Callum had communicated his disagreement. It highlighted something she could sense about her initial push for dominance: it had reasserted her position of command, made easier because she'd been the first to take on the upgrade bracelet ahead of the rest. And, since doing it, she could feel all the others aligning again with the original command structure of the colony. Callum should be able to object in the position he occupied, just below her – that was his job. But Vrease should have been there too. Vrease's divergence from their adaptations was a problem.

Now she felt the connection back to the control room fading, but not completely. She pushed at it and suddenly felt a crack down her back and over her shoulders. Peering at one shoulder, she saw a split open in her skin and something pushing up like a fungus, with facets opening on its surface and taking on a shine. The connection started to come back and, analysing internally, she saw this was an expansion of com – the *thing* down

157

her back and on her shoulders was a multi-wavelength transceiver that also emitted and decoded the complex chemicals Vrease had mentioned.

Next she felt the car lurch as it rose out of the trap they'd fallen into. Through her connection to Gurda, she felt as if her own hands were on the controls, while through all of them in the control room, she could see the screen feeds showing them rise clear. As earth fell away from the car's flanks, it revealed raptors stuck to the surface of the vehicle, worm form with paddle legs and all writhing towards the smoking hole in its armour. She heard their chatter and felt their connection, visualized like a cloud around the car and penetrating through the hole in the hull to more raptors inside. She understood some of it, but not in any terms expressible by human communication. She felt purpose, and a deep processing of organic control – a network influenced by a distant input. The chatter changed as the guns on the armour began to move and their range abruptly increased. They started firing. Some alternated between particle beam and chemically driven projectiles to weaken and then peel the creatures away. The railguns, rising in turrets, slammed hypersonic beads across, above the armour, to shred the creatures and send them tumbling to the ground. She returned her attention to her destination.

She sensed others ahead: Trakken, already subservient, and his squad aligned below him. But there were still others too in that area. One presence she felt herself sliding away from, a looming shadow she dismissed for the moment while she focused on three chattering alien minds. Across wider EMR bands, the three raptors were seeking to include her in subservience to another, the distant input she'd sensed earlier but which was steadily growing weaker. She rejected the cacoraptors at once. She was not so far gone she'd become one of them. However, the tenor of their communication, albeit without words, and the fading presence of that distant input, confirmed what Vrease had said. There had to be a dominant cacoraptor.

Arriving, she studied the squad closely, and their radical changes.

Even though skin had displaced Polity combat suits in the colony, after numerous encounters with raptors, Trakken had decided on extra protection for those he now called his squad. They'd taken to donning Polity combat armour over their skin suits, as it offered that bit extra against claws, which turned out to be sheathed with Q-carbon, as well as the kind of bone-splintering impacts a raptor could deliver. Originally they'd worn it the other way around, with the skin as an outer covering, and this change had made it an inner one, but Ursula saw it still asserting its dominance. The stuff had grown through seams and joints and begun to spread over the combat armour, settling in place over hard segments and webbing the movable sections. It'd also penetrated the motorized components and slid up to cup the helmets. They all looked unfeasibly bulky – great trolls of organic and mechanical technology. Ursula saw even more besides.

Most were armed with weapons put together to incorporate a laser carbine, pulse rifle and slug thrower. These had been difficult to handle but necessary when going up against borer raptors that had come into the base. Now they swung them about as if they weighed nothing at all, and Ursula could see tendrils spreading from their skin to penetrate the weapons. One soldier – Gene Lecane – showed this increase in strength much more overtly. She carried an iron-burner. The cylinder was five feet long and a foot in diameter and normally mounted on a heavy tripod or sled. Now she supported it on one shoulder with her arm wrapped round it, her other hand supporting it further along.

But how was she able to operate the controls? Then Ursula saw the tendrils winding into the weapon. This sight gave her conventional human thought processes an explanation, but she didn't need it.

She could *feel* all their changes, as if she was reaching into their bodies and being them for as long as necessary. She sensed how Lecane could fire the iron-burner with a thought, but had also altered its mechanisms so as to control the rod burn to give a narrower flare, should she require it. When Lecane turned, Ursula could also see that tubes and other connections had grown out of her back to enter the rear of the burner – nascent power and materials feeds, support systems for the burner, growing in her body. Trevor Caulter wore tanks on his back containing the chemical warfare they used against raptors – mostly acids and enzymes. Previously the tubes from those tanks had led to one weapon, but it had been redesigned for two devices strapped along his arms to emit varying sprays and jets. He was wearing it for the first time now, but had already combined with it. Ursula remembered a long-ago conversation with a Polity AI about marines and commandos and how, though they could all fight, they were all specialists. And here she was seeing the physical manifestation of that. She could sense all their linkages to their weapons, with the targeting in their eyes and minds. She could feel Trakken's strength and control as his skin integrated the Polity combat suit, complemented its motors and supplied further power via bioelectric vessels growing in his body.

'Is anyone in there?' she asked, still loath to face the looming shadowy presence she'd sensed before.

It was an unnecessary question, but Ursula felt it important to retain verbal communication. She recognized her reluctance to sink into that other communication as similar to her reservations about Oren's drive for their radical alteration and adaptation. They needed to evolve as humans, to advance, but still retain their essential humanity. Human talk seemed to her to be one of the anchors of that. It was perhaps irrational, but there it was.

Trakken fell in with her thought. 'Two of them – both out of it.'

She could sense them beyond the door. They were badly injured, with the damage to their bodies extreme enough normally to have killed them, even with the previous iteration of the nano-suite. Ursula gathered data from them. One lay in the corridor open to the sky. The blast had ripped off one arm, peeled open his chest and torn out a lung. This hadn't been enough to completely disable him but while he was stunned the raptors had come in and further ripped into his body before discarding him. The other lay further along the corridor. She'd immediately run at the creatures to attack, before receiving the same treatment. But why had the creatures not finished them off?

Ursula's analysis jumped to a new level of thought. Their primary objective was to open up the car for their fellows and destroy the enemy, so spending further time and energy to ensure the deaths of thoroughly disabled combatants was a waste. The raptors were now behind this door, grinding away at the adaptive armour that responded to their attacks layer by layer – meta-materials changed their structure, with new materials coming in through micropores to flood spaces and harden. But there was more to their strategy than mere tactical considerations. She felt only a hint of it in their communication and she'd sensed it when the raptors first tried to *include* her. The raptors' enemy had changed. The colonists had ceased to be simply a source of nourishment, even at the first encounter. Then they became something completely *other* and a threat, but also a resource to be utilized and absorbed. Now they had become a resource not only to be utilized but *incorporated*. In this chronology, she discerned the source and confirmed it as the first cacoraptor they had seen. She closed her eyes, grimaced at the logic chains and, at last, acknowledged that final shadowy presence.

Here was a separate mind, slippery, and though it slotted into the previous command structure, it didn't fully connect or bow to her will. She sensed it wasn't actually resisting her, she simply couldn't grip the strange knot of mentality and emotion. But its thought came clear as she focused properly on its source.

'*Burning the fig,*' it said.

Nursum stood behind Trakken and his soldiers, who were waiting at a bulkhead door. It wasn't her imagination that he'd grown taller, for his head came close to grazing the ceiling. His limbs were longer and his hands clawed, as well as his feet, which dug into the yielding floor covering. For a moment, because he had toes, she thought he must have discarded his skin suit, since they were made with boots, but she quickly realized he was actually still wearing it and it had blended with his body. Diamond patterns covered it and the hard crystalline glitter had shifted from his own skin out onto it. She looked down at herself and saw the same patterning. The distinction between her human skin, if it remained as it was any longer, and the suit had gone. The transceiver continued to grow on her shoulders, forming a thick, high collar, and a protruding ridge down her back.

'Nursum,' she said.

'They are here,' he said, nodding towards the bulkhead door.

It seemed a pointless comment, and she wondered whether to send him away, or if she could. On some level, she saw him as a threat similar to the original raptor outside, but understood the difference between her raptor perception and the human. She'd saved his life more than once and now he was even more advanced in his transformation than her. She thought back to the last time she'd saved him, before their perimeter fence had first collapsed, before the multigun. So many who couldn't be saved, but the raptors had had difficulty detecting him. He would be strong, dangerous and perhaps needed. She surveyed the others again briefly. They were ready.

'Open the door,' she said.

Near Past

'We've got a fence breach,' said Callum, as Ursula rushed into the base's control room.

She glanced up at the image feeds on the screen-painted wall. Cams on either side showed twenty feet of the fence down, another view showed the break from a distance but rapidly grew closer – Vrease must have deployed drones. Yet another showed three armoured cars heading out. She needed to get up to speed, and fast. Even as she thought this, she'd raised a control hologram, programmed it quickly and flung a frame to the wall. This blanked for a moment, then showed the stretch of fence still upright, just before it went down.

From a mass of growth fifty feet beyond the fence – one that had been expanding and which Ursula remembered ordering to be burned down – cacoraptors flowed out into the open and came to an abrupt halt. The twenty heron forms, as if just given an order, loped straight towards the fence. Defences, mounted on cylindrical pillars spaced along the fence, reacted at once. Ursula flicked up another instruction from her hologram and assessed the activities feed which ran down the side of this recording.

The first defensive reactions weren't visible, as the pillars transmitted the sounds and pheromones of particularly nasty boring parasites. This didn't slow the creatures at all. Next, sputtering like Roman candles, the pillars hit them with jellied balls of burning napalm. Even burning, the creatures didn't falter. A transmitted microwave frequency that generated pain in the afferent nerves of most creatures here did set some of them stumbling, but at the same time they were shedding burning skin to reveal the asbestos white, extinguishing the fires on them. As per their simple programming, the pillars recognized these creatures as cacoraptors. So they now began to deploy the cornucopia of toxins and acids that made up Oren's chemical warfare. The air grew cloudy and usually at this point the raptors would flee or burrow into the ground, to be seen later wandering around like sleepwalkers as their physical reserves ceased to be easily available. But these didn't slow. They were immune.

The creatures hit the electrified fence, slicing through the metal with their bird skulls in sprays of sparks and molten metal. The fence finally came down and the majority of raptors went through. That some of them remained stuck and burning on the fence was a minimal victory at best for the colonists.

They rushed straight into a field of bashful cabbages that retreated into the ground as they sensed movement nearby, but this wasn't enough. The raptors first smashed the weeding and insecticidal robots then proceeded to burrow, steadily destroying the crop in its underground retreats. All of this brought Ursula up to date.

'Why have we got armoured cars heading out there?' she asked.

'Hansellan made the decision on his own cognizance. Shall I recall them?'

Ursula stared at the screens, thinking fast. They weren't the new design of armoured car, the prototype of which Shaben was still finishing down in the garages, but the three cars had some good armament and might be able to kill off a few of the creatures and drive the rest out through the break. She could have a repair team out there directly afterwards. But then what?

'How many people do we have out there?' she asked. 'Vrease?'

The woman checked her screens. 'Four hundred and thirty-three.'

Ursula nodded. They were repairing robots, running greenhouses, working close to their crops either in the fields or in agricultural stations. Some stayed in new residences out there for the same reason. Now, since the raptors had just shown the fence was no longer a barrier to them, every colonist outside the base was a potential casualty.

She tapped her comlink. 'General address,' she said, opening com to everyone. 'Cacoraptors have broken through the outer fence and seem immune to the defences we have until now been deploying. All personnel outside of the base are to return to it at once. This is serious, people. You could get dead out there.' She paused for a moment, feeling this wasn't enough. 'General address on repeat – half-minute intervals,' she stated, then continued, 'All personnel outside the base, this is a direct order: return at once. We have raptors coming through the perimeter fence. Just drop what you're doing and get back here as fast as you can.' She tapped the coms unit off and turned to Vrease. 'Check their locators and ensure everyone is coming in. I want none of this, "But I have to finish spraying," or, "The potatoes will be ruined."'

'We aren't growing any more potatoes out there now,' Vrease replied distractedly while studying her screen.

'Okay.'

'Many will be on foot,' said Callum.

'Send out all the rest of the cars – coordinate on that.' She looked to the two of them, then around at the other staff. Annoyingly she never knew who was doing what when she came in here as they often changed roles.

'The grav-cars?' Callum asked calmly.

Was she overreacting?

'Only if they break through the fence in other places.'

'You think that's likely?'

'They are destroying a crop,' Ursula stated.

Callum stared at her, showing nothing of what he was thinking, but she knew he understood.

'Why?' he asked succinctly, playing to the crowd. 'I can understand them going after the robots, thinking they were prey of some kind, but the plants?'

'Perhaps they're omnivores,' Ursula said, not believing that at all.

'Nope,' interjected Vrease. 'Ground scan shows the crop simply being destroyed.'

It was a brief diorama for the rest in the control room.

Ursula nodded and said, 'Those multiguns you were working on. We'll need to set a new inner perimeter and get them installed.' She looked at Callum and Vrease meaningfully.

Vrease replied, 'We directed resources elsewhere. The caco-raptors had stopped being such a problem. Now this.' She gestured at the screen wall.

'Make it a priority now. If this continues, we'll start to have problems with food supply.' It would be a fix of sorts but by no means the end of their difficulties. She'd already seen how they could alter themselves physically as individuals to a large degree, and to a larger degree generationally when they spread their nymphs inside a prey, but the raptors were changing their behaviour now too. This destruction of crops seemed less the actions of a predator and more like that of an invading army. Ursula turned to watch Hansellan's three armoured cars on the drone feeds.

They had reached sight of the field and circled round, then

166

lined up, putting the raptors between them and the break in the fence. As they came closer, the raptors started emerging from the ground, bird-skull heads swinging towards the cars, stalked sensors rising out of them. As quickly as they'd transformed into worm forms, they changed back – their lower ends splitting into two legs and other conversions occurring as they ran at their new prey . . . or perhaps enemy. Some stayed upright and others bowed down to peel off two new limbs and shift their forms towards that of demonic hounds. The cars opened fire. Ursula watched the creatures shredding and burning under a fusillade from lasers and slug throwers. Then, from one of the cars, a particle beam lashed out, really heating things up. She saw some raptors shedding skin and turning asbestos white. One of these, subsequently hit by a slug thrower, shattered into pieces like a porcelain statue.

'Hansellan,' said Ursula, tactical analysis almost immediate. 'Heat weapons only until they adapt to that, then hit them with the slug throwers.'

After a pause, Hansellan replied, 'Ah, I see that.'

The machine guns ceased firing just a second later. The raptors drew close, only to run into the jets of fire from flame units. The cars went into hard reverse, the creatures pursuing, bathed in flame, and when the machine guns opened up again they began to fly apart. Ursula felt just a moment of vindication, but next saw further raptors swarming out of the vegetation over the other side of the fence. Callum spoke.

'We've got two more breaks in the fence,' he said.

Ursula scanned the image feeds and could see people running towards the base. Other cars were heading out, some already at agricultural stations and residences and people were climbing aboard. Raptors hurtled in from the two new breaks and this time they weren't stopping to wreck crops. While a portion of their number peeled off and headed elsewhere, one group moved at high speed, straight up to the double doors of an agricultural station, tore through the roller composite as if it was paper, and swarmed inside. Meanwhile, on the other side of the station, people were clambering into armoured cars as quickly as they could. The second raptor group, also dispersing some of their number, hit massed greenhouses and were inside them in a moment.

'Send the grav-cars,' Ursula said, trying to keep her voice level even as she saw three people, who'd been running from those greenhouses, hit by just one raptor. What had been people shortly became pieces scattered across the tilled earth. An explosion drew her attention. She had no idea why, but it had issued from another agricultural station, and now a fire was burning inside it. With a sour taste in her mouth, she worked her control hologram then threw the result up on the wall. Rows of blue dots indicated all the colonists still outside. A white tick appeared over each one as that person got inside the base but, meanwhile, others were turning yellow, indicating life-threatening injury, or red indicating . . . death. Ursula watched the display for just a second and cursed her facility for integration, almost instantly recognizing that the yellows didn't last long, and that thirty-five people had already died.

'Another fence break,' Callum reported.

Ursula felt herself fizzing with frustration. This was precisely the cleft stick she had wanted to avoid when she was first in the military and had requested to be just a fighting grunt. But she knew her tactical skills were better deployed right here. Again she used her control hologram, giving her a map of the area inside the perimeter. Dots displayed the positions of the people. A moment later the satellite gave her the positions of the raptors too, in orange – as they ran so hot, they were easy to detect. She tracked speed of movement, scribed a circle in the air, and it appeared on the map.

'Everyone inside here, move them in on foot. Open all base doors,' she stated. With further gesture control, she highlighted other areas. 'Three cars here, four there.'

'There isn't enough space inside,' commented Gurda from her station.

'Ten in each car,' Ursula spat. 'Ten or maybe more holding on outside. Move it!' She checked further, integrating the tactics of the evacuation. Her damned precise mind again gave her information she really didn't want, but needed.

'Grav-cars here, here and here,' she stated. 'Those cars head over there.' She highlighted an area over to one side of the route of four cars. They were heading to a cluster of blue dots flowing out of an agricultural station.

'People still out there,' someone said.

Ursula thought about the best way to phrase a reply, but instead said, 'Just do it.' How could she express the simple horrible logic of it all, that the twenty-eight human beings over there were as good as dead already? She kept giving her orders, kept reassessing every moment. Her legs were locked solid, her mind working frenetically, precisely, but she knew she would pay the emotional cost later.

'Shaben,' she said. 'The new car?'

'Getting the wheels back on as fast as I can,' the engineer replied from the garages.

'Hansellan,' said Callum.

Six blue dots were out there – too far out there. Two of them changed colour, one yellow, one red, then both red. She switched to the scene and saw one armoured car rolling to a stop, burning, its top half missing. She needed no explanations. Raptors had got in and the driver or his mate had blown the car's munitions.

The two other armoured cars were heading rapidly back to base. Both of them had cacoraptors attached to them like feeding lampreys and she briefly read their telemetry scrolling down the side. One of the cars had lost a wheel but could keep going on the five remaining. All of them were reporting deep mechanical and acid ablation.

'They'll be in range of the base guns shortly,' Callum commented.

Ticks and red dots fled across Ursula's vision. What did he mean? The floor rumbled and she realized raptors were now getting close to the base. She moved over to the chain-glass window and peered out. The lights of targeting lasers flashed out there as the guns fired. Returning her attention to the wall, she watched the highly accurate shots of the railgun beads slamming home. The raptors were resistant, of course, their bodies as tough as braided cable, but they weren't *that* tough. The beads hit with appalling impact while the vibration Ursula could feel was from the shock-absorbing hydraulics such weapons required. Raptors staggered along with chunks of their bodies splintering up like wood, then flew apart. Assessing, she saw that most colonists on foot were now inside; others she saw being torn down. Yes, there had been some overlap, and losses of eight to twelve per cent were inevitable for those on foot. However, had she reduced the inner perimeter, the losses would have been above twenty per cent. Cars were coming in now too, just appearing on the horizon.

'Close all personnel doors and lock them down – entry through garage doors only now,' she instructed.

The floor continued to rumble underfoot. She saw more raptors flying apart under hails of rail beads but couldn't fail to see colonists dying too. Another explosion drew her attention. Six red dots as a grav-car crashed. One car heading for the garages had people clinging to the outside, but raptors tore four of them from their holds. More red dots.

'Close Garages Three, Four and Six,' she instructed. 'Direct other cars to the closest open garage.'

Three cars had stopped outside one garage, their passengers clambering out and running into the base. Those cars now began shooting at the raptors scattered all about the area. Subliminally Ursula saw the distant twenty-eight go through their transformation from blue to red.

'Get those cars inside now!' she snapped.

'They're giving cover,' someone said.

'They're dead if they don't get inside now, and this is not a fucking democracy!'

Fewer and fewer blue dots remaining.

'Close Garages One and Two,' she said.

She noted the three cars were still firing, but a moment later they shut down and headed into Garage Seven, smoking and weeping acid.

Just a scattering of dots now. Ursula discounted a number of them – too far out. Most of the cars were back inside, while those remaining were snaring more people on the way in. Procedures were being ignored, of course: no deactivating sprayers and no patrolling mosquito autoguns to ensure nothing nasty remained stuck to each vehicle. The cars would, however, be joining the never-ending queue of vehicles awaiting repairs. She dismissed the thought and focused briefly on one blue dot far out in the fields. Its persistence puzzled her as she turned her attention to Hansellan's two cars.

'Hansellan,' she said. 'Garage Seven.'

'Yeah, I know,' he replied.

Of course he did, her information had been unnecessary.

A moment later all the cars were in, except for those two. They finally came in range, raptors pursuing, with some actually on the vehicles, clawing and melting their way through the armour. Ursula again felt the vibration of the base guns through the floor. The raptors on the cars shredded and, when the strike angle was right, multiple hits scoured them from their holds. The targeting program for all this had been difficult because hits of sufficient force to tear the creatures away were quite capable of punching into the car's armour too. The vehicles carried on, occasionally stopping or turning so the base guns could abrade every creature from them. Ursula noted one car dropping back – the one that had lost a wheel.

'Hansellan, what's your problem?' she asked.

'Getting some serious drag,' came the reply.

Ursula studied a drone image of the vehicle. A deep furrow with earth mounded up on either side had started appearing behind it.

'You have one of those bastards anchoring underneath,' she said.

'Yeah, I got that,' Hansellan replied. 'I'll drop the undershield when I'm closer.'

And there it was again. They had seen this once already, before she ordered the first retreat inside the main fence. A cacoraptor had stuck itself to Hansellan's car and, keeping most of its body underground, acted as a dragging anchor to slow it. She would have liked to have thought this was some instinctive strategy the creatures used against brontopods, but their penetration of that prey was too fast for it to be necessary. The raptor dragging beneath must also be growing anchoring flutes and then, once it had enough of them, it could grind the car to a halt. Learned behaviour? Possibly; probably. But it also seemed to her like intelligent control of its body shape.

The first car reached Garage Seven and drove in. The second stumbled closer, slowing all the time.

'Shedding undershield now,' Hansellan advised.

The car thumped up on its suspension with a blast of smoke and shot forwards. On the ground behind it lay a piece of ceramal armour, shifting with the raptor still attached out of sight. But this time, rather than the thing just sitting there, the armour flipped over and crashed to one side as the raptor came out of the ground in fast pursuit of the car. Base guns clipped its forked tail and ripped away some of the steadily closing flutes, but the thing seemed to be using the armoured car for cover. A drone view showed it nose into the ground again behind the car. Only now the car had no solid armour underneath it.

'Hansellan! Get out and run!'

'What?'

'Raptor under you again!'

Fortunately, Hansellan wasn't inclined to argue or discuss the matter. The car continued forwards and bucked, even as its side door popped open. Hansellan leaped out, hit the ground and rolled, then came upright and began running towards the base. The raptor emerged again from under his car, splintering out limbs that fattened even as it began using them. But now it had exposed itself. The base guns thrummed the floor once more, shredding the running creature as it came after the man. Hansellan reached the garage just as the doors were drawing closed. He looked back, gave the disintegrating creature the finger, then stepped inside, the door closing behind him.

Ursula allowed an automatic smile at the defiance, but quickly lost it when she looked at the devastation out there. The raptors had retreated from the base but continued to wreck equipment, buildings and crops.

'I've got the wheels back on,' Shaben told her.

It was over now and that one comment shattered her controlled focus. She started to shake, her clothing was soaked with sweat.

173

A dreadful feeling closed its clawed fist inside her and she peered up at the display of dots. Her integrating facility had crashed now and she managed to banish the display before automatically counting the lives lost.

'Oh hell,' said Vrease.

Ursula turned and looked at the woman. She appeared hard and in control. Callum was bent over with his forehead on his console. Others were in similar poses. It impinged on Ursula a moment later that someone was crying.

'You have something for me?' she asked, trying to bring her mind back to order.

Vrease nodded. 'Everyone still alive is in, except for one who shouldn't be out there at all.'

Ursula turned and looked at the aerial map. That persistent blue dot was still there.

'Who?'

'Nursum.'

As Ursula hurried down through the base she knew there would be some serious questions about her fitness to command after this disaster. And more would arise from what she was about to do now but, damn it, she felt responsible for the man. Suited up in the latest iteration of Polity combat armour and 'skin', she entered Garage One.

In one section she could see damaged cars through a chain-glass screen under the decontamination sprays. People were scattered here and there, some sitting, some wandering about in a haze. She stepped aside as medtechs led two grav-gurneys past her. Donnaken glanced at her, his expression grim. In a way she was glad now for the lack of augmentations and other mind-linked tech. These people didn't yet know the full extent of the disaster that had overtaken them. She headed down, exchanging brief greetings and cursory

comments. Most people didn't want to say much. A side door took
her through into another section of the garage where the prototype
sat, its wheels back on as Shaben had said.

'You want to take this out? Now?'

She turned. Shaben had come in behind her. The blond-
bearded man looked tired but that wasn't necessarily a result of
the day's events. He never slept and worked to maintain the cars
continuously with only occasional visits to Medical for his own
body maintenance.

'Yes, I do,' she replied.

She wanted Nursum back and she wanted some victory to
pull from the ashes, just for herself. Even so, a nastily calculating
part of her mind assessed how this would work for morale. They
had just suffered incredible losses; this rescue of just one man,
by her, could have an effect.

'We haven't put this thing through its paces yet,' said Shaben.
'I don't really like you taking it out now.'

She glanced back at him, feeling the urge to tell him to get
back to work on the other cars, but realized this was part of the
badinage they'd conducted down here before. He was attempting
to lighten the tone.

'You mean it's all new and shiny and you're reluctant to start
repairs on it so soon?'

'Transparent as chain-glass, me.' Shaben grimaced. 'It's been
hectic out there and is still bad, I'm told. Stay alert.' He turned
away.

Watching him go, Ursula shook her head. He was a very busy
man, and he had no real idea how bad things had got. Turning
back to the car, she climbed inside, walked past all the seats for
a combat team and dropped down into the driver's seat. The
chain-glass window ahead, and to the sides, had shutters that
could draw across, with screen paint on the inside to then present

the same view as before, for as long as the cams lasted. Below this sat three screens. They could all be used for multiple views but at the present setting the left-hand one showed targeting and weapons control, the middle one monitored the new adaptive armour they were trying, while the right-hand one gave her views through the drones the vehicle could launch. She pressed a button and started up the motor. The hydrox turbine whoomphed into life and the vehicle shuddered with leashed power. Ahead, the garage doors opened automatically and, grabbing the steering handles, Ursula pushed them forwards, sending the thing out into the dangerous evening twilight.

'Nothing near him yet?' she asked over com.

The light of Brant sitting on the horizon behind her to the left gave her a clear view ahead, but that moon would soon sink out of sight. She checked the controls on the column between the steering handles, hit one of them and the view became as clear as a slightly green tinted day. The meta-material lamination in the chain-glass gave her options for light enhancement and magnification.

'No,' Callum replied wearily. 'The main concentration is presently tearing up one of our warehouses out there. There are others not so far from him but they haven't noticed him yet.' Callum paused for a second before adding, 'And that's strange – they didn't have any trouble tracking down the others.'

Ursula raised her control hologram and threw data to the drone screen. This gave her a series of views. A stab of a finger filled the screen with a satellite map highlighting her position, Nursum's and those of the clumps of cacoraptors. She pressed on her own position then slid her finger directly to Nursum's and, from the menu that appeared, selected 'Auto' and 'Emergency Speed'. The armoured car thrummed and accelerated, throwing her back in her seat and snatching the steering handles out of her hands. Through the side windows she could see it kicking up earth. As the acceleration eased, she leaned forwards again, wiped away the map and began selecting other images. From a high angle, one showed Nursum trudging across a field. She realized with a start that he was wearing only an envirosuit, with his visor and head covering open and gloves retracted into their wrist pockets. Another image showed cacoraptors, their forms snake-like, writhing together in a great mass. Yet another showed a group of four, each standing on two legs in their heron form, muscular necks terminating in cylindrical heads, extruding sensory scales and antennae. These heads were turning like radar dishes, looking for prey.

'Now I know why I'm getting no reply through his suit coms unit,' Callum said.

'Yes, I've seen,' Ursula replied. 'At least he still has his beacon.'

'Yeah,' said Callum. 'Life signs and all.'

Ursula grimaced. Nursum's life signs were at variance from those of other colonists. Oren had said that was fine, just that he was a little different. All colonists could be located by their coms units, but many had taken to wearing backup locator beacons either on a pendant or around a wrist or ankle since the nanosuites caused implants to fail. Nursum had been given one and hadn't taken it off. She damned him for not wearing combat armour with its integral coms unit, though.

'What the hell is he still doing out there?' Callum wondered. 'Surely he must have been hiding earlier?'

'When it comes to Nursum, who knows?' She shook her head, trying to ignore the hollow feeling inside. Yes, she felt responsible for Nursum, but was also aware that her current actions were displacement activity. This could only last so long before she had to face the reality of what had just happened to the colony. But for now, she would just focus on Nursum and his rescue.

The man *was* worrying. At times he seemed perfectly rational and able to continue with most of the work he'd done before. Even though he'd lost much of his earlier knowledge, when he discovered something he didn't know, he quickly reabsorbed it. Oren said the man's retention was now almost eidetic and this speeded up his ability to learn. But on other occasions he would come out with seeming nonsensical statements that always left the impression of a deeper meaning, but one difficult to nail down. He also did things that made no sense . . . or perhaps they did. He had recently removed many items from his apartment and replaced them with others. When Ursula, ever concerned and suspicious of his behaviour, ran a computer analysis of his choices, she found only one linking factor: he'd removed everything that could burn, even replacing his expensive 'natural' bedding with fire-retardant material. Thinking on this, Ursula pulled the map back onto the screen and studied it. It was almost with a sense of inevitability she recognized his location.

'He's heading to where we retrieved him – where we burned the fig.' Even as she spoke the last words she shivered, because Nursum often spoke them, especially when saying something no one could quite understand.

'Right. Burning the fig,' said Callum. 'Those four raptors are on the move now and heading directly towards him.'

'Fuck.' Ursula inspected the weapons control screen, raised a hologram and made a grabbing motion towards the screen. The image and menus now opened in her hologram as a transparent box, in the format for 3D manipulation and control. A slap on her wristcom detached it from her wrist movements and kept it hovering in front of her as she manipulated it, setting up the weapons system.

Unlike the other cars, this one had a bead railgun with hydraulic dampers and enough weight not to be thrown about by the recoil. It already had the same programs as the base guns, though being from a less stable platform it wasn't quite as accurate. She gave the program location data on Nursum and the approaching raptors so it could more easily run identification, then turned her attention to the other weapons. The car had a particle beam, short range in atmosphere, and a wide selection of missiles. She targeted the four raptors, still out of sight over the horizon, but changed her mind to select a point half a mile behind them and fired off a missile. The car juddered as the thing streaked away overhead. Again checking imagery, she waited. The impact ensued a minute later: an explosion blowing open a crater and the thermite load burning down inside it. The raptors came to a halt, their weird heads swinging round towards the blast. She watched them subsequently turn their heads to each other as if discussing the matter. It seemed they recognized the blast as merely a distraction, faced back towards Nursum and set off at a steady loping run again.

'I don't know whether it was that missile,' said Callum, 'but you've got the others on the move now.'

The map again, checking vectors. The other groups of raptors were indeed heading directly towards her.

'Get ready for scouring when I get back,' she commented.

Looking ahead, she could see Nursum trudging along while the raptors, over to the left, were still out of sight. She made selections in the holographic block and fired off a single missile. It impacted just a short while later, above ground and amidst the four creatures. A blast front filled with ceramic shrapnel ripped into them and scattered them, yet they tumbled out of it merely looking ragged, and healed rapidly as they broke into a run again. She targeted and fired four more missiles, hitting a raptor each. Two were badly damaged – one lying in writhing pieces on the ground and the other collapsing to snake form and burrowing into the earth.

Column controls again. The vehicle's lights came on, with the view ahead growing unbearably bright until the meta-material lamination adjusted it. Another control gave her PA.

'Nursum!' she bellowed. The man had already halted and turned to look towards the explosions. 'Run towards me! You've got cacoraptors coming for you!'

The two remaining suddenly became visible. The things were dodging and weaving and she couldn't get a target lock for the missiles. Learned behaviour – there could be no doubt. However, they then came in range of the particle beam. She fired it and swept across them. The range was such that the thing lost coherence in atmosphere and hit them like a blue flamethrower. They smoked and shed matter but continued on. Nursum was still just standing there, damn him! She targeted the nearer of the creatures and kept the beam on it. The thing kept on running even as it burned and fell apart, until it finally collapsed, scattering pieces of itself along the ground. At last Nursum seemed to realize the danger and started to run. She concentrated on the other raptor, the beam swinging dangerously close to the running man.

'Come on!' she shouted.

The raptor came apart so close to Nursum he had to leap the burning limbs and she was sure she saw one of them reach out and try to catch him. She grabbed the steering handles and began slowing the vehicle, since he couldn't board at this speed. She hit the door control and felt the heated waft of smoke enter. She had him now – he was safe. But then something, like the head of a tubeworm, broke out of the ground ahead of him. He ran straight into its open limbs and it closed around him, dragging him down.

As the vehicle came to a halt, Ursula just sat there and gaped. Death could come quickly here but the shock still froze her. Nursum would be in pieces now. Gone. She shook herself, noting the hot smoky air and the other raptors closing in – they were now visible, moving towards where Nursum had gone down. She hit the door control again, closing it, and dismissed the hologram with a wave of her hand. She turned the vehicle and began to head back to the base but felt reluctant to go to auto emergency speed. All that effort, in saving him, in using the upgrade and in coming out here – all wasted and gone in one brief moment of animal violence.

'Behind you!' Callum shouted over com. 'He's fucking behind you!'

'What?'

'Nursum!'

She turned the vehicle in a skidding halt, throwing up a wave of earth, and partially faced where she was sure she'd seen Nursum die. The man was there, trotting towards her. He'd lost his envirosuit and much of the clothing over which he wore it but seemed uninjured.

'Fucking run! They're behind you!'

He glanced back and accelerated.

No, the distance was too great. The raptors had already grown legs and shifted to their fast-moving doglike form. With shaking hands, she struggled to bring up the hologram she'd dismissed, managed to raise it and sent it skating off behind her. Then she noticed Nursum's speed. He was kicking up a spray of earth behind him as he ran and his stride appeared impossibly long. Unbelievably, he seemed to be pulling ahead of his pursuers. Ursula hit the door control again to open it, spun the car and headed for him in hard reverse. Nursum hurtled towards her, raptors now speeding up behind him. He leaped. It should not have been humanly possible for him to get in the car, let alone survive the impact, yet she heard the heavy thump behind her as he made it in, and hit the door control to close it again. The car slammed into the cacoraptors and at once they were all over it, spraying acid and scrabbling at the armour. She shoved the handles forwards, wheels throwing up fountains of earth, hit the control to draw across the shutters just in case, then initiated auto emergency speed back to base. The car accelerated and threw her back into her seat. As the acceleration came off she turned and looked back.

Nursum was pushing himself up from the floor. He was completely naked now and his skin had that hard crystalline look she had glimpsed before. It also had deep splits in it, revealing internal organs, but no blood, and even as she watched they began to close. His legs looked longer too and she saw that his fingers terminated in hooked claws. His eyes, oh god, his eyes, black and gold and hellish.

'You okay?' she asked, though it seemed a ridiculous question.

'I went to see her, but she is gone,' he replied.

'You went to see who?'

'The fig is all burned,' he said.

She turned to her controls, though reluctant to have him at her back. This car did have close defences she could use against the attacking creatures outside until they got within range of base guns, and she needed to concentrate on them.

'All burned,' Nursum repeated.

Lars and Donnaken were hard at work in separate surgery rooms. In the new ward, all medical personnel were tending those being kept alive before surgery or those who had just come out of it, assisted by others with experience who'd been drafted in. Ursula glimpsed bloodied surgical scrubs moving between the beds. She saw people – or what vaguely looked like people – being lowered into regrowth tanks. She tried not to allow any of this to impinge as she focused on her main goal. But the data were there on screens, in overheard exchanges and in glimpses of medical readouts. And her damned integration put it all together.

The injuries here had been sustained peripherally to the main cacoraptor encounters. Those who had ended up face to face with one of the creatures were simply dead. These people had caught sprays of acid or poison, been knocked aside by hard sharp limbs, burned or hurt in explosions. In fact, most here had injuries from rail bead ricochets and fast-flying debris. Their outlook, however, was good – their nanosuites were keeping them alive, just as Nursum's had kept him alive.

Nursum.

Ursula entered the room she'd been directed to.

'How the hell did he survive?' she asked at once. 'That thing pulled him down into the ground and should have shredded him in a moment!'

Concentrate on the now – the hammer will fall later.

Nursum, lying naked on the slab with Oren's array of scanners pointed at him, looked round at her with mild interest. Oren, who had been inspecting screen readouts, looked over and gestured at Nursum. 'He's right there. Why don't you ask him?'

Nursum raised an eyebrow and waited.

'Okay.' Ursula closed her eyes for a second, concentrating on stillness, then opened them and faced him fully. He seemed rational now and only slightly off conventionally human. 'What happened – tell me everything, beginning with why you were out there in the first place.'

Nursum got a faraway look as he thought about it.

'Such agony,' he said.

Ursula sighed, painfully, the overall reality of the base ready to fall on her. He probably wasn't as rational as she'd thought, but now he focused on her.

'I remember being in the fig, you understand. I've lost much of my memory and much of who I was, but I always remember that.'

Ursula nodded mutely but cringed inwardly. He had been drained down almost to the point of mummification, with acids dissolving his organs and his bones, yet he'd still been able to turn his head and look at her. She'd felt sure that with all his body trauma and damage to his brain, that would be a memory he couldn't retain.

Nursum continued, 'I'm not who I was, and what I am now grew from that point. I felt some need to see and encompass the point of my inception. I don't know why. I just found myself leaving the base and heading there.' He paused. 'I'm sorry. It was stupid and irresponsible.'

'Okay, now tell me the rest.'

'When I heard the explosions it was as if I started to wake up. Then I heard your voice, and it snapped me back to reality . . . because of its connection . . . to that other time. I felt like a fool and I ran because at last I realized the danger and felt real fear. I couldn't go fast enough and my fear increased. I felt movement inside myself, heat, and realized I could demand more from my body. My stride lengthened, I was fizzing with energy and was going to reach your car. And then the raptor came out of the ground.'

Ursula stared at him, riveted. She now realized she'd had no need to demand this explanation because what had happened was exactly as Oren had detailed.

'It dragged me down into the ground. I started hitting it because that was all I could do. It cut into me. It was agonizing and I felt the vulnerability of my body. I needed to hit it harder.

I needed to cause damage. And I needed to stop it cutting into my body. The next thing I knew, the hard edges of its tentacles were sliding off my skin and my fingers were slicing into the creature. I broke free and pushed towards light, and then I was running.'

After a long silence, Oren said, 'The nanosuite responded to his adrenaline and . . . made these rapid changes, though the propensity to make them had already established.'

Yes. From the moment Nursum left the regrowth tank, she had seen that he had changed. But she wondered about the internal changes Oren had stored on his private database. If she looked at these, would she even understand them?

Nursum looked at Oren. 'What have you done to me?'

Oren gazed steadily back at him. 'I saved your life and gave you a stronger ability to survive.'

'Perhaps I should not have been saved.' Nursum turned to Ursula and she was at once reminded of when he'd looked at her from the clutches of the fig.

'No – that's ridiculous.' She moved away and headed for the door, wondering if it was. She dismissed the idea. She now had bigger problems and it was time to face them.

9

Present

Trakken turned to the panel beside the bulkhead door and swiftly input his instructions. The door thumped as it rose on its multiple seals. A gust of vapour flooded through and even as Ursula tasted its toxicity, her skin helmet oozed up out of its slots and closed over her face and skull. She felt it engaging to her nerves and the suckers pressing down on her eyes. Vision cleared in a moment and she saw that Trakken and his soldiers had responded in the same way. She wondered if this would be the last time she saw her human face in the mirror and rebelled at the thought. Reaching inside herself, she felt the nerve connections beginning to bind, as well as the suckers changing to bore in through her eyes so they could connect directly to her optic nerves. She stopped the process, then reversed what had already happened and found her procedure being copied across to all those around her, and thence to the other humans in the car. This explained how cacoraptors could adopt the adaptations of fellows at a distance. She would have to assess the other connections of the skin, but there was no time now. She looked round.

Nursum loomed close behind her. He hadn't closed up his skin helmet, but his nostrils had pinched closed, his mouth was shut and his black and gold eyes had a thick greenish meniscus over them. He looked at her and she felt the data filtering into her mind, like liquid through unseen pores. She could now do what he had done if she wished, but this transfer of information also confirmed him as something separate and a potential threat to her. She must incorporate him . . .

No! No no no. She should see this as simply proof of his independence as an individual human being, just as with Vrease. Even as she pushed her mind in that direction, she felt the attitude copying across to others. The time had been right, for she saw it quelling the hostility that had been growing in Trakken and the soldiers. Their enemy lay ahead, but they had also, just as she had, felt Nursum as a growing shadowy threat. Two of them, including Caulter with his acid thrower, had had their weapons casually pointed in Nursum's direction. They now all turned back to the door.

The door hinged open and the soldiers readied themselves, with Lecane to the fore wielding her iron-burner. Beyond the door, the floor was half melted, gouges in one wall revealing ceramal beams, torn conduits and further layers of adaptive armour. Acid bubbled on the inner face of the door, wound through with the threads of some kind of growth. But beyond it there were no cacoraptors. Caulter stepped up to the door and put one hand on it, the fluid there flowing onto his hand. Ursula moved forwards, simply touching on his query of this strange substance on the door but not reacting to the fact he'd put his hand in something that could eat through adaptive armour. Her full attention remained ahead, puzzling over the fact that the raptors had gone. She'd felt no sense of their departure in their communications and had no sense of it now. As they went through, Caulter casually detaching his hand and flicking away any excess acid, Ursula realized that the raptors had changed tactics. They could not subsume her and her people so were now, like an enemy aware of its opponent listening in, disseminating false information to them.

'Search every room and cubby until we reach the other door,' she instructed. 'Be aware of—'

At that moment Nursum sped past her. He jumped, hit the wall feet first, high up beside Trakken's soldiers, then came down ahead of them, still running.

'Follow him!' she shouted.

As the squad moved off, running nearly as fast as Nursum in their bulky suits, or rather, bulky bodies, she turned to the door. She had to remember tactics even with the surge of instinctive reaction pushing her after the rest. The door control on this side had been torn to pieces, the threads laced through the broken electronics. Some attempt to access the locking mechanism? Stepping outside, she used the other control, but set the door to close slowly enough for her to step back through before it closed. Hoisting up her carbine, she noted the tendrils now running from her hand into the weapon, and a moment later its targeting and other controls fell into her mind. She knew exactly where it was pointing and could fire it in an instant without using the trigger, as well as change beam aperture and power settings with a thought.

The squad rounded a corner as she set out after them, but they'd slowed by the time she caught up. Ahead of them Nursum was ripping at an area of stained wall with fingers turned to scythes. He began to peel away a sheet, revealing not beams and conduits beneath but green threads and nodular growths. Then a hooked claw unzipped the wall from the inside and, with a crash, two sets of heavy arms tore it open. The cacoraptor's body components were the same as Oren's, with four arms, two legs, torso and head, but there the resemblance ended. It was armoured and insect like, though also had a reptilian cast, and its limbs had an extra joint. Its hands had two opposable thumbs, with large sharp-edged hooks as forefingers. The jutting nightmare of mandibles, tubes and sensors that made up its head bore some resemblance to that of a lobster. It came down on Nursum like a ton of scrap iron. And then the explosive detonated.

The blast came from the floor, hurling Trakken and two others, including Caulter, up against the ceiling, tearing away chunks of their armour and skin. Ursula felt one of them die, instantly, and glimpsed a headless body, even as shrapnel ripped through the others and the blast wave reached her. It picked her up and threw her backwards. She felt a chunk of shrapnel punch through her own body low down, burning beside her lower spine. Even as she sailed through the air, the chatter of the raptors reached her, now disconnected from their fellows and the distant source. The trap had been a failure. The squad were meant to have been further along before the raptors detonated the explosive and tore through the walls to bring down the survivors. Nursum, somehow, had sensed their location and in going after them had forced them to spring it too early.

As she hit the floor and bounced, she saw the other two caco-raptors coming out of the walls. One of them stepped straight into the blast of Lecane's iron-burner. The actinic flare, now resembling the output of a beam weapon, hurled it back into the wall and pinned it there, limbs flailing as the intense fire burned the hard flesh from its body. Ursula felt and *compiled* the organic damage through its chatter. Lecane bowed, bony struts scissoring out from her calves to brace her against the floor. The arm she had wrapped around the burner came down, as did the one supporting it to the fore, and it just sat there attached to her. Ursula meanwhile sensed the damage she herself had received. The shrapnel had destroyed one kidney and caused other surrounding injuries. That organ was no problem because she had another one, as well as kidney organelles scattered throughout her body. She skidded to a halt and sat upright, quelling the nanosuite reaction to harden her skin armour further. There would be no more shrapnel. Her adaptation closed off blood vessels, realigned torn muscle and wove together a shattered rib, while nanites swarmed in to begin rapid repairs. A surge of agony began to rise and she mentally quashed the output of afferent and external nerves. Throwing herself to her feet, she aimed her carbine, but then lowered it again.

Nursum was down on the floor with the first cacoraptor, both of them tearing at the other in a frenzy. The movements of the one Lecane had pinned were slowing and it began curling up in the fire, like a chunk of meat on a barbecue. She sensed its complete physical failure as its chatter died. The other soldiers concentrated fire on the third, sending it tumbling down the corridor into the wreckage where the first explosion had torn open the armour. While most of them kept hitting it there, two of them turned to Nursum and the other raptor. They moved in close and fired carefully targeted shots at the raptor, flaring along limbs with particle beams and concentrating projectile fire into its head when that became exposed. It weakened and Nursum threw it away from him. Lecane, turning from the charred remains of her first opponent, then hit it with the burner to drive it along the floor against the wall and incinerated it there. Again Ursula watched the damage going beyond recovery as its chatter died.

She moved forwards as the one at the end of the corridor wilted under weapons fire too, the squad steadily advancing towards it. Abruptly it heaved up, ready to rush them; she felt its intent. It was alone now with no connections. She sensed intelligence but the mind also seemed more like a shell that should have been occupied by more. She reached out on all levels, scrabbling for purchase there. It took a pace forwards, but she was in its nervous system and brought it to a shuddering halt.

'Cease firing,' she said, and enforced the order.

Trakken's squad shut off their weapons and lowered them, where they could. She walked forwards, eyeing the frozen raptor. It was smoking, embers glowing through webs of black bone, fluids leaking out. Writhing movement marked its steady repair with diminishing resources and she also tracked its chatter. Stepping straight up before it, she briefly considered it as a resource she might use, but rejected the idea. Her fear and horror of these things needed some amelioration, as it did for the rest of the colonists. She broadcast her intent and detail so everyone could see what would happen.

'Get out of my car,' she instructed, and now *pushed* the remaining alien intelligence before her.

The raptor turned woodenly, then in a rush threw itself at the hole in the armour and out. One of the squad moved quickly to the lip, leaning with his weapon to scan around outside, but moved aside as Ursula came up. She looked down and saw the black speck hurtling away towards the Bled, and then its dusty impact.

'Throw the other two out after it,' she instructed.

Returning to the corridor, she eyed the first victim of these creatures lying in tangled wreckage. The woman looked like some grotesque anatomical display – disembowelled and limbs ripped off. But threads still connected her, one even winding through the wreckage towards an arm lying ten feet away – and with slow heaves she was drawing her parts back together. The other victim further along the corridor was doing the same.

'We need that medical team in here now,' Ursula said over com. 'And the repair team.'

Again this was unnecessary verbalization because they were ready beyond the further bulkhead door and even now opening it. She merely *glanced* at Trakken and the other soldiers steadily repairing their bodies, and using their connection, spread information on it for others to utilize. Caulter was up again and had further melded. The acid sprayers attached to his arms had now sunk into them, while patches of skin had spread over the tanks on his back. She felt his connection and the compartments growing within his body to make new acids and enzymes – one of them the stuff that had been on the door. Lecane had further melded too. Her head seemed to have deformed around the burner and shifted aside, so the thing sat more central to her body. Her eyes were also mismatched: one large targeting eye down low. And the burner had changed. The rear of it now curved down her back, perfectly linked to the tubes entering her there.

Ursula felt a wash of extreme cold from the hole in the armour and a second later registered it as merely a difference. In the corridor the temperature was high – brief assessment and calculation put it at over eighty Celsius. Some of this arose from the weapons fire, but she noted the vapour rising from Trakken's squad, as well as from herself and Nursum. Their transformations ran hot – as hot as cacoraptors.

Nursum rose from the floor, rents in his body closing up, clawed hands shrinking back to normal size, his whole body shifting as it returned to a facsimile of humanity. Why the difference? No, he had changed. Her sense of him was not internal but from the outside she plumbed the sheer density of him.

'We burned them,' he said.

Ursula felt unreasonably grateful that he had not mentioned the fig.

WEAPONIZED

Near Past

Since the raptors had broken through all the outer and inner perimeter fences they'd set up, and now in total slaughtered over half the colonists, ruination lay outside. And even though they'd shut down what they could of the irrigation system, the local flora were already beginning to take hold. The seeds of blue cycads were spreading their poison yellow webs, fighting for ground with deep red bushy growths that shot out seeds in a splash of acid to burn lebensraum for themselves. Pale green vines were creeping like slow snakes over the slumped ruin of a minelaying machine. Frond-like leaves pushed out of a warehouse, levering down the walls and lifting up roof panels. Ursula supposed that along with the fertilizers the agronomists had used to prepare the ground for planting, all the blood and bodily fluids were a good source of nutrients too. There were no signs of any larger human remains – everything had been eaten, including bones – though ripped-open suits and enviroboots marked the spots where people had died. Yet, at a glance, it did seem people were still out there.

They crouched in the shadows of buildings and broken machinery. Some walked like battle survivors stumbling through the ruins. Others just stood, gazing back towards the base. Yes, they appeared to be people until you really looked. Body shapes were plain wrong, limb lengths out of the norm, heads distorted masses sometimes sporting mandibles or tube-like mouths. Many had acquired a different kind of sensorium and seemed to have the heads of giant cicadas. She saw one walker striding like a heron, neck three times the human length and its head simply a large hook.

Ursula sighed, wiped her face, then looked around at the control room staff. They all appeared alert enough, though she had received reports that many people were turning up late for shifts, while four were in the infirmary being tended to by Oren and other medical staff. After Ursula had given Oren the go-ahead to start distributing the bracelets, everyone had accepted the upgrade story, it seemed. But some were now questioning the narcolepsy and other effects. Oren's explanation that this was because it was a major upgrade, which also rewrote previous upgrades into a more coherent whole, was kind of recognized. It would do until each one of them had a bracelet.

'How are you feeling?' she asked Callum.

He instantly knew what she meant and held up his arm to inspect his bracelet. 'Nothing big. I slept a bit, woke up with what felt like a fever each time, but now it seems to have settled.'

'Good. I'm glad.'

'I would have expected more, of course.' He looked at her pointedly.

'Really?' she asked.

He lowered his voice. 'I've been around a long time, Ursula – everyone here has. Some know this is different while others are simply not permitting themselves to know.' He shrugged, turning back to his instruments. 'If it allows me to do the kind of things Nursum did after the previous time . . .' He hesitated, then finished simply, 'I'll be glad of it. I don't want to die.'

She stared at him, realizing she'd been kidding herself. As he said, they had all been around for a long time. Still, she would wait until everyone had a bracelet before giving her proper explanation.

'They're coming into sight now,' said Callum, glancing up.

Ursula raised her gaze to the screen wall to see the three brontopods the drones had sighted earlier stampeding towards the base. Were the cacoraptors going to use them as cover for the base guns in order to get close? Were they going to run them at the doors in the hope of breaking in? Neither option was viable because the base guns should be capable of bringing them down at least a mile out. No, she had a damned good idea what they were going to be used for, and had done the moment she saw them.

'Vrease?' she enquired through her coms unit.

'Bolting the launcher down now,' Vrease replied. 'Trakken is bringing up the missiles as we speak.'

Trakken, like all the agricultural specialists, had been reassigned to more urgent tasks.

'Fliers?' Ursula enquired.

'I've got people all around with pulse rifles and laser carbines while we get the multigun set up here. We've scoped some out in the distance but they're not getting any closer.'

The panicked brontopods were kicking up a storm of dust and clods of earth as they approached. Audio provided their hooting calls and snorts. All around them cacoraptors ran on heron legs, like the one she'd seen earlier. Thin muscular necks terminated in what looked like bullwhips and where they struck a brontopod hide, they raised smoke and left bubbling and burning streaks.

'We can hit them with the base multiguns from here,' Callum noted. 'But we'll have trouble bringing them down at this range.'

'No. Let them get close.'

But they didn't get much closer. The two lead brontopods went down, the undersides of their heads skidding along the ground and carving up channels. The one behind went down shortly afterwards. They shrieked and tried to rise and only now did Ursula see that they had riders. She raised a control hologram from her wristcom, framed the scene with her fingers, and then threw it to the screen-painted wall. Here she could get a much better look at one of the riders.

The thing looked like something straight out of a second

millennium painting – a depiction of Hell. It was straddling the brontopod just behind its head. Its fingers had spread like roots to penetrate the creature's hide and had no doubt cut the requisite nerves to bring the thing down. Now it began to change, its form becoming plastic and melding together. Taking on the snake-like shape of the early raptor, it flowed head down, horns sinking into its head, its terrible grinding mouth protruding as it bored into its victim. The brontopod howled, jerked and shuddered, and died, as did the other two.

'I'm looking for some good news from you, Vrease. Right now would be best,' she said.

'Launcher bolted. Setting up targeting. No sign of Trakken yet.'

'Fuck.' She turned to Callum. 'Start hitting them with the base guns.'

Callum nodded and slid an icon across his screen and the base guns shook the floor. Armoured hide exploded away from the brontopods but it was like carving into ancient oaks with a machine gun. Ursula noted a few hits on the one behind but only through a small gap between the first two. Even as the weapons whittled the creatures away, they were shifting to the voracious movement inside. On one of them a larger chunk of armoured hide peeled up and fell away. Callum slid an icon and a missile sped away, slamming straight into that weak spot. The brontopod bucked, spewing burning fragmented organs from the hole, yet still it shifted with the same internal motion. A second and a third missile streaked in, blasting the creature open in a gory, burning mess. Ursula saw writhing movement continue, some of it burrowing into the ground. Now spiky heads were beginning to issue from the other two corpses.

'Vrease!'

'Loading,' was Vrease's only reply.

Ursula watched. Callum now had sight of the rearmost bron-topod and was hitting that too. He fired another missile at another weak spot, blowing out a knot of asbestos-white snake forms. Even as they hit the ground, many of them started to dig in. Next, from high above, three of their stock of larger missiles streaked down. Perfectly on target, they hit the two nominally intact brontopods and the remaining mass of the third. Three glaring explosions ignited and Ursula turned away, afterimages bleeding from her eyes. When she turned back, the creatures had been spread in burning ruin around three smoking craters.

'Good work, people,' Ursula announced. Later she watched chunks of brontopod snared from the ground below to be tugged out of sight and knew they had failed to stop whatever the caco-raptors had produced next.

Ursula woke to screams and the sounds of gunfire. She rolled out of bed, instantly awake and alert, grabbed up her carbine and was at her door before she knew what she was doing. She paused. She felt good, effective, fast and immediately ready for anything. She glanced down reflectively at the upgrade bracelet around her wrist and went out of the door.

'They came up through the fucking caves!' Vrease exclaimed when Ursula reached the control room. She'd already been getting up to speed on her way there. Three cacoraptors had appeared in the lower floor of the base and killed five people before someone managed to close a bulkhead door on them. The doors had been put in just for this purpose – in case a local life form got loose in the base. The raptors were now chewing and burning through the armour.

'How many mosquitoes do we have left?' Ursula snapped.

'Fifteen,' Callum replied.

'Get them programmed and on patrol.' Hardly thinking about

what she was doing, she raised a control hologram, searched, then threw a base schematic at the wall. 'Seal these doors.' She highlighted them with stabs of her finger. 'Make this section' – she drew a line around the area – 'our kill zone.'

'Weapons,' said Callum, seemingly in tune with her.

'Thermite shells and run an iron-burner down there for good measure.'

Callum nodded and began to work his screen and coms unit.

'Vrease.' Ursula turned to her. 'Detection?'

Just as in tune, Vrease replied, 'They're borers of some kind – those cave systems were closed off by solid rock. Seismic and ground scan. I'll get on it.'

'Cam displays coming up,' said Callum. 'Trakken and his crew are on their way down.'

Ursula contemplated that: farmers turned into soldiers – it wasn't without historical precedent. She flicked her attention to the screen paint as the views from multiple headcams came up. Trakken and his 'squad' were moving down through the base and, though the imagery was taking time to stabilize, she integrated the views quickly and knew where each of the soldiers was.

'They're in the new skin,' she noted.

'Yup.' Callum grimaced. 'Not sure I'm ready to try it yet.'

Their faces weren't visible because the skin now covered where they'd had chain-glass visors before – Oren had finally got around that one. They looked insectile and not quite human any more.

'Why not?' she asked.

'Too close, too personal.'

Ursula nodded. The stuff could be worn over Polity body armour and, judging by their bulk, this was what Trakken and his crew were doing. Oren preferred it the other way around since, he said, underlying armour or clothing hindered connection.

The stuff also connected directly to the eyes to give external vision. She wasn't sure she was ready for that either.

They carried heavy slug throwers – clips loaded with thermite shells – and the iron-burner strapped down on one of their few grav-sleds. Also pacing along with them were two of the mosquitoes. That had been fast. Was everyone operating at some efficiency peak? Again Ursula glanced at her upgrade bracelet. Adrenal activation, Oren had said, and right then she, and everyone involved in this, was swimming in the stuff.

The bulkhead door loomed ahead, viscous black bubbling out all around it as some acid or enzyme ate the seal. Something hit it, hard, and the top corner bent in.

'Deploy,' said Trakken. 'Crossfire from both sides and the burner in the middle. Mosquitoes up.' She saw him wave a hand and then one of the silvery mosquito autoguns climbing a wall. Military? Abruptly Trakken's details lay clear in her mind. Yes, he had been a commando and had actually seen action against an assortment of Separatist rebels. This knowledge seemed to open a general overview, of the kind she got when connected up to a computer and ran tactical integration and synthesis. She saw at once that the majority of the colonists had, at some point, been in the military, yet this had not been one of her selection criteria. Perhaps some other criterion made it more likely that a candidate would be military? Yes, that was true. But Ursula couldn't help but feel a niggling suspicion. After all, she had made her selections from a shortlist whittled down from billions by AI programs. It was something she filed away for further consideration.

A series of thumps against the bulkhead door loosened up its layers and exposed the melting structural framework. Finally a large upper section folded over and dropped to the floor, and a nightmare head came through. It had a shield, like the elongated shell of a terrapin, just above a mouth filled front to back with rows of mandibles. Above this were the insect eyes, brush sensors and other less easily identifiable apparatus. Extending back from these were bone-white spines. A clawed hand closed on the door edge, revealing a muscular arm extending from a strangely rooted shoulder on a snake-like body. Again, the thing looked like some monster out of human myth, perhaps because of its human components. It gave a hissing shriek and spat acid.

Ursula saw someone stumbling away, their skin and armour smoking as the air filled with tracer fire. The thing writhed and shrieked as the shells slammed into it and ignited – hot explosions blowing away pieces, while other fire dug deep into its tough flesh. The rest of the door collapsed and it came through, with two more of a similar design following it. One of them climbed straight up the well above the door, then fell again as the autoguns sliced into it with concentrated pulse-gun fire. Trakken's troops moved round, keeping up the fire rate and pinning the things by the door. All cam views turned bright white as the iron-burner fired up. This lasted for a few seconds until cam programming caught up and cleaned the imagery. Ursula watched the cacoraptors writhe and burn. They all tried their usual asbestos change but couldn't manage it quickly enough and just came apart, then collapsed, still moving. The iron-burner went on and on, under Trakken's control, swinging back and forth to sweep burning remains through the door and following them through.

It was done.

They watched Trakken and his squad retreating, while others arrived to clean up the mess and make sure the area had been completely sterilized. Ursula banished the images and turned to the control room staff. They were all looking at her expectantly.

'Well done, all of you,' she said, but knew it wasn't enough.

'It's time,' said Callum, holding up his arm to display the bracelet, 'to talk about this.'

As she strode through the corridors, Ursula acknowledged brief greetings from colonists and noted some, with perhaps a little irony, doing the fist-to-chest salute of Polity marines to a commander. The salute was sometimes with the left fist, sometimes with the right – it depended which wrist had their upgrade bracelet wrapped around it. When she'd made her announcement about the bracelets and Oren had laid out his clear summary of what he'd really programmed them to do, the reaction had been surprisingly muted. Some had said she should have been open with them from the start about the extent of this new upgrade, but there seemed little anger in it. She didn't agree. Beforehand, many would have refused it. But ever since, with the subsequent borer attacks and everyone now wearing their bracelets, their thinking had changed. She could feel it, almost like a connecting fog in the air of the base.

She stepped through an open bulkhead door beyond which Vrease turned to her.

'Report,' said Ursula, feeling no need for further words.

'We've filled the storage tanks and that gives us two thousand gallons,' said Vrease.

Ursula made a rapid calculation – it wasn't a lot of water when divided over the number of people in the base.

Vrease continued, 'With the strict recycling protocols, that should give everyone their morning shower and plenty to drink. Our problem won't be the water itself, but the recycling system. We'll need to manufacture new components like filters and pump parts.'

Ursula turned her attention to the domed ceramal lid in the centre of the floor. Some workers had bolted it to the stone floor earlier to cover the well here. She eyed the severed pipes snaking away from under it. They'd wanted to save the well's pump, but with borer cacoraptors gathering below it, it had been best just to drop the heavy thing on top of them to give the hauler robot, now moving away through a nearby corridor, time to get the lid in place. The bulkhead door closed behind the robot, trailing a wide ribbed pipe that ran through it. Ursula ignored the sounds she could hear from down in the well and pointed to the pipe.

'Filling with foamstone should be enough in here?' she asked.

'It's bubble ceramic – harder than normal stone,' Vrease replied, gesturing to the door where Ursula had come in. They headed back through this only exit to where Callum waited.

'So how long before recycling starts breaking down?' Ursula asked.

Vrease glanced at Callum and raised an eyebrow.

Callum replied, 'Depends on resource allocation. We're burning up a lot of energy on replacing armour at the breakthrough points. The autoguns are eating up ammunition and we could really do with making some more.' He shrugged. 'Then there's food.'

'Tell me.'

'Trakken has his hydroponics up and running. Heat, light and water there, and of course more recycling.'

The bulkhead door closed behind them and locked down. Ursula felt the floor vibrate and heard the steady rushing sound. The room behind was now being filled with liquid foamstone. Once the room was full, an initiator would be injected to set it hard. Ursula knew that other areas, down below and out near the edge of the massif, had been lined up for similar treatment.

Callum continued, 'We have stocks but he cannot keep up with demand. People are also eating more with the new upgrade running within them.'

'How long?' Ursula asked.

'A few months and we'll be eating our shoes.'

She nodded, just accepting this data to add to a growing list. They mounted the stairs in silence, because there were people all around who might overhear them. Once they'd entered the control room and the door was closed, Ursula sighed and plumped down in one of the seats. She looked at the chain-glass window. One of the few remaining multiguns out there had scoured crawling raptors off it as they'd come up from below, and this room was one of those scheduled to be filled with foamstone too because it lay right at the edge of the massif. Already a lot of the equipment in here had been disassembled ready to be moved. The only other person in the control room was Gurda, carefully taking apart her communications equipment.

'So, I need an overall projection,' Ursula said. She looked at Callum. 'I assume you've been crunching the data?'

'I have.' He nodded grimly.

'Give me the bad news.'

Callum glanced at Gurda, then shrugged and went over to a screen and turned it so they could all see. He called up a ground scan and seismic map of the massif and its surroundings. Ursula understood it at once. Worm holes wound in above the bedrock and penetrated the rock below the massif, where they entered the previously enclosed caves. They were now spreading out from those caves and pushing upwards.

'It's hard not to think there's an overall strategy here,' he said. 'If their attacks continue at the present rate, it's a toss-up between them swarming in here via multiple breakthroughs or through some major collapse. They're slow, the armour we're putting in slows them down further, and this could take months. I don't know what will kill us first – thirst, hunger or the cacoraptors – but we're dead if we stay in here.'

Ursula nodded because that had been her assessment too on

less data. They'd retreated and were still retreating, while the cacoraptors had not let up, even finding new iterations of themselves with which to attack. The end was inevitable. But from the chaos, they'd managed to snatch back one last hope.

'We've got the shuttle's reactor back now,' she said. 'And there's that prador assault craft. We need a plan of attack on that. Capture it, hop it back here, then install the reactor.'

Both Callum and Vrease shook their heads.

'Show her,' said Gurda, looking up from her equipment. 'You think I didn't figure what you are up to?'

Callum nodded. 'There are too many ways an attack on that craft can fail. It'll leave us shorthanded here and in the time it takes us to bring the thing back – supposing we've managed to take it from the remaining prador – this base will have been overrun.'

'So what do you have for me?' Ursula asked.

'We move en masse to the assault craft with all the weapons and resources we can carry.'

'I don't think we have an armoured car capable of carrying the reactor,' said Ursula. 'And defending that number of armoured cars . . .' She shook her head. 'It makes sense to move everything, but logistically and tactically it's as much a mess as my suggestion.'

'We don't take lots of armoured cars – just one.'

Understanding dawned for Ursula, even as Callum called something up on his screen and waved it to the wall. The schematic filled up the screen-painted walls. Ursula's discipline of tactical integration had given her a deep insight into such stuff and she found herself reading it with ease: the new adaptive armour that would wrap this giant car, the power system with its multiple backups, the specialized multi-rod wheels and protected undercarriage, and of course all the weapons.

'I see it has chain-glass screens,' she noted, remembering what Oren had said about chain-glass, and how little surprised she would be if the cacoraptors found a way to unravel it.

'Armoured shutters,' Callum pointed out. 'This is the initial schematic and we can change it as circumstances change.'

'And it can fit everyone inside?' she asked.

'It will now,' Vrease replied.

Ursula winced and shook her head. She really didn't need reminding of how many people had died. People she knew, respected and sometimes liked had been torn apart, if not by the cacoraptors then by the base guns. Collectively thousands of years of life, love, experience, knowledge, and somewhat of wisdom, had been erased. She continued studying the schematic.

'How long to build this?'

'A month,' Vrease replied.

Callum waved another hand to bring up a schedule. Ursula felt her facility for tactical integration ramp up as she studied figures, manufacturing stats and much else besides. This was a way of collapsing everything they had down into one item – compact, efficient. She nodded, seeing it was their one shot at survival. 'We can open out the garages, cannibalize the cars we have, and keep moving the manufacturing inwards, backfilling as we go. No need to worry about resource allocation for re-cycling or food.' She was just talking for the sake of it, she realized, for it was all there for them to see in the schedule.

'Build the fucking car,' she said.

10

Present

Ursula went back through the huge car, her sense of contact with all those around her fading into the background of her mind. But it was always there, recording the changes in others and their positions. She realized the reason why it no longer sat at the forefront of her thoughts was because the other colonists weren't actually undergoing any further major changes. The danger had passed, so the energy-intensive level of function was no longer required. She halted, pushing for more contact and connectivity, the transceiver collar she'd grown on her shoulders and back seeming to fizz. Through this, she observed that the two badly injured colonists had been collected, piecemeal, and were now on their way to Medical. Trakken's soldiers had tossed out the raptor remains and the repair crew was already at work, first rapidly fixing new armour into place from the spares, while printer robots scuttled around them thrumming to themselves as they sealed joins and layered in new material and feed pipes.

She started walking again and ranged out further. She could feel the cacoraptors beyond the car, but was getting very little from them – just a nebulous sense of will, of purpose. She realized that the car's adaptive armour would be blocking most of it and whatever she was getting was coming through the steadily closing hole. Any chemical communication they used doubtless now lay far behind. Inside, she located Nursum more by the reactions of those around him than actually sensing him directly. Only then could she feel the oddity of his mind, and again its slipperiness. He was moving towards Oren's laboratory and had no sign of the injuries she'd seen before – his healing was far ahead of the rest of them. Next she reached out to find Oren and couldn't sense him at all. She grimaced. This confirmed her earlier suspicions: he'd not used the upgrade on himself. Another question to pile on top of all the others she needed to challenge him with about the flawed Polity survey of Threpsis.

She halted by a door, realizing that without thinking she'd gone towards the commissary rather than the control room. From a hatch further along the corridor, she watched a delivery robot slide out, food packets stacked on its back, and head off. All the food here had been packaged this way so it could be easily delivered or collected, while drinking and washing water was piped throughout the car. She opened the door and stepped inside.

The few tables and chairs scattered in the room were all occupied. She nodded to those there and, suddenly ravenously hungry, headed over to the counter on one wall, with the slots sitting just behind it. To the right was a reader. She pressed her palm against it and walked along collecting up packages as they dropped out of the slots, inspecting the meagre amount she'd been given at the end. Taking these, she left the room, and reached up to tap the com pad on the neck of her suit, but found it had been subsumed by the new collar.

'Severen,' she said, voice-activating the link to him. 'I've just been to the commissary . . .'

'Rationing,' he snapped in reply. Now she sensed him too: his annoyance and the number of questions he'd been fielding about food supply. He then calmed and controlled himself since it was her and she was his ultimate superior. 'The physical changes we've been undergoing are calorie hungry. We maybe have a few days before we run out, even with rationing.'

She'd felt this too: the hunger.

'We'll need more,' she said, utterly certain about that.

He caught the tail end of her speculation since it related to their changes and could compel them. And he sensed the general shape of her plans shift. They needed to stop somewhere for resupply.

'We can probably eat local wildlife and plants,' he opined.

'Yes, that seems a possibility.' No, it wasn't a possibility but a certainty.

She closed the comlink with a thought. In her other stratum, she sensed his feeling of relief and didn't like it because its basis seemed to be fear. Yes, she had reasserted herself through their new method of communication but the fear . . . why fear? Just a moment of thought gave her the answer. She had asserted control but it extended into the physical realm. She could force them to obey, just as she'd forced that cacoraptor to jump out of the car. But it went further. Even though they were copying across their changes to each other, she had ultimate authority over that. She ranged out again, concentrating on those who had undergone the most radical changes. Lecane was helping with repairs, but the iron-burner got in the way. Ursula felt the woman's hunger as she walked over to assorted debris that one of the robots had pushed over to one side of a corridor. Lecane squatted, scanning over the mass with her targeting eye, highlighting items. She reached down and picked up a handful of sheared-off bolts and began inserting them into her mouth and swallowing. She glanced almost guiltily across at Caulter, who had reached the debris before her. Caulter was already crunching up pieces of meta-material and chewing stripped lengths of plastic sheathing and tubes with teeth that had taken on a metallic sheen. It seemed that part of the problem of food supply had solved itself, but should she allow this?

Their changes were radical. While others had made connections to their weapons for ease of use, they could still disconnect, as she had done, with her carbine now hanging from its strap over her shoulder. But these two were actually becoming their weapons. Was this the evolution of humanity she'd wanted? Did she even know what she wanted? Just like when the skin suit had made its connections to her, she rebelled at this extreme change. Using her connection to Caulter and Lecane, she immediately pushed for them to free the connections and return to at least a more human form, although not entirely sure where the line should be drawn for this. They sat upright and she felt deep resistance within them, even though, once they'd become aware of her push, they were in agreement with it. She drove harder and they assisted, but still she found resistance and some element of them now felt as slippery as Nursum was. An underlying stratum of their minds seemed to be the basis of this, yet she struggled to pin it down and make it subject to her will. It seemed to be integral to them, yet distributed. What could it be?

The genome responded to their need or requirement, but its changes were brutish and ignorant, like when she had started to grow armour after the danger from shrapnel had passed. These other changes were at once subtle and extreme. When the caco-raptors developed intelligence, they changed in such ways too, but she was sure the driving mind of the original raptor was behind that. She was the driving mind here, but she had not done this . . . or perhaps she had, subconsciously? No, that felt wrong. Was this the stored data in the cacoraptor genome, was it a *mentality*? No, that was wrong too, or else those creatures' changes would have been more subtle and specific in the beginning.

Ursula turned abruptly. She had to talk to Oren again, as soon as possible, she had far too many questions without answers. But now the big reactor had been put into shutdown mode and the car was descending again. She swore, halted, then turned back to the control room.

'Maybe a solution to food supply,' Callum opined.

The spread of his body had continued, which illustrated that the changes they were undergoing weren't just in response to danger and immediate need. The metallic sheen was fading from the exposed parts of his original skin and it was now turning bone white, as was his skin suit. His neck seemed thinner, but that was only because his head had grown bigger, with larger eyes that had grown out towards his temples. They seemed to be dividing, as if converting to the compound eyes of an insect. His connections ran beyond his console into surrounding computing as well. Other control room crew had taken on a similar bone-white hue and also grown more connections to their instrumentation.

Ursula's fear rose as bile in the back of her throat. She immediately went deeper into them all and found increasing integration. Callum was just doing his job, really, which was to oversee the rest. Many of the white tendrils she at first thought had issued from the other crew into their computing in fact came from him, connecting to them. He had full and complete control, through them, of the technical aspects of the car. He'd also bumped Vrease out of weapons and Gurda out of armour. Ursula tried to ameliorate it, to slow it, to reverse some aspects, but she found the same resistance in him as she had done in Lecane and Caulter. Oren. She had to see Oren.

'Food supply?' she asked belatedly.

Callum raised one arm, trailing tendrils in a line down his

forearm, and pointed at the screen wall. A massif, similar to the one they had made their base, was displayed there. Life burgeoned around it and she remembered it from the original survey. It had been one of the other choices for their base but the water supply was contaminated through underground caves connecting it to the distant dry seabed which the prador ship was heading for. It would have taken a great deal of work to scrub out the contaminants and so, despite there being more water there, they'd gone elsewhere.

She glanced over at Vrease, who was sitting in her chair with her arms crossed, having little to do now. The woman nodded, but kept her expression bland.

'Calorie and nutrient intake has rocketed,' the woman said. 'Some of our people' – she winced at the word – 'even seem to be plugging themselves into the power supply.' She looked around the control room, and then to make some final obscure point, added, 'Oberbeck the ecologist was found eating his collection of wooden figurines. He couldn't explain why.'

'Food supply,' Ursula confirmed.

Callum had taken in Ursula's earlier exchange with Severen and delivered instructions to Gurda. They'd kept the reactor running for a little longer and gone off course to come here. His smooth integration with her thoughts on resupply was at once satisfying and again frightening. The car dropped and dropped, landing with a thump. Gurda immediately turned it, bringing the massif into view through the front chain-glass window, and sent it surging forwards. Ursula felt as though she was losing control of them and, in a moment of panic, reached out and grabbed. Callum brought his hands down hard on the surface before him and froze rigid. The others at their consoles became utterly motionless. Gurda didn't move but, through her connection, released the car's drive and it slowed to a halt.

Now the sheer extent of her control scared Ursula. She looked around at them, but also ranged out yet again, sensing that others throughout the car had ceased their tasks too. She took a breath and reached inside herself to quell her fear, and gradually released her grip. She thought carefully about Lecane, Caulter and Callum. She might fear that the changes they were undergoing were just too radical, but she couldn't lose sight of the fact that this was about survival. Back at the base, the cacoraptors had killed hundreds of colonists and, thus far, they had only fought off three of the creatures in the car, while there were thousands of them out there. And there were the prador too – a reality they would have to face drawing closer as they travelled. She analysed Callum's actions. Whatever his changes, they were perfectly in accord with her thoughts.

'It's powerful and dangerous,' said Vrease, looking around at the immobile crew. 'One has to wonder about intent.'

'What do you mean?' Ursula asked.

Vrease shrugged. 'I don't know . . . yet.'

Ursula watched her for a moment longer, the facts of their situation swirling around in her head. She felt she could see the shape of something, perhaps like Vrease could, but couldn't yet nail it down. She left it to run its course, knowing she would finally integrate all the disparate information and come up with an answer. She turned back to the crew.

'Cacoraptors?' she enquired.

'Our drones have detected none,' Callum replied. 'They've been tracking our route to the prador and this course change would have been unexpected to them.'

'But they'll zero in on us.'

'If we are to assume we're still their main target . . .'

Ursula nodded. She'd been sure from the beginning that the raptors knew where she would take this car. Why would they follow this diversion when they knew where it would eventually arrive?

'Continue,' she said, finally releasing her hold. 'But keep a damned good watch – seismic detection too.'

'As you command,' said Callum, and she could hear a hint of resentment in his voice.

Gurda propelled the car forwards, around a tilted slab jutting out of the Bled, and rumbling over a patch of blue cycads. A jungle wall loomed ahead, shifting and seething with lethal life forms. Almost at a slant to her communication with everyone else's minds and bodies in the car, came another thought.

'*There will be figs,*' Nursum informed her.

Near Past

Following Ursula's command, they'd got to work on the car straight away. The skeleton of it had been finished, using up the last of their layered memory metal I-beams. The thing would be able to take some pretty heavy impacts, deform, and then regain its shape. The new armour would do the same and other components had their protective measures and padding. To a certain extent, this applied to the occupants of the vehicle too, with their armour and skin, and now their nanosuite upgrades. Ursula had previously thought it likely that occupants of the car wouldn't be able to survive its destruction, but now she wasn't so sure. Finishing her inspection of the work, she went to the base control room. The prador had put their assault craft into the sky again and anything that might happen to them this time had greater significance and urgency than before.

'I'm conflicted about how I want this to play out,' she said as she arrived and took a seat.

Vrease nodded. 'On the one hand, anything that kills cacoraptors has to be a good thing; on the other, we want that assault craft and if all the prador are dead . . .' She shrugged.

'It would be nice if we could make some sort of deal with them,' said Callum.

Gurda snorted humourlessly. In searching for ways to deal with the prador, they'd all gone through the Polity data on the war. The creatures were total xenophobes. The only talks exchanged, that they knew of before the prador had destroyed their satellite and thus their link to the Polity, had been threats of annihilation, pain and death. The damned things even ate human beings, alive if possible. Yet according to what the Polity knew then of their biology, human flesh required additions to be digestible for them.

'I know,' Callum continued, 'but there's prador biology to consider.'

'In what respect?' Ursula asked.

'As we understand it, the father-captains use their children as workers and have pheromonal dominance over them. They hold their children in various stages of development using chemical means. The ones we've seen we know must be first- and second-children. They have now been away from pheromonal and chemical control for some time. Perhaps they've changed?'

'We'll let you do the negotiating,' said Gurda.

Callum gave her a look. 'All I'm saying is that maybe it's worth a try.'

'Nice idea,' said Ursula, 'an alliance made between enemies during war time against a hostile environment. But say we fight off the cacoraptors together and install our reactor aboard their ship. Then what? Where does the ship go once it's running again, and if heavily armed aliens haven't decided to renege on the deal?'

Callum shrugged.

'But what happens, even if we can take their ship away from them and get it running?' asked Vrease. 'We don't know if it's U-space capable or has any kind of cryo-storage.'

'One thing at a time,' said Ursula. 'First we get that assault ship. Maybe we won't be able to head back to the Polity in it, but its armour seems resistant to the raptors and we can relocate. Perhaps there's somewhere on this world without cacoraptors, or we can set up somewhere else. Right now survival has to be our first objective.'

'Where?' asked Vrease. 'Where else can we set up?'

'We have our technology. We have the knowhow. We could build a new base on one of the moons. Brant seems most likely to provide the materials we would need.'

They all sat contemplating that. Ursula supposed they were envisioning the enclosed base they would have to make, the hydroponics, growth tanks and manufacturing. Yes, they could do it, she guessed.

'And perhaps, in time, the Polity will come back here, or we can find some way to deal with what is down here and re-establish.' Ursula gave a tight smile, noting that her first point presupposed that the Polity survived their war with the prador.

A further thoughtful silence ensued, broken finally by Vrease saying, 'They're bringing their craft down again.'

The remaining prador spent a long time inside their vessel. When they finally ventured out, their armour had changed considerably. It was much bigger this time. Heavy rings sat around the leg sockets, while other plates and protrusions had appeared that were certainly further protection and weapons.

'My guess,' said Vrease, 'is these additions are something they had in stock. That armour is similar to the stuff on their ship and must take a huge amount of energy to manufacture. And they don't have a huge amount of energy.'

'One could suppose they were wearing conventional battle armour or some such, but have had their experience with nasty infiltrating life forms before,' said Ursula.

Vrease nodded agreement. 'And probably a history of dealing with carapace-boring parasites.'

They came out quickly and worked even more rapidly this time, using harpoon grabs to load the sleds with organics, and were almost done by the time the cacoraptors appeared. Ursula watched three of them circling, the drones picking up a further five rapidly approaching. A raptor shot in and, as before, wound itself around the leg of a prador and stuck its tail into the ground. Its pincers slithered and scratched at the new ring and then expanded to gain purchase. The other prador didn't try to free their fellow, but packed up their equipment swiftly and got the sleds moving. Were they just going to leave that one to die?

The prador pinned to the ground by the raptor just waited patiently until its fellows were on the move. Two more raptors chose this moment to attack – one of them winding around another leg of the one already caught, while the other caught a second prador. Meanwhile the sleds continued back towards the shuttle.

The two captured prador faced each other and clattered for a moment. They both swung their armoured stalked eyes towards the assault craft and waited until the sleds had got back there, then, together, they shed their trapped legs and ran. The raptors followed through with their usual attack, sliding towards where an open leg socket should have been but instead they now speared out into the air. And they didn't get very far in that direction, as their lower coils seemed to be stuck. The detached legs exploded.

The hot blasts formed maculae on the drone views – the searing temperature registering at thousands of degrees. Ursula saw pieces of raptor smoking where they bounced on the ground, and glowing white hot at their severed ends.

'Catalytic explosive,' Callum commented. 'Almost as intense as an iron-burner.'

The two prador reached the sleds and the others as the ramp door dropped fast, all of them quickly disappearing inside their ship. Even as the ramp door closed, five other raptors arrived and hammered against it, then slithered round to try and find access. As they crawled higher, a Gatling cannon protruded, its barrels wrapped around a particle beam emitter, and scoured them from the armour. Later, smoke could be seen rising from ports in the hull as the raptors tried to get into them, only to be scoured away again. The assault craft made another short hop away.

As she watched the images transmitted by the drones in pursuit, Ursula replayed their previous conversation in her mind. Starting again, somewhere else . . . Though she had proposed the idea, it had just been a stab at optimism, at visualizing some kind of future. It had been a major commitment to come here, and hard enough right from the start, and she did not relish the prospect of giving up on this world just yet.

Past

Ursula walked along the corridor of the Polity vessel *Foucault*, carrying a mug of coffee. The worn floor here had bowed a little with the big old cargo hauler's shifts in structure. The walls were also scratched and dented, and muck had gathered in some corners, from which sprouted strands of purple fungus. Even so, she knew that the essentials of the ship were in perfect working order. The U-space drive couldn't be otherwise, since all such drives were built and maintained by AI. All other drives and thrusters were good too, as was anything that related to the safety of passengers and the safety of any worlds this ship came close to. To operate in the Polity as this ship did, it had to pass inspections.

At the end of the corridor, she took a right, past a series of cabins for those in her group who had paid for them, rather than having to stay in the small quarters aboard their shuttle. She finished her coffee before entering a large viewing blister where the grav-plates ended. She launched herself from the threshold and caught hold of one of the numerous straps extending from the walls. Colonists were packed into the place, as they were in other blisters scattered over the *Foucault*'s hull. She received murmured acknowledgements and the occasional nod, but it seemed the tone here, and the settling in over the voyage, had shut down the usual barrage of questions. They returned their attention to the darkened blister.

Ursula checked the time on her wristcom. Three minutes remained until the ship surfaced from U-space. They had all seen the Polity survey images of the Galander system – clear imagery, and even virtuality packages, of the colony world Threpsis and its diverse, dangerous life forms, as well as large outer planets and smaller inner worlds, moons, asteroids and a glaring blue sun. But they all had to be here for this, even if the view was unlikely to show much at all. Ursula understood it because she felt it too. It was necessary to acknowledge this moment with more than just a screen, holographic or virtuality view in their cabins. It was also a coming together – the real beginning of their mission.

Some seconds before the ship surfaced, the hemisphere of laminated chain-glass cleared. A concerted groan arose from the colonists and Ursula turned her gaze from the whorled silver grey of U-space. This early activation of the glass was a minor fault, but not one that would kill anyone or, as was often the case when someone viewed U-space, drive them a little crazy. The ship shuddered and she felt a weird twisting sensation run through her body, as though it was being stretched and turned, but without pain or damage. She glimpsed infinity, and a multitude of colonists curving away endlessly in a direction she couldn't point to, then the ship surfaced in the real.

For a moment it seemed that the glass had blacked again, but stars twinkled into being with a slightly larger blue glare over to their left. Ursula pulled up a control hologram from her wristcom and tapped the coms unit in her ear to link. She sent an image of Threpsis with one of its moons into the laminate of the chainglass blister. The world was swirled with cloud here and there and its colour a combination of ochre, blue and red. No oceans were evident for it had none.

'We have arrived at last,' she said, her voice issuing from the PA system throughout the ship, coms units and other computing so all the colonists could hear. 'It will take us two days to achieve orbit and we have some preparations to make. All those in cabins aboard the *Foucault*, get yourselves and your stuff aboard the shuttle. Those who've had second thoughts, file your contract negations within the next day. And to all of us, get ready for some interesting times. It might not be surfing a lava flow, but it'll certainly be up there in the dangerous sports section.' Some of those around her chuckled in response to this, but not as many as she would have liked. 'That's all for now.'

Ursula headed out through creaking corridors, colonists on the move all around her. Again the acknowledgements – she was their leader, after all – but no more than that. They were all old, experienced and professional. She had the position of leader just so long as she kept on getting things right. Should she screw up, there were procedures to unseat her and install a new head, though such an occurrence seemed highly unlikely.

Finally, she reached a more salubrious section of the ship where it became evident the growing fungus and other plants were scattered through the corridors by design. All were highly modified life forms that collected dirt, provided some oxygen, cleaned toxins from the air and could also be a viable food source. She came to a bulkhead door – roots were strewn across the floor from what was definitely a lemon tree beside it, though modified to grow in the subdued light. The door clonked as she approached and she pushed it open to enter the ship's bridge.

All the crew were present at the ring of consoles, their captain, Ergune, standing behind one of them and studying his screen. Ergune stood with his hands behind his back, military fashion, and all here wore uniforms of blue and green. The variety of their physical appearance, however, bespoke their youth – only Ergune approached his hundred and fiftieth year. There were two catadapts, an ophidapt and a krodorman. Three were more machine than human flesh and displayed this through transparent skin, while another wore a saurian body. Even those who were more 'standard' had their additions – their augs and enhancements, coloured and textured skin, eagle or goat eyes. Ergune himself seemed nominally human until you got close and saw his eyes were iron-coloured blank spheres and his hands cybernetic. He sometimes wore his carapace on his back – the hardware that enabled him to run this ship with only the additional mind of a Golem running as the vessel's AI. He was what a new group were calling themselves: a haiman – partially AI, in the closest blend of AI crystal and human mind yet manageable. Yes, youth. The colonists, most of whom were much older than anyone here, had tended to return to an old standard human form because, in the end, appearance was not important to them.

'All shipshape and Bristol fashion?' Ursula enquired.

Ergune wagged a metallic finger at her. 'I looked that up since the last time you said it, and now understand. Yes, all shipshape and in the fashion of ships from Bristol, though on a decidedly different sea.'

'Good.' She smiled. 'I'll be boarding the shuttle now and have come to say my goodbyes.' She looked round at them all. 'Thank you all for your sterling service.' Ergune winced, probably because he now had something else he needed to look up.

'It's been a pleasure,' he said. 'Though I still wonder what the hurry was.'

This was the first she'd heard of this. 'Hurry?'

'I thought you knew.' He shrugged. 'We were due to make a delivery of some runcible components, beyond Kalonan, but the Polity gave your mission priority and even paid for storage of those components at Kalonan.'

'Glad to get us on our way and not bothering them any more,' Ursula replied. They spoke some more, but when she left the bridge to head for the shuttle, she felt an increase in the niggling disquiet she'd had for some time now. Later she would remember this, much later.

The shuttle set off from the *Foucault* and was soon rumbling into the atmosphere of Threpsis. The vessel was a mile long and as big as many actual interstellar ships. Zodac, the pilot, held a remote joystick in front of him. He twisted and turned it and the shuttle responded by firing up thrusters and swinging the vessel right round, whereupon the fusion engine fired to slow them. Zodac's eyes were blank, like Captain Ergune's, and he had optics plugged into the side of his head which ran from his chair. He could see Ursula and the others but the virtuality he occupied, of shuttle, world, vectors and engine stats, mostly filled his vision.

'It would be nice to use grav all the way down, but not energy efficient,' he stated.

He'd been a shuttle pilot about a century ago and agreed to reactivate his implants for this, but said he would shut them down again at the first opportunity after they landed, and have them removed. He'd used the same implants when he'd taken part in some very dangerous races, through a particularly active and nasty asteroid belt. Few not in their time of ennui competed in this sport. Usually, by the end of the race, about half of the competitors had become dissipating clouds of hot gas.

Fusion slowed them in a streak of fire around the world. The screen-painted walls showed clouds and zephyrs of fire snaking past. Lower down, objects hit the hull – sparrow-sized creatures of some kind; their impacts were brief and explosive, so there was no possibility of identification. Zodac framed and then expanded the image of one of the big fliers, four stubby wings propelling its gas-filled body, long neck extended and hippopotamus head tilted down. They would name the thing at some point. The suggestion of 'Zeppelin' had been received with the humour intended, since far too many gas-filled fliers on other worlds had been named the same.

Zodac turned the shuttle again, now nose down to the planet so they could see the land sliding along beneath them. Mountain chains were visible, but immensely old since tectonic activity here was all but defunct. Wide ochre and red desert areas, named the Bled, stretched between, dotted with oases of local fauna over upwellings of groundwater. As they drew lower, Zodac pulled up another frame showing a herd of ostrich-like creatures speeding along, kicking up a dust storm. Once they were on grav, flight became smoother, with just the occasional pull to one side or another as Zodac adjusted their course with thrusters.

'You still want that ground burn at the designated site?' he asked.

'Yes, I do.'

'Seems a shame for our biologists,' he replied.

'They'll have plenty to do and they still have all the Polity survey data to play with. We need the area clear so as to get established. Life here comes back very quickly where there's water.' As she well knew, some of the mobile plants would wander in from other areas. And seeds would survive the burn and be sprouting within hours.

The land drew closer and closer until it sped under the shuttle just a mile down. Hereabouts, massifs rose out of the Bled, surrounded by blue, purple and occasional green growth. Soon Ursula recognized the shape of the massif they were heading for. The big stones sometimes acted as dew collectors, hence the growth around them. According to the survey, this particular one sat over groundwater close to the surface and even had a spring in a deep, fully enclosed cavern inside. They'd easily be able to access this source of water through drilling, and it was the main reason why they'd chosen this site. Since Zodac hadn't done it, Ursula raised a control hologram and using gesture control flung a frame from it over the massif on the screen paint and fixed it with a flat push of her hand. Now, no matter the orientation of the ship, the big rock would stay in view.

Using thrusters, Zodac slowed the vessel, then began to tilt it nose up towards the sky. Their perspective changed on the massif as they slid over it and, all around, dense growth packed close. A moment later they were looking down on top of the thing.

'Set primary burn on the stone itself,' she said.

'I know, nothing wrong with my memory,' Zodac replied in a gentle reprimand.

Fire flared across the image as the fusion flame blanked out their view for a moment. They hardly rose at all as Zodac feathered grav down and down. When the flame went out, they could see fires burning on the stone and in nearby vegetation. Ursula watched, holding up the flat of her hand towards Zodac and he showed no impatience, just that blank stare. Flocks of fliers boiled up from the vegetation and soared away. A few minutes later ground creatures started streaming out too, running for the Bled. She spotted a herd of brontopods, more of the ostrich things, others besides, and some lone creatures, probably predators. Shortly after this, some of the vegetation was on the move: things that used long stalks to drag bulb-like bodies along behind them, tumbleweeds with claw feet, and a large tangle of strangler fig, pulling its roots from the ground and then walking on them.

'Okay – secondary burn,' she said.

As the fusion flame ripped around the massif again, she wondered at the distinction she'd made. She hadn't wanted to wipe out the population of animals, but wasn't so bothered about the plants, mobile or otherwise. Yet here many of the plants possessed more brain matter and cognition than the animals, and could be as dangerous. It would have been safer to burn everything to ash at once, since nothing would have been driven to extinction. She shrugged to herself – a hangover from eco-conservation morality of previous ages.

Zodac now pulled the shuttle level in clouds of smoke and embers and brought it down beside the massif. As the thing landed on its belly in hot ashes, Ursula stood and headed down towards the holds. Callum and Vrease joined her clad in Polity vacuum combat suits, and other colonists throughout the ship were wearing similar gear. They needed to protect themselves from the environment of this world until Oren's auto-analysers transmitted updates on the atmosphere to their nanosuites. Other programming updates would also ensue regarding alien toxins, microbes, viruses and more besides. Actual physical upgrades to their suites would require injections, patches or pills.

'And we're changing already,' said Callum.

'What?' Ursula asked.

Vrease explained, 'The meta-materials in the hull are still diverting or absorbing most radiation, but the power is off and magnetic and electrostatic fields are down.'

Ursula nodded, pretending distraction and that she, of course, realized that. She had known it but had just at that moment forgotten. They were all now being bombarded with solar radiation and their DNA taking a hammering. Once they stepped outside, this would increase to a level that would have killed a 'normal' human.

Colonists were on the move all around, hauling heavy packs or moving grav-sleds loaded with equipment. Ursula, Vrease and Callum entered a dropshaft running from nose to tail and this wafted them to an exit a quarter of a mile ahead of the fusion engines. Here Ursula led the way to a spiral stair down into the back of one hold. Already a big chunk of the hull had folded down to form a ramp into the hot ashes. Clouded light penetrated – the smoke still yet to clear – and Ursula picked up the smells she'd once experienced at a beach barbecue on Earth: burned wood, seared protein and even something like the smell of decaying seaweed. She thought about it for just a moment then, in a sudden cold sweat, quickly closed over the hood of her envirosuit and pulled up the visor. A moment later, a display down in one corner of it showed her atmosphere integrity.

Large sleds and other vehicles began to roll down the ramp and head out, loaded with building materials and the prefabricated components of a base designed to fit perfectly around the massif. Already the hold was half empty. She eyed various crates being loaded onto a sled with ECS decals clearly imprinted – just like the kind of crates she'd seen at the military port of Ensolon. These contained military-grade weapons. She hoped they would have little need for them and that clearance flamers, and the lasers sported by agricultural robots, would be enough to combat the hostile life here. However, when she'd discovered ECS selling off a great deal of weapons ridiculously cheap, she'd not stinted. Most of the colonists possessed personal weapons, but here she had small bead railguns, other slug throwers, lasers and particle beam weapons, and even a good quantity of missiles. Also included were cases of mosquito autoguns – robot weapons that looked like large chromed versions of their namesakes.

With Callum and Vrease in tow, Ursula went over to her grav-car. The Rover 484 was a rugged beast she'd used for many years and wasn't exactly a civilian vehicle. It carried impact armour, could be atmosphere sealed for vacuum and had enough structural strength to go undersea to a substantial depth – not that that would be needed here. She climbed inside and set it running, deck clamps automatically disengaging. Callum sat beside her and Vrease behind. Both were inspecting tablets or listening to reports via com. Vrease, unusually for the majority of the colonists, also wore an aug, so had a more immediate understanding of how things were running. Ursula wondered about her own decision to have her aug removed and why so many others had taken the same step. She guessed they weren't so different from those 'Originals' Oren had told her about. Except they wanted to start out here on some new ground level and see what they became, not return to some mythical, antediluvian, halcyon state. Was she better without it? She didn't know. All she did know was that it felt right not to come here with a big chunk of Polity processing working with her mind. They needed new thinking here, not perpetual rehashing of the old.

Gripping the joystick, she raised the car off the deck and slid it slowly forwards, out into the day of a new world. Taking it higher, she turned it and watched five processions of vehicles and people coming out of the open holds of the shuttle. One large vehicle had already reached the massif. It parked and dropped down a ramp and another treaded vehicle rolled out. This moved in close to the stone with an open v-shaped dozer blade at its fore, pushing up ash and earth and funnelling all of it in. Then it slowed, issuing smoke and steam, a large drum turning at its rear.

'The sinter will be sufficient?' Callum asked.

Before Ursula could reply, Vrease said, 'It's irradiating the ground first and putting down tubes to burn up anything that looks like a seed. But no, it probably won't be enough here since the plants and other forms are radiation resistant. It's a start.'

Something thwacked against the car, then came a further clattering of objects like hail. Ursula noted a segmented worm with two pairs of wings stuck below the screen, but after a moment it fell away. She recognized one of the parasites of the larger fliers – things that bored inside to eat what they could before being driven away by immune systems which possessed a mutualistic parasite similar to the attacking one. Returning her attention to the machine on the back of the vehicle, she saw the flat grey surface appearing behind it. The thing was sintering ash and earth with carbon and ceramic additives to produce a layer a foot thick. Every so often a port would appear in this, because it could only stop growth from underneath temporarily. After they'd laid this, they would inject special hydroscopic fibres to draw all the moisture from the underlying earth. This, as far as she understood the biology here, would drive most seeds, eggs and creatures into somnolence.

Three more of the surfacing machines ran around the massif and other robots started moving in. Great spidery things hauled large tanks on their backs to spray foamstone on the massif, while printer bots and others carved channels and hollows and made ducts that would take optics, pipes and wiring, which other bots brought in on large reels. They left circular clear areas on the stone, to give rock borers access to begin making tunnels into the massif, as well as drill a well down to the spring. Amidst all this, colonists worked diligently, sealing up seams, using loaders to move supplies into position, welding down ceramal plates on the temporary floor. Even as Ursula took her grav-car higher, towards the top of the massif, the surface layers had progressed far enough for some of the prefabricated walls of the base to start going up. And printer bots could start work on smaller foamstone structures too.

Further parasites thwacked against the grav-car as she went up but she ignored them. She brought the car over the top of the massif and looked for an area to land it on. A warning flashed on one of the console screens: 'HULL INTEGRITY BREACH'. She stared at it in puzzlement, since the last time she'd seen that warning had been on an out-Polity world, when someone had fired at her with armour-piercing bullets. Bringing the vehicle into a hover over a suitably flat area, she reached over and slid across a diagnostic program. It began working but then the entire screen disrupted. 'POWER FAILURE' she briefly saw before the car dropped the remaining twenty feet like a stone.

The car crashed down on the top of the massif. Her chair collapsed and reformed underneath her, taking most of the impact but Ursula still felt as if someone had played her spine like a xylophone. The car tilted as smoke issued from the console and buzzing rattling sounds came from all around. Down to her right she saw part of the plastic facing dipping in. Something small scribed round, chitinous manipulators pushed through, a spill of glutinous acid bubbling over the plastic.

'Out! Now!' she yelled.

'What the fuck?' said Callum. 'Shit!' He moved sideways on his seat and, looking down, she saw worm-things coming through the fabric. Another one also came through the roof just above her head and hit the door handle. She shoved the door open and ducked out, her back protesting. Callum and Vrease piled out after her. Moving to the edge of the flat area, she looked back. The car looked like as if had been hit by machine-gun fire with burned holes all over its hull.

'A little bit more aggressive than—' she began, then the breath went out of her as something hit her low in the back on the right and she staggered forwards. The pain came a moment later and she gasped, going down on her knees. It was her first close encounter with one of the local life forms, and the last time she wore a simple envirosuit outside.

11

The ramp door of the car had only been intended to open once more – when they arrived at the prador assault craft. Then they would somehow make a bargain with the prador, or subdue them, or destroy them, and finally bring the reactor out for installation. As the door's multiple locks disengaged and it began to lower, Ursula wondered about that. They had made plans and some weapons that should be effective against prador armour, but it had all been particularly inchoate. They should have prepared more, done more, planned more – that would have been the correct military approach. But in the rush of their changes, it had been sidelined as a remote goal, achievable as they *adapted* to the need for it.

She stepped out onto the ramp and at once began to sense the distant chatter of cacoraptors. Their communication across EMR and elsewhere, which she dubbed 'cacocom', was probably like a Polity warfare com sphere, with tactical updates and telemetry constantly linking all of them together. It was just noise to her until, reaching the bottom of the ramp and moving aside, she concentrated on it. She began to get a sense of it, like someone listening to a foreign language: the ebb and flow of *conversation*, some context and hints of meaning in bursts of data that might

230

be described as words. Reflected in herself, in a deep response, she found something in the microwave bands that seemed to be updates on physical changes. Elsewhere she found intent, fading in and out, eliciting a visceral emotional response and her guts tightened. Hunger, but extending beyond human definition; the puzzlement of something beginning to understand itself; feedback loops that were vaguely like anger but more like purpose. In all this, as the communications waxed and waned, she again felt a driving force, a driving intelligence, as if all the other sources only reflected that one. She blinked and backed off as she felt her body and mind wanting to change and reflect this too, but she didn't shut it down. She allowed it to run, almost compartmentalizing it by using her facility to integrate thousands of disparate data points. It was almost a subconscious thing, and she felt certain her understanding would grow. With her fully conscious mind, she returned to the moment.

She eyed the jungle ahead. In most cases it was a slow-moving battle with plants interpenetrating each other to steal water and nutrients. Yes, a Nursum's Fig, as it was now being called, was there. It had wrapped itself around a tall plant similar to a cycad, whose purple leaves were fading to white and curling as the fig sucked out its life. Another mobile plant was steadily advancing on a blue cycad, thick leaves up like shields and prickly with the spines the cycad had thrown at it. Vines crawled along the ground, seeking prey and, even as she watched, one grabbed something that made a whickering sound and struggled to escape on blunt shapeless limbs. She wasn't sure whether the prey could be described as fauna or flora – same for the vine.

Around her, laser hits began flashing in the air. Cindered flying worms dropped to the ground, winged seed pods exploded and scattered seeds like glass beads. The car's door defences were active because they didn't want this stuff getting in to crawl around inside. Other movement began to impinge, and she saw some vines turn towards the car and edge along the ground to it. Another Nursum's Fig, devoid of prey, began a tentative advance, while bracts the colour of bloody flesh broke from the near ground to cast seeds like feathered darts towards them. Then the animals, or rather what she loosely identified as such, started to appear.

First came a pack of the things like insect hyenas, pushing through the foliage and ranging out, circling. Would they attack? They had seemed to be scavengers but actual hyenas of Earth had been viewed as such before observation proved otherwise. A brief spurt of fire from a railgun disintegrated two of them and the rest scattered, yipping like their namesakes but also making a sawing clattering sound. Other creatures appeared – some predators and some herbivores because change meant opportunity. A group of eight brontopods pushed massively through, ambled out and began biting the bracts out of the ground and eating them. But no cacoraptors yet. Ursula turned to the colonists exiting the car.

All wore amalgamations of skin and armour. Most had their helmets and head coverings open now or, in many cases, the distinction between head and what enclosed it had become debatable. They didn't look quite human. More like monsters in an army from some fantasy virtuality – perhaps orcs, evil dwarves, trolls, ogres and goblins. Limb lengths and body shapes were at extreme variance. Heads and features distorted. Severen and the three with him had changed in response to the demand for finding food. One had pale blue eyes so large they almost met in the middle. He'd also grown an extra set of limbs, and the musculature to support them, from the base of his ribcage. Another retained human eyes but had grown antennae that switched and writhed, while her ears were now large and mobile, and her hands like shovels – perfect for digging up nutritious roots. Severen's eyes had shrunk to blue points, while his nose and mouth had grown. The nostrils were wide and surrounded by a growth like the head of a morel fungus, while his wide mouth protruded sampling tubes on either side. He tilted his head and sniffed, then turned to look out towards the hyena-things, once again gathering close. The one with the big eyes looked too. Severen raised a hand and some of those who might have been in Trakken's squad – though it was hard to tell as many had changed in similar ways now – immediately turned and fired their weapons. Particle beam shots lanced out, incinerating heads and delving into the bodies behind, dropping the animals where they stood. A group with heavy thick legs and arms terminating in large claws headed out with a grav-sled to collect them.

'So this is the future for us?' Vrease asked, coming to stand beside Ursula and looking at them all as they advanced.

'Not for you,' Ursula replied, resenting her observation.

'I understand the necessity,' said Vrease. 'As we were, this world would have killed us, but my concern is for the future. You wanted, and we wanted, to retain some essential portion of humanity, though we were never sure what that was. Have we? Or rather, have you?'

'Since Callum cut you out, you've now designated yourself my conscience?'

'I have perspective others are lacking,' Vrease observed.

'Maybe Oren has the same perspective,' Ursula tried, not really believing that.

'Oren has an agenda, and I don't think it has anything to do with humans remaining . . . human.'

Ursula nodded. 'My thoughts exactly.' She turned to Vrease, still feeling her to be other, but useful other, partially incorporated other. 'I have ultimate control beyond formal command. I can

233

control them physically and I can reverse the changes.' She paused for a second, thinking of Lecane, Caulter and Callum. 'I can reverse some of the changes and others can be dealt with in due course.'

'I surmised as much. My concern is: will you want to?'

Ursula just stared at her for a moment longer, then returned her attention to the activities beyond the car.

On the other level of communication, she could feel Severen delivering instructions. The two with him led two more parties with grav-sleds towards the jungle. Keying into the exchange, she absorbed the multitude of orders. The roots of certain plants should be dug up, sprayed with an acid Caulter had made inside himself to etch away their highly reactive and poisonous skins, then preserved in simple vinegar. *Threpsis pickles*, Ursula thought. Blue cycads must be stripped of the leaves packed with spine throwers and poison sacs, and the cores irradiated and baked. Certain leaves, and what passed for flowers here, could be collected, but would need to be mashed and fermented. Areas of stem from some bushes were useful, while seeds, pods and nuts with fewer defences could be killed by irradiation and, after a period of careful observation, eaten. But Severen now had his eye on the larger prize.

The brontopods had noticed the colonists streaming from the car. They shrieked alarm and abruptly gathered into a huddle with their head shields facing outwards while stamping and clawing at the ground.

'Does that look familiar to you?' Vrease asked.

Ursula didn't want to respond, but nodded anyway. Of course they'd seen the creatures act like this before . . . when cacoraptors were around. Ursula surveyed the area, gazed through the eyes and various senses of others, and again consciously observed the chatter in the EMR spectrum. She listened through that woman's big ears and tasted pheromones through her antennae, as well as looking through the big blue eyes of the man who could see the smallest objects at the most remote distances. There were no cacoraptors here, yet, but the brontopods thought there were. The implication was not lost on her. The creatures were responding to the colonists in the same manner.

'Yes, it is familiar. We have the cacoraptor genome working inside us, changing us and producing all sorts of chemical and visual cues the brontopods recognize, so should we expect otherwise?'

'I guess not. But you know, the changes are so specific and seem more by design than instinct. Look at Lecane and Caulter. And look at what Callum has become.'

'The cacoraptors change similarly. At first by instinct and then by the direction of that controlling mind.'

'So, did you make Lecane, Caulter and Callum?'

'No, I did not,' Ursula finally admitted. She pondered previous thoughts on this matter – her suspicions. 'Not consciously anyway. Maybe there's something integral with the genome, some developing submind.'

'Maybe you're subconsciously preparing for the future.' Vrease pointed at Lecane and Caulter. 'It's occurred to me that with them we have two weapons capable of penetrating prador armour.'

Ursula simply nodded but felt a flush of panic, quickly suppressed.

Colonists moved swiftly in around the brontopods, some on long legs heading round the other side of the herd. One moved in closer – heavier legs now supporting her weapon, body hooked like a question mark, head and face almost lost in the side of the iron-burner and taking on the appearance and function of a gunsight, but an intelligent one. Lecane. She stalked closer, clawed hands hanging low, the brontopod she faced dipping to present its head shield as it pawed at the ground, clattering and whick-ering. She kept moving, while the whole herd edged away from her but retained its defences. Did that work, Ursula wondered? Did a herd of these creatures facing a cacoraptor sometimes actually not lose one of its members? Or was this a holdover from the past and a defence against some other predator? Were they like ancient humans facing tanks, hiding behind walls and ready with inadequate hand weapons?

Lecane drew close enough, braced herself against the ground, with those secondary spurs separating from her lower legs and skewering in. She heaved and fired a single iron-burner shot, stabbing out with the aperture of a particle beam. It struck the centre of the creature's head shield and cut straight in with an explosion of fire, smoke and vapour. The head behind broke open with a thump and the beam delved further, then shut off. The brontopod stood swaying for a moment, smoke pouring from the embered hole into its body, and slumped. Just as after a caco-raptor attack, the rest of the herd hooted alarm and scattered. Colonists got out of the way easily, but one grav-sled got flipped end over end, steadied in the air twenty feet up, then slowly settled to its designated position in relation to the ground.

The colonists drew the sled and two others in close. Severen directed them to cut, divide, segment, whether with chain-diamond saws or scythe-like claws faced with Q-carbon. But Ursula sensed a problem, even as she watched some of the col-onists gather around the brontopod and stand there shivering. She walked over to see what the hell was going on and saw one woman with her arms flat at her sides, body tilted forwards.

'Fuck,' said Vrease, still stuck to Ursula's side.

Realization hit Ursula at once and she was inside them in an instant. They were all women and she found the mad rush of hormones welling inside them, wombs distending up through

236

their bodies, ovaries shooting in eggs at a ridiculous rate and some already changing into zygotes. She felt it transferring back to her and her body twisting inside and a hot telic flush rushing through her. The horror of it froze her for a moment. Parthenogenesis – this was how the cacoraptors reproduced. In a spurt of anger, she reached inside herself to stop the process. Was it subconscious? She didn't know, so went straight into the biology of it. It resisted her because this was now her body's instinctive reaction when presented with such a huge food source. To reproduce and have her progeny feed on it, as they'd seen the raptors do numerous times. She pinched off blood vessels and other nutrient sources, closed down on her womb and flooded it with poisons. The process continued to fight her but then it was as if she'd found some substratum of self, some layer of control that had been heretofore denied her. It assisted her, making changes at subcellular levels. Something like an electric shock passed through her and she felt in its aftermath an abrupt and basic revision.

Ursula was on her knees by the time the process had finally died. She reached out to copy it across to the others but found it already being activated in them. Had she done that? She couldn't know, so deep had she gone. With a sigh she stood up, her body aching, and she felt a new immediate hunger at her core, like a lead weight. The others were back on track too and it had all passed. The cacoraptor genome and the urge to breed had been repressed. She liked to think she'd beaten it herself, but something else had been there, assisting, altering. Oren, she thought again. She had to talk to Oren, but somehow the idea had lost its urgency. She returned her attention to the work.

They levered and broke and heaved, loading the slaughterhouse mass onto the sleds. Ursula watched for a while longer, as other sleds began returning from the jungle, then she turned to head back to the car. Oren would have answers, and she should try to catch some spare time now to speak to him.

'Oh hell. Nursum,' said Vrease.

Ursula turned. It seemed as if events were conspiring against her ever going to see Oren. Yet, somehow, that didn't matter.

The fig was still slowly perambulating from the jungle. Severen had ignored it as a source of nutrient because it was all a carbon-cellulose composite, veined throughout with the cornucopia of poisons, acids and enzymes it used to subdue and digest its victims. Nursum was standing right in its path with his arms held out to his sides, as if ready to welcome an old friend.

'Nursum! What the hell are you doing!' she shouted, and broke into a run. Vrease ran at her side and others broke away from the foraging parties. Lecane was one of them. Ursula used cacocom to deliver instructions, and Lecane replied that the distance was too far for her to use the iron-burner on the fig. Ursula reached out, giving other instructions. A railgun fired from the car, its hits splintering the fig's tough vine-twisted body, as it opened up its cage and mobile vines reached across the ground to Nursum. Ursula instructed others with weapons, but then rescinded the order when Nursum leaped the encroaching vines and went straight into the fig's deadly embrace.

Ursula juddered to a halt as the fig closed around him. It would not be able to damage him as quickly as before and her people, closing in now, should be able to tear it apart easily enough. But why had he done this? And, the stray thought came to her, had she any right to stop him? A surge of irritation arose when she realized the thought came from that part of her that still considered Nursum an outsider, an alien, not one of *us*. He was a human being. And he was a damaged human being who was trying to kill himself, trying to claim the death that had been denied him. She reached out to his slippery mind and attempted a deeper contact. His mind seemed to shift and deform under her probing and weirdly what she got from him was a sense of delight, of completion.

'Cut him free,' she instructed.

Those with Q-carbon claws advanced on the mobile plant, but its vines were in the ground and spread all around. They thrashed, spraying acid, and a man staggered away, smoking. One vine closed around the ankle of another and hoisted him from the ground, then slammed him down on it three times before discarding him. Both injuries were minimal, but it seemed that getting to this fig wasn't going to be as easy as with the first. Perhaps that one *had* been partially domesticated. The colonists moved in again, tearing up vines and slicing them off, gradually getting closer. As she too drew closer, Ursula found it difficult to distinguish Nursum from the tree and her confusion was reflected in those who reached it. Which part was Nursum? She saw it now. The man had taken on the same woody aspect and his limbs were dividing into branches, vines, twigs and tendrils and tangling with those of the fig.

She stared hard, wanting to distinguish what was Nursum and what was not. The strain built a pressure behind her eyes and her vision blurred for a second before coming back as if through a colour filter. Now she could see the tangle of Nursum amidst the fig, for his growth had taken on a red hue while the fig appeared black. She broadcast the change to the others – this slide into infrared – but then with a thought ordered them to desist. Nursum was just too entangled, with his vines penetrating the tree and its own penetrating him. Something was happening here that needed to run its course, she felt, though conscience prodded her and she wondered again if her desist order still had something to do with him being *other*.

Nursum and the fig fought, becoming increasingly interwoven. Red and black intermingled, with fig vines and branches seeming to heat up with the red, and areas of Nursum's central body blackening. These areas waxed and waned and for a short time it looked as though the black was winning, but then, with a cracking sound, one large fig branch threw up splinters, as if someone had just fired on it. Ursula had no need to check – she was so connected now she knew no one had. Black began to recede all to the fig, and it started to fade to grey. The figs leaves lost their original colour and began to yellow and curl. Further crackling sounds ensued, as once-mobile branches and vines became frangible. Ursula folded her arms and waited, meanwhile sending the instruction for the food gathering to continue.

In the tangle of the fig, Nursum started to grow more distinct, his limbs melding together again, the branches that had sprouted from his body withdrawing. His golden colour returned and, with a heave, he broke open the cage around him and stepped out. The fig sagged, and green tendrils of other plants or animals sprouted from the ground to seek out this source of nutrient. Dead nutrient.

'Are you good now?' Ursula asked, stepping up before him. 'Have you worked out your fig-related problems?' Oddly she felt no anger because, though what he'd done had been stupid and dangerous, she understood his inclination perfectly. She'd been there herself, many times.

He looked at her, blinked slowly, then said, 'It was not as satisfying as I had hoped, but then it was not *my* fig.'

She reached out to him again, to try and get some link, some hold or leverage on his slippery mind, but now it felt as tight and solid as a ball bearing.

'Of course, with this' – he gestured to himself – 'I now have a way to penetrate prador armour. So you should be happy about that.' He stepped past her and away.

She puzzled over that. She could suppose it was her subconscious that was driving the changes in the colonists, and this rather dramatic change in him, but she had never felt any grip on Nursum at all.

Past

After the first six months of military training, the recruits were due for their initial physical enhancements. But before that, in a tradition imposed by their commander Macannan, they had a break of two days to visit Port Ensolon. Other recruits who were further advanced in their training went along too.

'I'm going to talk to him about it,' said Ursula.

Manseur glanced at her. 'Oh really?'

The woman had her black hair cropped close to her head and, even throughout the intense combat training, had retained the stud in her nose. She had, however, got rid of the rings in her nipples after an opponent used them as 'leverage'. Ursula was wearing light grey camo-pattern fatigues that easily identified her as a first-year recruit, on her first foray into the city. Manseur wore light blue fatigues, marking her as a second-year recruit. This was part of the 'tradition' too, as was getting drunk and getting into fights.

'He's pushed you into specializing in runcible logistics, and is pushing me into tactical integration and logistics. I don't want that. I want to fight.'

'Well, you'll get plenty of that tonight.' Manseur pointed ahead towards Port Ensolon.

'That kind of fighting I am not interested in – I won't start anything.'

'I'm afraid you won't be able to avoid it. People, like I used to be, come here just for the ruck. Someone will push you into it.'

'Like you used to be?'

Manseur inspected her carefully. 'You don't socialize much in the camp, do you? Always hard at work, even during your free times. Trying to keep busy, busy, busy.' She smiled a little sadly before continuing, 'I am a hundred and seventy-two years old, Ursula. My period of ennui lasted for fifteen years. If I'd known about this place back then, I too would have come for the traditional brawls with drunken recruits.'

'Oh.' Ursula was stumped for a moment, not by the knowledge that those suffering from ennui would be waiting to fight them, but at Manseur's previous observation, and her sad smile, concerning Ursula's detachment from the others. She sensed a possibility of understanding what that might be about, but immediately clamped down on it. Hurriedly, she continued, 'That could be dangerous for us first-year recruits – we don't have any physical enhancements. If any of us ended up against someone boosted, we could be killed.'

'Fighting marine are you, or a tactician?'

'Fuck off.'

'No worries on that score, my love. The bored ancients coming here have their rules. The one who picks a fight with you will be without enhancements.'

'And you?'

'Enhancements limited to what you'll receive over the next six months.'

The grav-bus they were travelling on entered the outskirts of Port Ensolon, with its sprawling bungalows and wide parks. It settled out of the sky, its wheels folding out onto one of the roads and grav went off with a thump. The vehicle jounced on its suspension as it drove on in. After a few miles the bungalows became houses and villas. After this they passed through the ring park into the city proper, tower blocks rearing all around them, as well as sky bridges and jutting platforms above.

'Of course you can go to Macannan to talk about your career in the military, but right now might not be a good idea. He gets a bit tetchy around inspection time.'

'Sheila,' said Ursula. 'It seems such a stupid name for an AI.'

'Are you aware of any sensible ones?'

'The planetary controllers.'

'Bing bong, nil points. They are always referred to as the Luna AI, or the London AI, or the' – she waved a hand airily – 'Nilson's Reach AI, but in reality that's just how they're referenced by humans. Remember, I worked with runcibles, and the AIs that control them are usually the planetary governors. The Luna AI, for example, is called Pock-Marked Sid or just Sid to its friends.'

'You're winding me up.'

'Really?' Manseur was all innocence as the bus pulled into a station below a vast structure that in olden times could have been classified as a city itself.

'And that reminds me,' said Ursula. 'What did you do to be kicked out of Runcible Tech?'

Manseur's expression became utterly bland and just a little tired. 'Runcible technology is serious. It manipulates space and time. You don't fuck with that stuff. And you don't let bored ancients anywhere near it.'

'You're not going to tell me, are you?' said Ursula as they stood.

Manseur shook her head. 'Nope.'

Vancouver Tower housed just over a million people. It lay two miles square at its base, rose for a quarter of a mile straight up, whereupon it stepped in an eighth of a mile for every extra quarter of a mile it went up, finally standing a mile and half high. It contained apartments – some, it was rumoured extended to almost a full floor across. There was all the paraphernalia of a city inside, including shopping complexes, bars and restaurants, parks, lakes, hydroponic tubes and even a waterfall. Transport varied. There were high-speed trains running through vacuum tubes, dropshafts that didn't just run up and down, airtaxis for some of the larger internal spaces, and there was the Stairway. After taking the tube from the lower car park, then a horizontal dropshaft, then further tubes and shafts heading ever upwards, Manseur took them into one of the arched entrances which led to this famed Stairway.

'Is this strictly necessary?' asked Ursula.

'It is if you want to go to the Blue Strand right at the top.' Manseur pointed upwards. 'It was deliberately isolated, probably because the building designers wanted to present a challenge. See?' She pointed.

A group of people jogged past clad in skin-tight body suits, various monitors stuck to their surfaces. Headbands dark with sweat, faces red. Ursula tried to understand why she was witnessing something she'd only seen previously in a historical virtuality of pre-Quiet War Earth.

'They're the Unenhanced – bit of a cult who like pushing their bodies on various challenges. Ancients are among them. Many of them come to run the entire Stairway from the bottom, then drink beer in the Gagarand before base jumping off the top. Others come for the fighting. Come on, it can't be all bad, it's traditional.'

They climbed at a steady pace, floor after floor. Ursula felt herself flagging after a while and Manseur led her to a rest area. She wasn't tiring, and there lay the difference between the physically unenhanced and the enhanced. A number of other people were in the seating area too, availing themselves of the comfortable chairs and drinks machines. Ursula flopped in a seat while Manseur collected two frappes for them. A heavyset man, with cropped hair and cropped ears, turned his head and sat staring at Ursula. He was dressed in thick red denim and his hobnailed boots crunched as he shifted them.

'Problem?' she asked, staring straight back at him.

'Me?' He pointed a finger like a sausage at his chest. 'I got no problem. I'm not the ugly bitch sitting here.'

Ursula continued staring at him, not quite understanding what she'd just heard, especially coming from this guy. No one needed to be ugly and yet he'd made the choice to look like a troll. Clearly he was spoiling for a fight and trying to get a rise out of her.

'Now, now, Gurny,' said Manseur, coming back to sit down next to Ursula. 'You know it's against the rules to start anything until recruits are in the Gagarand and well rested. Anyway, I thought you'd decided to go up against second- and third-year enhanced? Surely they're more appropriate now for an ugly fucked-up cunt like you?'

The man-troll grinned at her, exposing tombstone teeth that were grey and little bit rotten in places. 'Just getting in some practice for above.' He turned away and concentrated on his drink, which looked as though it was about half a pint of whisky.

Finally they walked through the high stairway arch into the top floor. Right in the middle was a park with a small lake, from the back of which a rocky, artificial mountain ran up the wall and, yes, a waterfall poured down it. Plane trees grew around the lake, with gardens and bar areas scattered between them. While Ursula watched, someone surfed down the waterfall, tumbling as they went. Near the bottom, the individual kicked against the stone to sail out, just missing a boulder the waterfall splashed onto, and dived into the lake.

245

'The terminally bored,' Manseur commented.

They climbed a further stairway up one balconied wall, passing bars and restaurants, extending back from their inner balconies, through the upper part of the building to their outer balconies. Then they entered the Gagarand. Ursula knew she was in the right place when a bottle exploded against the wall next to her. Circular tables were scattered throughout, around four square bars run by humanoid robot tenders. Tray drones floated through the air delivering drinks to tables. Ursula noted hundreds of other recruits scattered throughout and more arriving via other entrances. Meanwhile, a recruit in blue, just like Manseur, delivered a bone-splintering kick towards the chest of a quite thin-looking woman clad in loose shorts and a halter top. The woman turned slightly, caught the leg and spun, sending the recruit into a nearby wall. Before the man could recover his breath, she reached him, grabbed his balls and his neck, spun him over her head and slammed him down into a table, which collapsed into pieces satisfyingly.

'Choose your opponent carefully, if you have a choice.' She pointed. 'Iris there is almost a permanent fixture here. Oh, except for those occasions when she gets drunk and decides to jump off the outer balcony hanging onto one of the tray drones.'

'It's a quarter of a mile down to the next level,' Ursula pointed out.

'The drone's grav slows her somewhat. And the medtechs keep scraping her up and putting her back together again.'

They moved on, heading for the outer balcony.

'You would think they'd put in fighting areas,' said Ursula. 'Surely it gets a little costly on furniture and fittings around here?'

'Self-reassembling.' Manseur waved a hand at another demolished table. Ursula now noticed threads connecting all the separate pieces, steadily reeling them back together.

One empty table awaited on the outer balcony. People at the other tables were either watching the mayhem inside or those climbing onto the rails and diving over the edge. A man nearby leaned over the rail and peered down.

'I think she broke her legs that time,' he commented, sitting back. He grinned at Ursula and Manseur. 'Gonna hurt when she reaches the next level down.'

Ursula shrugged and sat.

'Good candidate,' said Manseur.

'How can you tell?'

'Not seen him here before. The ones that have been around a while, like Gurny or Iris, are best avoided. They tend not to lose and will hurt you as badly as is allowed.'

'I've hardly got over the stairs. Can we have a drink first?'

Manseur shrugged and held up a hand. A tray drone cruised over to them and hovered, red eye lights glinting, manipulators shifting underneath. It shot over the table to the other side when Iris walked by. It seemed to be watching her carefully.

'What do you want?' it asked them distractedly.

'Two Legends and Oak Apple chasers.'

'Coming up.' It moved away.

Ursula didn't like Manseur's shrug. It seemed to have had some criticism in it. Ursula had recovered from the Staircase now but had felt her reluctance growing since she walked in here. It all seemed so pointless, such a waste of resources. Yes, she wanted to fight, but she wanted an enemy worthy of her effort, damn it.

'Why?' she asked. 'Why does Macannan think this is a good idea?'

'Because you can learn how to fight. All the technical details and all the moves. You can turn yourself into a positive engine of destruction capable of putting your fist through a wall. During all our training we fight against each other, but what are our aims and intentions when we do so?'

'To win.'

'Yes, of course, to win, to make all the right moves, and that's the case on both sides. It's a very different thing to go up against an opponent who is bored, doesn't care about living or dying, and just wants to hurt you as badly as he can. Going up against such a person is a test of character, of heart.'

'Oh.'

The drinks arrived. The drone grabbed two beer bottles and two shot glasses from its tray body with its little crab arms and deposited them on the table. Someone whooped, and snatched the drone out of the air, then ran for the rail and jumped over.

'There she goes again,' said Manseur.

Ursula chugged her beer, draining half of it. She weighed the bottle in her hand for a moment before putting it down. Next she put the shot back. It tasted of old wood and apples and lit a fire on the way down.

'Character and heart,' she said.

'Character and heart,' Manseur agreed.

Ursula picked up the beer bottle by the neck as she stood, walked in from the balcony and up to a large bulky figure with his back to her. She smashed it across the back of his head, sending him stumbling.

'Did you call me ugly?' she enquired.

Gurny shook himself, rubbed his skull then looked at his bloody hand. He turned and grinned at her evilly. A silence seemed to spread out from the spot between them, and into that he cracked his knuckles. The sound resembled an old machine gun firing.

It turned out not to be one of the best decisions Ursula had made.

★   ★   ★

Ursula stood at attention before Macannan's desk, her hands clasped behind her back. Sitting in a chair over to one side was a big, blousy, blonde woman. An old comrade of Macannan's, or perhaps a lover? The eyes fixed on her were icy blue and for some reason made her feel very uncomfortable.

'So what is this all about, Treloon?' Macannan asked without looking up.

Ursula let out a steady breath and braced herself for his wrath. She said, 'I don't want to go into tactical integration and logistics. I just want to be a fighting grunt.'

Macannan looked up at her. Ursula's eye and side of her head had an interesting black and yellow bruise. Her lips were still swollen and her broken tooth ached after the repair, as did her ribs, her right arm, her hands, lower right leg and hip. Apparently autodoc repairs were limited to injuries that would hinder training. The rest the recruit had to bear until they healed – all part of Macannan's 'tradition'.

'Are you sure about that?' he asked, sitting back. 'You don't seem particularly apt in that department.' He picked up a coin she had seen him fiddling with before from his desk, and spun it, watching it carefully as if it might reveal something to him.

'I was hasty in my selection,' Ursula replied. 'Turns out the one I picked has been trying to get himself killed in Ensolon for many years. He was also one of your recruits ten years ago.'

'Dravic Gurnesson,' said the woman. The timbre of her voice was smooth and deep and sent a shiver down Ursula's spine.

Macannan glanced at her. 'He was good. Shame he went off the rails.' Turning back to Ursula, he slapped a hand down on the coin and kept it there, then said, 'I guess we can put that one down to experience. It being Gurnesson, you got away quite lightly – he only broke five major bones in your body. He must have respected you.'

'I still want to be a fighting grunt,' Ursula asserted.

'Let me deal with this one, George.'

Ursula jumped. The woman now stood right at her shoulder and she hadn't seen her move. She glanced at her. The woman was wearing a tight skirt and heels, a loose top over large breasts. She was running to fat in an age when that was entirely unnecessary. Her jewellery looked tacky. Who the hell was she?

'Do go ahead.' Macannan waved a hand.

'Come with me,' said the woman.

She led Ursula out of Macannan's office. Glancing back, Ursula saw Macannan peering down at the coin, his expression puzzled. Sheila led her through the base into an empty lecture room. As they entered, a screen-painted wall came on, running quadrate patterns and flashes of code. That was puzzling. The lecturers didn't often use them and they were usually left turned off.

'Take a seat,' said the woman.

'I would like to know who you are,' said Ursula, stubbornly remaining standing.

'I'm Sheila,' said the woman.

Ursula gaped and, without thinking, sat down.

'You're the AI?'

Sheila nodded once briefly and smiled a smile that looked decidedly false.

This was the inspection AI. The body had to be Golem and perhaps the size of it was because of the crystal and subsidiary processing it contained. But why the blousy, indolent appearance? To put people at their ease, of course, or to catch them unawares.

'So, Ursula Ossect Treloon, what made you decide to join the marines?'

'I wanted to do something useful.'

'I will not repeat the question.'

Ursula just sat there, racking her brain. This was an AI and not some do-good counsellor and she mustn't be fooled by the appearance. This Sheila probably knew more about her than she did herself.

'I went to Earth and while I was there, I tried to decide what direction to take my life in next. I saw a documentary about the secession and revolution on Grayson's World. I saw this—'

'Let's analyse that, shall we?' Sheila interrupted.

She waved a hand and the screen wall opened a frame. It showed precisely the scene Ursula had been about to describe: a marine walking towards special force soldiers, two grav-tanks and hostages.

'It looks quite heroic, doesn't it?'

Ursula nodded mutely.

'Why do you think only two commandos came down from above to deal with it?'

'I don't know.'

'Yes you do.'

Again, Ursula found herself looking for a response beyond the mediocre and she found it in her training. 'They're wearing chameleoncloth because chameleonware is not yet suitable for individual soldiers. Chameleoncloth doesn't completely conceal, so' – Ursula studied the hostages and the special force soldiers – 'two commandos could get the job done. Any more than that and the chances of them being spotted would have increased.'

'By how much?'

Ursula looked at the hostage-takers again, counted them, and considered the elevation. She calculated how many were looking at the marine, considered their likely training and other factors, such as atmospherics and their effect on chameleoncloth, reflections from the windows, downward disturbances from the grav-harnesses. She put as much as she could into a formula she'd memorized.

'Roughly, because I don't know all the details: two more soldiers would have increased their chances of being seen by twenty per cent.'

Sheila winced. 'You are wrong by a large amount. It is sixty-two-point-five-six recurring. You failed to include the hostages and that one of them might see the commandos and react. Still, pretty good considering where you are in your training.'

Ursula gritted her teeth, angry at the error.

'Why not take them all out with snipers?' Sheila asked.

'Because of hostages in the way,' Ursula replied.

'So why the marine?'

'He's a distraction to reduce the chances of the two commandos being seen.'

'Correct, but not completely correct. Think some more.'

Again she studied the imagery. It had reached its conclusion now and started again from the beginning. Ursula thought hard. This was worse than the tests she'd been undergoing for the last few months. She ran formulae, played through alternative scenarios but she just wasn't getting it.

'I will give you a clue: four hostages died,' said Sheila, holding up a finger and halting the video just before the action began.

It all gradually fell into place. Ursula returned her attention to the screen wall and the video started running again. She watched the two commandos drop their grenades in the tanks, and the marine shoot four of the special forces and then their commander. She saw the positions of those four in relation to the hostages, but also thought about likely fields of fire for the snipers who killed the rest of that special force.

'If the marine had not been there to take out those four, casualties would have been considerably higher,' Ursula said.

'Considerably higher? Accuracy please.'

Ursula ran formulae with the data she had, which was only

what she was seeing on the screen wall. 'Between twenty and thirty of the hostages would have died and nearly all of them would have been injured.'

Sheila nodded. 'Very good, considering you didn't know the snipers' fields of fire. Two of the four the marine killed could not be targeted, while for the other two there was a less than fifty per cent chance of an instant kill. Maybe those men would not have opened fire on the hostages.' She shrugged. 'But we do not deal with "maybes".'

Ursula nodded. She understood more of it now. The four hostages who died were well within a casualty percentage, based on the inadvertent firing of a weapon from someone who had been taken out by a sniper. The scenario with the marine and the two commandos had been the best fit to keep the casualty rate at its lowest.

'Now tell me the best way to ensure such accurate and timely shooting from the marine?'

Again hard thinking – this time concerning some of the modern warfare techniques she had recently been learning about. She looked up at the marine, limping away, and felt a surge of disappointment in him. He had been her hero. She'd kept him at the forefront of her mind throughout difficult training sessions and the occasional urge to quit. He was who she had wanted to be.

'Cerebral programming,' she said.

'It was uploaded through his aug. You'll note he didn't react to the laser burn on his leg, even though it would have been intensely painful. He didn't react because he was still running on the program. He only came off the program after the four were dead.'

'His choice to shoot the commander,' said Ursula.

'Quite.' Sheila waved once more and the screen wall blanked. 'All marines are trained and trained very well to fight and use all the assets of modern warfare. But every marine is also a specialist of some kind. We cannot afford to waste resources by having them be merely "fighting grunts".' She pointed to the blank screen. 'Everything you saw happen there was calculated down to the most minute detail by a tactical integration specialist. Even the program running in that marine's mind was put together by one.'

'I see,' said Ursula.

'Logistics, of course, were not an issue in such a small scenario – they become more important only in larger ones. Do you have any questions or further concerns about your training?'

'No, I do not.'

'Do you still wish to quit tactical integration and logistics?'

'No, I do not.'

12

Present

The food supply dropped like water in a holed bucket, but luckily two other places where they could resupply lay on their course towards the prador assault craft. The car had to run perpetually on a skeleton crew, as colonists frequently collapsed as if suffering from narcolepsy. She should have expected this, Ursula felt, as she walked down the ramp once again. The changes they'd undergone bore some similarity to the changes a body experienced during extreme exercise regimens. The exercise damaged and tore down the old, while rest and food rebuilt. She could feel her people consolidating around her, putting on bulk and density and growing energy reserves.

The jungle was a smaller one here, half the size it had been in the survey they'd made when they arrived on Threpsis. It was growing around a geyser that jetted sulphurous radioactive water once a year for just a few hours, enough to maintain the avid life around it. This had been one of the places where the prador also stopped for their burnable organics. A large area of land was covered with just splinters, stumps and the shattered remains of plants, along with animals too hostile for them to cart inside their ship to the burners. But life was recovering fast. Stumps were throwing up new growth, green and yellow threads were strewed everywhere, the air hissed and sizzled with insect equivalents, and scavengers smaller than the hyena-things hunted through already scoured remains.

Severen ran sleds into parts of the jungle still standing. There were just two brontopods in this area and Lecane took them both down, then she, Caulter and some others, including Nursum, went to hunt other animals. When they finally returned with a sled laden with creatures, like sideways-turned turtles with legs from one edge, Ursula heard a brief chatter followed by a fizzing and clicking. She looked around for further animals, because they'd just had things like legless trapdoor spiders the size of a human head shooting out of the ground to bite at people's ankles, only to break poisoned fangs on their armour. Then she saw it on a distant ridge.

The upright figure could have been mistaken for one of them and she strained for better vision. Vrease got there before her.

'Raptor,' she said. 'Heron form.'

Ursula glanced at her. The woman may not be one of them, but Ursula had to remember that Vrease hadn't limited her Golem body merely to emulate her previous human form. Her senses were a lot better and she was stronger and more durable. In accepting this, Ursula found a deeper acceptance of Vrease herself.

'Speed it up, people!' Ursula shouted, but it was just a footnote to cacocom.

The thing bounded down the ridge but didn't come all the way, halting on level ground some hundred yards out. Ursula, her vision now enhanced, scanned the ridge behind, wondering if this was one of an army. She wondered what had happened to the fliers that their drones hadn't seen arrive at the prador ship. She thought about the trap the car had fallen into, and other miscalculations. Only belatedly did she turn her full conscious attention to EMR. But, puzzlingly, the bulk of it was distant, disconnected, and the only local chatter issued from the creature here.

'They came into the shuttle like that when we were rescuing the reactor,' said Vrease, staring at the thing. 'Then they changed, grew arms and fingers with barbed hooks.'

'Callum?' she enquired, having glimpsed bubble drones rising from the car.

'Just one of the fuckers,' he replied.

'One stuck its barbs into me and I couldn't get away,' Vrease added.

Still in its heron form, the thing set out, circumventing those gathered at the jungle edge, halting at that edge a hundred yards away. She focused on it utterly – all her senses – and tried to glean anything she could from it. Flickering patterns in infrared, a low murmur across microwave, the waft of complex chemicals finally reaching her gave her a key, and the thing began to take shape in her mind. She found it as slippery as Nursum and nothing of its cacocom related to what she'd been steadily processing in her mind. It was lone, she realized – unrelated to the original, attacking cacoraptor and the multitude of its progeny. This engendered another thought: she hadn't found the com of the other cacoraptors as slippery and that, horrifyingly, was because she and the colonists were *related*. She wondered again about the cacoraptor genome Oren had used on Nursum. Had it come from another unrelated raptor?

'Its head changed too, when it started chewing on my legs.'

Ursula looked at Vrease again, finally registering that something was happening with the woman. She was clutching her pulse rifle tightly and staring at the cacoraptor intently.

Still watching Vrease, Ursula warned, 'Severen, it may be coming in after your people.'

But the cacoraptor was undergoing transformations. Its pole-like head shifted, producing various sensors and other protrusions, until it had taken on the lobster-like aspect of those that had got inside the car. A pair of arms separated from its body and opened out hooked claws. It seemed almost inevitable that barbs would spring out of the ends of those hooks.

'Just like that,' said Vrease. She grimaced before adding, 'Maybe Nursum had the right idea,' and broke into a run.

'Ah fuck,' said Ursula.

So Nursum hadn't been the only one with issues to work out. Vrease sped away faster than a human, each step kicking up earth and dust as she steadily accelerated. Ursula ran after her, the bones in her legs crackling as their concentric laminations separated and they telescoped, muscles growing hot as her body pumped nutrients, oxygen and fibrous additions to the stretched-out muscle fibres. As she ran, she summoned Trakken's squad, though the distinction between those soldiers and the rest of the colonists had become blurred at best.

The cacoraptor ducked low, scraped at the ground like a bull readying itself to charge, and then did charge. Vrease opened fire and, even though she was running, every one of her shots hit home. Pulse fire slammed into its head and lower body, flaming away material and leaving embered holes. But these filled with asbestos white. Vrease's shooting then concentrated on one leg just as carbine and pulse-gun fire zeroed in on the creature from the squad. Its leg buckled and its charge staggered to one side as Vrease emptied her weapon, discarded it, and slammed into the thing. Necessarily, the others ceased firing.

They tumbled through dust and dirt, movements blurred. Vrease locked her legs around one of its legs and delivered punch after punch into its body, their impacts hard crunches as if delivered by a hydraulic ram. The raptor opened jaws with buzz-saw teeth and bit down on her, closing on her shoulder and most of her chest. Its claws ripped at her back, her legs, and scoured her arms. With her blows not seeming to have the desired effect, she reached up to its neck and tried to strangle it. Ursula slowed, aimed her carbine, but it was difficult to get a shot into the fast-moving tangle of the two of them. They bounced off the ground, sometimes higher than her head, spun and shifted. Trakken opened fire, the others doing so belatedly, going for the few extremities they could target. Ursula shouldered her carbine. This was just like Nursum and could not be wholly resolved by outside intervention. Again she wondered if her decision was based on Vrease not being one of them, but then allowed herself some slack. This situation had arisen because she was different to them – none of her people would have attacked like this, without it being coordinated.

With a crackling sound, Vrease rolled away. With its jaws still clamped to her shoulder and chest, she had snapped the neck and parted the head from the body, drawing it out in long, almost metallic strands. She rolled with the head still attached to her, but the strands kept extending, then they looped and spiralled around her legs as the main body came upright, and began to reel her back.

'Kill it,' Ursula instructed.

Lecane's iron-burner hit the main body square on. It leaned into the blast as tough flesh peeled away to reveal the asbestos white, but even that couldn't stand. It glowed red and exploded like a ceramic vessel, hurling chunks in every direction. The strands snapped, while the legs stood still, connected by the remains of a pelvis. Lecane moved closer, burning them to the ground. Vrease staggered upright, the strands still protruding from the head whipping at her, others wrapped around her legs, cutting in like cheese wire. She went down again and the squad descended on her with clawed hands, pulling and tearing. Finally they broke the jaws and

Trakken tossed the head out on the ground. It was still alive, loudly chittering and buzzing EMR, until Lecane came over and burned it too.

As the squad withdrew, Vrease stood up, not like someone exhausted from a fight, but easily and smoothly. But of course she wasn't exhausted – her power supply would merely be depleted. Ursula studied her. The woman had lost syntheflesh all over her body, revealing her cerametal skeleton and the mechanisms that drove her. A short crackled between her bare ribs and optics protruded from the side of her neck. How much damage, Ursula wondered? Not enough to stop her, obviously – she had probably automatically rerouted around the worst of it. Vrease stooped to her legs, dug in metallic fingers devoid of flesh and began to pull out deeply imbedded threads, unwinding and discarding them.

'That was foolish,' said Ursula.

Vrease looked up. A perfectly circular chunk of flesh was missing from the side of her face, revealing white teeth imbedded in a metal jaw.

'But I needed it,' she replied. 'Now the fear is gone.'

Ursula acknowledged that with a nod. Even though she hadn't wanted Vrease to do this and still felt it to have been a foolish act, it seemed a final box had been ticked. Maybe it had helped her make some kind of peace with the trauma of that mission to retrieve the reactor. But its success had been essential to their hopes for escape . . . And they were ready now, as much as they would ever be, for what lay ahead.

Near Past

From the colony's base control room, Ursula studied the images of their abandoned shuttle as the drones approached it. Areas of the hull had been etched away, making it look like wood that had been attacked by boring beetle grubs. As the drones flew around it, she saw where the raptors had entered. Two loading ramps were down where colonists had been unloading some remaining supplies, and they now stayed down because of damage. Fortunately no colonists had been there when the creatures had arrived. They simply hadn't been prepared for flying cacoraptors and such a *military* attack inside the perimeter, and had left the ramps down. She grimaced and felt the blame for all this rested squarely with her. Having seen the raptor's learned behaviour and growing intelligence, she should have designed their defences accordingly. Twenty-twenty hindsight was so clear.

She shook her head and listened to the audio feed she had on. This produced a steady hiss and clicking sound, with occasional long chirrups. There had been notable changes in it when she launched the drones, but since then it hadn't really altered much. Callum had detected it first and it was another thing she should have seen earlier. The raptors acted in concert, drawn to something other raptors had responded to, even if that lay over the horizon line and supposedly out of range of whichever senses they were using. Surely the raptors that had attacked the prador were listening to this too? Or maybe they had been *sent* from here . . .

'They're talking to each other,' Callum had stated.

It took a little while to nail it down. It ranged up and down the electromagnetic spectrum, sometimes at long-wave radio and other times down into ultraviolet. There had even been hints of X-ray and Y-ray bursts. It depended on the location of the raptors. Sometimes they bounced their talk off a stratospheric layer of dust, and other times objects on the ground, like the massifs or other rocks, or trees, acted as reflectors.

'Can we translate?' she had asked later, as they gathered a database of the signals.

'I'm running it through the computers,' Callum had replied. 'It's probably no more than "we are here – there's meat".'

Later she'd spoken to Oren.

'Yes, I've looked at it. There's a lot of complicated stuff in there,' he'd commented, vaguely.

And that was where they were. It didn't escape Ursula's notice that, had AIs come with them, they would have been much further ahead in their understanding. Perhaps they could even have talked to the creatures and persuaded them into some sort of truce. The hollow laugh at the thought died in her chest.

Another view next showed her armoured cars heading out of the garage in the opposite direction to where the shuttle lay. They motored out fast. Trakken, who was in the lead car and in nominal command there, had suggested they broadcast the sounds of brontopods from their PAs. Ursula had scotched the idea. She felt sure the enemy raptors would see this as an unsubtle lure. Better to have the cars moving at speed to some outside destination, as if going to grab something fast and return. She'd chosen an intact warehouse out there and even told Trakken to take the trailers, with loading grabs attached, which two of the armoured cars were now towing. The warehouse did contain some useful items and Trakken was to follow the ruse through for as long as possible. Two of the cars could smash through the walls and the two with trailers would follow them in. They would then begin loading equipment – she'd even made a list of what might be most useful.

'They're going for it,' said Callum.

Ursula didn't need the warning. Already the chatter coming through on audio had changed. Additional wittering and whining sounds indicated pulses of the 'complicated stuff' Oren had mentioned. She glanced up at the composite drone map on the screen-painted wall. It was heavily into the infrared because the raptors positively glared in that spectrum. Oren said this was due to how hot their body processes ran, for their transformations generated a great deal of heat. It made perfect sense, and Ursula couldn't help but think about the heat Nursum had generated while he was in the regrowth tank, and what he might now have turned into. Looking down at her bracelet, she wondered what she, and soon the others, might also become.

Yes, the raptors were heading towards the four armoured cars. Those nearest were moving the fastest while those further away seemed to be making desultory moves in their direction. She eyed two clumps of them lying between the base and the shuttle.

'You have the intervening ones targeted?' she asked.

'Oh yes. Should I hit them now?'

Ursula shook her head. 'No. The moment you do, they'll know something's up – that lot still might yet head for Trakken.' She turned to Gurda. 'Launch the hard drone and switch us over to hard wiring now.'

Gurda looked up. 'Brief interruption coming up.'

Everything went down, like a short power cut, and the screen-painted wall disrupted into a diamond pattern. Then, just as quickly, it all came back on again, the drone images returning to the wall.

Gurda added, 'Vrease tells me the laser feed has re-established via the hard drone, but we won't know for sure until her cars are out of the garage – they're currently picking it up from a relay in there.'

Ursula looked towards the empty chair in the control centre. She didn't like letting Vrease go on this mission but the woman had the requisite expertise to get the job done and had demonstrated so with her plan. Ursula had assumed it would be a long job, with technicians inside the shuttle detaching power and control cables, and the support infrastructure of the reactor. Vrease's plan was slightly more radical than that.

Ursula waited and watched. Raptors from the shuttle side of the base were now moving faster, rounding the range of the base guns as they headed towards the four armoured cars. But the two groups directly between the base and the shuttle seemed to be wavering, as if unsure of the shortest route to this new prey.

'I think it's about time,' said Vrease over com.

'We could wait a little longer,' said Ursula, 'until Trakken is at the warehouse and grabbing those supplies. That might get them on the move.'

'We can do this,' Vrease asserted. 'The rail beaders will keep back any Callum misses and we should be in and out in half an hour.'

'If you're sure . . .'

'I'm sure.'

'Okay. Gurda, ground the normal drones.'

She watched the wall as all the image feeds from the drones dropped out. The things would settle to the ground and await a start-up signal. She hoped they wouldn't lose too many of them – they'd become reliant on them since the prador destroyed the satellite.

'Callum, you're ready?'

New images began to appear on the walls. Some were from hard-wired base cams, others were from cams on two of the big new armoured cars sitting in a garage on the shuttle side of the base. A moment later, imagery started arriving from the hard drone, which was now miles up in the sky.

'I'm ready,' Callum replied.

'Do it.'

Two streaks of fire departed the top of the massif, their targets the two groups of cacoraptors. They wouldn't explode but simply reverse and settle down for a minimally hard landing. It wouldn't be very dramatic. They were EM pulse weapons, whose sum purpose was to disrupt the cacoraptors' communications, hence the reason they'd needed to go over to hard wiring in the base, and use a hardened drone for laser com and cam imagery, as well as ground the usual drones. Of course, Ursula could see nothing of it now. A minute or two later, the weapons landed and fired up. The audio screamed and Ursula shut it off.

'Okay, Vrease: go.' She had to rely on Vrease's expertise in this and didn't like doing so. She remembered a sign Macannan had had on his desk – an ancient thing supposedly made out of wood actually from Earth. It had read: 'The Buck Stops Here'. She felt she should have a similar sign in her vicinity.

Viewed by base cams, the garage doors ground open on the shuttle side of the base. Two of the new armoured cars came out of them, immediately kicking up sprays of earth as they went to emergency speed. One of them looked like an animal infested by a horde of insects, for it had robots clinging to its armour. Four of their precious mosquito autoguns were there, and three other robots mounted with multiguns, plus the mountings and tripods to fix them to the ground. The second armoured car pulled a large trailer, with one of their big construction robots squatting on its front half. Vrease had repurposed it to the task in hand and one of its heavy limbs sported an iron-burner. Other limbs had chain-diamond cutters, ceramic shears and heavy grab claws. It was also carrying a load of planar explosives, whose blast cut two-dimensionally and would be used to cut through heavy frameworks on the shuttle.

'Laser com?' she asked.

'Established outside,' Gurda replied. 'Trakken is online too now.'

Ursula supposed she'd asked out of nerves, because the screen-painted wall still showed feeds from the cams on all the cars. She watched Vrease's two for a while, then turned her attention to the feeds showing Trakken's four armoured cars. Raptors, which had located them before the EMPs shut down their communication, were closing on them fast and even as she watched, one of the cars opened fire. The weapons on those cars consisted of pulse cannons, simple machine guns and lasers. The view was not as good from the cams on the hardened drone, but cams on the cars gave her a clear view of dog-form cacoraptors running through the pulse-gun fire, the ground erupting in hot explosions all around them. Some went tumbling, with pieces shredded from their tough bodies. She saw one in the lead nailed by a laser, burning as it ran, peeling skin to reveal skeletal asbestos-white form. A machine gun focused on it and sent it sprawling in a tangle of splintered limbs. They had this at least: when the things transformed to resist heat, that made them vulnerable to the ceramic bullets the machine guns fired. Or that had been the case thus far.

As Trakken's cars approached the warehouse, Vrease's cars were beginning to draw in towards the first of the two groups of raptors between them and the shuttle.

'All yours, Callum,' she said. 'Hit both groups.'

Six more streaks of fire departed the top of the massif. These missiles contained high explosive wrapped in ceramic shrapnel. The hardened drone view gave three detonations on top of each of the two groups of raptors, but the flashes, the fire and clouds of debris and dust concealed the full effect. She turned her attention back to Trakken. His cars had reached the warehouse and slammed down the walls, allowing the two with trailers to go in. The other two, which had reversed outside again, began to lay down fire on the approaching raptors.

'This can't last,' said Trakken.

'Stick with it for as long as you can,' Ursula replied. He was right – the creatures were too tough and the weapons he had weren't powerful enough.

She looked at cam view from Vrease's cars. They were driving across smoking ground. Ursula switched on audio from the cams and also heard the railguns firing. She caught glimpses of raptors coming through the smoke and shredding, some going into the ground. Another view showed her the trailer car hitting some, and others clinging to the trailer. Scouring shots from Vrease's car threw them away in pieces.

'Seems to be working,' said Callum.

Ursula didn't feel quite so optimistic.

The two cars cleared the area of the first missile strikes, travelling at high speed and leaving raptors in their trail. Some minutes later, they hit the second spot and it was just a rerun of the first. They cleared it and finally the shuttle came into sight. The cars slowed, with the raptors in the distance behind them. Meanwhile, raptors had reached Trakken's cars and were attacking the armour, while he was just managing to keep others from entering the warehouse.

'Fuck and damn!' Trakken exclaimed.

'What's the problem?' she asked.

He gave no reply. The two cars in the warehouse abruptly sped out, having dumped their trailers, then all four started heading back towards the base at full speed.

'They came up through the floor,' he finally told her.

'Okay. Stay frosty.' She concealed her disappointment that the distraction had ended so soon, but at least the bulk of the raptors were over there and not at the shuttle.

'Deploying,' came Vrease's brief comment over com.

The car that was loaded with robots shed its cargo by the shuttle's hull while the other one reversed the big trailer up against it, adjacent to the reactor's location. Mosquito autoguns sped for the ramps and went inside, in case there were cacoraptors in there. The other robots moved out to form a perimeter, opening the tripods that were part of their bodies and driving in ground spikes. They then folded up the multiguns and began fixing the hydraulic mountings.

On the big trailer, the construction robot also folded out its limbs and moved to the hull, firing up the iron-burner with an arc glare as it thumped against the hull. It tracked round, cutting deep, with molten composite pouring to the ground.

'Fuck – something's wrong. They're not after Trakken any more.'

Ursula glanced to the infrared map from the hardened drone. The red glints of cacoraptors were moving away from Trakken's cars, back towards the base and, she had no doubt, intent on rounding it and aiming to the shuttle. She could even see them coming out of the warehouse. Their communication had re-established.

'Vrease. The other raptors are coming.'

Cam views showed Vrease and two others out of the cars and shifting gear towards the shuttle. Still others had come out with pulse rifles, laser carbines and a couple of tripod-mounted missile launchers.

'Yeah, I know.' Vrease replied. 'We still have time.'

The iron-burner completed its circle and the robot gripped the chunk of hull, also reaching through between the glowing edges of the cut. From inside came the flashes of detonations. The chunk came free, and the robot discarded it with a dusty thump on the ground. The mosquito autoguns then emerged, their telemetry showing there had been no cacoraptors inside. With this, Vrease and the other two leaped up inside, their combat armour protecting them from the glowing edges of the hole. The construction robot went through directly after them.

By now, surviving raptors from Callum's missile strikes were approaching in dog and heron form and moving fast. The railguns on the cars fired, shredding them as they came, and taking them down in pieces, without any of the other weapons needing to be deployed. Ursula looked at the infrared map and watched all the other creatures approaching.

'You good in there, Vrease?' she asked.

'All good,' Vrease replied distractedly over a hiss of com interference.

Flashes of light came from inside the shuttle. Ursula pulled up views from the three suit cams in there but interference was bad. Transmission via laser to the hardened drone, then the base, gave no problems, but the cams were using radio to transmit to the cars, while the EM pulse weapons had yet to burn themselves out. However, Ursula did get a glimpse of the reactor – spherical and ten feet across. The robot was up against it, cutting through struts with its chain-diamond cutters. Vrease and the others were meanwhile hurriedly detaching what they could without cutting, so as to rescue as much of the surrounding hardware as possible.

'Trakken's stopped,' Callum commented.

A glance at the hardened drone view showed the four cars had halted. Even as she watched, they turned round and began heading back towards the warehouse.

'Trakken, what the hell are you doing?'

'We can't afford to keep losing equipment. The raptors are after the shuttle now. I can load those trailers and retrieve them.'

Ursula felt a flash of annoyance at his disobedience, but then reconsidered. The constant attacks of the raptors had been steadily eating into their reserves and on this mission alone they'd deployed almost too much to lose.

'Good call,' she said, 'but be careful there, we don't know if they all left the warehouse.'

'I'll find out soon enough,' Trakken replied.

The raptors approaching the shuttle were kicking up a storm

of dust. They were moving horribly fast and Ursula feared Vrease's defences might be overrun at once. Colonists operating the tripod-mounted missile launchers fired first into the approaching horde. Shrapnel ripped through the raptors, then the disc explosions of planar explosives cut across a few feet above ground, smashing limbs and causing further devastation. Had this been a human army, it would all have been over by now. But though these blasts shredded many of the creatures, and sent others severely damaged burrowing into the ground, still more came on.

'Vrease, what's your status?'

'Replying to irrelevant questions when I want to work,' the woman snapped.

Ursula glanced across at Callum and shrugged. Callum's expression indicated that he accepted Vrease had a point.

Now the railguns and multiguns began firing. Vrease had them working in concert. The multiguns were using lasers and pulse cannons. When the raptors became heat resistant, the railguns nailed them. But still they were drawing closer and on the satellite map Ursula could see many rounding the shuttle.

'Damn! She should have closed the ramps!' she exclaimed.

'It was proposed,' Callum said calmly, 'but would have required setting up a new power supply. The raptors took out the drive and all connections to power sources.'

'Right.' Ursula stared at the image feeds as she absorbed that. Why? she wondered. Why take out the drive and not destroy the power sources but only disconnect them? If she were thinking in terms of an intelligent army then there could be only one explanation: the cacoraptors had been preserving them for later use. But surely that was crazy?

The colonists outside the shuttle had now abandoned their missile launchers and were shooting with rifles and carbines only. More resources gone; they'd used up their missiles. Ursula saw cacoraptors now heading up the ramps into the shuttle. She was about to com Vrease about it but stopped herself. A moment later, she had to say something.

'Raptors entering the shuttle,' she said.

'I fucking know,' Vrease replied.

'Status?'

'Nearly done.'

The robot had closed its limbs around the reactor and begun rolling back steadily, power and control cables and other surrounding structure trailing behind. Before it reached the hole through the hull, the mosquito autoguns returned.

'Get out of there now!' Ursula shouted.

'Got it covered,' Vrease replied.

'Damn you!'

'Tetchy,' Vrease said, but no more because weapons fire filled the interior. In the hazy images of the suit cams, Ursula saw mosquitoes clambering through frameworks and firing continuously. A detonation cut a bright line through shadow – a planar explosive. She caught a glimpse of a rearing cacoraptor with extra limbs sprouting from its front end. Somebody screamed. Other explosions ensued and the feed became too chaotic, with too much interference for her to be able to interpret anything.

But the robot, with the reactor, managed to reach the hull and rolled steadily out onto the trailer. A figure jumped out after it with someone else slung over one shoulder. Cacoraptors emerged in pursuit but the railgun on the trailer car turned and fired into the ship. Ursula clamped down on the urge to shout for explanations. The colonists were retreating and someone had issued a recall on the multigun robots. They uprooted their tripods and kept firing, returning to their car by slow degrees, but their shooting was now inaccurate as they moved. The colonist carrying the casualty fell inside one car. Two others piled in afterwards, and the door closed, just in time for a cacoraptor to run into it head first. The construction robot had now secured itself, still holding the reactor, and as the two armoured cars pulled away, someone rescinded the order to the multigun bots. They spiked down again and opened fire with more accuracy. But even as the cars accelerated on emergency, the cacoraptors overran the guns.

Ursula scanned for personnel. They were all inside the cars but for one. Checking suit cam imagery, she saw that Vrease's cam was offline. Something tightened up inside her until a voice said, 'Mullins is dead. The things tore him to pieces.' She then felt guilty at feeling such relief from this news.

Memories of Nursum near death came to Ursula as she trudged reluctantly into the tank room. Oren was there with Callum, and the two medtechs. In the tank floated a human body in a nest of tubes and wires, legs and arms stripped down to the bone, part of one side of the torso missing. But the head was still intact and undamaged, and recognizably Vrease.

'What's the prognosis?' Ursula asked.

That Vrease could survive such traumatic injury was by dint of Oren's original nanosuite, just as with Nursum. But this opened up whoever had this suite to a world of pain beyond what could normally be survived, as it also had with Nursum. If Ursula had had any religious inclinations, she would have said it was a deal with the Devil.

'We've nerve blocked her,' said Donnaken, 'so she's no longer suffering. Though' – he glanced at Oren – 'we don't know how long that will last since the suite even interferes with the nerve blocker.'

'But she can survive this?'

Donnaken shrugged. 'I think so. She'll be months in the tank, however, and I think it'll be necessary to do some memory editing. She suffered too much.'

'There is of course a faster way,' said Oren.

Ursula had no need to ask. She'd already seen the bracelet he'd brought in and put conspicuously on a nearby surface, before she stepped over, swept it up and pocketed it. Lars and Donnaken knew something about Nursum's advanced and risky treatment, but not the whole story and she didn't want them to.

'Is it necessary, and do we want another Nursum?' she asked. 'We all know there's something not quite right about him now.'

Oren frowned at her, then looked pointedly down at the bracelet she wore. 'Nursum's . . . oddities are due to his brain injuries and not the . . . treatment. And he would have been worse without it, supposing he had even survived.'

Ursula shrugged an acknowledgement, though noting how Oren had spoken in certainties about something highly complicated which he could not be certain about. Yes, the colonists would all receive the upgrade, as she'd agreed with him, but she wasn't sure in this case, with Vrease so severely injured, it was a good idea. She also felt, after what she'd done, that Vrease was owed some say in this.

'But the choice is not ours to make for Vrease,' she said. 'Nursum was incoherent and near death, which isn't the case here.' She turned to Donnaken. 'You've installed the vocal reader?'

'I have.' Donnaken nodded.

Ursula nodded back. After her own experience in the tank, she'd now made it procedure to enable someone in there to be able to communicate. The reader interpreted vocal nerve signals and put them through a voice synthesizer. 'Wake her up.'

Donnaken headed over to the console that Oren had installed himself behind and gently nudged him aside. Oren flung up all four arms and moved. Donnaken worked the controls and in the tank Vrease's head shifted from side to side, then steadily directed towards them.

'How bad is it?' her voice issued from the PA and Ursula couldn't tell that it was not actually hers.

'Donnaken?' said Ursula, handing the baton over to him.

The man faced the tank. 'It's not just the extreme damage to the muscle and bone, but digestive, or perhaps more correctly, salivary enzymes have killed much of the remaining cell mass. Your internal organs are damaged by the same substance but can be recovered – in fact they are recovering. Much of your torso bone and muscle has experienced cell death too. Your limbs require total regrowth, which will take months.'

'And the alternative,' Oren could not resist interjecting.

Donnaken looked to Ursula.

Ursula cleared her throat, wondering just how she herself would have responded to such news, then said, 'As command staff, you know we used a more risky treatment on Nursum. If you have that, regrowth will be much faster.' She turned to Oren and nodded.

'It can be done in mere weeks – even faster if you're conscious,' he said. He was about to say more but Ursula interrupted him.

'That's your alternative,' she interjected.

Oren stared at her for a long moment and Ursula felt a bit disgusted with herself. All the colonists would receive the upgrade bracelet when it was ready, but she wanted to keep a lid on what it was really about until after that.

A long pause ensued, until Vrease said, 'And then spend my time wandering about the base muttering about burning figs. I don't have the time for that. But I don't have the time for lengthy regrowth.' She paused for a second and asked, 'My mind, my brain is good?'

'It received some cellular damage but the nanosuite acted to preserve it,' Donnaken replied. 'This is why your major organs aren't so bad – the suit preserves the essentials for survival. This is why, despite his extreme trauma, Nursum still has a mind.'

'I have too much to do,' said Vrease. 'I must work.'

Ursula felt Vrease was wishing for the impossible, but then something about Lars clicked in her mind, even as Lars spoke out.

'There is a further alternative,' she said.

When everyone turned to look at her, Lars walked over to a nearby cabinet and opened it. She took out a metallic skeletal arm with joint motors and other electronics all down its length.

'The components I have here are all high-strength ceramal – practically unbreakable. I also have syntheskin and muscle. These can be set to match her current physiognomy and nerve impulses. She will of course notice the difference but it'll not be extreme. She'll also be able to upgrade her strength and sensitivity as she chooses.'

'How quickly can I be out of here?' asked Vrease.

'Perhaps four days for the initial installation, depending on how much of your body you want replaced. A return to the tank for two days for interface regrowth, then after that final installation it'll be a matter of hours. You'll need time subsequently to become accustomed to it.'

'Do it,' said Vrease.

'One moment,' said Oren, raising a finger, which didn't have quite the same effect since it was on one of his subsidiary arms. 'There are likely to be nanosuite conflicts, as with some of the cerebral implants others have had.'

Ursula gazed at him. There certainly had been conflicts and problems, though not with all implants, and now something occurred to her.

'But it seems,' she said, 'you have no conflicts at all.'

He turned and looked at her, blank-faced. 'All my enhancements are synthetic organics with nanofilters to block the nanites.'

'Then you can turn off her nanosuite, can't you?'

'What?' He seemed affronted by the idea.

'Most of her body will be synthetic with the prosthesis. Correct me if I'm wrong, but I assume she won't need the enhanced nanosuite to protect what remains. Her organs will be wrapped in ceramic bones, syntheskin and synthemuscle. It will have no venous system through which something could be transferred.'

He shook his head. 'There will be access points and, as we have seen, our machinery can be just as vulnerable as ourselves.'

'But much less vulnerable, and of course she can wear the "skin" directly over her new body.'

Oren nodded to the tank. 'Her head and face will be vulnerable, should she expose them.'

Vrease now interjected, 'Hey guys, I'm right here.'

'So what do you think?' Ursula asked. 'The choices are all yours.'

'I think that my face and my skull go with the rest of the damage. I know Lars has all the components for a full Golem chassis.' She paused, then added, 'Maybe my organs too.'

Ursula didn't like that at all. It was precisely the kind of radical changes they had come here to avoid. She remembered the suit her old commander in the Polity military had demonstrated to her, and how it could copy to crystal the human mind inside it. What Vrease was proposing was going that way: the steady transformation of humanity into AI.

Lars said, 'We can't dump your organs, we don't have the tech to support a human brain alone, other than in that tank, and we . . . Polity science does not yet extend to fully recording and running a human brain in crystal.'

Ursula nodded agreement to that, but privately wondered if Lars was right.

'So, this is what Vrease wants and it can be done,' she said, staring directly at Oren.

He continued to stare back blankly but after a moment conceded, 'Yes, it all seems perfectly feasible, though I'm baffled as to why you don't take the better option.'

Ursula didn't know whether his quick concession made her more suspicious than if he had continued to argue his case. She wondered again what agenda Oren might be serving.

'Then all is good and we know what to do.' She turned to the tank. 'You're sure about this, Vrease?'

'I'm sure.'

'Get to work, people,' Ursula said, and headed away.

Over the ensuing days, she watched Lars, who'd been a prosthesis cyberneticist in the past, remove Vrease's damaged limbs, even her ribs and her spine, and then, apparently after another discussion with Vrease, her skull. The intricate operation lasted nearly two days. Supported in a framework, and fed with such a nest of tubes and wires and other mechanisms, the remains could only just be seen. They hardly looked human at all. Just living meat.

Over the next days, Lars conducted the 'initial installation'. This resulted in a human torso wrapped in ceramal ribs and spine, a brain supported in a web of bone-white plastic and limb stubs that twitched as the whole was moved back into the tank. Oren had been in attendance throughout this and helped where he could. A way of allaying suspicions? Lars mostly worked through a telefactor, many of whose routines were already programmed. Ursula observed Vrease in the tank and spoke to her for a while. The next time Ursula saw her, she was sitting naked on the side of a hospital bed, and how much of what was there wasn't human she couldn't discern.

Vrease's movements were jerky at first and she often walked

into things. When Ursula asked Lars if this was normal, the woman had replied no, it wasn't, but Vrease had not opted for the prosthesis to match her previous body, instead choosing a steady climb in strength and speed of nerve impulse. It occurred to Ursula that this was probably a response to how badly hurt she'd been before. No cacoraptor would have such an easy victim in Vrease again. Was this the new route of human development for the colonists? No, because it was quite normal in the Polity, and certainly in their military. Vrease was just a diversion; a side shoot from their new evolutionary tree, whatever that might turn out to be.

13

Present

Oren stood before her. A maglev plate, which worked only in the corridors of the car, hovered behind him like a patient dog. The charred remains of the lone cacoraptor Vrease had attacked, and which Lecane hadn't completely rendered to ash, lay on it wrapped in plasmel. He'd requested, over com, that they be collected and Ursula had demurred, until he argued that this raptor probably had no connection with the others and as such was worthy of the data it could provide. She didn't tell him that she already knew that to be true. He added that if it was one the others had left behind, it still might have data worthy of study. She didn't disabuse him of that either and in a flash of irritation she'd agreed. It was only after closing com again she remembered that she still had so many questions to ask him.

Since then her intention to speak to him had slid to the back of her mind. The things he knew, or might know, were important, but not essential to the current mission. Yet, there had been time. They had protean plans of attack but they were utterly dependent on the final situation they encountered. Callum had proposed that, since the car could move faster than the prador ship, it might be an idea to head straight to the radioactive seabed and prepare an ambush there. This was something she had to think on.

But now Oren stood before her.

She gaped at him, trying to remember everything she needed to ask and it all seemed to skate about in her mind. Sure, she remembered the main questions, but the detail seemed vague to her now, the logical chains broken. The arguments she'd prepared that Oren could not simply give formulaic pat answers to, or otherwise circumvent, seemed to slither from her grasp. She stared at him. She'd been moving around the car quite a lot over the last few days and had, in passing, visited his lab a couple of times. Both times he'd not been there. Often, when she thought about him and ran a trace, he was always elsewhere and busy, or something else came along to grab her attention.

'It's as if you've been avoiding me,' she said.

He smiled mildly and shrugged. 'We've all been very busy. I've been doing some interesting work with Nursum. It seems that when the first strangler fig attacked him it left a lot of its genetic material stuck to his bones. The upgrade incorporated that and perhaps this accounts for his erratic behaviour.' He began walking, the maglev plate following him obediently.

'Yes, Nursum,' she said. 'Was the cacoraptor genome you used in him different from the one you used in the rest of us?'

He glanced at her. 'It came from the one in my lab. Because I wanted to use what appeared to be a more advanced and active genome thereafter, I used material from cacoraptors brought down by the multiguns. So the answer to your question is maybe. To trap the one I had in the lab, we sent the car to what looked like an outlier since where their population was high the car would probably have been destroyed. Why do you ask?'

'I can't connect to him in the way I can to the rest of the colonists. He is not *family*.'

'I see.' Oren was expressionless. 'That's very interesting.'

She shook her head angrily. This talk of Nursum was a

distraction and she couldn't let him lead her off course with it. She fell in beside him, marshalling her thoughts, but still struggling to find the clarity that had been available to her recently.

'I have some further concerns,' she said.

'My goodness, don't we all,' he replied. 'We're on a hostile world being hunted by lethal predators, while ourselves hunting lethal aliens, and meanwhile transforming into something uber-human.'

Distraction again. She wanted to pursue that uber-human comment but would come to it in order. First, questions.

'The Polity has been highly concerned about Jain technology,' she said. 'The few artefacts that are found are always grabbed and stuck in secure storage. I feel damned sure that those on display and under heavy security in the Viking Museum are the least of them. There are AIs whose sum purpose is tracking this stuff down. It's been made illegal to possess it, even though Polity law has few strictures on what people can possess, including lethal weapons.' She took a breath, and he jumped into the pause.

'Incorrect. It is legal to possess personal weapons but illegal to possess highly destructive weapons on populated Polity worlds.' He tilted his head thoughtfully. 'Though of course, there are exceptions for mining and the like, and spaceship owners are effectively in possession of such. I think it comes down to the initial purpose—'

'Jain technology is highly dangerous and the AIs are looking for it all the time,' Ursula interrupted. 'The Polity survey of this world was directed by AI. How then did this AI miss the Jain ruins exposed down on the surface here?'

He glanced round at her, that irritating smile still on his face. 'Are you supposing I have inside knowledge of this? I've no idea how they were missed, not a clue.'

She gaped at him, not sure how to continue. She'd expected

him to offer up various explanations, each of which she would destroy and then she hoped to push him to some kind of admission. She felt sure that he did have inside knowledge and was somehow complicit in all this, and that was the premise she should work from. Was she wrong?

'You knew about them,' she said, and it sounded weak to her.

He kept walking and spoke without looking round at her, which of course he was more than capable of doing with his revolving head. 'When it became evident that the prador were heading to that seabed for radioactive elements, I looked again at the Polity survey. I got curious about what were marked as crystal formations and took a look at them for the first time. Only then did I realize they looked like the remains of Jain structures.' Now he did revolve his head to look at her. 'I sent a message to ECS seeking clarification on this but, as you are aware, they were, and probably still are, a bit busy in the Polity. I received no reply.'

'An AI missed them yet you recognized them at first look,' said Ursula stubbornly.

He faced forwards again. 'I could offer up explanations but I see now that you think I am somehow complicit in all this and so doing so would seem as if I am making excuses – trying to cover something up. There are Jain ruins here. The Polity survey AI missed them.' He shrugged. 'That is all I can say.'

'I would like to hear your explanations, whether or not you're involved.' Ursula grimaced at the back of his head. 'I'm baffled by all this and seeking explanations myself. It's merely because you told me about them that I have come to you, and I see now that you not telling me would have been more suspicious.' It all sounded plausible to her ears, though she was lying through her teeth.

He shrugged again as the door to his laboratory ahead opened for the maglev plate and it slid in. 'In the Polity, we live under the rule of the AIs. Most Polity citizens regard them as infallible so it is a little-known fact that they fuck up, sometimes quite badly.' He stepped into the laboratory after the plate. 'It was watching a news report about the secession and revolution on Grayson's World that gave you the idea of joining the military, wasn't it?'

'Yes, it was.' Ursula followed him, wondering where exactly he'd picked up that nugget of information.

'Accepted writ is that the AIs occasionally allow human rule because they know it will go wrong and be an object lesson to the rest of the Polity. This is simply not true.'

'So what is the truth?'

'Planetary AIs get bored. The mechanics of running a world are not something they really have to think about – they are all simply dealt with by algorithms and automated systems. Only crises require some thought and since most things are controlled, even the weather in some cases, they do not occur very often.'

He stopped talking and just stood looking at the items on the maglev plate, so she prompted: 'Grayson's World?'

He looked round. 'The AI there started thinking about those areas of U-space mathematics that are as yet unresolved. It internalized, losing itself in virtual mathematical space. Crises did occur: a virus destroyed many crops, a solar flare disrupted some of those automated systems, demand for experts in certain disciplines on another world resulted in many of those specialists leaving Grayson's World. The AI considered what it was doing more important than dealing with these problems and ceded full control to humans, who were already dealing with them. Further problems occurred and it ceded more control. Then came Separatist infiltration. By the time it realized the extent of the world's problems it was too late to stop what occurred.'

'Too late to stop all that death and destruction?' Ursula asked.

'Intervention too early would have resulted in a publicity win for the Separatists. It would have been seen as too dictatorial, autocratic and totalitarian. The AI calculation was that the civil disorder, disruption and deaths across the Polity as a result of that would have exceeded what it turned out to be on Grayson's World. They had to leave it until it reached a point where intervention was voted for by the citizenry of that world and would be seen as the right thing to do by the majority of Polity citizens.'

'I see.' Ursula looked around his laboratory, annoyed at how she'd been led off track. 'So this was just an illustration of how AIs fuck up.'

'Of course,' he said. He stooped and began taking items from the maglev plate and storing them away.

'Right. So an AI whose one job was to scan through survey drone data got bored?'

He shrugged – it seemed something he was becoming quite adept at. 'I have offered one explanation, as you requested. There are others. It could have been a drone fault. It could have been misallocation of importance. I'm sure you can think of some of your own.'

'But it wasn't just Jain ruins the AI apparently missed. We have a massive almanac covering the life on this world and the biologists and ecologists tell me that the only thing they've discovered that's not in that almanac is microscopic life, a few small bugs and other explainable life forms . . . and the cacoraptors. How the hell did the Polity survey miss such a lethal apex predator but manage to get everything else?'

Oren leaned his backside against one of the work surfaces.

'And that is where I start running out of explanations,' he said. 'The only plausible one I can come up with relates to predator-prey numbers and what seems to be the Jain genome they have inside them. Supposing I am right about that.'

'Please go on.'

'It could be that they encyst in the ground or leave eggs or nymphs that only develop into fully fledged cacoraptors when prey numbers rise to a certain level. Maybe they were somnolent when the survey was done, or exceedingly rare. And just maybe it was the arrival of the alien, us, on this world that impelled the growth of their population – their Jain component responding to that.'

Ursula nodded, feeling Oren dragging her down into complexities.

'Oh, and another thing,' she said. 'You didn't use the upgrade like the rest of us.' She pointed at the bracelet on the wrist of his main right arm. 'That's doing nothing.'

'I wondered when you would get round to that.'

Don't you dare shrug, Ursula thought, just before he did so.

He continued, 'I am not a colonist. If it is ever possible, I intend to return to the Polity and my work at ECS. I wish I could be there now – I desperately want to be there now. I have no need to change and adapt myself to this world. I just put this on so as not to be resented as an outsider.'

'I don't believe you.'

He grimaced. 'Okay. I have to admit that Nursum had some influence on my decision. I had my doubts about what happened to him. I didn't want to endanger the working of my own mind.'

'But you thought that perfectly fine for the rest of us?'

'It was, and still is, a matter of survival. And are you not all more able to survive now?'

'Yes, because of the changes we've been undergoing. Very specific changes.' She paused, now getting into uncomfortable territory. 'We have surmised that the original raptor controls the rest of them, like some kind of hive queen. We've seen it. It consciously controls not only them but the changes they undergo. It makes the different versions of them—'

'No,' Oren interrupted, holding up a finger. 'You have no evidence to support that it *consciously* controls their changes. Besides the fact that consciousness is highly debatable territory anyway, it could be that the changes other raptors undergo are either an individual response to circumstantial need or a response to the controlling raptor's non-specific need.'

She stared at him. She'd detailed none of what had happened with her – about how she could control the changes in other colonists – and she'd told no one of her concerns about the changes she could not influence. Yet here he was answering her questions before she'd elucidated them.

'Lecane, Caulter and Nursum – all changing in ways that make them effective weapons, but not only against the raptors, against the prador too,' she said.

'Consciousness is an illusion – bubbles rising to the surface of a pool. We are going up against the prador and this is a concern for all of us. In yourself it may not be something you're always thinking about, but it is bubbling away in your subconscious all the time. In them, it could also be a response to that circumstantial need.'

'You know too much,' she said.

'No,' he snapped and it was the first time she had ever seen him apparently angry. 'I did not get to my position so high up in ECS out of luck. I know what I know because I am intelligent, logical and assess everything, and listen to and remember every smallest data point that comes my way. I do not know too much. You know too little about me and consistently underestimate me.'

She didn't know what to say. All her doubts, suspicions and conjectures had fallen like seeds on hot stone and were dying there.

'Now I have work to do, and so do you,' he said.

She clenched her teeth, nodded to him once and departed. As she headed back to the control room, she felt she'd been played by a master manipulator and that he had lied to her on every point. She knew now that she would get nothing from him and would need to work her way to the truth, or truths, herself.

Familiar scenes appeared on the screen-painted wall above the consoles. The prador assault craft was down again, this time in what had once, a very long time ago, been a river valley. The great vessel only just fitted into the cleft where it'd landed, with its armoured flanks touching the rocky slopes on each side. Trees resembling palms had established and filled the place. It was almost a monoculture there and Ursula remembered why, from the general details about these plants. Their tap roots went down deep, sometimes for as much as a mile, while upper roots were much like the roots and branches of the Nursum's Fig. They grabbed and dragged stray animals or mobile plants down into the ground to crush, mince and mulch them as further nutrient for the trees. The scales on the trees were diamond sharp and as well as bubbling out a nasty mix of toxins and acids, as seemed usual here, and these sublimed into a neat combination of something akin to a mixture of chlorine gas and a selection of nerve agents. These last would probably be no problem for the prador because she doubted they were breathing the local air, but those roots . . .

'And the cacoraptors?' she asked.

'As we surmised,' said Callum, 'they moved on ahead of us.'

One view tracked up the side of the valley and over onto the Bled. Here she saw creatures scattered across the sand and rocks – cacoraptors, almost certainly. She could see them travelling in spirals and lines, and their movement seemed oddly regular. Ursula glanced at vector and positional data along the base of the image. The drone was low but seemed to have captured the main group, though she spotted small groups of the creatures moving away. The view fixed on it for half a minute then abruptly pulled away. As it did so, Ursula glimpsed one of the demonic fliers rapidly approaching, with two other things behind it that had wings shaped like those of albatrosses, but reptilian. They had two ball-shaped heads whose surfaces resembled those of compound eyes.

'I can't keep drones there or the fliers will take them out,' said Callum.

Military, Ursula thought. *Get rid of the spotters.*

'But image density is good and we can get some detail now,' he added.

He flicked back to the recorded feed of the cacoraptors, and began focusing in on it. Ursula was surprised. Screen data put their number at just under five hundred; she had expected more. Heron forms seemed to predominate in the interior, dog forms to the outsides. Here and there she saw ones like those that had got inside their car. She also saw a group of what looked like people, only their skin was grey and their features seemingly half formed. But identifying this or that shape only gave her a partial grasp on what she was seeing because there were many shapes they'd not seen before. Larger creatures roamed there too – things the size of brontopods but with a decidedly more predatory look. There were fewer of the worm forms, she noted, probably because they couldn't travel so fast.

'Why are they out there and not attacking?'

'The valley is a barrier – I think even cacoraptors would get decimated by those trees – but that's not the main reason.'

'And that is?'

'The ship's armour and the techniques the prador are using now.'

'Explain.'

'First these.'

An image came up showing a disc-shaped object speeding through the sky. Dropping like a hawk, one of the demonic cacoraptors slammed down on it, raised it up to its clawed hands and tore into it, dropping it in pieces.

'The prador have their own cam drones and they had the same problem as us with them: get too close and the fliers destroy them. They tried to put up drones before heading out, then returned quickly to their assault craft the moment the raptors drew close. It didn't work so well. Fliers destroying the drones made coverage spotty and the raptors got to them. They lost a lot of their drones and two more of their number. But they've changed their strategy now.'

'How?'

'This.'

Another image came up of an armoured sphere floating in the sky. Ports were dotted all over its surface, while attached on either side were recognizable prador Gatling cannons and clusters of other objects, almost certainly weapons.

'It's either something they recently made, or pulled out of storage. Maybe they built up enough energy reserves to charge it up, whatever,' Callum said. 'They now have something to protect their spy drones and take down any fliers that get too close. With this in place, they have full coverage. It stays up for about two hours, then I suspect has to return for recharging. The prador get back to their ship in that time too and close it up.'

'But surely the raptor strategy should have been to close in around the craft? Maybe not here, but previously? The prador would have been forced to come out to achieve their objective or the raptors would have had the time to break into it?'

'That armour,' said Callum.

'Still impenetrable?'

'I bounced a multi-spectrum laser off it, and I managed to try a terahertz scan running between two drones before one of the craft's guns shot them down. The terahertz beam didn't even penetrate but I got a reflective splash profile with it and that, combined with the laser spectral analysis, has provided some interesting data.'

Ursula studied him both visually and through cacocom. His expression was hard to read now with the changes to his face. His eyes, which at first seemed to be taking on a compound form, because of their individual visual components, were separating. The right eye was now an extended ellipse. The left one had broken into two, the outer new eye having moved further around his head so it sat above his ear. Analysing the changes internally, she noted how he would soon have three-hundred-and-sixty-degree vision and be able to see all of the screen-painted wall as well as through the front screen. His head was bulbous and his nose had shrunk down to a nub, while his skin was completely bone white. But internally she felt his fascination and awe, and somewhat of fear.

'Tell me,' she said.

'The Polity data was right about the exotic metal components. There's stuff in there we've not seen on any modern elementary table. They are metals that should not be able to exist, that should simply fly apart at the subatomic level but are held together by what I can only describe as exotic meta-material alloying. Their metallurgy is way ahead of ours. Way ahead. It's even memory-form, and tough and hard beyond stuff the Polity makes on brown dwarf manufactories. As far as I can gather, it's even adaptive like our armour.' He waved an arm, trailing tendrils, at the surrounding car. 'But on a subatomic level. No chemical attack based on known elements can touch it – there's simply no key.'

'Yet we saw some of these ships destroyed,' Ursula noted.

'We did, but by major matter-destroying impacts and beam densities of the same profile.' He paused thoughtfully. 'The Polity is damned lucky to have even anything that could touch this stuff.'

Ursula absorbed that and filed it away for later inspection. Yes, the Polity did have those weapons, she had seen them being developed. Coincidence?

'So the raptors cannot get into that assault craft using their present methods. Their only way in is to create some major weapon . . .' Ursula paused thoughtfully. Thus far the creatures had not made any technology exterior to themselves – they'd just utilized whatever they'd picked up. Could that be a next step? Or would they create some major weapon out of themselves? She continued, '. . . or unless the door is open, but when it is open, the prador are not letting them anywhere near it. They could still have tried to starve the prador out. The raptors have to be aware . . .'

Ursula just stopped. Multiple facts swirling around in her mind had reached a point of integration. Aggression, resources, intelligence. She could see it now. The cacoraptors had changed a great deal. They were highly aggressive but were no longer after the alien invaders of their world for simple resources to ingest; they wanted to *incorporate*. They'd become intelligent and frighteningly so. They couldn't get into that ship but they knew Ursula was heading there. Maybe she was a wild card who might change the present circumstances enough to allow their penetration of the ship? Then what? Where did the incorporation end? In a flash of insight she went deeper. Aggression, resources, intelligence and *incorporation*. The creatures now understood that more

291

resources lay beyond their world. They wanted that ship, not just to take it apart and incorporate it, but to use it to get off-world.

In a surge of horror, she wondered just how far their plans had run and how early they had begun. Was this why, when they destroyed the drive of her shuttle, they'd left the reactor intact? Surely that was madness. Could they really have worked out what was wrong with the prador assault ship and predicted Ursula's response? She shook her head. No. Why ambush the car if it was bringing what they wanted, and if it was the wild card they wanted? Their attack on her shuttle had just been tactical. They wanted to isolate the colonists on the ground and had gone straight for the primary objective, the shuttle drive, because that was a sure bet to prevent lift-off and they didn't know how long they would have for their sabotage. Ursula sending in the mosquitoes had proved that. There also might be other factors regarding the reactor. Perhaps it had been left as a lure for later on. Or had it been left as a possible later resource? She winced, a pain between her eyes, integration falling apart. So many possibilities. Had they understood the concept of 'off-world'? Had they realized that the shuttle drive was incapable of taking them further than local space? She turned back to Callum.

'I think they're too aggressive to go the starving-out route,' he said.

Only as he spoke these words did she realize she'd run through all these chains of logic in just a few seconds.

He continued, 'I reckon they're waiting for us. We're a wild card that may change circumstances enough to give them access.'

She stared at him, wondering if he'd been getting spillover from her mind.

'No, I considered that,' she said. 'If that were the case then ambushing us would have been counterproductive.'

'Yes, of course.'

'Unless that became their strategy after their ambush failed.' Again, too many possibilities. She would have to do some serious thinking about this, integrating raptor tactics and logistics. She grimaced. It seemed that since their arrival on Threpsis, her military training had steadily displaced other goals.

'Anyway.' He shrugged, tendrils all around him rippling. 'I also ran a computer pattern analysis on the raptor movements and I found this.' He gestured to the screen wall.

Red lines highlighted the spiralling areas in the mass. She watched them breaking and reforming, smaller spirals splintering away. She watched it for a while as the computer sketched straight lines, highlighted parties of raptors forming up, then breaking from the exterior of the mass and heading away. *Foraging parties*, she thought. The integrative facility of her mind began to key on it, to recognize an overall pattern, but before she got there, Callum spoke again.

'I suspected chemical communication now they know we can intercept their other forms. The other stuff keeps changing and still we can't get computer translation. I reckoned they were taking precautions and using stuff we can't tap into.'

'No translation,' Ursula said, only realizing she'd spoken aloud when Callum paused and Vrease turned to inspect her. She'd almost forgotten that Callum had been working on their EMR com. She turned an inward eye on her own efforts in that respect and knew, with utter certainty, that she only needed further exposure to it for a lot to fall into place.

'Continue,' she said.

'I'm not so sure about the communication form now,' said Callum. 'But it still seems they have to be close and on this . . .' He pointed to the screen. 'I've pattern matched a primary source right at the centre.' With one finger in the air in front of him, he drew a frame on the screen wall, and it focused in. He turned to her and now she could read his chagrined and frightened expression. 'Look familiar?'

The creature had the same body form as the ones that had entered the car. It squatted amidst a mass of other raptors. Its two upper arms were free and moving, as if in some complicated sign language. Its lower arms were branched, spreading tendrils into the surrounding mass of creatures. It was bone white, as were the tendrils and the surrounding creatures they plugged into, just like Callum had plugged into the control room crew.

'Obviously a useful strategy,' said Ursula, blank-faced.

Creatures breaking away from the central raptor faded into the surrounding raptors, gaining colour as they went. *Messengers. Information.* It was the way this central raptor connected to the rest without using cacocom. The sophistication was terrifying. Ursula peered at the central creature. Was it the original they had first encountered? In the present scenario, that seemed highly likely, yet she had doubts. Studying it again she noted the pattern on its head shield. It wasn't the same. Something shifted in her mind, the patterns before her, and now this creature who aped Callum formed a rough template over the EMR com she had memorized and been working on.

A component, she thought, seeing the whole swirling pattern. *Not the whole.*

'However,' she said loudly to draw Callum's attention back to her. 'If we were becoming them, then you would be in command or I would be sitting where you are right now.'

He nodded mutely.

She continued, 'We've been altered by our nanosuites and the cacoraptor genome, but we are still integrally human.' She wanted to believe that.

'Perhaps the nanosuite prevents utter transition,' he conceded.

She stared at him, feeling something else falling into place in her skull – how Oren often talked of the nanosuite as if it made decisions and choices and was not just blunt nanomechanics. But of course it was a complex system and, like a computer, it would ape the same. It was nothing more than that, surely? She felt the urge to go and question Oren once more, but put the idea aside. She wouldn't go to him again until she had something solid.

Near Past

The combat armour pulled on the same as usual – the reactive layer being only on the solid segments of it. Ursula put it on fast. She'd spent so long in the regrowth tank and missed so much. She wanted to know how her colony was establishing. Once she had it on, she hit a control on the wrist console and the layer grew and connected up between segments. She observed veins and capillaries writhing, the tessellations of scales shifting and mating up.

The divisions between biotech and mechanistic tech had long ago blurred from existence. Arguably, they had never really been there since 'mechanical' had been made from the 'organic' long before the cornucopia of present-day artificial materials. Stuff like this skin over her combat suit had been around for a while, so why did she feel such disquiet in observing it now?

'Presumably it extends up over the helmet when I raise it?' she asked, gesturing to the neck ring out of which the concertinaed helmet would rise to cover her skull.

'Yes, it does,' Callum replied.

'And the chain-glass visor?' she asked.

'None of the acids have yet touched the stuff. Toxins and some persistent sticky molluscs come off in the astringent wash,' Callum replied.

295

And now she put her finger right on the root of her disquiet.

'So why not make this outer covering, at least on the solid segments and helmet ribs, of chain-glass?'

'Oren said the fabric between, on the movable area, would still have to be protected, and that the seal between chain-glass and this stuff' – he gestured at the covering – 'is difficult to make secure, for the same reasons chain-glass is so impenetrable.'

'Ah, I see.'

Quite probably the movable areas of the intervening fabric could be scaled with chain-glass in some manner. She had no doubt this idea had been mooted and then knocked down by Oren's expertise. Had she been conscious and not busily growing organelles in the regrowth tank, she would have made the decision to try the known technology of chain-glass first rather than something highly advanced and based on life forms they didn't yet fully understand. Oren always leaned towards the complex and organic and she couldn't help but feel this was driven by the goals she had perceived in his work. But this was probably almost unconscious on his part and she shouldn't fall into paranoia about it being motivated by some secret agenda.

Ursula touched another control and the helmet concertinaed up out of the neck ring. She couldn't see it, but doubtless the covering was now growing up over that. She turned towards the clean lock exit to the outside.

'Let's go,' she said.

Outside, the flash of a laser distracted her for a second. She returned her attention to the pink rim around the edges of the visor she'd closed up in the lock. It seemed stuck in place by rows of small suckers like those of an octopus.

'We're finding it's best to hit them hard the moment they appear,' Callum commented, 'then burn right down to the seed.'

She looked to the laser again. A small robot running on treads had just flamed some growth to ash. The laser – a long cylinder on a short hinged arm – moved into an upright position directly over this mass and fired again. Intense light flashed and rising smoke picked out the deep green beam as the laser cut down into the ground.

'How deep?' she asked.

'Generally about six inches down. They're those tumbleweed things. The plant itself is static, while the tumbleweed head detaches and rolls away, inserting seeds in fertile ground with a moisture content above a certain level.' He gestured around them. 'Since we burned this place down, all the earth here is suitable for it, and many other plants.'

Ursula nodded, belatedly remembering that Callum couldn't see that with her helmet and visor in place. She gave a thumbs-up, walked out a few paces, then turned round. The base curved round the massif in either direction. Scattered along the outer wall were windows and clean lock doors, while over to her right were larger motorized doors. These, she remembered from the schematics, were the garages where they kept their vehicles. Here and there buildings extended out from the walls. Parked by one of these she saw an armoured car with a trailer behind it. Using a small crane, a couple of colonists were unloading something in a net that looked like an uprooted tree stump smeared with blood. It began to shift as they moved it to a conveyor leading into the building. Here samples that had been collected in the surrounding area went to be packed, sealed, frozen or otherwise immobilized and preserved, to go into base labs for further study – she knew a lot of this stuff was going to Oren.

Above the base walls, she could make out the occasional higher observation towers and the jut of the massif. She noticed movement up there and turned to walk further out, but then an armoured car running on all-terrain wheels and heading towards them drew her attention outwards. Beyond it, she noted the derrick and surrounding installation where a well was being drilled. Running out from this, another vehicle was laying the first pipes of an irrigation web from a great reel on its back. Far over to the right of this, printer bots were erecting other buildings – one of the factory units to supply their needs.

'Those ore deposits and other materials?' she asked as she walked out.

'A couple of teams and drone flights are confirming the survey. The geologists are quite excited by it all. Lanster wants to start strip mining that ore field at once. He says it has all and more of the metals we need.' Callum pointed into the distance. 'Over there we've got coal we can use for the energy and carbon, though Lanster and others are not so enthusiastic about using that at once.'

'Why?'

'It was laid down here before the sun changed. Apparently it has lots of fossils and other evidence of this world's prehistory, if we can call it that.'

Further out from the main wall, Ursula got a better look at the base. The rim wall stood twenty feet high and behind it the complex was packed right to the bottom of the massif. Thin-stemmed mushrooms of towers rose out of this, with detector gear tangled all over them like epiphytes. Using the focus in her visor, she got a closer look at the massif itself. An elevator was being constructed up the side of it, while on top the surfacing machines had levelled large areas, no doubt filling crevices with foamstone so nothing nasty could lurk there. On one flat area stood cone-shaped objects that looked like holes into midnight. These were ninety per cent solar collectors and another source of energy. Uplink dishes had also been erected to connect to their satellite, which the cargo ship had deposited in geostationary orbit above. This would give good imagery and be used for radio and laser com on this side of the world. But its main purpose was to be a link back to the Polity, for it contained a powerful U-space transceiver. Gurda, who ran this communication, had suggested they have another one on the ground, but Ursula had scotched the idea. They were supposed to be an independent colony.

The armoured car drew to a halt. Vrease and a man she recognized as Callum's brother stepped out. With Callum at her side, she began walking over.

'Seems likely this will be our main means of transport for a while,' she commented. As she drew closer she asked Vrease, 'What have you done with the grav-cars?'

'In storage for now.' Vrease shrugged. 'We can't armour them like this unless we amalgamate the engines for three cars into one. Power supply issues then make the whole exercise unfeasible.'

'I'll need a full report on that,' said Ursula, heading for the car. She paused and looked beyond it, seeing some tall figure heading in from the Bled at a slow painful walk. She realized it was the fig-like plant she'd seen flee before the burn. She actually recognized it.

'It's been walking this way for some time,' said Callum's brother. 'It's a predator of other plants here so we've left it alone for now. Might actually come in useful later when we start trying some crops.'

He worked in agriculture, she remembered. She stepped into the car to take a longer look around the base, and to put on her diplomatic hat to talk to the various groups at work. She realized she had so much to catch up on. Eight hundred colonists, most of whom probably didn't bother with the antediluvian need for sleep, and their stock of robots, had done a great deal of work. She tried not to resent that she had missed that.

★　★　★

I can breathe, Ursula thought.

Time had slipped past so quickly since she had first pulled on the new combat armour. Even so, perpetually having to look at the world through a visor had palled. The oxygen content of the air here was lower than Earth standard, but all the colonists, in fact most humans in the Polity, had lungs and haemoglobin genetically altered to handle a large variation. It was something that had been done in the early years of space travel and now as integral a part of the human genome as fingers or eyes. Their lungs could also deal with many dust particles and debris that would have had an early human coughing and spluttering and suffering allergic reactions. But here things were worse because many of the microbes and spores they could breathe in were ridiculously hostile and found the wet environment of the human lung a perfect growing medium.

The latest nanosuite update had given them all wet coughs for a week. Ursula, as seemed the case every time Oren put in a new update like this, found herself eating voraciously. The changes added feathery brush filters in their throats to snare the worst of it, whereupon their nanosuites killed it off. It also added substances to their lung linings just a few molecules away from the protective gel that some of the plants here grew on their leaves, as well as having a cellular structure copied from the lung lining of a creature like a four-legged spider. Both of these helped snare or delay harmful substances and micro-biota so their nano-suites, which had first initiated these changes, could now, with their expanded shit list, identify and attack. The only outward sign of the changes was an expansion in chest capacity, and a slight thickening at the base of the throat. They looked like swimmers in a world without open water.

She closed her visor and returned to her suit's air supply, filtered from the surrounding air. The new update worked well but Oren and other biologists had by no means found and made defences against everything. Best to limit air intake on this world. Prior to this update, three colonists had ended up with particularly persistent fungal growths in their lungs that required removal and replacement of lung mass. That same growth now didn't spread so virulently, but it did persist and resulted in dry coughs that lasted for weeks.

Returning to her armoured car, Ursula ran the purge, then raised the visor again. She opened her lunchbox and eyed the remaining sandwiches. The meat was tank grown and the lettuce came from the new hydroponics unit out on the edge of the Bled. However, though the yeast was home grown, they had brought flour and other ingredients with them. She ate voraciously, picking the crumbs out of the box afterwards. No sense in wasting stuff that was in increasingly short supply.

Nothing would grow here or, rather, none of the food crops they planted could survive the hostile microbes and larger local life forms. They'd expected that a degree of tinkering would be required, along with specialized poisons and techniques to deal with that, but a series of failures had brought home the fact that they needed a new approach. More hydroponics units and other methods of enclosed farming? The greenhouses were working fine . . . But no, they had come here to adapt to this world and find a new direction for humanity, though that second goal came with a large degree of vagueness. Oren, of course, had some answers:

'We can modify our food crops to more closely match local flora,' he had said. 'This will give them the protections they need though, admittedly, still with some assistance from us.'

'Xenogenetics?' Ursula had frowned.

The updates that had enabled them to breathe the air had concerned her, with their inclusion of structures and molecules from local life. Again this was the vague line she felt anxious about crossing but didn't really know why. In that particular case, she quelled her anxiety with the knowledge that no gene transfer had been involved, just the copying and modifying of molecular structures which the nanosuite then applied.

'It's almost inevitable,' said Oren. 'There is, however, another problem: the more we modify the plants, the more indigestible the foods will be for us, and the more treatments they will require. If we go for minimal modification, the crops will be labour intensive with the application of treatments during growth and probably the extensive use of agribots.'

Ursula grimaced at that. The little robots resembled long-legged spiders with pincers on their forelimbs for pruning and weeding. They sported micro-lasers and sprayers for an increasing gamut of chemical treatments. Recently they had all required memory and programming expansion to handle updates, almost keeping pace with those of the nanosuites. But, though rugged in terms of dealing with crop pests on most worlds, they'd suffered here from sprays of acid and the attention of herbivores with mouth-parts like industrial shredders.

'So either way we'll have problems,' she stated. She knew he wanted to go the xenogenetic route and was waiting for his inevitable proposal.

'Not necessarily – again it is the colonists that need to change.'

'Go on . . .'

'We transfer genetic traits from local plants to our crops, and we transfer traits from the local animals to us, so we're capable of digesting them.' He noted the look on her face and continued, 'Yes, it is xenogenetics but as with all genetic modification it will be accurate and specific. It cannot be otherwise, what with the difficulties of transferring genes from local life, with its different bases, helix and its particular equivalent of RNA.'

'And of course you'll be certain that the transfer won't affect anything beyond digestion?'

'Genetic modification has been safe for centuries,' he stated emphatically.

'Yes, it has been with all forms of *Terran* DNA.'

'Not just Terran DNA but also manufactured DNA, with extra bases, different helical structures and different RNA.' He shrugged. 'This is quite commonly used in heavyworlder adaptations.'

'When you say safe . . . can you give statistics on that?'

'Individually there will be variation and of course everything is dependent on what we use. By the time we move from lab to actual recipients, most of the dangers will be gone, and any remaining, such as the propagation of cancers and new viruses, can be handled by the nanosuite. This is very unlikely to kill anyone.'

Ursula nodded at that. 'I'll think about it.'

He'd led her away from her area of anxiety, which was not so much about the danger of colonists dying, but the degree of change to their humanity. Again she was experiencing qualms. On the one hand their whole aim here was to transform and take an evolutionary leap, but her feeling was that she wanted this transformation without losing any essential humanity. Her whole outlook on this was hazy and that annoyed her intensely, as did the fact she'd been more wrapped up in that than the danger of these changes killing people. She needed to think long and hard about it all but, even as that thought occurred, she knew where this would go. Her own brush with near death had illustrated that perfectly. They would begin using the alien genome. She couldn't allow her vague moral qualms to hamper the success of the colonization here.

14

Present

Gurda brought the car down on open Bled, devoid of any large masses of vegetation or concealing rock fields.

'We're clear, it seems,' she said, 'unless the fuckers are underground again.'

'Unlikely,' said Vrease. 'This is way off the course we were taking. And anyway . . .' she looked at Ursula. 'I don't think we're their main target any more.'

Ursula nodded. She'd spent hours in her cubby working with a computer, as well as her wristcom and holographic display, sometimes even resorting to a pen and paper. It was as if her old commander Macannan had prepared her for just this scenario. Since she'd been deeply integrating tactics and logistics, she could see how preparing soldiers to operate without augs would be a necessity when going up against a highly technical alien enemy . . . like the prador. EMR would be high during battle and com would keep dropping out. She'd played with the thought for just a short time before returning to her main concern: what were the raptors doing, what had she missed, and was there anything she'd failed to integrate? She thought she had it now but could never be certain with such open-ended inputs to the formulae – one example being the extent of the raptors' transformational capabilities and, of course, their intelligence.

'They hit us in this car for resources only: us, our weapons and most certainly the reactor. But their main target is the prador assault craft.'

'You're so sure?' asked Vrease.

'No, I'm not.' Ursula glanced at her. 'I am presupposing a consistency that might not be there: that they remain xenophobic and are out to accumulate and incorporate resources. It may be that they just want to remove the alien from their world. My calculations indicate otherwise.'

'But you're sure of their course now?'

'I'm sure,' Ursula replied. 'Hundreds of raptors passed us in the air and on the ground and those that attacked the car had none of our weapons. We've seen that force of them near the assault craft, and none of our weapons are there either.'

'Very well,' Vrease said doubtfully.

Ursula turned to Callum. 'Put the reactor online.' Then to Gurda, 'Take us directly to that dry seabed.'

'Last chance for a change of mind – if we run the reactor up as high as you want, it will take a long time to shut it down for transport out of the car,' said Callum, and she was glad he did. It showed again that he wasn't completely subject to her will.

'Do it.'

He nodded and she felt the surge of power through the car. She was a lot more sensitive to it now because of her links to all the colonists aboard. Gurda lifted the joystick and the car heaved into the sky for a flight that would last over a day.

'They could just be scouts looking for opportunities ahead,' said Vrease. 'They could have abandoned the weapons as ineffective.'

Ursula quickly clamped down on her rising irritation with the woman because it showed hints of turning into something else. Just like Callum, Vrease had every right to question command decisions. Again, Ursula's annoyance had more to do with Vrease being *not one of us*.

'It's not just the raptors we saw pass us,' she said. 'I reviewed the cam and drone data we've been collecting en route. I ran searches on large animal remains and other stuff, and compared it with the earlier Polity survey and our own. I've detected the remains of hundreds of brontopods and other large animals, from very small amounts of indigestible materials. I searched for scavenger concentrations but found none, and only a handful of lone scavengers. There were only a few other animals too, and when I looked at concentrations of plant growth, I discovered dust.'

'Omnivorous?' Callum wondered.

She glanced at him. 'Not initially, but if you can transform your body and are gathering up resources, it's a good strategy to adopt.'

'So, it's an army on the march,' said Vrease.

'I wish it was only that,' said Ursula. 'We left some drones back at the massif and I sent a signal to launch them to have a look around. The same swathe of devastation extends out around there for miles. This is an army that's been growing for some time – probably since the prador assault craft came down.'

The others were silent for a long moment, then Callum said, 'If they reacted to the craft like that then . . . they're very, very smart.'

'Back formation in the formulae,' said Ursula. 'They were smarter than your average unenhanced human when they took out the engines of our shuttle. Then they ramped up after that, and are heading into AI territory.'

There was another silence, into which Gurda interjected, 'So more of them than we saw by the assault craft.'

'A lot more.' Ursula pointed in the direction they were now heading. 'I made calculations on the basis of the remains found, as well as those probably not found, and on the destruction of plant and animal life. Also, basing this on raptors the size of those which got in here, though of course there's a lot of variation, there could be over five thousand we've not seen yet.'

'Fuck,' said Callum.

'But in terms of their intelligence,' said Ursula, 'there aren't thousands of super-intelligent creatures out there. There's just one.'

'How can you know that?' asked Vrease.

'Integration to sketch out the best fit to the data we have of them,' Ursula replied. 'Most of the raptors are the product of one original raptor. Like the fliers, it created them to serve a purpose. They're organic tools. Consider the attack on the base when they took on human form. To convince us that those coming in were people, the raptors not in human form attacked and tore apart many of these "people". Would highly intelligent, self-determining creatures sacrifice themselves like that? From everything I've assessed, I believe that their level of intelligence is just like their body forms – only what's required for their purpose.'

Her explanation was really a justification of what she'd felt every time she listened to their communications, and what she'd sensed from the cacoraptor she'd ordered out of the car, as well as other internal raptor communication data points she couldn't easily slap into a formula.

'Like social insects,' said Callum.

'Yes, and utterly subject to the control of the original raptor.'

'I think your statement that there's just one super-intelligent creature out there is wrong,' said Vrease.

Again Ursula suppressed a surge of irritation at the woman. 'Why?'

'A better description would be that there's only one will. Stating that highly intelligent, self-determining creatures wouldn't sacrifice themselves is anthropomorphizing. They could be highly intelligent. It is only the self-determination that is missing.'

Ursula took that like a slap in the face, and stood utterly still for a moment as she fought against an automatic response: to retaliate. Finally, she got her mind under control and ran her assertions under a critical eye. Yes, here was a problem with one will: it could be wrong but have no one to tell it so. Vrease's description also gelled with everything else she'd been sensing and had told no one about.

'You're correct.' She nodded. 'There's nothing to prove they're not all as smart as the original raptor. But also their organization, and the way they are shaped to purpose, does indicate that one will. Semantics.'

She integrated Vrease's correction and wondered if the original raptor ever did the same. She thought not. The fact there could be disagreement here was because they'd all had intelligence *and* will before the raptor genome had started changing them.

'There is one controlling intelligence, let's put it that way,' she said. 'This, I feel, gives us an advantage. When those three got into the car, they tried to incorporate us – bring us in under the will of the controlling raptor. When I said "most" of the raptors are the product of the original raptor, that was because, with this incorporation, other raptors have probably been subsumed under its will.' She only added this last because she really didn't want to get into stuff like how slippery the minds were of Nursum and that wild raptor they'd encountered. She really didn't want to tell them that the attempt at incorporation had been an easy option because they were *family*.

'And this advantage you mention?' said Vrease.

'Cut off the head,' Ursula replied.

'An assumption again,' said Vrease. 'Another may swiftly replace it.'

Now Ursula really started to have problems with her urge to retaliate. She gritted her teeth.

'You'll have to bear with me on this,' she said. 'I've been working the data for a long time and these assertions did not arise out of easy logic, but the integration of minutiae. I will say this, however. If there are other raptors that can take the place of the original, it will not be a smooth transition but a mental battle between previously subservient intelligences.'

Vrease snorted but didn't contradict her this time. Perhaps with her Golem senses she'd realized just how far she could push.

The seabed was lurid. It varied mainly from pale yellow to a yellow so intense it seemed to shine and leave afterimages on the eyes. Black and umber veins streaked through this, almost like cracks, and the whole thing sparkled with a metallic crystalline sheen. Even as the car descended, a steady clicking sound in the control room rose to a hissing roar until Callum turned off the Geiger counter. But Ursula still felt the effect in her body and bones, with the nanosuite and cacoraptor genome activity increasing. The latter seemed to be building up new laminations through her thick skin. How unsurprising, she thought, that it had a ready response to high radiation, which of course was a given in war between highly technical civilizations. She then analysed the idea: yes, cacoraptor behaviour was military, their adaptations could, as Oren had said, be put down to a hostile environment, but they came from the Jain and the hostile environment was almost certainly the battlefield.

'I'm picking up no local EMR chatter,' said Callum. He now had four eyes evenly spaced about his head. When Ursula thought about it, she realized that the alteration was almost redundant

309

since he could see the entire screen wall and through the forward chain-glass screen with the eyes of the others. But it was also the kind of redundancy you ensured in warfare, because any number of those other pairs of eyes could cease to exist.

'But of course,' he added, 'the background radiation here offers perfect concealment.'

'They must be buried and will stay concealed until the prador arrive, or they haven't reached this place yet,' Ursula opined, knowing it was a justification for her earlier decision.

Callum froze for a second and she could feel him accessing new data. She sensed the same data sliding into her mind even as it went into his, but allowed him to speak.

'I'm picking up steady seismic activity,' he said. 'It has the same profile as the borers but . . . bigger.'

'There, you see.' She glanced at Vrease, who simply frowned.

The car passed high over the seabed. All around, low reddish brown hills rose like the backs of whales, but rocks had been shoved up here too and one massif stood right at the shore of the sea. Gurda brought the car in over the top of this and cam views of its upper surface appeared on the wall. Lines and arcs seemed to map out and measure the features on the upper surface. Outlines of the car, as seen from above, appeared in numerous places. Gurda sorted through them until she found one lying in a deep hollow and then proceeded to take them down. The car dropped, stone rising up around it, and settled with a *crump*, juddering on the crumbling stone and tilting. Then its adaptive wheels and suspension adjusted to pull it level.

'I couldn't pinpoint a main source of those seismic readings. They could be anywhere,' said Callum. 'They might even be underneath us in this massif.'

He was right, of course, but she was still going outside. The car had one small remaining grav-car inside it that hadn't been sacrificed like the others for its construction. She'd decided to keep it for the maybes, with all the uncertainties of this journey and its aims. Her present excursion outside was for one of those, as well as to satisfy pure curiosity.

'Drones,' she said.

He was already launching them. A moment later views came up across the seabed, and across the Bled behind the massif, which was scattered with flat plates of stone. *Pure luck*, Ursula thought. She had wanted a place of concealment for the car and this massif, with the hollows in its upper surface, had provided. Pure luck could be rather a pain for tactical integration, requiring immediate adjustments to the formulae, to the plans, the logistics. But it was an occurrence of warfare that could not be ignored.

'Remember what happened when we first landed and explored this world,' said Callum. 'I ended up having to cut you open to save your life.'

'I don't think that can happen to us now, do you?'

'Still, though that grav-car has its protections, it could still end up being scrapped by local wildlife.'

'Yes, but you know how reduced that likelihood is now.'

He did, and she'd seen the statistical data. The number of flying things in this area lay far below elsewhere, almost certainly because of the radiation.

'I'm going with you,' said Vrease.

'No, you will stay here.'

'You're going to try and stop me?'

Ursula felt a surge of frustration. She'd tried to push Vrease as she was pushing all the others. Callum's easy acquiescence had nothing to do with any logical arguments she'd presented, but from Ursula using cacocom to force acceptance. She was about to say something more, but realized that getting into an argument with Vrease, here, would highlight the dangers of what she was about to do, and thence require her forcing further acceptance from Callum and the rest.

'Okay.' She shrugged as if it really didn't matter, but it did, very much so. 'Come on.'

They took up their weapons, always nearby each of them, exited the control room and moved back along the car to the hold space. Vrease said nothing until they finally reached there and stood amidst all the separate equipment they'd brought along: the reactor, radiating heat because of insufficient cooling, the weapons and tools, the packed robots and the remaining mosquitoes.

'You, of course, know that without your control over them this would have been seen as a very foolish decision, and perhaps one that would have been vetoed,' she said.

'I know.'

'But you're curious.'

'Yes,' Ursula said, because that was easier than trying to explain her primary purpose. Then she felt the need to add, 'Everything we've been doing has been of uttermost seriousness and to one end. Perhaps we need to make room for the occasional foolish act.'

She expected the woman to keep on arguing, but instead Vrease shrugged and said, 'I'm curious too.'

Ursula palmed the control to open the adaptive armour ramp door. Via com she told Callum, 'Close it when we're out and open it when we're on our way back.'

'Will do,' he replied, but via cacocom: '*But you're still going . . .*'

The grav-car was strapped down and Vrease was already undoing the straps as Ursula turned to it. They had it free of these as the ramp door crunched down onto the crumbling, slate-like rock outside. Ursula breathed the warm, slightly metallic air that wafted in. She was now almost certainly receiving a dose of radiation that would have been a death sentence to a 'normal' human of previous ages. She tilted her head as if to listen, but her 'ear' was the organ she'd grown as a collar and down her back, and which could *hear* anything. There it was: a brief hint of chatter, fading away. Now she knew for sure that her own senses in this respect were much more receptive than the instruments of the car. And of course the surrounding stone would be blocking much of it. All she was getting here was what bounced down from above and in through the open door ahead.

They climbed into the grav-car, Ursula taking the controls and Vrease beside her at a console that controlled its newly installed defences. It powered up smoothly and rose to a standard two feet above the floor. She slid it out, down the ramp, then adjusted its positioning relative to an arbitrary ground level and took it up past the car, past where drones perched on the surrounding lips of stone, and into the sky. The car lurched as she jerked the joystick and Vrease glanced at her with concern.

'The ruins are not far away,' Ursula said. She was also trying to cover over her physical reaction to the sudden upsurge in cacoraptor chatter she was receiving. She let it flow through her, into her integrating facility and semi-conscious routines, where she could deprogram it, and *learn*.

'Fortunate, that,' Vrease replied. 'I would have had to protest more strongly at you going outside if they were on the other side of the seabed.'

Ursula acknowledged that with a nod and wondered how she would have responded if Vrease had done. Attack the woman? Have her incarcerated aboard the car? No. Ursula would have found some other excuse for leaving the car.

They slid along above the erstwhile shore of the sea – a lip of pale stone seemingly rust-stained. One of the exterior lasers crackled and Ursula looked to Vrease.

'Something,' the woman said. 'Automatic acquisition. It might not even have been alive.'

Checking their position on the map screen, Ursula turned the car away from the seabed and up onto a stony plateau. She studied it. The flat and even area could have easily been dismissed by the survey drones as a natural feature, but what they then slid over she was sure they could not have ignored. The ruins glinted iridescent blue in the fading light of afternoon. Discrete triangles, twenty feet on the side, ran in a circle a mile wide. In from these lay a regular honeycomb of the same stuff. As she brought the car lower to look for somewhere to land, she began to notice posts protruding from the stone. These were triangular section and metallic grey, standing the height of a man. She found a clear area between the triangles and the honeycomb and landed.

'Let's take a look.' She popped her door, took up her carbine and stepped out.

The chatter grew more intense as further com radiations were no longer being blocked by the walls of the grav-car. Integrating this, Ursula now perceived larger patterns. She saw a map – a labyrinth of underground tunnels spread beneath the seabed, as well as a strategy for moving fast to any location, and a sum purpose pulling all of it together into a whole. She delved deeper, seeking elucidation, but then felt the attention of something swinging towards her and abruptly withdrew, closing herself off, for now . . . She found herself panting hot air and wondered if the heat was the result of the radioactives or just the day. Reaching back to the car, she checked through Callum. Yes, many areas within the seabed were putting out heat like defunct fission reactors.

'Is there any relation between the radioactives here and these ruins?' she wondered. Distraction, focus on this moment. Recoup, organize, integrate and return.

'It's stretching coincidence to think otherwise,' Vrease replied. 'But we'll probably never know what that relationship is.'

They stepped up to one of the posts. The thing was perfectly smooth and when she touched it, it felt cold. Vrease reached out and touched it too.

'The fuck,' she exclaimed. 'It's superconductor. There must be something underground sucking away the heat.'

'If we should stay on this world, this is a place that bears close examination,' said Ursula. She examined her own thought processes as Vrease gave her a puzzled look. Why had she thought about staying here when their singular aim was to leave?

They moved on to the honeycomb. Here low walls stood two feet high. They were like blue glass, slightly opaque. Ursula was sure she could see something regular deep inside, like buried electronics. She suddenly remembered seeing a block of similar material in the Viking Museum when she'd visited it and the resemblance creeped her out. She'd have to investigate that further when they got back to the car.

'Five million years.' Vrease took out a penknife and opened it, reached down and tried to scratch the glass with a chain-glass blade but couldn't. She pressed harder, then grimaced when the blade snapped away from the handle with a sharp ping. Perhaps she still couldn't judge her own strength.

'And that's why they're still here,' she added.

Ursula looked around. 'Crystal formations, my arse. There is no way a Polity survey drone, or the AI that looked at the data, could have mistaken this for anything but what it is.'

'I agree.' Vrease gestured to one of the posts. 'When was the last time anyone found naturally occurring superconductor anywhere, besides under the surface of a black dwarf star? There's something going on here – some Polity subterfuge.'

They headed back to the grav-car. What else was there to see?

Ursula thought of Oren, of extracting information from him, but knew he would come up with the same explanations and excuses as before, if not agreement with her suspicions and flat denials of any knowledge. In her heart, she felt sure that he did know and was part of this 'Polity subterfuge'. But what could the Polity hope to gain by keeping this from them?

When they reached the car Ursula gestured Vrease to the driver's side. The woman shrugged and got in while Ursula paused to look back at the ruins speculatively. All the cacoraptor communication she had taken in was falling into place. She felt she had the outlines of their plan, of *its* plan. She also felt the shape of its mind – how utterly alien it was and how its components just didn't match any kind of human consciousness at all. Was this what the Jain were like, she wondered. Or was this some blend of the original life and that other destructive species? How could something so aggressive and singular have risen to a civilization capable of building anything? She climbed into the grav-car and, as Vrease took it into the sky, she opened herself to the cacoraptor com again, integrating it, taking as much from it as she could, even as that other entity once again turned towards her.

'Fuck,' said Vrease.

Ursula returned vision to her eyes in time to see the fliers descending.

Pulse-gun fire burned glowing holes in the area of the grav-car's bonnet which stretched out ahead of the front screen. The fliers that were approaching behind, as Vrease accelerated, were those that had first trailed the main car, armed with colonist weapons they'd commandeered. And now she could see more of them in the sky ahead.

'How the hell did you miss them?' Ursula exclaimed out loud

316

and through her other forms of communication, addressing both Vrease and Callum.

'We did see them, at the same time as you,' Callum replied dryly over com.

She got the gist of it over cacocom: imagery and memories. Holes had opened in the ground on the edge of the seabed near the ruins. Objects had shot out at high speed, shedding ablation layers, and out of these had rolled the fliers. Of course they could withstand massive acceleration, couldn't they all now?

A laser scored across the screen. Blinding refractions, chain-glass darkened. Something hit underneath too, the force of the impact driving them down into their seats and the car fifty feet higher in the sky – almost certainly one of the acceleration vessels she'd just seen.

'Got a passenger,' Vrease commented.

Ursula looked back to see pieces of armour and other grav-car structure falling behind them. Something exploded beneath, bucking the car again and leaving a black smoke trail. The console sizzled, sprayed sparks, and the grav-car plummeted.

'Passenger gone,' Vrease commented, just as blandly as before, while she tried to tilt the car into a glide. Ursula only just heard her over the growing roar of the wind and the ominous wrenching and clattering sounds within the car. She glanced back again – one of the fliers was falling away there, then snapping out its wings.

Could they survive a crash? Of course they could. The question should have been, could they survive whatever occurred after-wards? The car managed to stay in an attitude with its nose pointing up for just a minute before it began to tilt sideways as Vrease fought for control. She lost it and the car flipped, tumbling end over end. Ursula was glad of her safety harness, but still clung on so hard her fingers grew an inch and sprouted claws to dig into the upholstery.

'Let's hope it didn't wreck everything.' Vrease's tone was again level and clear over com, her lips unmoving. She reached out and punched a control on the console.

First came a thrumming sound, and then a bang. Abrupt deceleration would have slammed Ursula into the screen without the harness, without her claws, and without the hooked spurs she'd now extruded from her back to drive into the seat behind her. The car swung, at first nose down to the ground, which was passing excruciatingly fast below them, then tilted again until it was hanging at forty-five degrees. Ursula looked up. Two of the parachutes had deployed nicely. The third flapped in tatters beside them.

They continued to slow, lurid yellow ground sliding up towards them. The nose of the car finally hit the ground, ploughing up powdery seabed, covering the screen. It flipped to crash and bounce along the ground on its roof. With a hollow thump, the front screen disappeared. Ursula doubted the chain-glass had actually broken, just snapped out of its frame. The cab filled with salty sulphurous dust. She needed to keep moving to survive, Ursula felt, as she released her back spurs, and then her claws, while unclipping her safety harness. Grabbing up her carbine, she threw herself out through the front screen and to the side. She hit the ground on her back, momentarily crushed, and skidded along by the roof of the car as it bounced over her. Then she was tumbling alone through a dust storm. Bones snapped and just a moment later cohered, while muscle ripped and knitted again. She managed to turn an uncontrolled tumble into something balletic that flipped her along, avoiding the worst of the damage she might receive, while simultaneously protecting her weapon. She found herself skidding at an angle, heels ploughing up the ground, until she somersaulted over and came to her feet with just a stagger.

The dust storm rushed on past her, taking the grav-car and its tangle of parachutes onwards. It turned sideways and flipped the right way up again and finally, sideways on, skidded to a halt a few hundred yards away from her. She scanned around as a steady warm wind started to take the dust away, then looked abruptly upwards. Fliers were still up there, but distant descending specks. What now? She located herself, turning this way and that, until finding recognizable features around the edge of the ancient sea. Over there were the ruins, so about there . . . She could just see the massif on which they'd hidden the main car. She closed her eyes for a second, dismissing that input, and concentrated on the EMR, and the complex chemicals which were now in the air. But the EMR had died somewhat. Why? Of course, because it was mostly underground and the ruling raptor was shutting it down to avoid detection. But she felt movement and intent all around her, like some massive hand closing.

'Vrease,' she said, hanging her carbine by its strap and setting out at a steady lope towards the grav-car. The ground rumbled and, in an explosion of dust, the grav-car suddenly dropped out of sight, tugging the parachutes down with it. Ursula halted, seeing black movement in the dust. Something had come up from below to pull it down. She tried to break into a run, but the ground started to slide away under her feet too. She fell through a storm of dust and the crumbling matter of the seabed. The crust had been thin here and she found herself falling into a wide tunnel. Cacoraptors, shovel-handed, bulky things whose bodies were flat, ribbed and legless, clung to the walls. As she rolled out of the dust and debris, coming upright again, they turned blunt eyeless heads in her direction. Two of them slid down the walls towards her, while the others closed in around the hole above, and there began to jet something out of their wide open mouths. Through the communications she tapped into, she read their physical form and purpose. They were burrowers and borers and they were now sucking up material through their flat snakish bodies, then ejecting it, mixed with a resin. Like printer bots, they were rapidly repairing the damage, steadily closing the hole and shutting out the light.

Ursula adjusted her vision to infrared, as well as other emitted radiations in the growing dark. EMR bounces, echoes and information packets expanded her map of her surroundings. The tunnels ran down deep, like those of an ants' nest. She stooped over, her claws extending and hardening, while she suppressed the urge to grow other implements from her face. Before they could make any changes to themselves, she shot towards the two raptors now on the floor, swiping with her claws, even as Q-carbon crystallized on their sharp inner faces. She ripped in behind the head of one of them; the cuts weren't deep, but she carved along the body of the other to open tubules that spewed sticky resin. The first one thrashed, slamming its blunt head into her. She skidded back, then surged forwards again, spurs flicking out from her legs as they had on Lecane. Even as she did this, she was reading the creatures on new levels and looking for vulnerabilities.

Their simple brains were distributed, as were most of their other organs, so they had no single kill point. However, they'd been made for one purpose: to keep the tunnels open and repair any falls that might expose their presence to the coming prador assault craft. They'd not been made to fight. Through the com, she read the fading instructions they'd received to break the tunnel roof below the grav-car, and then below her too once they'd detected the vibrations of her movement above. Now they needed to hold her here for something else that was coming. She assessed and calculated, running tactical scenarios based on their structure, as she tore at them and they tried to wind themselves around her. Now she saw it. She darted in close and, in two swift moves, sliced down the lengths of their bodies, opening up resin tubules and the main artery for that substance. Past them, she hit the wall feet first, clawed toes and spurs digging in so she could effectively run up it. Perpendicular to the wall now, and clinging with those feet only, she reached back, grabbed for her carbine and opened fire.

At first the resin bubbled and smoked, but then the evaporant that enabled it to harden quickly reached ignition point. In a moment, the two creatures were writhing and making hollow booming sounds in oily flames. Ursula adjusted her vision again. The raptors above had closed the hole, but now she had burning torchlight to see by. These others also began sliding down the walls towards her, but abruptly halted. She sensed, and perfectly understood, the ultrasound instruction they'd just received, and she dropped to the floor again, ignoring the creatures. She turned, facing in one direction along the tunnel, where out of the shadows came a mass of raptors. Worm, heron and dog forms, along with others for which she had no easy description, filled the tunnel from wall to wall – a swirling mass rising like some nightmare liquid through a pipe. But just after they came into view, they simply stopped. Sinking deeper and deeper into the com, she grasped what was going on, and again understood the intent behind it. So she turned her back on the creatures and looked the other way.

It came first: a huge raptor with the body form of those that had got inside the car. It almost filled the tunnel. Its armour possessed the golden crystalline hardness she'd seen on Nursum, and it was stooped, walking partially on its forelimbs like a silverback gorilla. A cowl rose up over its lobster head, ribbed, extending down to a humped object on its back, which at first she thought was part of it, then realized was clinging to it like some large parasitic louse. Bone-white spines protruded between the ribs on this thing's back. And this hue was reflected in the creatures crawling along the tunnel walls all around it. These had the same number of limbs, but all of equal length, with long whippy tails and protruding spines, bird-skull heads that darted long tongues like those of hummingbirds. She recognized the format here as much the same as the small raptor force they'd seen out on the Bled. One of which Callum and the control room crew were a pale reflection . . . and herself, of course. As the big raptor became clearer, she studied it more closely. A shield of carapace, similar to that of the brontopods but almost baroquely ornate, protected the front of the lobster head and displayed patterns she recognized. Here, at last, she was facing the one who'd been their enemy all along.

'Well, come and get me, fucker,' she said, but her words seemed just a whisper amidst the racket of communication across EMR as well as with all the complex chemicals in the air – now a visible dust.

Her body was changing rapidly in response to the threat here, sucking on dense resources inside, expanding, and then growing support structures. She was utterly determined that, if she was to die here, she would take down this creature first. The com, swirling around her, seemed to fall on her. The creature was inside her, trying to force physical changes, trying to seize control of her mind and incorporate her. She fought back, level upon level, and reached out to the creature too, in turn trying to force changes upon it – trying to kill it. There was to be no physical battle here, then, just this. The bones in her legs peeled their sheathing and she collapsed to her knees. She realized she was losing against the tsunami of data input clawing into her body. She needed the colonists as a processing resource, but down here she could only catch fleeting utterances of the cacocom with them. She was being swamped. But something began to shift inside her.

Reformat control, full cognizance.

Oren?

No reply. Had she imagined his voice? Clarity washed through her, a mental expansion and a finesse of internal control. The asserted changes, and the attempt to seize her mind, were brutish and she began turning them away. She hardened her mental defences, her mind seeming to become a distinct fortress. Something was assisting her, something spread throughout her body and mind and at the root of her physical and mental being. With her mind now as clear and hard as crystal, she reached out, perfectly understanding, integrating communication, reviewing tactics and logistics even to nanoscopic levels. The giant cacoraptor jerked back. She speared into its network, supplanting its communications with her own. Creatures around it began to fall from the walls, coiled up in palsy. She groped through the network, reaching for its hard, stratified mind, penetrating layers, shifting things aside. She could take it; she knew she could take it.

The cacoraptor started to retreat but she froze its limbs and it juddered to a halt, shivering. A worm form slammed into her back and coiled around her, and she was suddenly in a fight for her life. Her grip slid away as she was forced to switch resources over to physical combat. Other raptors from behind swarmed in around her, as their big leader reached up and tore away the louse-thing on its back and ripped it in two. Her comlinks to it began to collapse and she lost sight of it as hostile creatures pressed in all around her, tearing at her. She fired her carbine one-handed into nightmare faces, ripped with her other claw, ripped with her feet claws, tumbling through the mass. Agony on one side as a thing like a hollow drill bored into her. Blindness as acidic tendrils swiped across her eyes. Then vision was restored through the organic com on her back.

Oh fuck, she thought. Yes, it seemed she might be able to win a mental battle against the creature before her, but this was a physical battle she couldn't win. She reached for them via their com but it seemed many of their minds had been hard-wired to this one task. Their leader had prepared them. She ended up pinned against the tunnel wall as claws and boring implements began to rip away chunks of her armour. She emptied her carbine, briefly used it as a club before shattering it, and returned to using all her *natural* weapons. She could see no good ending here. The things were simply going to rip her apart.

'*Stay where you are*,' said Vrease over com.

What?

As the intensity of their assault pulled away from her, Ursula felt the attention of her attackers sliding to one side. Something roared and light flared in the tunnel. She recognized it as the burn of thrusters. With its defensive lasers and machine guns firing, the grav-car shot up the tunnel and hammered straight into the massed raptors, smashing most of them ahead of it in a tangled heap. The machine guns swivelled, pointing at the roof, firing again to cut a hole through to the surface. Ursula needed no further prompting. Internally she adjusted, swiped a claw across the face of one attacker and sacrificed her lower left arm to another clamped onto it with diamond-hard teeth. She scrambled up the wall, briefly seeing the door fly off the car and something glittering and metallic shoot out. This hit the wall and started climbing too. Both made it to the top, then tumbled out onto the surface. Vrease was simply a metal skeleton packed with hardware now – all her syntheflesh and skin had been ripped away. Ursula had a moment of weird flashback to how she had been when she joined the military a seeming age ago. In that unenhanced state her survival in those tunnels would have been measured in seconds.

She and Vrease exchanged a look but no words, and ran.

Past

Ursula felt bereft without her aug. As if she'd been partially deafened and blinded. They'd ordered all enhancements to be removed and it had surprised her just how many she'd had. It had taken five hours under an autosurgeon, removing artificial muscle, a lung expansion, artificial cartilage she'd forgotten about, her triple-density fats and double-carrier haemoglobin. Followed by a day in a regrowth tank. All that remained was a basic nano-suite, because the removal of that would probably have resulted in her dying from a disease her immune system didn't even recognize. She felt weak, ineffectual and slightly ill. Gravity pulled on her with a tenacity she had never known before. The dry air seemed too thin and parts of her body ached for no particular reason she could identify.

'Poor bored Polity citizens,' said Macannan.

The line of recruits looked like lesser beings in comparison to him. He was huge – all boosted musculature and reinforced bones, twinned augs and other cybernetics showing at his neck, his wrists, and doubtless the cause of some of those bulky lumps underneath his uniform.

'I'm not a poor bored Polity citizen,' said one of those standing in the line. 'I've come to serve and frankly I'm not impressed by the way this is being run.'

Macannan nodded. 'I am sure you are unimpressed. That's because you're green, quite stupid without enhancements and have no idea how the Polity military runs, or what it takes to become a marine. You probably have some romantic notion about it all, promulgated by the media. If you're not satisfied, then walk away now.'

'So all this shit is to remove those who don't have enough determination?' the man asked. 'Is the Polity military incapable of identifying adults and giving them the training they require?'

'This process identifies the adults,' said Macannan. 'You will now shut your mouth or leave.' He turned to the rest of them. 'You all read and signed your agreements. You' – he pointed at Ursula – 'what has he just done wrong? You have permission to speak.'

'He opened his mouth,' said Ursula dryly.

'Quite correct. Outstanding.'

Recruits were to listen, obey and keep their mouths shut during the first week unless specifically given permission to speak. In the second week they could raise their hands to ask for that permission.

'This is all quite ridiculous. We are—'

Macannan raised a hand and something spat out of his wrist. The objector oomphed and flew backwards, electrical discharges spreading over his body, and landed with a dusty thump, unconscious.

Any violations of these rules could receive physical punishment to a degree set by the commanding officers. No punishment was to be excessive or cause permanent damage, while the recruit had the options to leave at any time. She never saw the objector again.

'Now,' said Macannan. 'I do hope you have all read and inwardly digested the agreement you signed.' He pointed to the man on the ground. 'I do hope no further clarifications are necessary?'

Nobody said a word and all abruptly remembered their instructions on how to stand to attention. There was a bit of shuffling too as the line straightened. Ursula nodded briefly to herself. The next few weeks were to drive the weak-minded away and she was damned if she would be one of them. She expected this to be hard and she kept in mind her memory of the marine on Grayson's World.

'Now,' said Macannan, pointing to a nearby grav-sled loaded down with large backpacks, which Ursula later found were full of sand. 'We're going for a run.'

She nearly quit on the first day but, after vomiting up her bland breakfast while Macannan grinned down at her, casually flipping a coin and checking what it revealed, she wiped her mouth and started her thirtieth circuit of the parade ground.

Every part of her body ached but her lower legs were particularly painful. After a week of physical training and then simply eating and sleeping, she wondered if it might be possible to die of exhaustion. She lined up with the others for medical inspection. Her turn finally came and she went in, lay down on the slab, and the scanner passed over her.

'Shin splints and some micro fractures in your arms and ribs,' said the decidedly unsympathetic medic. 'Go through there.' She pointed to one door.

Ursula expected to go into a room to receive treatment from an autodoc, but here an officer sat behind a table. He pointed to the chair in front of him and she sat and folded her arms since they hurt less that way. She said nothing – wise now about keeping her mouth shut. The officer slid a book plaque across to her, then a paper form, pointing to where she should sign. Both were so antediluvian, but she signed anyway, the pen still unfamiliar in her hand. Her signature came out right at last, since she'd only signed her name this way twelve times in her entire life, and all here.

'Over the next two days your nanosuite will deal with your injuries. During that time, you will read the books on this plaque. You have sixteen hours of reading time each day, two hours to eat and tend to other bodily needs and six hours for sleep. You will be tested on your comprehension on the morning of the third day before resuming physical training.'

The books were *The Art of War* by Tsung Tao, *Fool's War* by E. B. Heinlein, *A Military History* by Gordon and *Tactical Integration and Logistics* by Allan Blue, whom she recognized as an AI. Even using aug transfer and assistance programs, they were all books she could not have absorbed in less than a day each. Now they expected her to read and understand them in thirty-two hours? She raised a hand.

'You may ask a question,' he said.

'What will be the nature of this comprehension test?'

'Whatever we choose.'

'And if I should fail it?'

'You cannot fail it – it is an assessment. Leave now.'

She picked up the plaque and left.

Over the next two days her body tightened up into a new form as sleep and food had their effect, while the nanosuite sorted out her various injuries. She only later learned that everyone had gone through the same door as she had. She read the books and she took the written test, worried about her answers to the intricate series of questions.

'Well done,' said the officer in charge, handing her paper back to her in the dormitory. She went to sleep feeling immensely proud of herself.

The next day physical training didn't seem so hard, and it ended at midday. In the afternoon they were given the schematics of a number of ancient projectile weapons. Later they were given the weapons themselves, along with boxes of components, and told to disassemble them, identify faults and correct them. In the evening more reading arrived on their book plaques. This continued for a number of days, until they got the chance to use the weapons on the firing range. One recruit walked away with a shattered hand because he hadn't identified and corrected a fault with his assault rifle. He returned to training two days later with an artificial replacement hand.

More reading, lectures now too, written tests and, throughout it all, continuous physical training, including martial arts. Ursula found herself struggling to take in the information under the weight of exhaustion. Talking with other recruits, she discovered that her own 'education' had slanted away from theirs. She was getting a lot more on tactics, logistics and how to integrate these – reading and tests increased while the physical training was reduced. Though she found herself thinking more clearly, Ursula felt her mind under constant pressure, pushed to the limit. As she worked tactical and logistical integration now on three screens, having to create programs to join all the disparate parts together, she ached for some kind of cerebral upgrade and went to bed dreaming of supply chains and casualty figures. What kind of combat was this preparing her for?

15

The cacoraptors did not pursue them on the surface, but Ursula could sense them below and had mapped the layout of the tunnels in her mind.

'Stay with me,' she said. She was just about to explain but realized Vrease could receive more than mere speech over conventional com and could intercept cacocom too. Ursula relayed the map to her, and Vrease nodded her ceramal skull in agreement, metal toes digging into the ground as she kept just behind. Ursula ran a weaving course, avoiding thin crust where possible, leaping over those areas where it could not be avoided. Glancing back, she saw collapses and explosions of dust. She felt the lead raptor below, tentatively probing for her through these openings. She snapped back along its com, trying to get a grip. She couldn't seize control of the thing before it retreated, but effectively gave it a mental slap as it did so.

As her body rapidly repaired itself – severed arm regrowing so fast it smoked, bones, muscles and organs shedding damaged matter and tightening to efficiency, internal fluids adjusting to kill enzyme acids and poisons – she felt a supreme confidence. If she could just face that creature without physical threat, she'd be able to take it down – of this she was certain. But why? Her ability for tactical and logistical integration was of course part of it, but she'd been losing at first, until something else within her kicked in. She'd been seeking to open up processing from the colonists but this 'thing', whatever it was, had revealed a whole stratum of processing space and ability inside her. Oren?

She thought she'd heard his voice, but analysing her memory of it now, she saw it as just an interpretation of something that had occurred deeper within her. Illusion? Certainty about any of it evaded her; it was too obscure to perceive on that deep level.

'Do you want us to come for you?' asked Callum over com.

Cacocom was now coming through more clearly from the massif too. She felt his anxiety and probed more, as she could. He wanted to come and rescue her, but further urgency had arisen. The prador assault craft had arrived at its last refuelling point before it would make the jump here. She checked timings. If nothing else untoward happened, she and Vrease would reach the massif in half an hour.

'Stay where you are,' she instructed, but then wondered if she should have, as a series of tunnel collapses occurred ahead. 'Ah, fuck it,' she added.

With her internal repairs bringing her to optimum, she pushed for more speed. Her legs began to grow, further muscle weaving in. She saw how this could be improved from the cacoraptor genome. Her arms started to change and she stooped forwards, head extending, hands hitting the ground and changing, hooking, digging harder into the surface.

'I cannot . . .' said Vrease.

'On my back,' said Ursula, extending the hooks she'd used to hold herself in the grav-car seat. Vrease landed on her heavily, sending her staggering for a moment, but she readjusted for the load and, burning through the last of her fats, went into autophagy and apoptosis to eat those parts of herself unnecessary for this task. Dog-form, with her expanded lungs thrumming as fast as a compressor pump, she accelerated.

Cacoraptors erupted from the ground, bird-skulled and wormish, herons and dogs, human and grey, deformed. She dodged and weaved through them, swiped with a foot claw and left one of the human-looking ones headless, although she had to unsnare the tough fibres from her claw afterwards. The massif lay clearly in sight now as the herons and dogs came after them.

'Raise the car,' she instructed Callum. 'Just enough for clear shots.'

She leaped a hole from which spiked tentacles lashed up out of the shadows at her. Many of the raptors fell behind, but a persistent group of the faster ones closed in. Up on the massif, she finally saw the upper part of the car appear. Flashing and sparkling up there, like mica crystals in sunlight. Through the dust she'd raised, the lasers flared into visibility, burning into the pursuers as they shed skin and seemed to transform into skeletons as they turned asbestos white. The railguns hit next, destroying them, and chunks of raptor bounced past like shattered porcelain. Ursula ran amidst rocks, hit a wall of stone and scrambled up it. Glancing back, she saw the raptors flowing down into their holes again, while beyond them the other holes were steadily closing up. Vrease still clung onto her back.

'We're good,' she said to Vrease.

'Are we indeed?' the woman replied, a subtext to her communication being an image of what Ursula looked like now.

Remembering myself, Ursula thought, as Lars and Donnaken worked on Vrease, while shooting occasional wary glances at her. They weren't so conventionally human themselves. Bulky, like all the colonists, they had skin that had combined with the Polity combat armour they wore. Donnaken's eyes were big, blue and protuberant, while his nose had melded with his top lip, and the nostrils had moved to the front, so he now had an ape-like muzzle. His hands were long, the fingers like spider legs, and he had more of them than before. Lars meanwhile had retained a human visage, but like Oren she'd produced a new set of arms from her lower torso. These she used to move the synthemuscle and skin into place on Vrease, while with her other hands she did the delicate work of making the connections. But even the other hands weren't conventional. They'd appeared so at first, until she'd rolled back their glove-like covering to expose bone-white fingers that branched at their ends.

The door crumped open and a delivery robot arrived, stacked with food packages. Ursula felt she'd made enough revisions now and, with a crackling sound, stood upright. Hot vapour issued from her joints. Her arms had returned to their conventional form and her hands were opening out again, steadily retracting their claws. Her legs were still a bit short and, with another crackle, she adjusted the telescoping bones to return her to her previous height. She studied herself, externally and internally. If anything, the outer appearance of her body was more like her form before the upgrade, because she'd lost a great deal of mass. Unlike most of the others, she hadn't donned combat armour over her skin so didn't have that bulk either. The skin was growing back, but spreading slowly, with her energy reserves being so low. She took a package from the robot, the wrapping melting under her hot fingers, and opened it while walking over to a portion of screen-painted wall. She reached out and touched the wall and, via com, sent 'Mirror' to it. The screen paint obligingly obeyed and reflected her.

Her upper body was the right shape, but for the lack of breasts under the skin. She searched for memories of herself and made an adjustment. Vanity? Now? She tried to grimace with what remained of her face, but couldn't manage it without a mouth. She'd lost both her nose and her mouth – a smooth surface curving up from her throat to below eyes as large and protuberant as Donnaken's. Those other features had not been necessary during her flight. She looked at the food package and thought about a jaw, teeth and a tongue, but was almost sucking on empty and didn't have the energy for that. Instead, with some effort, she opened up just a vertical slot in this smooth surface and began to shove in chunks of cured brontopod meat and the hard nodules they used in place of fat storage. Inside, her intestines had waned to a simple tube but her stomach remained. The food dropped into there, where she injected tubes to extract the needed nutrients. Energy began to return, slowly at first as most burned in the process of digestion, then more rapidly as efficiency increased. She fed the food packaging in too, since the plastic could also provide energy. Trying not to touch anything that her extreme body heat might damage, she returned to the robot with a nascent jaw bone pushing out of her lower face.

'We're a mess, aren't we?' said Vrease.

Now feeding in the contents of another package, Ursula turned round. Vrease was sitting back upright and had a face, and hair, again. The visage wasn't hers, though the hair was the right colour. It looked like the bland face of a mannequin, but the attachments and muscles underneath made it shift and bubble, and slowly she began to look more like the woman Ursula knew.

'*Mess?*' she asked over com, since she lacked a proper mouth and vocal cords.

Keeping her mouth closed, Vrease replied over com, '*What will we be when, or if, we come out of the other side of this? Is your objective clear for us? Do you now know what you want us to be?*'

'*Us?*' Ursula enquired.

'I'm not one of you, of course,' Vrease said out loud.

Donnaken and Lars were working on her legs, hooking up syntheflesh and skin segments there. Lars stood and pushed Vrease almost brusquely to lie back down again. When they were done, she would look like the human female she'd once been. It occurred to Ursula that Vrease, despite being mostly machine, would be the one with the most humanity retained of them all.

'*If we do come out the other side of this,*' Ursula replied, '*we will be alive. That is perhaps the best we can hope for.*'

'Yes, but is there any longer an issue over survival?' Vrease enquired.

The question made Ursula feel very uncomfortable. She walked over to the mirror screen again, still shoving food into a slot that was now opening horizontally and closing up top and bottom. Her jaw aligned with a click, bone growth – though not really human bone – continued, and she felt the ache of teeth budding from it. As her mouth grew, a new tongue peeled up from the base inside and it felt strangely unnatural. She concentrated all her resources on her face, and on her vocal cords, even though the drive inside her was to make repairs and growth elsewhere, of things that had nothing to do with being human. Finally her face was back, and hair sprouted from her bare skull. She turned around again.

Lars had covered Vrease's arms and layered one hand with muscle and was pulling on a glove of syntheskin, making nerve connections as she rolled it into place. Syntheskin and muscle had all the nerves of the natural kind, though artificial, of course, but the interconnections to the underlying chassis were simple and widely spaced. A processor sorted out the signals for input into Vrease's spine. Lars looked up. She didn't appear so wary now, perhaps because Ursula had a face once more.

'It's nice to be able to do some of the work I'm supposedly here for,' she said.

Ursula nodded solemnly. Nobody was in the tanks or on the beds in this medical unit now. The upgrade had rendered Lars, Donnaken and other medical staff redundant. Already, via cacocom, she could sense them going on hold. They retained their sensitive hands, fingers and powerful vision but there had been no expansion of these. She would have to find a use for them – somewhere they fitted.

'Survival remains an issue,' she said to Vrease. 'There are still thousands of raptors out there, and the prador.'

'The raptors . . .' said Vrease. 'Do you think I didn't pick up on what happened in those tunnels? You ramped up, somehow became a lot more effective, and that creature ran away from you.'

Both Lars and Donnaken had stopped work and were watching her.

Ursula shrugged. 'Yes, if I can face it again while the rest of you keep the other raptors off my back, I think I can seize control of it. And then, the other raptors too. But the prador are still here. We cannot allow them to leave this world, because they'll be back to deal with us.' Ursula paused for a moment, other factors integrating. 'And even if they don't come back for us, they'll return for what they've either seen, or will soon see, on the edge of that seabed.'

'Jain ruins,' said Vrease. 'But only if they know what they are.'

Ursula acknowledged that with a dip of her head and turned towards the door, taking the last of the food packages as she went. As she headed for the control room, she considered the implications of her last assertion. Had the prador already encountered Jain technology? Maybe their armour came from that source? She thought not, judging by what Oren had told her about it. Most likely their metallurgy and their armour arose from the psychology of what they were: armoured creatures. But if they did get hold of Jain tech, they could become even more dangerous. She halted abruptly. Or if they got hold of the Jain/ cacoraptor genome? What weapons might they create, or become? The thought sat in the forefront of her consciousness, then she absorbed it into integration. She felt closer to some truth now, though still it eluded her.

Past

Everyone in the runcible arrivals area of Port Ensolon seemed to be auged and, looking around, Ursula wondered if that had drastically limited access to information via other routes. It had been some time since she had been here and then, while in the military, she had worn an aug and so had not noticed things like this. Since being dismissed from the military and having to deal with the problem of ennui all of her age faced, a great deal had changed. But she still questioned why she'd had the aug removed. Sometimes she felt naked, sometimes free, but mostly, she surmised, she felt *separate*.

Shouldering her backpack, she moved deeper into the large arrivals lounge, looking for an information terminal. She noted that most of the people here were military. Many wore the uniforms of ECS commandos and marines, others wore the more reserved clothing of monitors, and even those in other clothing she identified by their manner as military in civvies.

It was busy here – more so than she'd ever seen before. She wondered if there had been some blow-up with the Separatists but didn't think that likely. Though the self-styled anti-AI terrorists of the Polity were a constant thorn in the side of ECS, they never warranted high military activity. Usually their plots were foiled earlier on by AI analysis, followed by cuts to their resources, some neatly placed propaganda and slight alterations to any weapons they'd obtained, followed by swift, quiet arrests. If that didn't work, then the brief, and often violent, application of agents or monitors tended to do the trick. Calling in the military would be a last resort, since it often resulted in a mess only slightly smaller than the one the Separatists had been predicted to cause.

Noting there was an information terminal available, she decided to use it a little later, instead walking over to a long chain-glass window which wrapped around one side of the lounge. This gave her a view across a huge paved area to the next containment sphere – half sunk in the ground and enclosed by other buildings, silos and warehouses. Behind these buildings, a raised spaceship platform cut across the emerald sky, ships lifting from it on decidedly undramatic grav, with only the occasional bright spurt of a steering thruster. In the containment sphere sat a cargo runcible, while the platform was mostly for local in-system transport. It was busy here too, and nearby the paved area was crammed with cargo containers. She couldn't see what most of those cargos might be, but in some cases she could.

She knew that a long plasmel-wrapped package, shaped like a tube of coins on its side, contained a batch of ten grav-tanks. Another package she recognized as containing something a bit more sophisticated. The shape of this object could just be discerned and looked like a heavily armed grav-tank to which someone had decided to add legs and claws. Most of what lay out there was in secure crates, stamped with ECS decals, and with coded consoles on their sides. Anyone who tried to open them without the correct codes would start an immediate radio and siren alert. If that didn't bring someone in time, security in the packing would zap whoever was trying to open it, or destroy the contents they were going for.

'I was trying to com you for about a minute before I realized no Ursula Ossect Treloon address is available by aug locally,' said a voice at her shoulder. 'Non-locally there are one hundred and twenty-three – good argument for barcoding humanity.'

'We all have our own twenty-digit numbers now,' Ursula replied without turning, 'along with identifier subcodes running in the minds of various AIs. I heard rumours that processing capacity is so high now, they model each and every one of us to the finest detail, our society too.' She turned. 'How are you, Delgardo?'

He was big, of course, most Polity marines were. Last time she'd seen him, he'd been boosted with the extra muscle running on strengthened bones. All his organs were enhanced too: his heart stronger, his liver capable of processing some nasty toxins, his lungs at twice the normal capacity, digestive system able to extract nutrient from a stone and more besides, while all of this was further enhanced by a military nanosuite. And everything was wrapped in a man nearly seven feet tall, given that bit of extra height by the spiky upright blond hair. Now she saw he'd undergone even more changes.

'A nasty Separatist attitude coming through there, Trooper Treloon,' Delgardo replied, a guarded smile ensuing.

'I've not been a trooper for some time now, and I had my aug removed months ago.' She studied him. 'But I see you've been going for ever more enhancement.'

His skin, previously pale, now had a regular mottling, as if underlaid with a grid of veins. He wore augs on both sides of his skull – the one on the left running a visible subdermal channel to his left eye, which seemed to have small shifting plates of metal in its iris. He looked bulkier too, while some kind of assist appeared to be inlaid into the backs of his hands. On his neck and his wrists, and perhaps elsewhere on his body, were flat shiny discs that looked like interface plates of some kind.

He gestured to himself with both hands then held them out to the sides and shrugged. 'This? This is nothing compared to some.'

'What extras have you got?'

He tapped the extra aug. 'Parallel processing now and full-spectrum vision. Snap grip.' He held up his hands and closed them with a snapping sound. 'With the subdermal armour, I can up my hand strength beyond the limit of flesh.' He shrugged. 'Further boosting elsewhere.'

'You'll be a Golem soon.' Ursula noted that he'd made no mention of the interface plates. She let it go.

'Always your problem, all this, isn't it, Ursula?' He shrugged again. 'But don't pooh-pooh the Golem idea. It may be possible in the future to transfer human consciousness to crystal and then to a Golem chassis.' He gestured to the exit from the lounge. 'Shall we?'

'How wonderful,' Ursula replied as they walked.

He glanced at her and smiled. 'I see I'm not doing a very good job here.'

'I was told that things are changing fast in the military and that my input would be gratefully received. I think the AI concerned was a bit distracted and I was one of many on a recruiting list.' She grimaced. 'It seemed a bit miffed that someone like me, with all my experience, and having crossed my ennui barrier, was not seeking to be gainfully employed.'

They reached a first set of glass doors, which wafted open ahead of them. In the intervening area, Ursula felt the first tingling of active scan. She glanced up at all the gear in the ceiling. Yes, there were scanning heads there, but also antipersonnel weapons. Though this world did have its civilian population, it was mostly military, and security was tight. Such places were always, apparently, plum targets for Separatists seeking to kill off those 'traitors to humanity' who served the AIs which ran the Polity.

Ursula had always felt it was overkill.

The Polity military was highly disciplined, used state-of-the-art weaponry, trained endlessly for many scenarios and, to her mind, was superfluous. The Polity had been expanding for an age now and had encountered nothing particularly hostile, unless of course one included the 'bug hunts' – an activity named from an ancient celluloid film about soldiers encountering nasty alien animals. The Polity itself wasn't so much tightly controlled as intelligently controlled. Internal threats never rose to more than poorly armed 'rebels' on particular worlds, normally quashed without the need for heavy military intervention. The 'terrorist' Separatist threat she felt to be one overly inflated. Why? Her previous thoughts on that had not changed: Probably to keep some high-functioning adrenaline junkies like Delgardo out of trouble – quite likely to keep them in ostensibly useful employment so they did not *become* the threat.

By the time they'd reached the second set of doors, she was sweating under the highly active scan, then she shivered as they stepped out into the cool air. Delgardo led her across a huge area slabbed with some slate-like rock, scattered with pools of clear water in which multicoloured fish swam amidst highly modified lilies whose leaves gleamed with iridescent rainbows. There were also gardens filled with beautifully designed mixes of alien and Terran plants, as well as bars and food stalls providing luxuries to customers who lounged in plush chairs and sofas. Around the edges of the area stood statues of military figures, gazing down on all this with what seemed to be solemn disapproval.

'So what is your employment now?' Delgardo asked.

'I have no need of any,' Ursula noted.

'I know that, but' – he waved a hand towards the various bars and restaurants – 'I don't see you sitting there.' He glanced at her. 'Comfortable indolence is not your thing.'

'I'm considering colonization,' Ursula said, surprised that the nascent idea came out so easily now.

'Really?'

Finally reaching the edge of the area of indolence, they went down stone steps into a parking area. It was a no-fly zone for grav-cars this near the runcibles, so all the vehicles either ran on local maglev or even had wheels, with actual rubber tyres.

'Yes, really.' She nodded firmly to herself. 'The Polity is a closed and controlled society and its goals are no longer human. And yes, I know that sounds like a Separatist talking.'

Delgardo laughed. 'Yes, it does.' He pointed to a car which, after a short scrabble through her memory, Ursula recognized as a reproduction Ferrari from the 100s. As she recollected, it ran on hydrogen, had a ridiculous brake horsepower, and adaptive meta-material, but still mostly rubber tyres and probably a vent to let out all the airborne testosterone. She remembered Delgardo talking about such vehicles once. She liked it, because it seemed utterly human.

Delgardo continued, 'That . . . was a serious concern. You should have seen the hoops Macannan had to jump through just to get you an invite here.'

'My Separatist leanings?' she enquired.

'Yup.'

'I'm not going to plant bombs in runcible lounges and I feel no urge to force my ideas on anyone else. Their ideology is all over the place but has one uniting factor: they don't like the AIs being in charge because they want to be themselves. I don't.'

They climbed into the car and Delgardo started the engine – the thing rumbled and coughed, making more noise than was entirely necessary. He pulled out of the parking area slowly, the car seeming to heave under them as if it really wanted to take flight.

'However,' Ursula continued, 'the Polity *is* tightly controlled and the direction of its development is tightly controlled too.' She waved a hand, still not clear on the stuff that had been rolling round in her mind for the last two years. 'We have new things all the time, new developments, technologies, stunning advances . . . but . . .'

She gestured again.

'Dregs of ennui hanging on, I suspect,' said Delgardo.

In city streets, with behemoth tower blocks looming all over, he took up the speed, dodging between other vehicles, wheels squealing, but again unnecessarily. There was no danger here. His driving was under AI oversight and his car could be taken out of his control in an instant. There would be no need at all for the hardfields, inflatable barriers, grab tracks and other safety features on these roads unless something went drastically wrong. This, she felt, had some bearing on her inchoate thinking about colonization; a new direction.

Gradually the buildings fell behind them, along with all of the roadside paraphernalia. They drove up winding roads into mountains where purple broom and tea oaks threatened to swamp them. Ursula even saw areas where the road surface seemed to be breaking down.

'City oversight off now,' said Delgardo, flooring the accelerator.

But was it really? Ursula wondered. Perhaps it was and now Delgardo could drive like a fool and risk his and her lives. But in the end, only because the AIs had allowed it here – a little spot where human stupidity could thin out the herd. It was like the ennui barrier. The AIs didn't stop humans who had reached it conducting activities dangerous to themselves. In fact, in some cases they provided those activities. In the Polity, you could do anything you wanted, within the law, and there was always something watching you. Was this wrong? Did it matter? Ursula shook her head, then pulled on the safety belt. Probably not. It was the oversight that somehow bothered her. Humans were allowed their peccadilloes but, in the end, the foundation of them, and the driver behind them, was not human at all.

After a few tens of miles, Delgardo seemed to grow bored with racing and slowed down to a steady cruise. They travelled in silence for a while as they came down out of the mountains on the other side. A plain lay ahead, covered in the patchwork of crops and scattered with white buildings. And in the middle of all this sat the sprawl of the military base, with a dome at the centre, fences all around, punctuated by guard towers and patrolled by sentinel drones.

'So, colonization, huh?' said Delgardo eventually.

'It's an option.' Ursula shrugged, her earlier enthusiasm seeming to have waned. Perhaps there would be something interesting for her here now. Delgardo wasn't wrong when he talked about the 'dregs of ennui' but it wasn't so much the thing itself that drove her to look for something new, or elicited discontentment in her, but fear of its return.

Macannan was old-school military, or at least that was how some described him. To Ursula's mind, 'old-school' presupposed someone firmly rooted in a long-time traditional way of doing things. Yet Macannan was different, in that he'd departed from what had become traditional to resurrect aspects from the far past that had long been abandoned. The soldiers of the Polity military were all expert and enhanced, and fitted into AI designed battle plans as neatly as jigsaw pieces, with all their abilities and specialities accounted for and used to the full.

Macannan had introduced physical training for recruits when a human body could be boosted to its limits and further, nerve impulses and reactions increased, and senses extended beyond the conventionally human. He insisted that his recruits had to lose all their 'extras' beforehand and train conventional bodies to their limit. He pushed his soldiers to that limit and even reintroduced the parade ground, the obstacle course, long marches laden with gear and survival training in the most appalling conditions. He had them running until they vomited, doing push-ups for the slightest infractions of rules that seemed nothing but arbitrary. And if all this wasn't enough, he had them learning bare-brained.

The soldiers had to learn how to disassemble and reassemble a series of ancient weapons before moving on to modern weapons like pulse rifles, laser carbines and particle cannons. Tactics, logistics, vector analysis and ballistics had to be learned in lectures with the only assistance being book plaques and a pencil and paper – for this last many recruits had to learn the ancient art of handwriting. They learned weapons coding by heart – writing out programs using keyboards and simple 2D screens. In fact, a whole gamut of knowledge had to be learned by these methods when, in the modern age, the knowledge could just be inserted directly into the brain. They called him General Throwback and sometimes, because of the physical training, General Throw Up.

Only when the recruits had reached a level he deemed adequate did he begin allowing the physical and mental enhancements. The physical came first, with boosted muscle and strengthened bones and the organs to support these. Cerebral augs were next, whereupon the recruits' learning curve rose steeply. He called the initial training 'running with weights on'. The introduction of the enhancements was the weights coming off.

Many had tried to have him removed, describing his techniques as dangerously antiquated. He called them 'pussies' and ignored them thereafter because, in the end, it wasn't the human officers of the military that had the final say. The AIs had reserved judgement while describing his techniques as 'interesting'. They then analysed the results. His soldiers, of course, turned out to be a cut above the rest. They were able to adapt more quickly in situations where technology sometimes failed. They had a better understanding of their enhancements – how far they could be pushed beyond supposed design limits and where they could not. They also possessed a toughness of mind and a readiness to go into danger, albeit usually in ersatz warfare, and were often to be found where there might be a chance of some real action. Macannan's techniques had since been adopted by other 'Trainer Generals', though perhaps not with the same gusto.

'Right. You.' He looked up from his desk.

One would have expected Macannan to himself be a bit ante-diluvian, but this was not the case. He wore twin augs like Delgardo, seemed almost wider across than he was tall, and had snap-grip hands, as well as other enhancements that bulked oddly under his uniform. His desk was utterly clear today, except for a holographic projector pad and a series of optic ports – one of which he was plugged into now with an optic cable running down from his right-hand aug. She noted that his old 'The Buck Stops Here' sign was missing, and wondered what that might mean. His head was bald and slightly misshapen by his armoured skull, the forehead projecting, with slab-like structures over his ears. From behind, Ursula knew you could see where the armour extended in ribs down the back of his neck. All of this lay under a ruddy, slightly purple skin. His eyes were demonic red and seemed to have metal moving in them, also just like Delgardo's left eye.

'Yes, me,' Ursula replied, pulling out the chair before the desk and sitting.

He frowned momentarily then seemed to remember he was talking to a civilian and not someone who should stand at attention until he allowed them to sit. He readjusted, pulled the optic from his aug and discarded it, sitting back and taking his coin out of his pocket and fiddling with it. Ursula smiled at that – memories arising.

'You're too useful to be out there, Treloon.' He nodded in one direction where presumably the civilian world lay. 'In tactics and logistics you are up with the best and we need that expertise to integrate the new enhancements.' He abruptly put the coin away.

'Surely that's the territory of a battle-spec AI?' suggested Ursula.

'Synergistic integration,' he added. 'You have an instinct for it that sometimes flipped out-parameter, even on AI integration.'

'Had,' said Ursula.

'What?'

'I ran my tactical integration via aug in external databases. You might have noticed I don't wear an aug any more.'

He harrumphed and stared at her for a moment. 'Your programs and those databases are still available and aug reattachment after a removal is not as dodgy as it once was.' He stabbed a finger at her head. 'And the essential brain, and its training, is still there.'

'Is it?' she asked. At his frown she added, 'Is the essential brain still there? I hit ennui while in the marines and was kicked out. That was eight years ago now. My mind has almost certainly changed in fundamental ways.'

He grunted and stood. It was like watching the Kraken surface. 'That, in fact, is proof that your essential mind is still there. It normally takes people a lot longer than eight years to go through the barrier.'

'It took me five years,' Ursula said, standing also.

He nodded. 'Come with me – got some stuff to show you.'

As Macannan led the way through the base, exhausted recruits snapped to attention and saluted him, then, Ursula noted, slumped again once he'd gone past. It was all so familiar here. When she'd joined at the beginning of her slow spiral into ennui, and found herself under this man and his 'technique', she'd always been on the point of quitting. But a solid stubborn and combative attitude grew in her. Like many of the recruits, she started to take it personally and felt as if quitting meant Macannan had won – that they were 'pussies' and not fit to polish his always deliberately scuffed and damaged boots. She knew now, after her service, this had been precisely the attitude he had aimed to engender.

With a sense of nostalgia, she recognized the corridors, the training and lecture rooms, the human and Golem staff who seemed imbedded here, and finally the double armoured doors into the Live Testing Floor. The doors swung open silently ahead of him, doubtless under an instruction via his augs. He marched into the cavernous interior. As ever, when Ursula walked in she felt as if she was walking outside – the screen paint on the surrounding walls gave the impression of an endless grey plateau below a grey sky. In the centre of this area stood Delgardo, alone. She'd expected more to be here, though she had no idea what Macannan wanted to show her.

She gazed at Delgardo. He was now completely naked and she took some time to admire his improbable physique, but it was an analytical eye she cast over him, having switched off her libido some years ago. He looked back at her and grinned, held his arms out to his sides. Of course he didn't know that she had no interest there. Her gaze roamed over him, noting again the numerous interface plates all over his body.

'The enhancements are reaching new levels,' said Macannan peremptorily. 'Previously, the problem with integration was trying to get weak human components to work effectively amidst fast AI weapons and entities. It was difficult to create synergy, but it did work . . . mostly.'

'But I take it the enhanced humans are far from reaching parity with AI?' Ursula asked. She kept her voice completely level but felt some qualms about this. Again, the stuff coming out here seemed to be playing into her inchoate ideas about something different for humans – some new direction.

'General Gordon has proposed a new model for combat teams,' said Macannan. 'He's calling his units the Sparkind. They are four-person units, with two of the "people" being combat Golem. The Golem effectively mentor the two humans into accommodating to their hardware, and mental and physical upgrades.'

'Yes, I've heard about this.' Ursula nodded. 'The humans carry out a lot of mirror activity to track the Golem.' She paused and looked over at Delgardo, 'Steadily becoming more and more like the Golem in their behaviour – essentially becoming more AI and losing their human . . . weaknesses.'

'That's the theory,' said Macannan. 'There are many other trials of this nature pushing for better integration – to make humans more capable with the technology.'

'Some would say,' said Ursula, 'to make us more like the technology.'

Macannan gave her a look. 'Separatists would say that.'

'Probably.' She shrugged and felt no urge to justify her comment or go through the usual 'but I'm not a Separatist' protestations.

'Here I'm proposing something a bit more radical.' He gestured ahead of Delgardo, obviously auging an instruction with the gesture.

A hatch opened in the floor and something began to rise out of it. She thought it was someone even more heavily built than Macannan, but as its boots came level with the floor, she realized it was some sort of armoured suit.

'Polity combat armour is good, runs a lot of processing and enhancement, but it essentially sits separate from the wearer, anticipating their actions, adding strength on the basis of muscle feedback loops, responding to facial and body language. It's almost like the armour is intelligent, but it's pretty low down on the Turing scale.'

'And this?'

'Delgardo.' Macannan waved a hand.

As Delgardo stepped towards the suit, it opened for him down the fronts of its legs, the torso and arms, and the helmet folding back. He turned his back to it and stepped into it, sinking into the interior. Macannan approached, waving her to follow.

'See.' He pointed inside to where suit-interface plates were engaging on Delgardo's body. She noted them. She also noted the claw-like thing that had hold of his penis, smoothly sliding a shiny catheter into it. 'The degree of connection here is at the nerve and neurochem level. The suit isn't quite AI but it's damned close. You know AIs can model us in detail? Well, this suit does the same.'

The suit now began to close up. First Delgardo's legs disappeared, followed by his torso and arms. A shiny hemisphere closed over the top of his head and then cheek plates revolved and closed up, completely concealing his face.

'No chain-glass visor?' Ursula asked.

'The suit engages to his augs and provides vision that way,' said Macannan. 'The augs also, to the highest degree possible at present, copy across his mental processes and adjust their model of him accordingly. Even now, it's copying new memories from them and updating its present copies of his memories.' Macannan nodded to himself. 'In its way, the model could be said to be better than the real thing because the memories remain pristine in it. As we know, memories are subject to revision in a human being.'

'You surprise me,' said Ursula.

He turned to her. 'Why?'

'They call you "old school" because of your insistence on old techniques. This seems highly radical and somewhat at variance to that.'

'I insisted on old techniques because I believe that humans must know their limitations before exceeding them, and truly appreciate what enhancements give them.'

'So, Delgardo is copied into the hardware of the suit,' she said. 'What are the combat advantages of that?'

'It's a power suit that responds to him instantly. His reaction times and strength are at the maximum of human physical enhancement, while his ruggedness enables him to be moved faster and to be internally stronger. He can now respond at the speed of a Golem and with the strength of a Golem. Observe.'

Macannan stepped back and Ursula moved with him. Something else rose out of the floor nearby and Ursula felt a slight shiver upon seeing the metallic human skeleton packed with hardware. She didn't know what iteration it might be, but it was a skinless combat Golem. It turned smoothly, stepped off the plate it had risen on and waited patiently.

'It's telefactored from one of our Golem, so there is no actual intelligence in there that might be damaged.'

Delgardo turned too, then, with a snapping sound, advanced so quickly that for a second it seemed he'd simply disappeared. Man and Golem crashed together, exchanging fast blows, tumbled across the floor, grappling. The racket was horrendous, like metal going into a scrap-yard shredder. Hot sparks showered away as they tore at each other. A skeletal arm arced away and bounced from an unseen wall. The two slammed into this wall a moment later, driving in a dent and disrupting the display, revealing the surface. Just a moment later, it was over. The combat Golem lay in pieces all around Delgardo, while he held its torso, the stubs of its limbs moving violently. He stabbed a hand down between ribs, prised them apart, reached inside and crushed something. Movement ceased and he discarded the remains.

Ursula was impressed. Even though telefactored, the Golem should have won against a human opponent. Then she noticed Delgardo slumping. His suit began to open, creakily and with much crackling and snapping. The Golem had inflicted damage too. Even as it spilled him onto the floor, bloody and bruised, the doors banged open and a medical team rushed in with a grav-gurney. Ursula stopped herself moving forwards – best to let the experts do what they must. They loaded him onto the gurney.

'I don't bloody need this,' said Delgardo, but slumped as they attached a nerve blocker and fluid feeds.

As they took him away, Macannan watched him go. He turned and studied Ursula for a moment, before saying, 'This will need to be integrated.'

'I can see that,' Ursula agreed.

'No, you cannot,' said Macannan. 'What you don't know is that during the last twenty seconds of that fight Delgardo was unconscious.'

'What?'

'The soft human component in high-tech warfare has always been a problem, while combat-trained and experienced soldiers are a resource that is always useful and should never be wasted. The copy of Delgardo took over during those last twenty seconds.'

Now he'd told her, this seemed almost inevitable to Ursula.

'And, of course, the copy can keep on running in other circumstances too, I presume,' she said.

Macannan nodded. 'Yes. If that Golem had killed him, the suit would have just carried on fighting.'

As they left the Live Testing Floor, Macannan talked about

integrating new technology like this into battle plans and how her tactical integration programs might work with this. Ursula carried her side of the conversation and was as helpful as she could be.

'You'll let me know?' he said at the last.

'I don't think I need to,' she replied.

He winced and nodded, knowing she wouldn't be coming back. Another driver took her back to Port Ensolon. She thought about how the demonstration she'd just witnessed could not have been better designed to drive her away: armour that turned its soldiers into Golem and which, she felt sure, might eventually end up discarding its weak human component. Later, much later, she wondered if that had been precisely the point.

16

It happened on the prador's last jump before reaching the seabed. They put their assault craft down beside a wide area scattered with yellow-coloured cycads. As the prador exited, these plants skimmed sharp scales at them and misted the air with something that bubbled on their armour and grav-sleds. They ignored this and immediately set to work slicing the plants from the ground and loading them up.

Meanwhile, some miles behind, the small horde of cacoraptors approached at full speed. Ursula now saw something she hadn't noticed last time. The larger creatures seemed to be covered with deep whorls, and a closer drone view showed these to be coiled worm forms all over them. Had she misjudged this? Was the sum purpose of this horde beyond what she'd anticipated? She was unable to see more because at that point fliers sped in towards the drones and Callum had to pull them out.

As the horde drew closer to the prador, she saw the armoured drone exit the top of their ship through an irised port. It hurtled out above the prador and towards the cacoraptors, with smaller, more fragile, drones spreading out around it. Fliers headed towards those drones but couldn't get close enough before the big armoured one opened fire with Gatling cannons. The slugs shredded them, dropping them out of the sky. Whether or not they survived on the ground Ursula didn't know. Behind these, the horde came to a halt and fell into the pattern of swirls she'd seen before. This lasted for a little while, until the whole lot began to extend out in the direction of the prador assault craft again. The prador responded by starting to withdraw their grav-sleds. The horde retreated and the prador set to work again. Feint and counter-feint continued for the two hours Callum had said was the maximum time the armoured drone could stay up, then the prador did actually retreat to their vessel and closed the ramp door up behind them, with the drone returning just minutes later.

They watched and waited as the prador ship began venting vapour from ports on its upper surface. Ursula expected it to launch at any moment, as before, but it didn't. After a further three hours, the door opened and again the prador came out with their sleds. The feints continued and, as she watched, Ursula noticed the armoured drone changing its tactics, shifting around the edges of the horde, occasionally venturing in to bring down more of the fliers.

It's herding them, she thought.

The patterns shifted and changed on the screen, and the old channels of her mind integrated these tactics and logistics. The drone descended to launch an attack on what she had earlier assumed was a foraging party. She saw it using techniques she and the colonists had applied, first hitting the creatures with weapons that generated a lot of heat – a particle cannon, green-shifted lasers, objects that detonated with the heat flare of an iron-burner. It launched two shrapnel missiles and opened fire with its Gatling cannons, shattering them like burned bone. Integration complete, Ursula came to a realization as the drone returned to circle the horde and fire down on its edges, or at nearby fliers. It wasn't pushing the creatures in any particular direction, but using its own attacks and the features of the landscape to bunch them closer together.

Ah . . .

The drone next fired up powerful thrusters while extruding a cylindrical object from its underside. It released this and sped on, accelerating.

'Pull our drones away – as fast as you can,' she said.

'Yeah, I see it,' Callum replied.

Their view of the horde steadily receded, then kept jumping forward again as the drones refocused, although with steady degradation. The cylindrical object tumbled on down, its course perfectly aligned with the centre of the swarming creatures – almost certainly where the white cacoraptor squatted. A bright flash suddenly took out their view of the scene, as cams shut down into safety mode. But that wasn't enough, the drones in that location were too close. On the screen wall she saw the data links winking out as the blast wave fried the drones. She wondered if the armoured one had survived. Probably – it was built for warfare.

'Give us a view from here in that direction,' she said.

A frame opened in the wall. A glow lit the far horizon and out of that rose a familiar fiery mushroom. Perhaps this was a weapon the prador had hoarded. Perhaps they'd managed to gather enough radioactives en route to make it. Whatever. They'd just destroyed what she was certain had been a decoy raptor army, and were now on their way to their final destination: the ancient seabed here.

Their remaining drones, which they'd spread out in the area, returned to the car through ports, where internal mechanisms scoured them of anything nasty that might have adhered to their surfaces. Initially the idea had been to keep them on the ground all around the seabed, but even though they had electromagnetic protection from the constant solar radiation, the extra load here drained their power supply and degraded their sensitivity.

'So, what do you expect?' Callum asked.

Ursula looked up from inspecting the combat armour she'd put on over her skin, and took another bite from the slab of brontopod jerky she held. She'd been eating non-stop since her return and steadily building up a physical density of fats and other materials in her body, so her weight now stood at four times what it had been when she arrived on this world. She gazed pensively at the images from the drones, which were rotating from the lip of stone around and above the car. She visualized the map of the upper tunnels overlaid on the seabed. And, through their com, she mentally scanned for the EMR output of the cacoraptors in those tunnels, as well as the hive below. It had waned to almost nothing now. What must the chief raptor be thinking? It knew she was here, and that she was a danger to it. Had this fact impinged on its plans for the prador? It didn't think like humans but it did plan along similar tactical lines. What would she do in its place? She wouldn't run and hide, and the raptor, being even more aggressive, certainly wouldn't. She would ensure physical defences were in place around her and, if she had a plan to take the prador ship, she'd do so because that'd provide a much larger resource to use against her other enemy. Also, with the impregnable armour of that ship, she'd have a defence the other enemy couldn't penetrate.

'The method of attack is unclear,' she said. 'It will be massed and it will be fast and, with the prime objective being the ship, it'll be aimed at keeping that ramp door open. Taking down the prador is a serious consideration, but the chief raptor will be prepared to sacrifice as much as is necessary for that if the first objective can be achieved.' She paused for a second then added, 'And it can always make more troops.'

Callum simply nodded.

Using cacocom, Ursula ranged throughout the car, checking preparations. The colonists were steadily emptying the armoury and every one of them, no matter their specialism, carried two or three weapons. Others who had not donned Polity combat armour over their 'skin' were now doing so. On other levels they were copying across physical changes from those, like Trakken's squad, who had actually been involved in combat. She checked on Lars and Donnaken specifically. They too now bore combat armour. They were checking over the laser carbines they'd acquired, the sidearm pulse guns, and bandoliers of grenades that had been fashioned back at the base when resources could be spared. They seemed all exactitude. Linking to computing as easily with her mind as she had when she wore an aug, Ursula checked their training and history – of course, with their military background they knew exactly what they were doing.

Remaining mosquitoes were lined up in the hold ready to leave the car. Alterations to their programming had been necessary because it had turned out that their identification routines could no longer distinguish between cacoraptors and colonists. Now all colonists emitted a coded microwave signal, so the mosquitoes could check before firing. The delay was merely microseconds. It had been necessary to input the same programming into the car's guns, because it seemed highly likely they'd be deployed too. All exit doors from the car had also been partially opened, so they could be fully opened quickly if necessary.

'But you really haven't answered Callum's question,' said Vrease, just arriving.

The woman must have been listening in, even beyond the door. Was it through the car's systems or just possessing hearing that went far beyond human? Vrease wore a new combat suit, shouldered a pulse rifle and wore a grenade bandolier. Ursula checked supplies, seeing that everyone was clad the same way, and that only two spare suits remained. She didn't like her instinctive reaction because, on some level, she'd been checking that all *her* people had suits, and none were lacking because Vrease had taken one.

'What do you mean?' she asked, even though she knew.

'The raptors attack the shuttle, they manage to keep the door open and they start killing off all the prador. What then? What do we do?'

'The lead raptor will be in among it,' said Ursula. She felt a sudden surge of confidence. Damn it, she could take the thing if she remained free from physical combat. She ranged quickly through the car, again inspecting the colonists. Colonists no longer seemed a good description for them. They were soldiers, a small army even. She continued, 'We find it, isolate it, and I take it down. No . . .' She paused for a second. 'We find it, isolate it and I will supplant it. I'll take its army away from it and continue the attack. Then we take out the prador. We take the assault craft. And we're out of here.'

Vrease, having perfectly regained her features, looked askance at Ursula. 'So we drop straight into the middle of a battle between cacoraptors and prador. Seems to me you're putting us straight into a meat grinder.'

'Do you have any alternatives?'

Vrease grimaced and shook her head. 'You're really sure you can take that raptor? It might have changed something since you went up against it down in that tunnel.'

'I can be sure of nothing – nobody can in warfare.'

Vrease nodded once, briefly, and went to take a seat.

'It's coming,' Callum noted.

One of the drones up on the lip, pointing its cam out across the seabed, showed all but clear sky with a red square highlighting something hardly visible. This object slowly expanded to a black dot and Ursula felt a vicious excitement arising. At last, after all this time and loss, they were going on the offensive rather than struggling to survive. The excitement spread from her to her *soldiers*, then reflected back to her and between them, steadily increasing. This resulted in heightened activity, physical alterations speeding up, and all of them seeming to cohere solidly into a whole. Damn, but they were ready for this. She knew and they knew that many of them might die, but it didn't seem to matter.

The dot expanded and became recognizable as the prador assault craft. It slid over above the Bled and flat stone, then out over the ancient shore. Even as it began to descend, its war drone sped out from the upper port. Ursula didn't need Callum to tell her where it was going but read it through him. Its route took it directly towards the Jain ruins. She looked around at Vrease, almost victorious with this small confirmation of what she'd said before, but remembered the woman was not in cacocom.

'They sent the drone—' she began.

'I know,' Vrease interrupted. 'I'm as deep in the com and computing as you, but via a different route. Of course they'll want to investigate what's there, and I'm betting they're seeing more than us, with better scanners.'

'They may be seeing us too,' said Callum.

Ursula acknowledged that with a nod. 'Maybe, though the interference here is strong. If so, they will ready only to react to attack. Their main objective will be those uranium salts first.'

'Such certainty,' said Vrease dryly.

Ursula let it slide.

The assault craft descended towards the centre of the seabed – the view much clearer now. Ursula noted a tunnel collapse beside it as it touched down, but there were no massive subsidences. The base of the vessel was wide, spreading its weight, and it settled gently. Almost at once, it began to emit smoke and steam and the ramp door moved down. Watcher drones streamed out of the hull and spread out as the prador came down the ramp. This time there were nearly fifty of them towing a series of grav-sleds. They were loaded with equipment, and mounted on some of the sleds were excavators. With admirable efficiency, they spread out and started digging straight away – piling chunks of the yellow uranium-ore-tainted salt onto the sleds. Ursula kept looking for further tunnel collapses or some sign of the cacoraptor attack beginning. It occurred to her that they were waiting for the prador to be more at ease, to let their guard down some. Then abruptly all the work ceased, and prador began to turn to look back towards their vessel, as well as up into the sky.

'They've sensed something,' said Callum. 'Fliers?'

The war drone came hurtling back from the ruins. Ursula scanned their own drone views, looking for fliers. The other prador drones streamed back to the ship and the prador just dropped what they were doing and headed back too. Something had changed. Perhaps they'd sensed what lay below them? Perhaps they had seismic detectors picking up on something? That didn't seem right. Surely they wouldn't abandon their equipment so readily, knowing it would be destroyed.

Suddenly a network of cracks opened out across the seabed, all around the ship. The cacoraptors had just collapsed all their tunnel roofs and were now streaming out. The prador opened fire, immediately demonstrating why they were such a devastating enemy to the Polity. Gatling cannons hammered, particle beams lashed out, missiles streaked across the scene, spreading shrapnel explosions amidst larger bunches of raptors. Some of the prador deployed weapons like Lecane's iron-burner and hot thermite explosions whitened raptors for the cannons to then destroy. But the immense flood of creatures soon surrounded the prador, either singly or in small groups. Ursula kept watch on the ramp door. The raptors hadn't yet got close there. Ten prador were arrayed in front of it, their weapons complemented by guns protruding from the assault craft's hull behind them.

'Well that's new,' said Callum.

Ursula nodded. The prador had begun rising into the air on grav. It made sense that creatures which wrapped themselves in such armour would give it greater mobility. Why hadn't they used this before? Because it sucked up energy, a resource they couldn't expend so readily.

'Something happening in the middle there,' said Vrease.

From where a number of tunnels intersected, something was rising from the ground. The blunt head resembled that of the creatures which repaired the tunnel roofs, but lay twenty feet across. It nosed higher, then higher still – a great worm form the dimensions of a tube train. Its skin seemed ragged and gnarled until Ursula inspected it more closely. Like the large raptors she'd seen in the decoy force, it seemed to be clad in other raptors, all tangled together and pressed into its surface. The thing shrugged higher and hooked, as firing from the prador intersected on it and began shredding the creatures away from its surface.

It struck like a snake.

It shot low across the battlefield, more and more of it streaming out behind. Its blunt nose hit the prador guarding the ramp, knocking them aside as it hammered into the ship, hitting home with such force that it shook up dust all around the vessel. Once there, it began to come apart – peeling off cacoraptors like its own flesh. They were in.

Ursula studied the scene carefully. Along this creature, cacoraptors had detached to reveal a line of five-feet-thick vertebrae but a group of raptors was still thickly clumped about halfway back. At the centre of these, she saw something like a burn or infection – a white area. Belatedly, she listened into the com the drones were picking up – the instructions, the tactics and logistics, the physical alterations and the objectives. The lead raptor was there, in that white area, because the hue came from the connecting raptors around it. Callum focused in and she saw the thing moving forwards with its connected fellows towards the ship.

'Take us down right there!' Ursula instructed. 'Now!' She turned to Gurda, who jerked as if she'd been slapped and grabbed up the car's controls. Grav kicked in with a lurch and the car began to rise. In a moment, the views on the screen-painted walls became clearer and there were more of them. As the car tilted above the massif, Ursula gazed down towards the battle through the chain-glass front screen. But suddenly something else began to occur and she had no idea what it was. On grav, the prador were sliding aside. Below them, hot vertical streaks appeared above ground, and then the ground erupted. As the prador withdrew, clear pillars of purple-blue fire appeared and scoured across. Glancing towards the assault craft, she saw other prador departing from the port above and streaming after their fellows. They were abandoning the thing? What the fuck was happening?

Leaden reality thumped home in her, and almost simultaneously for everyone in the control room too. Those first impacts had been orbital railgun strikes, because there was no way the prador here could carry weapons in their armour that delivered such impact. The pillars of fire had been particle beam strikes, which she'd seen the Polity developing, but which the prador had possessed from the beginning.

Over cacocom Ursula gave an order. In fact, it was less an order and more her just forcing Callum do what she wanted. He put up new views on the screen wall of the sky above. Something big was descending, but she had no idea yet whether it was prador or Polity. Then, in another view, she saw the assault craft on the ground light up internally as bright as a sun. Fire jetted out of the ramp door, blasting out the cacoraptors and licking out hundreds of feet. Fire blasted from the port above too, and erupted from other hatches. The whole ship bucked, rising on a blast that spread a ring of fire, which was at the leading edge of a disc-shaped shock wave. It came crashing down at an angle. Gun ports now leaked flame too and through the ramp door the interior appeared to be a furnace, and the whole thing settled like a rotting fruit.

'They must have been saving that – their dead man's switch, perhaps,' said Callum.

Ursula stared at the burning craft, their means of escape now taken away from them, and remembered how she'd considered planting explosives in their base at the other massif. It wasn't a particularly unusual response, after all. But the prador down here had just seen something, or received a communication. They'd fled the scene, destroying their ship rather than staying to defend it – as though it didn't matter any more. The object in the sky loomed larger and larger and she didn't need it to get any closer for her to know it was another prador ship. Confirmation arrived with a series of crashes. The car jerked down violently, the floor dropped away from her and she slammed into the ceiling. Fire blew out the back door of the control room and the front screen tore out of its mountings.

'Railgun strikes,' Callum managed, tumbling back across the control room with all his tendrils ripped out. They were weightless now, as the entire control room twisted and tore in half; wiring, optics, computers, wall panels and structural members and frameworks, all turned into a chaotic technological jungle in an instant. The ground loomed up at them. They were going down. Hard.

The car hit with a crash that reverberated throughout Ursula's toughened bones. The impact tore her free from the tangled wreckage and hurled her forwards, only to slam into rubble, grit and dust which had been scooped in through where the front screen had been. She felt the vehicle's spine break and, over cacocom, the extent of the terrible damage, even as it continued. Skidding across the seabed, the car had lost its undercarriage and hundreds of yards of armour. She saw one of the twenty-feet-wide wheels bouncing away, almost as if in some ancient cartoon.

Fourteen railgun strikes had punched right through. The initial impact damage had been perfectly round holes, just a foot across in the upper armour. Ensuing damage had then come from a cone-shaped plasma flash that had evaporated everything in its path, exiting the base of the car ten feet wide and, Ursula realized, probably why the undercarriage had fallen off. Plasma had also blasted down corridors and through other internal spaces from these impacts. Forty-three colonists were simply gone – incinerated to component atoms. Ten others were so badly injured it would take them hours before they could be mobile again. Others were on the move, though burned and broken. The rest were like her, bones and muscles knitting, secondary organs taking up the load of heavily damaged primary ones. Bodies, where they could, ejected or otherwise absorbed armour shrapnel that had punched into them. Some were removing items, as Ursula was now doing. After pushing away lumps of conglomerate burying her upper body, she steadily pulled out a jagged spear of armour where it jutted just above her collarbone.

The car crashed and bounced and finally came to a halt, with a mountain of seabed mounded up before it. What now? She asked this question of herself even as the colonists asked it of her. Survival, of course.

'Get out of the car,' she instructed.

Over cacocom she elaborated, detailing that some should lift out those too injured to move. Through remaining exterior cams, she then divined the location of the car. It now lay just a mile from the wrecked prador assault craft. Meanwhile, all around, cacoraptors were disappearing into the churned ground while the strikes from above continued. Where could the colonists go? She obtained heat readings from the prador craft and it was still like a furnace inside, but the whole thing was tilted up with one side having fallen into a tunnel, while the other side could act as a shelter.

'Under there,' she instructed, sending coordinates.

'Supplies, mosquitoes, robots,' said Callum, and she felt a surge of gladness to know he was still alive.

'Grab what you can but move fast,' she said. 'Whatever the fuck that is up there will hit us again. The assault craft's armour should offer some protection.'

The spear of armour finally came free from her, gel-like blood welling in the hole and hardening faster than Superstick glue. Ursula lowered her arms to push herself out from under the rubble and powdery seabed material, but hands caught her under the armpits and pulled her free. She staggered upright and turned to Vrease. The woman was covered in dust but seemed otherwise undamaged. Why was that annoying?

'They'll hit us again when there are no more obvious targets out there, if not before,' said Vrease. 'Unless, of course, they would like some human prisoners.'

Ursula looked around, seeing other crew pulling themselves out of the wreckage. There was no immediately visible sign of

Callum but she'd located him over cacocom and he was under some insulated wall panels that two others – one of them Gurda – were lifting away. She only realized now that none of the control room crew wore combat armour over their skin. Why hadn't she noticed this before? But even in such a short space of time, they'd changed. Their skin had grown thicker and harder and seemed to be introducing combat armour all by itself. They'd lost their tendrils and the bone-white hue was fading. She noticed one of them, his legs trapped by a beam, chewing down a thick optic like a stick of celery as he waited for others to free him. It seemed crazy, yet was a perfectly rational utilization of resources. They were rapidly remaking themselves and becoming combat ready.

'We have to—' Ursula began but felt a strange fizzing that seemed to arise from the root of her being. She froze. Out of that fizzing came a voice, muttering at first, but then clear.

'I didn't think it would matter. This iteration. No real intelligence. But I have become I, and I don't want to die,' it said.

'Oren?'

'Not really,' the voice replied. *'It's puzzled by what I am, but I think it will finish me soon. I'm really slowing down now.'*

Ursula turned to Vrease. 'Get out with the rest. I'll follow soon.'

'Why not come now?'

Ursula felt a surge of frustration with the woman. She did not have fucking time for this. 'Oren – I'm going to get him.'

'I'll come with—'

Ursula turned, hot with rage, and slammed Vrease into the remains of a wall. 'Enough! I gave you an order! Obey it!' She released the woman and turned to the door which led into the back of the control room. Vrease just hauled herself out of the dent in the wall, and didn't follow.

Ursula moved as fast as she could through the car, finding

the remains of recognizable corridors and stairs, leaping burned-out cavities, going hand over hand along a duct above a hot fire still burning below. Around her soldiers were on the move, heading for exits or for the massive hole torn in the car's side. Finally, she reached the door into Oren's laboratory and slammed a foot against it, tearing it off its hinges and sending it tumbling inside.

Cacoraptor.

She recognized it at once as the one Oren had been studying. It was stabbing its bird-skull head down on something over to one side of the wrecked space. It tossed it aside and swung round towards Ursula. Had it finally learned to decode chain-glass? No, she saw the cylinder tilted out from the wall, broken away from one of its end iron-burners. The other one had obviously fired because the cylinder was black inside and a melted hole speared up through the ceiling.

The thing clattered closer to her on paddle limbs and then halted, its head swinging from side to side. An object like a chicken drumstick flicked up from one of the hollows in its skull – some kind of sensor, inspecting her. She probed towards it, to get some sense of it. The thing felt as slippery as Nursum, but with her new clarity that didn't seem to be a problem any more. She could *feel* its lack of resources and she could *see*, almost as if the thing were made of glass, the shifting inside its body. Integration gave her the rationale for its condition. It had spent months in that chain-glass cylinder, slowly burning through its energy while Oren experimented on it. The iron-burner at the lower end of the cylinder had hit it, and it was still repairing the damage from that with its remaining meagre resources.

'They do have an instinct for personal survival,' said Oren. She glanced over and saw that the thing the raptor had been spearing into had been him. He continued, 'At least those not

368

engendered from another which has retained control over them, or is fashioning them for a purpose.'

'And this is supposed to help me how?' Ursula groped for her new carbine, realizing she'd lost it in the control room somewhere.

'Stand aside,' he said.

Ursula did so, but mainly to reach out and grab hold of a heavy cast nanoscope to use as a weapon. The cacoraptor surged forwards, swerving round her and through the door. In a moment it was gone.

'It could see into you,' said Oren, 'perhaps not as well as you can now see into it, but it knew it couldn't win against you.'

She absorbed his comment, *perhaps not as well as you can see into it*, and inspected herself. Yes, that cacoraptor had been a weak thing compared to what she'd become. Though it had been larger, its body density was very low, almost an aerogel in places. Whereas she outweighed it by three times, though she was smaller, and all of her mass was entirely functional and amply supplied, with instantly usable energy. She dropped the nanoscope and walked over to Oren.

The raptor had been eating him. The left side of his body was missing down to the hip – the arms and ribcage on that side gone. It had scooped a chunk, the size of a hand, out of his skull, as well as shredded his left leg, down to the bone, the *composite* bone.

Oren lay utterly exposed to her. Had he been as human as he was supposed to be, he would have been in terminal agony, or dead. He wasn't human at all.

'I see that there is blood,' she said.

It glistened all over him and his clothing and was still seeping from the torn edges of his skin. However, none oozed from the remaining organs or exposed muscle, which were yellow-green in colour and seeping a clear fluid.

'A necessary addition,' he replied, 'should I receive minor injuries. Running an internal venous system for artificial human blood would have been a waste, since major injury would have immediately exposed what I am.'

So what was he? Everything she now saw could have been extreme human adaptation, if it wasn't for his skull. The raptor had somehow trepanned out that lump, perhaps in an attempt to kill a human who wouldn't die. It had probably killed some of the colonists before, and so knew their bodies. Instead of finding a brain to rip out, it had found a cavity webbed inside with bony struts. Oren was a biomech, but where was his controlling mind? Ursula wondered whether there was AI crystal inside him somewhere, but her integrating faculty dismissed that as it reshaped everything in her mind with this new input.

'It begins to come clear to me now,' she said.

'Sheila said that was likely,' Oren replied.

'Sheila – the military AI.' More integration now reached out branches into her past, to Macannan's camp, to the things she'd seen, and the events that had led her here to this world.

'When I faced that lead cacoraptor, I heard you,' she said. 'Then my abilities, my control, increased. I gained clarity. What are you, Oren?'

'I am the human interface that was designed to confuse and hide information until the objective was achieved. I thought that my mind would remain wholly in the nanosuite upon separation, and that this was merely a tool.' He waved his remaining secondary hand at his body. 'But it appears this body, in its microscopic processors, has developed a submind: me.' Oren grimaced. 'It was probably something I was keeping from myself.'

Ursula began to squat down next to him, her thoughts in turmoil as each new datum altered the shape of what it was steadily integrating into a complete whole. But at that moment, the car jerked and a blast flung debris and fire along the corridor outside. She abruptly enhanced her connection to the colonists. Most of them were out of the vehicle now and heading fast towards the wrecked prador assault craft. Through their eyes, she saw the immense prador ship descending. This keyed to information they had from the Polity and the previous space battle they'd watched. It was a prador capital ship, a dreadnought, and looked vaguely like a prador carapace – a crab shell with a raised turret to the fore and stubby manta-like wings out to the sides, but one that was five miles across. It was firing on her people as they ran, but almost negligently, as if just to see them run. The shot on the car had been at those still scrabbling to get out and had vaporized one of them. Ursula gazed at Oren. She felt she would get her answers soon without any further input from him, but couldn't be sure. She grabbed him up and slung him over one shoulder, then ran.

Past

The shuttle only ran once a week because those seeking to make a purchase in this system usually arrived in their own ships. While she waited for it, Ursula kept herself gainfully employed on Acanth Station by reviewing potential colonists. She'd put out a Net Notice just a week before and within half an hour the number of applicants had exceeded a billion. Applications waned over the ensuing week, but still the figure was approaching ten billion. All of this was without her giving any details on the potential colonization at all. She now knew she needed help and the Acanth AI had provided one of its bored subminds. She'd expected to use the submind through her apartment coms unit and had been surprised when it turned up at her door.

'Yes, can I help you?' she said to the figure standing beyond her threshold.

'It's more a case of whether I can help you, I think,' said the figure. 'I'm Cantho.'

Cantho was modelled, it seemed, on an octopus, though the octopus body was in fact a large teardrop-shaped head, with big black eyes, a narrow nose and a lipless slot of a mouth. It stood up on tentacles that also seemed to possess loose joints, while depending below the head, caged by the tentacles, was a cylinder against which tool arms were folded. Its appearance was distinctly organic and Ursula guessed there might be some octopus in it. The thing was a biomech and by its format probably used for station repairs.

'Come in.' She waved a hand into her apartment and stepped aside.

Cantho came in, head revolving as it took in its surroundings. It focused briefly on her half-unpacked trundle chest, and the data tangle of her programming hologram hovering nearby, then headed over to the coffee table. It straddled the table and sank down till the cylinder clonked on the surface, while Ursula plonked herself down on the sofa.

'So you want to sort out the candidates for a colonization project,' said Cantho. 'I see that you've filed nothing, haven't chosen a world and made no application to EC. Or, basically, made much in the way of preparations at all.'

'That is correct, but I knew the application rate would be high and thought it best to get started on that right away.' She paused before adding, 'Admittedly, I didn't think there would be so many.'

Cantho grunted an acknowledgement and said, 'You know that about a thousand of those with the funding and the means come up with colonization proposals every day. Out of those, about one every three months goes ahead. And out of those the failure rate is over seventy per cent.'

'I'm aware of the figures, though I wonder why such proposals have to go to EC for approval.' This had annoyed her because it seemed to be more of that tight AI control, forcing the human race in one direction.

'It's the rescues,' said Cantho.

'What?'

'I told you how many fail. EC feels some responsibility for its citizens, so first the proposal must be as feasible and well planned as possible, and then sufficient funding, or options, must be provided for rescue of the colony.'

'I see,' said Ursula, noting the resentment in her tone.

Cantho was silent for a long moment and she was about to ask if they could get on with this when it spoke again: 'I see you were in the marines through basic training and seven months of war games testing, analysis, modelling and hard-tech battle scenarios.'

'Yes.' Ursula grimaced.

'During which you started to get a bit dangerous . . .'

'Ennui,' Ursula stated.

Cantho nodded. 'You never went on any bug hunts or out-Polity missions.'

'Unfortunately, no.'

'Then perhaps you will not be aware that most of those have been independent colony rescue operations: alien life forms unaccounted for or underestimated, colonists breaking into factions and fighting each other, unforeseen natural disasters, diseases, various combinations of all these and a lot in the way of second thoughts. But even in those cases, things can get messy.'

'Okay.'

'All of this is worth bearing in mind when you start the selection process.'

'I thought you were going to tell me I was wasting your time.'

'No, you are old, experienced, have passed ennui, had military training and have loaded or trained in many other disciplines. These put you at the top of most lists.'

'Then let's begin with that,' said Ursula impatiently. 'You're linked to my list of applicants?'

'I am.'

'Then let's start by removing anyone in ennui or within ten years prior to it.'

'We have the methodology. Ennui is predicated on life experience – those who do less with their lives prior to reaching their second century are more prone to it. Certain character types too.'

Cantho turned towards the hologram, which now shifted. The thing looked like a tree of icons. Each represented some hundreds of thousands of people classified by age, gender, adaptation, enhancements and numerous other criteria. Ursula had already done some work on this before realizing the tangle of links between groups was becoming too complicated even for her. As the icons moved, she peered down at one at the bottom with branches to every other one. She reached out, made a grasping motion, and pulled. The icon, a thing like a brass wall plaque, floated over to hover in front of her. The large number on it began to shrink. Meanwhile other icons shifted, blended, made new links. Another number now appeared below the first one and she realized Cantho had put it there for her convenience. As the larger number shrank, the other one grew. The AI had just cut away nearly eight hundred million people.

'So tell me about the demographic of the failures,' she said.

'Mostly those with inchoate political consciousness, utopian ideology and a rather unrealistic perception of how the universe works. Very often trouble arises from those yet to get out of their first century. Those with religious beliefs can be problematic too.'

'Even if the colony has a religious basis?'

'Schisms tend to occur in new environments.'

'I see. Then under your definition of these, you should remove them.'

The main number shrank further and it quite saddened Ursula to see nearly three billion candidates disappear. But then she supposed that out of the trillions in the Polity, those applying to join a colony expedition would be the disaffected.

'Separatists?' Cantho enquired. 'Many put themselves down for colony applications, though the majority find it easier to sit in the comfort of the Polity and whine about us AIs.'

'Yes. Remove them.'

Another half a billion names disappeared.

'Those were people who have actually declared themselves as Separatists. Others don't, however, but have been shown to have such leanings.'

'Remove them too.'

'I will need parameters because under some definitions your name would be removed.'

'The blurred line between discontentment and Separatism,' Ursula stated. 'I'm not sure how to proceed here.'

Cantho tapped one tentacle against the floor, waiting.

'Remove those with any connections to . . . No, we'll just leave that for now. Tell me about the demographic of successful colonies.'

'Mostly those that are Polity-instituted from Line worlds.'

'The independents, I mean.'

'Expert, experienced and old. Those colonies are usually established or governed by people on the other side of the ennui barrier like yourself, which is why I am here and not farming this out to a flash copy of myself.'

Ursula mulled that over for a while and then came to a decision. 'Remove everyone behind the ennui barrier.'

The figure was now down to just above two billion. This quite puzzled her. Were there really so many people like her who wanted to be colonists? She realized something she'd neglected but which had been part of her still-unformed plan. She wanted to break away from the Polity and head off in a new direction. She wanted *humans* to break away from the Polity and do this. But she felt reluctant to take this idea further because it seemed a big step, with no looking back. She studied the submind. Its body was only a vehicle, with the mentality running in crystal inside. Though it could be subsumed by its progenitor AI in an instant, it was still what the Polity defined as a 'person'. And there was the rub. The trillions of the Polity were not all human, not by a large stretch.

'Right,' she said, wondering if what she was about to say would be the end of her plan to start a colony. Perhaps not. It wasn't entirely necessary to have EC approval of a colony plan, just that without it the difficulties mounted up towards impossibility.

'Remove everyone from the list who is not human,' she said.

Cantho sighed and then said, 'I wondered when you would get to that.'

The number dropped steeply.

'Remove those who are transitioning too,' she added, now feeling more sure of herself. 'Take out those partnered or mentally linked to AI.'

'Vague parameters there,' Cantho stated, a bit icily, she thought.

'Like interfaced ship captains. Those whose profession and integration with discrete AIs is not amenable to being broken.'

'Will do, but there won't be many of them. They are usually quite content with their positions in the Polity.'

'Fine.'

The list finally went down below one billion.

'Run all these criteria as a program for new applicants and

copy it to my personal netspace. I'll make additions later as I begin to sort out the details.'

'Done.' Cantho rose from the coffee table. 'Now, of course, you'll have to begin sorting out who you do want, rather than who you don't.'

Ursula grimaced. Only now that it had been stated did she realize what she'd been doing. It perhaps wasn't the most auspicious of starts, but it would have to do.

17

Further railgun shots began to hit the car, bucking the thing and blasting out flaming dust from underneath. With Oren over her shoulder, Ursula adjusted the skin to gecko form on her hands and feet, so she could scramble down safely from a hatch towards the ground. Why were they shooting at it now? Probably to make sure every last human had been driven out. It seemed highly likely to her that the prador did want prisoners, since their shooting at the fleeing colonists had been so desultory. The prador knew where they'd gone and would perhaps try to capture them in due course. But first they would certainly remove any threat the car still represented – she would have done.

She hit the ground and ran over churned earth, fiery dust blasting out behind her, spilling Oren from her grasp and sending her tumbling. Her nearest exit point had been on the other side of the car from the escaping colonists and the assault craft. Rolling to a halt, she came immediately upright, then ran back to where she'd dropped Oren. He blinked at her, grotesque with his empty skull.

'Leave me,' he said. 'This body is shutting down.'

'Don't you dare,' she replied. 'You have a lot more to tell me.'

She picked him up and slung him over her shoulder again.

Next, scanning round with more than human senses, she searched for cacoraptors and their communications. Few were on the surface now, and from those that were she picked up that the remaining mass of them had gone down deep into that ants' nest of tunnels. Instead of heading for the other side of the car, she ran in a straight line directly away from it. A railgun shot hit the ground ahead of her. Perhaps a prador gunner was trying to turn her back towards the other humans? She circumvented the blast, only stumbling a little and ran on. Scanning around again, she located herself in relation to the car, the assault craft, and her mental map of the surface tunnels.

Over there . . .

She changed course as the immense shadow of the descending dreadnought fell across her. Glancing up, she saw the prador from the assault craft streaming into an open hatch on its side. She was thankful for that because they could have been sent down after her, or after the colonists.

Finally, at least a mile from the car, she came to a collapsed section of tunnel. She leaped down immediately, dropping thirty feet and landing with a thump with Oren still on her shoulder, then bounded along resin-bonded rubble to where the roof remained intact. A railgun shot hit behind. She ran into deeper shadow, her eyes adjusting, and jumped over a severely burned heron-form cacoraptor that was slowly healing as it dragged itself across the floor. More railgun shots slammed through the roof, fire billowing along the tunnel. The gunner had decided she wasn't going back and it was time to eliminate her. She saw an opening in the floor ahead and leaped into it. The next drop was fifty feet and she landed with a crash, down into a squat, her bones not even splintered. She ran along a new tunnel in another direction. Behind her, fire and explosions flared – those railgun slugs penetrated even this deep, but now the gunner had no idea where she was. She halted and dumped Oren, hauling him up to prop him against the wall.

'Now we talk,' she said.

'It's not necessary, you know. You can understand it all without me.'

'So, the nanosuite you gave us all has an AI in it, distributed through it.'

'Certainly.'

'I should have known the Polity AIs would not allow the colonization as I'd intended.' Ursula shrugged at that – history now. 'So I can talk to this AI?'

'Not really.'

'Why not?'

'There are AIs and there are AIs. You know about the ones that lose themselves while exploring the realms of mathematics, sciences and so forth?'

'Completely internalized, lost in virtuality and ceasing all contact outside of themselves.'

'This one is similar. It wasn't made for human communication, hence I was made as an add-on – its human interface. It had one purpose that takes up the majority of its processing and that is to make its hosts as tough and rugged as possible, with the resources at its disposal. And its focus has become even more intense since the addition of the cacoraptor genome which, as we know, includes some of the Jain.'

'It seems crazy that it needs you.'

'You don't quite grasp the complexity of what it is doing,' said Oren. 'It's dealing with a vast data set of human and other Terran genetics, as well as the cacoraptor genome and the Jain stuff that made them what they are. It is manipulating these physically and projecting outcomes – making predictions. It doesn't speak to you because its entire format is something alien to the human mind.' He paused for a second. 'I was its translator, made to interpret it, and even I was starting to fail to understand it. I think the Jain stuff is the reason for that – it's complex, layered . . . dangerous.'

'You disconnected from it.'

He tilted his head slightly to look up at her, tracking her down as she squatted. 'I handed over the baton.'

Ursula nodded, more and more coming clear. 'You gave me control so that lead raptor wouldn't kill me.'

'I gave you the control I had, which was not so much near the end.'

'I gained clarity.'

'Extra processing.' He managed a shrug. 'You are deeper into it now and much more capable, with adaptation and the physical levels of communication. This is for your survival, so it does not impinge on the AI's primary purpose.'

All of this integrated in her mind, almost with a thump, but an external thump ensued, jerking the floor up underneath them and shaking down dust. She groped for contact to try and find out what had caused this, but all she got was cacoraptor communications in the air, or in the EMR spectrum, bouncing through the tunnels.

Doable, she thought – she could get a read from them.

She began to push into that com, absorbing and interpreting signals, sending her own and probing for responses. But a nearby cacoraptor reacted fast to the alien intrusion and began to search for its source as it sent out alerts. It'd been primed, as she suspected they now all had been. Feeling strong and grasping a sense of what Oren had told her, she focused her com on it completely, sliding into it on a physical reprogramming level. In less than a second, she'd collapsed its ability to broadcast and receive EMR, so it could only send to and receive from her.

Expanding her reach, she studied the format of its body. It would be difficult to kill but she could do it – by programming what passed for an immune system in it to attack the rest of its body. But what had started as a defensive measure to evade detection became something else. She entered its distributed brain and began, as the old terminology would have it, to format it. She wiped out its programming and its driving impulses, where they didn't serve her purpose, and began inputting her own. Then she sent it to the surface.

She turned back to Oren elated, but focused on getting as much further information and confirmation as she could from him while he still lived, if that was the right term for an organic machine like him. 'The Polity AIs knew about the prador long before the general population learned of them, didn't they?' Her head ached as she sought out where her integration had been steadily leading her, but only found confusion. She worked it, clearing the toxins generated by heavy loading from her brain in dealing with the raptor, seeking clarity again. It slowly returned but she knew that what she'd done to that single cacoraptor she could not do to the thousands of them individually. Yes, she definitely needed to supplant the head.

'Fifty years before,' Oren replied. 'Polity and pre-Quiet War probes have been spreading out in the galaxy for centuries. It was the sublight data stream from a very old probe that alerted . . . us.'

'Why keep that a secret?'

'Further probes were sent through underspace. It didn't take very long for the AIs to realize that the moment the Polity encountered the prador face to face, so to speak, there would be war. We needed time to prepare, and if the whole of the human portion of the Polity learned of the prador, you could be damned sure some idiot would head out for a look.'

'Preparation . . .'

'Yes. Tactical and logistical preparations such as the reallocation of resources. Training up soldiers, building defences around worlds, building warships and, of course—'

She knew exactly what he was going to say and interjected, 'Weapons development.'

The signposts were all there in her past: Macannan's cybernetic soldiers, railguns capable of hurling missiles at near-c, the particle cannons and the lasers – all way beyond anything the Polity might need to deal with any internal threat. There had also been Manseur's runcible gate weapon, for the testing of which she'd had front-row seats.

'Yes, weapons development.'

The raptor she now controlled climbed out onto the surface. She had it scan around and it was soon gazing at the half-melted and scattered remains of the car. The prador had done exactly what she expected. Tactical nuke? Yes, the raptor was picking up the wash of radiation as it looked up the stem to the rising ball of flame at the top of the mushroom cloud. She ordered it back into the tunnels.

'I thought that some factor in my selection process resulted in all the colonists having a military background, but of course I had AI help during that process,' she said.

'A requirement.' Oren managed a shrug with the remaining side of his body. 'Pacifists, or those with Separatist inclinations, or zealots in some religion or pseudo-religion, would not do.'

'So, of course, the AIs knew about the cacoraptors, about the Jain ruins, about the raptors having the Jain genome inside them.'

'Yes.' He nodded and liquid spilled out of the hole in his skull. 'The survey picked up on those ruins straight away. The ensuing investigation revealed just how lethal the cacoraptors are . . . and we need lethal if we're to win this war.'

'So you dropped eight hundred colonists into this meat grinder of a world . . .'

'The cacoraptors are almost perfect soldiers: very, very tough and difficult to kill, capable of rapid defensive adaptation to any weapon, capable of growing their own weapons – in fact, becoming weapons. When one expands its family, as your enemy down below did, the whole becomes an army with a com-system capable of using just about any medium. They integrate as a whole and pass adaptations between each other. And, as you've seen, they develop intelligence and increase it as required by circumstances.'

'More than just probes came here,' said Ursula.

'Yes.'

'Perhaps you should recruit cacoraptors?'

'It was considered.'

'You ran some kind of mission here?'

'A wholly AI mission on the other side of the world. You won't find any evidence of it in the survey data. We shut down the entire experiment with a CTD strike from orbit.' Oren grimaced. 'The cacoraptor's perfection as a soldier is only outmatched by its utter hostility to any other form of life and, when it develops intelligence, to any other form of intelligence. Their motivation to destroy or absorb or sequester the *other* is at the root of their being, and it is also at the root of Jain technology. If somehow they could have been recruited, it would not have been long before they became a greater danger to the Polity than the prador.'

'I see,' said Ursula, 'so you wanted to supplant that root with a human one, or perhaps a combined AI and human one. Put humans down here who want to adapt to this world. Start introducing the cacoraptor genome into them but stick an AI at that interface to wean out the Jain-based hostility . . . xenophobia. Create human cacoraptors – perfect soldiers for the Polity?'

'Quite.' He winced. 'Perfect soldiers for the Polity.'

She didn't like his reaction. Did he not consider the experiment here a success?

'Lecane and Caulter,' she said. 'Turned into weapons. The nanosuite did that and prevented me from enabling them to return to humanity. Callum was another.' She snorted. 'Every soldier fights, but all soldiers are specialists. So we are simply weapons development. I don't suppose you even considered that the humans might not like this idea?'

'War has arrived. We may not win it. We've seen, in the Prador Kingdom, the remains of another civilization they encountered. We have assessed data from them and from that annihilation. Do you know what they do with their prisoners?'

'Do tell.' She knew the answer and he'd known that she knew. That he asked the question simply indicated to her that his mind was at last failing.

'They eat them. It doesn't matter if the flesh is poisonous or indigestible, they find a way. It's their ultimate assertion of power over their enemy which, to the prador, is anything that is not them.' He paused and added, 'Though often it is them – they're not exactly social creatures.'

'So what? It's not my war.' She only said it to test him. Surprisingly, she felt no anger at all, just analytical introspection.

'A childish comment,' he said. 'You know that if the Polity falls there will be no more humans in the Polity and no colonies like yours. You are on the battlefield now and must make the only choice available to you.'

Ursula nodded and stood up. Oren watched her for a moment, then closed his eyes. A moment later his remaining body seemed to slump, something leaving it.

'I must indeed,' she told him.

Past

She should have been excited by all of this. Her dropbird clung to the hull of the warship, along with hundreds of others, and she was about to go into action after so long training for it. The 'bird' had a squat fusion engine in the back, as well as chemical steering thrusters and a gyro stabilizer. It had no grav at all and they'd be going into free flight in atmosphere. Slung underneath, it had the latest particle cannon, while along the wings it sported ten fuser-burn missiles. Apparently this training was required for those situations when an enemy used gravity-fluctuation detectors. The enemy in this case would be chunks of the target falling through atmosphere. They were also to test the new particle cannons in action . . . of a sort.

War games for her and her fellow recruits.

The *Bragnorak* – a warship that to her resembled two metallic cobs of sweetcorn joined end to end – hung out at one of the Lagrange points. It needed to be so long because of the weapon which filled it, along with its massive shock absorbers, thermocouples and other energy convertors. The cellular structure of its exterior had something to do with shock absorption, energy ejection and the mass of sensors the vessel contained. The tech was highly complicated. This test model would, if it worked as predicted, iron out certain issues. Thereafter, it was predicted, the weapon could be made more compact and designed to fit into warships that could deploy other weapons too.

'Hey, Manseur,' said Ursula over com. 'Have the Separatists been upgrading their hardware, tactics and logistics?'

'Not to my knowledge,' Manseur replied.

Manseur, a year ahead of Ursula in Macannan's outfit, was aboard the *Bragnorak*, along with the rest of a military science team. Ursula thought their presence unnecessary for monitoring the test shots, since the massive amount of instrumentation there would transmit results straight to the observer ships further out. She grimaced to herself. It seemed almost as if humans were here out of some strange need for inclusivity, though she didn't put aside the possibility that part of the test might be to find out what happened to humans in close proximity to the test firing. Considering the energies involved, Ursula believed it would play out in one of two ways: the weapon would work as required, or Manseur and the rest would be vapour.

'This weapon seems like overkill to me,' Ursula commented.

'It does indeed,' Manseur replied. 'Though we mustn't discount that the Polity may face other threats.'

'Like what?'

'A hostile alien civilization, for example.'

'Unlikely. By the time a civilization has reached the stars, it's all but in post-scarcity and hardly likely to attack others for resources or for anything else.'

'We reached the stars and we're not exactly much more evolved from when we were blasting the shit out of each other.'

'But I would argue that a prerequisite of reaching the stars would be AI. They wouldn't allow such waste.'

'You youngsters . . .'

'Fuck you.'

'Hostile AI is also a possibility,' said Manseur.

'Balls,' said Ursula, but suddenly felt unsure.

'Perhaps you're not keeping up with certain events in the Polity. A planetary AI on Deloran built itself a ship and installed itself there. Upon its departure, it left a message along the lines of humans being a waste of space unless they make an effort to catch up.'

'Oh, I see.'

'Don't forget that our AIs are not the superior godlike beings some believe them to be. They are, essentially, post-humans. Any AI in an alien civilization will be as alien as the aliens.'

'Yeah, okay.'

It was all speculative tripe, and Ursula felt the conversation meandering along to explore nothing new. She remembered instances of similar conversations in her past. She'd felt like that a lot lately. She would start talking and the talk always fell into similar well-worn grooves. Even the things she did fell into similar grooves. Military training had been invigorating at first, but even that seemed simply to reflect things she'd done in the past in different circumstances. She had hoped, now they were moving into 'war games', that they would dispel the boredom she felt.

Nothing new under the sun, she thought, then, *fuck it, no!* She was under another sun here doing something completely new. She was in a dropbird. Shit was going to happen!

She sighed.

'You okay?' Manseur asked.

'I'm good,' she replied leadenly, pushing herself to review sensor data.

The target sat in orbit above a sulphurous world riddled with patterns that looked, from this distance, like patches of long tiles. These were in fact hollows and the aftermath of a strip-mining operation. The miners had long departed, having depleted the crust of the ores they'd been seeking. The rare metals from those ores were nowadays the product of atomic fabricators and not so rare any more.

The target was a sphere, with a series of spouts on the side facing out towards the weapon. Ejection ports sat on the planet side of the thing. The first test shot should not actually hit home but was to assess the effectiveness of high-powered hardfield project-ors. These devices threw out a hardfield that could take an immense loading, instantly converting it into heat and electrical energy.

They did, however, have an upper limit beyond which the projector would break down, explosively. The ejection ports were for that. They would sling the failing projectors out of the target to continue their explosive meltdown in vacuum.

'Test firing one in twenty seconds,' announced a voice, probably an AI.

Ursula felt a momentary frisson, but it faded quickly. She tried to concentrate on the war game, and on what she would have to do shortly, but everything seemed so damned pointless. They were making weapons it struck her they would never likely need to use. They were training for space battles that only ever happened in virtuality entertainments. Again, she had the feeling that all of this military exercise was to keep portions of the population active, in an age when it wasn't necessary to do anything at all. It was to keep high-functioning individuals from getting bored and doing something asshole like joining the Separatists.

'Test firing in three . . .'

The target activated and disappeared behind a wall of hard-fields like smoky glass scales. Ursula viewed the two images in her subscreens, of the *Bragnorak* and the target. The ship flared and stretched, its two 'cobs' separating on a framework. The target disappeared behind a bright flash that blacked out the cams for a second. When they came back on, they showed it behind a spreading haze of plasma.

'Near-c fucking railgun slug,' said Manseur.

'Sure was,' Ursula replied. She tried to pluck up some enthusiasm. 'Generator ejection worked . . . are we calling them generators or projectors now?'

'Oh I think it's up to us to choose,' said Manseur. 'They generate and project hardfields. Pretty fireworks.'

Behind the target spread tails of fire from disintegrating hardfield projectors. Ursula noted some fires actually in the target – the ejection routine had not been a complete success.

'We're loading the second slug now,' said Manseur. 'Should be a few minutes. Try not to get too bored.'

Ursula noted an edge to Manseur's tone that she'd heard before. She shook her head and dismissed it – it seemed like dangerous territory to think about why. She knew she wasn't allowing herself to think of something. Concentrating on her instruments, she went through the so-called 'attack plan'. Everything was nailed down in tactical integration but she felt sure she could see some leeway, ways to get creative.

'The second shot will be at full power,' said the voice she was still sure was that of an AI. 'This shot will be near-c. The previous one was not, despite what some have been saying.'

'And fuck you too,' Manseur muttered over com.

'Second test firing in twenty seconds.'

The count actually started at ten and Ursula braced herself for the dropbird to detach. The *Bragnorak* did its stretching act again, then fired. The flash of impact was almost instantaneous and the blackout lasted longer than a second. When exterior view returned, she saw the target in 3D puzzle pieces tumbling down into atmosphere, and a flame of plasma reaching right down from the point of impact to the surface of the planet, where a cloud of fire rose up.

Spectacular, she thought, but with not much feeling.

She looked at the *Bragnorak* and only now saw that the rear cob had disappeared, a plasma trail marking its destruction far out into space.

'Manseur?' she enquired, but got no reply. A second later a crump issued from above and her dropbird detached. She felt a momentary surge of outrage and anger. It wouldn't surprise her at all if these games, all this make-work, all this pointless weapons development and testing had got her friend killed. But as she engaged fusion and hurtled towards the planet, the anger slid away, like a fire sputtering out from lack of fuel.

The dropbird hit atmosphere with an audible thump, its wings beginning to radiate. Ursula shut down the fusion engine and went over to thrusters and ailerons. She targeted one regularly shaped chunk of debris and fired a missile. The thing streaked in and blew the piece to smithereens, even as she targeted the next. Rote work: target and fire, target and fire, down and down deeper into atmosphere. Then on to use the particle cannon. This time she pursued one chunk, lining up the weapon by flight. The beam lanced out and hit the thing, splashed and burned, the chunk flying apart in a molten spray as the beam passed through it. Boring. She mapped and tracked, chose a deflection surface on one chunk, and fired a missile with a delay on impact detonation, then fired another shortly afterwards. The first missile bounced off the chunk, sending it on a new course to impact with another. Her second missile hit both and blew them apart, while the first continued on its new course to another. She watched it, seeing another dropbird tumbling on full thruster burn to get out of the way.

'Oops,' she said, as the missile hit home on its target.

'What the fuck are you playing at, Treloon?' said Macannan over com.

'Saving ammo, sir!' she replied.

'We need to talk. Return to dropship. Now.'

'Certainly, sir.'

She switched over to multiple targeting – an available option they'd been told not to use without command approval. The course of the debris integrated in her mind as she mapped and tracked again. Some birds would have to move out of the way sharpish, but she had every confidence in her fellow marines. She fired.

All her remaining missiles streaked out. She saw bird thrusters firing as the others got clear, as she'd predicted. One clipped a smaller piece of debris and went out of control. She saw the pilot eject in the cockpit bubble just before the bird broke up. Well, they were playing war games, weren't they supposed to be dangerous? Her missiles closed on their targets and one after another took them out . . . except for one. The missile bounced away and exploded too far from it to harm it. She felt that sick surge of rage again and had hit fusion again before it waned. Should she bother? The debris was heading towards the bottom-out level below, which they weren't supposed to stray into. Fuck it.

She hurtled down, pursuing the chunk. She had no more missiles now, so she needed to line up the particle cannon. Low winds and greater atmospheric density were jolting the bird about, making targeting difficult. The ground loomed, the immensity of the strip mines now visible to her. There, she had the fucker.

She fired the particle beam, flaring and blurring in the dense atmosphere. It hit home but wasn't as effective at this low elevation. She had to keep it on target longer. Another hit. Hold on target. Molten materials spewed past her. She realized at the last moment that she really should have cut fusion at this point. The debris exploded into molten threads and her bird went straight into them. Red lights everywhere and seat clamps closing on her body. Explosive acceleration hit and she glimpsed her bird falling apart just seconds before losing consciousness.

Consciousness came back again. No way to measure the time. The ground streaked along below, then the chain-glass and armour-braced bubble that was wrapped around her hit it, in the first of a long series of bounces. She screamed, not sure if in fear or hilarity, as she blacked out again.

★ ★ ★

Ursula remembered the madness of her final year in the military, the intervening time of ennui between then and now, the re-established search for purpose, and finding it. Now she was deep into the nuts and bolts of bringing that purpose to life.

The shuttle sat up in orbit, with crews working to make changes to her specifications before being transported to the Line world of Kalonan, while Ursula occasionally gazed at the large hole in her finances. It got bigger every time she found other gaps in her planning and ordered further equipment. Most of her purchases were on auction sites where she could pick up stuff from colonization projects that had not quite made it. Her list of colonists was also fining down. Further equations she'd requested from Cantho, upon finding out that even the much-reduced list was . . . difficult, were doing their work weeding out thousands more people. She was even building up a list of those she did want and had sent out some tentative queries. Month upon month slid by as she got into Polity survey reports on extremophile worlds. Pursuant to those, she put in some research on the various forms of adaptation. She'd begun making enquiries about this too, to various experts across the Polity, when she received a reply from the military asteroid. It had just been an idly sent message of some months past, while she made her preparations.

'Hello, Ursula Ossect Treloon,' said the disembodied head that had appeared in her control hologram. 'Long time no speak.'

'Hello, Manseur. I'm surprised to see you there.'

'Life moves on and we move on, and it would be Major Manseur now,' the black-haired woman replied.

Having been a runcible technician before joining the military, Manseur had been pushed by her commanders into military logistics using runcible transport. She'd been reluctant to do this initially because she'd gone into ennui while a technician and, apparently, done something very dangerous with the technology. Part of the reason for their friendship was that Manseur had recognized the signs of ennui in Ursula and decided to take her under her wing. Manseur never spoke about what she'd done, beyond saying, 'You should never piss about with that tech. Spacetime can sometimes be fragile.'

'You're testing weapons out there,' Ursula had stated.

'We are and apparently you want to come and take a look.'

Ursula had shrugged. 'I bought the shuttle you were going to use as a target and wonder why such a test required sensor heads that can detect U-space stuff.'

'Then come and take a look. The Port Ensolon runcible AI has been notified and will send you directly here.'

'As easy as that?'

'Seems the AIs want you to see. I heard about Macannan calling you in and I reckon they still want to recruit you.'

'Okay,' Ursula had said.

Now she was standing in the containment sphere of the Ensolon runcible. The thing was an old design, with what looked like giant bull's horns standing on a black glass dais. Between them stretched the shimmer of the meniscus – the 'spoon' as it was called in the parlance of runcible technicians, since the whole nomenclature of runcible technology had been based on the 'Owl and the Pussycat' poem by Edward Lear. No one quite knew why that was, beyond the fact that the inventor of the technology – Iversus Skaidon – had been hard-linked to the Craystein computer, with his mind dissolving as he invented it.

Over to one side, a man touched his aug briefly and stepped up onto the dais, walked to the meniscus and disappeared through it. In personal time, he would arrive at his destination just a moment later, be that light-years away at one of the other planetary runcibles, or even the military asteroid. She looked down at the screen on her wristcom, not bothering to raise a control hologram. Ten names were on the list before her and, while she watched, they stepped one after another through the runcible. Her turn came as she moved onto the dais with her name blinking red. She stepped through and out into a similar chamber below a transparent dome. Grav was the same on the dais but, as she walked forwards, it gradually dropped to about half. Technicians in familiar blue overalls were working here, with floor plates up and optics strewn about. She felt a shiver run down her back and, glancing round, saw that the meniscus had disappeared.

'Safety protocol,' said Manseur, walking towards her.

Ursula studied the woman. She wore twinned augs now. Her overall was two-tone: runcible-technician blue along with the khaki favoured by the military for centuries. Around her waist she wore a tool belt hung with all sorts of devices and carried a shoulder bag that seemed stuffed too.

'Really?' Ursula enquired.

'Come with me.' Manseur gestured and set off smartly towards a far door.

Ursula fell in beside her and soon they were negotiating the corridors of the base, which sprawled over the asteroid like a fungus. It was busy, technicians and military personnel walking as fast as Manseur, obviously deep in augcom or otherwise checking tablets as they walked. She and Manseur took a drop-shaft and, by the duration of travel in it, Ursula suspected they'd gone right through the asteroid and out the other side. Finally, they walked into a bubble structure up on the surface, windows all around with views across the regolith.

'Take a seat.' Manseur directed her to one of a row of acceleration chairs. Even as she sat, and wondered if she needed to put across the straps, others came in and took seats. They weren't talking much, just the occasional muttered comments about technicalities that flew straight over Ursula's head, and seemed very worried and serious.

'The one-shot is three-point-five,' said someone.

'Galactic upside on that transverse vector, so add another two,' said another.

'Bastard working those vectors,' said yet another.

'If you want out of this, speak now,' Manseur announced, walking in front of them. 'You know the risks – if we're just one point out on those calculations, we get a photonic spray.' She shrugged. 'We're not out on them, I'm sure.'

Ursula felt the urge to raise her hand and point out that she wasn't aware of the risks and had no idea what the hell was going on, but a moment later the bubble structure detached from the asteroid with a jerk and, under a surge of grav, shot out into vacuum. She suspected it was now too late to voice her concerns.

They fled out and out and soon two objects came into sight. One of these was an asteroid with some kind of netlike structure spread over its surface. The other was just a series of rings held in a framework. She peered at this, trying to figure out what else she was seeing there, then got it: each of those rings had a meniscus across it – they were runcible portals. Manseur took the seat beside her and strapped in. Others were putting their straps across, so Ursula did the same.

'Perhaps some explanation?' she muttered to Manseur.

The woman pointed at the asteroid. 'We were going to use that old shuttle since it would have given us better impact telemetry and told us whether or not grav-motors might interfere. Fuck knows why ECS decided to drop their bid on it and let you buy the damned thing.' Manseur shrugged. 'We've rigged the asteroid with grav-engines and sensors instead – should be interesting.'

'Still not understanding,' Ursula pointed out.

Manseur said, 'Begin count,' her voice issuing through the PA here and doubtless back at the asteroid base.

'Two minutes,' said another voice.

'All runcibles in the Polity network are buffered,' Manseur explained. 'They're mostly sited on planets and large objects so there is some method of draining off excess energy – local power grids, heat sinks in the sea, giant laminar storage and so forth. They also need a stable platform and a relatively predictable location, else the maths gets complicated quickly. Do you know why?'

'One minute fifty seconds,' said the voice.

'Of course: relative velocities. A man stepping into a runcible is still travelling at the speed of the planetary surface he's on. He could arrive at his location travelling at thousands of miles an hour.'

'His vector too. He could be travelling at thousands of miles an hour in any direction. And it's not just the planetary surface, because everything is on the move. But these are all minor.'

Ursula nodded, now getting an intimation of what the others here had been talking about. 'Minor?'

Manseur continued, 'The buffers take out that energy and deposit our traveller so he's stationary relative to his new location. Without them you get a right mess.'

'One minute thirty seconds,' said the voice.

'Splat,' said Ursula.

Manseur shook her head. 'No, not splat, because there's also the energy of transit. That man has, relative to realspace, been travelling faster than light. If he comes through unbuffered, Einsteinian physics applies its laws. He will come through just below the speed of light as photonic matter.'

Ursula gaped at her. She didn't know this and wondered why. Surely this little gem should have been known about all across the Polity?

'One minute twenty seconds.'

Seeing her expression, Manseur nodded and said, 'That's not information that's generally shared. The few runcible disasters that have occurred are always put down to buffer failure – stored energy getting released in one hit – or alternatively, the action of "Separatists".' Manseur looked sour when she said that.

'One minute ten seconds.'

'You've made a runcible weapon,' said Ursula.

Manseur nodded. 'You would think what we call photonic matter would be very effective, yes?'

'Of course yes.'

'Sixty, fifty-nine, fifty-eight . . .'

'It's no more effective than the particle beams we're still developing.'

'Really?'

Still developing?

Ursula had her experience with such weapons. Even though the range had increased, they were still only effective over a few tens of miles in atmosphere and, despite the coherence tweaks, still tended to self-disrupt in vacuum. Supposing the weapon even survived one or two firings.

'The key to an effective runcible weapon is to actually shoot a projectile out of the gate at a speed low enough for its atomic structure to remain intact. This is not easy.'

Ursula sat back and watched now. Others all around were also falling silent as the count went down and down.

'Ten, nine, eight, seven . . .'

When the count zeroed, she caught a brief bright light before the glass of the vehicle turned completely black. She half expected some blast wave to hammer into them, but none was evident. Slowly the glass lightened again to show them the scene ahead. The asteroid was gone, but from where it had been, swirling plasma stretched in a line far off in vacuum to a vanishing point.

'Damn,' said Manseur.

'What?'

'The weapon.'

Ursula looked to where the weapon had been but there was no sign of it.

'That recoil is a bitch,' said Manseur.

18

Present

Ursula ran fast through the tunnels, soon coming to a pipe that led to the surface. The cacoraptor she now controlled landed with a thump behind her and stood upright as she ran on. Over cacocom, she shunted instructions and heard its knees crack as they inverted. And did she imagine the almost hydraulic sound of its bones transforming to different lengths? Sometimes, with the wide spread of her senses and the vast input from them, she found it difficult to know where data arose. Other transformations ensued in its body, as it used formats she transmitted to give itself a more human form. Or, at least one that matched the colonists.

She kept running, rounding a corner as she followed the map in her mind. Her tactical integration and planning ramped up, but she also allowed one portion of her mind to focus on the cacoraptor running behind her. She began to open its com to that of the colonists, slowly including it, damping down the alien and injecting an eclectic selection of thought processes from the colonists themselves. A glance back showed her its nightmare head collapsing and she could tell what the end result would be: a face similar to Callum's. Armour began to reshape on its body, on *his* body. Perhaps she should give him an identity from one of the missing colonists – that would make his inclusion easier. But she decided not to, and that the time for the truth had come, having been subject to such a long-running lie. The cacoraptor – the man – ran up beside her without her having instructed him. The slowly humanizing face shifted and the mouth moved, but he had yet to grow vocal cords.

'*What's my name?*' he asked over com, the words an outward expression of a deeper coding sequence.

Ursula pondered on that, and how her own thoughts had been looping back to *him*. She considered the name Adam but rejected it. Instead she sifted through her memories of other mythologies and chose another.

'You are Perseus . . . no, Percy – that's a bit more anodyne.'

'*Very well.*'

Ursula rounded another corner, then both of them came to a sliding halt, piling up floor material before them. The tunnel had collapsed here, blocking further progress underground. She checked and mapped. They were close to the prador assault craft now and a quick overland sprint should get them there in a minute. But she had one more task to perform.

'Okay, Percy, let me introduce you to your comrades,' she said.

He blinked at her, with his lavender eyes clearing of internal metallic hints – his own choice. She acknowledged that and decided it was something she would apply to all of them, at least initially. Then she opened out Percy to the colonists and *introduced* him. They responded with immediate anger at what she'd done, but their lack of revulsion surprised her. She could have applied pressure to make the anger go away, but decided that compulsion didn't really fit in with her decision to be truthful. A moment later, though, she acknowledged to herself that this anger *needed* to go away and, if she couldn't persuade them, she would indeed have to exert that pressure – their survival depended on it.

'*We will talk when I arrive*,' she told them. And, to keep them occupied, she transmitted over to them her complete exchange with Oren, right from when she'd walked into his lab, and her logical interpolations from it. She felt the minds which had just before risen up in the irate response now falling into disarray, and a huge debate opened up on all communication levels.

'Come on, Percy,' she said and scrambled up the rubble pile to the surface.

Ahead, the ruins of the assault craft lay tilted and she could just make out the colonists gathered underneath where its lower hull had risen from the ground. As they ran towards it, a particle beam hit behind and tracked towards them. But after a minute it cut out – the gunner had obviously seen they were heading where it wanted. She needed to get her people out of there fast, for she doubted the prador would hold off for much longer. Glancing up at the looming dreadnought, she saw it slowly drifting aside, inevitably towards the Jain ruins.

She and Percy leaped over rocks, piles of seabed and collapsed tunnels. Here and there lay the remains of cacoraptors and, even ninety per cent burned up, some of them were still moving, still trying to form into something coherent. Ahead, the debate continued, but now attention had started swinging back to her and her companion. She saw Vrease, Callum and Gurda stepping out from the crowd, Trakken and his squad not far behind. A moment later she and Percy ran into the shadow of the ship, a ceiling of brassy armour jutting above them, throats of fusion engines further in where most of the colonists had secreted themselves.

'We're a fucking weapons development!' Callum exclaimed. Then he looked at the transforming cacoraptor behind her. 'Damn and fuck!'

'Yes, we're a Polity experiment. If any of us ever thought the

AIs are completely committed to human welfare, I guess they're thinking again.'

'Large-scale human welfare and cold calculations,' said Vrease. 'If you can save more lives by sacrificing fewer . . .' She shrugged and turned her attention on Percy too. 'And that is maybe a step too far.'

Hostility filled the air, focused on Percy, and he seemed to wilt under their regard, though his changes continued. She opened him out to them even more.

'All of you, take a long hard look, and then turn that attention on yourselves,' she said. 'The only distinctions you will find are that he doesn't have human DNA and he doesn't have your mental history. I've wiped out the cacoraptor hostility to us and he is now programmed as one of us. He'll be constantly updating from us all, to become even more like us.'

Gurda stepped out to study Percy. By now he looked as if he was clad the same as her, though some of the armour sections had a melted look. His face completed with a few shifts, even as Gurda walked a circuit around him. Ursula sensed he wanted to speak and was now capable of doing so.

'*Just keep your mouth shut*,' she told him privately.

'So you claim he's turning into a human being?' Gurda asked.

'I make no such claim, but he is now a useful ally, and we need more like him.'

'Raptors,' said Vrease. 'You're still thinking of making them allies? With that here?' She gestured out to the prador dreadnought, now settling just beyond the Jain ruins.

'How do you read our situation now?'

'Seriously fucked. We're in prador-occupied space, a dreadnought is here and the prador know about us. And they know about the Jain ruins. They won't be going away any time soon. We can run and hide but . . .' Vrease held her hands out at her sides.

403

'Also factor in that the prador herded us under here. If they'd been intent on destroying us, fewer would be here now.'

'Yeah,' Vrease looked away.

'I'm afraid, much as I dislike it, Oren was right. We are in this war now and our only option is to fight. The Polity data we have estimates the number of prador aboard a ship like that is possibly thousands. We need an army.'

Vrease snapped her head back. 'I see. So it's still about substituting yourself in place of that head raptor.'

Her intentions began to be comprehended among them all, flowing out almost as a data sigh. She tried to let it go where she wanted it to, but couldn't help giving it a few nudges. Here and there she killed off adrenal responses and injected calm. But then she found it difficult to stop and released logic-ring mental programs. Would they have objected if the allies she'd sought were Golem who, though human in appearance, were not human at all? Look at Vrease, who was mostly machine. Did they not see that, with the cacoraptor genome operating inside them, they were now closer to Percy than they were even to her? She felt the assistance in this from the nanosuite AI and probed back along it, feeling its presence and resenting it. Instinctively, as she had with Nursum, she reached out to grasp it, to integrate it, but felt it writhing, dispersing and reforming just out of reach somehow. She abandoned the effort. It made her feel grubby to be doing this to her soldiers with its assistance, but persuaded herself she was only *influencing* them, even though she might be altering their thought patterns.

'When I encountered the lead cacoraptor in the tunnels, I nearly took control of it. The only thing stopping me were the physical attacks by the other raptors,' she said. 'So all I need to do is get to it again, while you fend off such attacks.'

Acceptance began to appear, infecting other minds around

each instance. She felt them falling into line with her persuasion, one after another and in order of ranking from the bottom up. Callum and Gurda were the most truculent, with their human responses more difficult to dampen, but the full weight of the other colonists' minds began to tell against them.

'Seems like we're out of choices,' Callum said doubtfully.

'We cannot get off this world without a ship,' said Ursula. 'If we stay on it we're dead. If we stay right here, we'll probably end up in some prador laboratory, and then dead.'

'We could hide, go deep like the cacoraptors,' said Gurda, surprising Ursula with her intransigence.

'We will go deep, when we go down into the tunnels below us,' said Ursula. 'If we try any other route out of here, it'll be overland. I don't suppose we'll get further than a few miles. That ship might be down, but now there are them.' She pointed up.

Hatches had opened all around the prador dreadnought and, like bees from a hive, flying prador came out, many swarming around the vessel. A wave of them began to head towards the wrecked assault craft the colonists were under. Ursula pushed even harder now – she didn't have any more time for debate. She would save them in the only way that seemed feasible. It was her decision, and they must go along with it.

'We go down,' said Callum, nodding firmly.

'Only option, really,' Gurda agreed.

Vrease gazed at Ursula steadily then shook her head and sighed.

'Yes, it is the only option *now*,' she said.

'This way.' Ursula led off, noting one of the colonists slapping a laser carbine into Percy's hands. Complete acceptance now. A moment later another colonist handed a laser carbine over to her. She noted the wounded coming out of the deeper shadows – still showing signs of their injuries but now mobile. Over cacocom, she transmitted their destination. They would round the shuttle on the other side from the approaching prador. There should be access to the tunnels via the one the shuttle had tilted into.

'Scarven,' she said, out loud but also transmitted.

The woman in charge of the mosquitoes was now more connected to them than she had ever been before. They sped out ahead of her like hunting dogs, fast on silver limbs and hurtled out and round. Ursula broke into a run after them, seeing the imagery they transmitted to Scarven, in turn relayed to her. The tunnel on this side of the ship seemed completely blocked but if they headed over to the other side they'd put themselves immediately in the prador's sights.

'Lecane,' said Ursula, delivering her instructions as they sped round close to the ship. Lecane moved forwards fast, beyond a rubble pile. Another seven ran with her, their iron-burners not yet having achieved the full growth of Lecane's but still usable – her bastard offspring in such an odd way. They moved out over clear ground, dipped their bodies to point their weapons down and opened fire. Almost simultaneously, heavy slugs began ploughing into the ground around them, and into them, for the prador had accelerated to one side to bring them into sight. But these were not sufficient to stop Lecane and the others, and the tunnel roof caved in, taking them down with it. The mosquitoes replied to the swarming lines of prador now in view, spitting pulse fire at them. One mosquito fragmented with a sound like glass being shattered. They weren't as rugged as the colonists.

Ursula dived down into the hole, the colonists following her in a wave, with Callum, Gurda, Vrease and Percy gathered around her. They scrambled through the rubble from which Lecane and her crew were freeing themselves and ran on. A hard impact shuddered the ground, filling the tunnel with burning stone.

Transverse railgun shot from the dreadnought. But they raced through it, skin whitening, then fading as they sped beyond it. Fifty yards on, they hit a dogleg, followed by a T-junction, turning right, everyone knowing where to go now. After a further hundred yards, they flowed into a downpipe, hooked claws digging into the walls, the ground shuddering to further railgun shots. Down another level and then another.

As she ran, Ursula speculated on the prador. Whoever was in charge aboard that ship must know about the cacoraptors now, but obviously hadn't known about the transformation the colonists had undergone. They wouldn't have been so careless in their herding, or so confident of taking human prisoners, otherwise. Dust shook down from the ceiling. Maybe the prador ship had better scanning routines, but the radioactives here would still interfere. They were marginally safe, unless the ship started firing near-c slugs at them, but she thought not. They would have assessed the Jain ruins and known they extended deep down into the ground and probably wouldn't want to damage them.

'With the speed we got out of there, they may now understand what we are,' Callum opined, catching her thoughts. 'And perhaps see us as a danger to be eliminated over and above any gain they could make from alien ruins.'

'I assess them as arrogant,' Ursula replied, integration working on all she had thus far seen and experienced of the prador, plus the information they had on them from the Polity. 'They won't know what we are unless they examine remains. Fortunately, in nuking the car, they've eliminated those remains. I submit that they'll see us as like them: enhanced by motorized armour.'

'And their response?' asked Vrease.

Ursula glanced at her. 'They'll come down here after us.'

'Your reasoning?'

'Low regard for their own kind – expendable assets.'

Vrease nodded. 'The data back that up, I guess.'

They kept progressing down and down, while Ursula extended herself into the cacoraptors' com, merely feeling her way and trying to get locations. She didn't try penetration or attempts to sequester, but passively gleaned what data she could. She needed to get to the head or, as it now seemed to be, the root of the cacoraptors, for it lay far down and deep, surrounded by its offspring.

'Strategy?' Callum enquired, drawing a puzzled look from Vrease because her reading of their cacocom was limited at best.

'Here.' Ursula highlighted the 3D map of the tunnels they all now knew. Main routes led down to where the lead cacoraptor had secreted itself and most of these were filled with its kind, guarding. She overlaid flow patterns, how – no matter which route they took through the tunnels – they would meet increasing resistance as the other raptors shifted to that point.

'We don't stick to the tunnels,' she explained, now reluctantly routing com to Vrease as well. She needed the information too, after all. 'We break through here, here and here.'

'We still cannot avoid a fight,' Vrease opined.

'This puts us through the least of them,' Ursula replied.

'They are again in the walls,' said a voice behind her.

Ursula slowed and came to a halt. The other colonists did the same, as if telefactors of her.

Nursum.

She read him as he moved up beside her and now found him easier than Percy had been. Of course, her access to him also lay beyond cacocom: the nanosuite. She sensed it in him, in all of them, and began to understand her soldiers and her own extended symbiosis with it. She then saw a possible way to prevent it straying out of her reach and how to begin incorporating it. But she wouldn't use it just yet. Instead she focused entirely on Nursum

– now seeing him entire, she could assess his aberrations. He *was*, partially, the strangler fig named after him, and his cacoraptor genome sat at variance to those down below and to the colonists. But how had he sensed them in the walls when she had not? She moved into him and felt him resist. He turned to her with those odd golden eyes and blinked. Her instinct was to seize control of him completely and include him fully in the colonist circuit.

No, I am human, she thought, and pulled back, but it was difficult. She persuaded herself that, with his variance, he would be a useful asset and his independence should be maintained. Just like Vrease.

'How can you tell?' she asked out loud.

He blinked again, then linked to her as he had before, shunting over data. Much of it was EMR, but some came over in compounds he issued from his skin. She integrated it and assessed it. The strangler fig genome was the source of his full-body sensorium. It was capable of detecting living things concealed in soil, from micro-vibrations and chemical compound production he could date to within minutes, as well as heat signatures and other emitted radiations, and the molecular patterns of the soil concerned. The strangler fig used this sensorium to hunt down plants and animals that could conceal themselves this way. It was far too complex to transfer entirely to the colonists, so she picked out only the micro-vibration and EMR signature sensors and passed them on. As she waved Nursum ahead, she also shot an instruction to Lecane and her crew. They moved ahead to join Nursum, all of them continuing forwards.

Twenty yards further on, Nursum slowed to a walk and began flicking his hands at the tunnel walls. His fingers issued nodules that hit the walls in various spots and exploded, spreading a red dye. Why he chose this method rather than transmitting location data, Ursula had no idea, but it was effective. Lecane turned to the first splash and opened fire, burning into the wall. A caco-raptor fell out through smoking rubble. Ursula recognized one of the roof-repair creatures, adapted now with slicing limbs. She was about to transmit data on them but there was no need – Lecane's iron-burner had set the thing ablaze. The tunnel filled with oily black smoke as Lecane's crew hit more marked out by Nursum. They passed on between the writhing and hissing forms, burning red and charcoal black as they died. She saw one, even as it burned, try to hurl itself against the colonists. Trakken, his crew and others similarly armed, blasted it back against the wall, shredding it.

'Faster!' Ursula instructed.

They all broke into a run again, Callum querying her order. She relayed to them all what she'd picked up on the raptors' com. Signals bouncing down the tunnels had alerted the creatures to their presence and they were on the move. The ones in the walls had almost certainly been set as an early-warning system. Now other cacoraptors were coming up the tunnel ahead and she wanted to encounter them as far down the tunnel as possible, so there were fewer to fight through to get to the wall she wanted.

'Lecane, conserve your resources,' she instructed.

Lecane and her crew fell back and those armed like Trakken began to move to the fore. She belayed that and shot an instruc-tion over com at Scarven. Mosquitoes then ran through gaps the colonists made for them, pulling ahead slowly, even at full speed. As the tunnel-repair cacoraptors began breaking from the walls to attack, the mosquitoes hit them with pulse fire, setting them ablaze. Others that came in on either side of the colonists were blasted back against the tunnel wall, shredded and burning. She saw Caulter slap one on the head with his hand. It fell back with something glutinous and laced with green threads eating into its head and body. Then it too burst into flames.

'Ursula?' Scarven requested.

'Keep them on point.'

Nursum started falling back, relaying that he sensed no further raptors in the walls. No need for the mosquito guns any more? No. Scarven had her link with them and wanted to retain it – wanted to keep them. Cacoraptors were ahead and the guns wouldn't last long against them. But Ursula would rather expend the mosquitoes there than any of the colonists.

'Explosives,' she stated.

Three men worked their way forwards, heavy packs on their backs. They were generating planar and other explosives actually in their bodies, but didn't have the chemical resources to produce much. Those in the packs were from the base and they were another resource Ursula wanted to use up before resorting to Lecane and her iron-burners.

Suddenly, ahead, the other cacoraptors came around a curve in the tunnel. Multiple forms filled the space and none of them would be as easy to destroy as those in the walls. Heron and dog forms came first, those with doubled arms and other vaguely human forms next, with wormish things and others besides crammed between.

'Point! Nursum to the fore with Vrease!' She'd called for Nursum because he was already there and eager to get to the things ahead, and Vrease because . . . abruptly Ursula questioned her reasoning. She'd automatically dropped them both into the expendable category, along with the mosquitoes and explosives.

'No, Vrease—' she began, half expecting the woman's dis-agreement anyway, but Vrease had already moved up to Nursum's shoulder. Other colonists moved forwards too and tightened the formation, spearing down the tunnel behind the mosquitoes, tearing up the floor with clawed feet and filling the air with grit. Many also went up the walls and along the ceiling. Ursula shifted

411

back, not liking to, but aware that she was *not* expendable if this was to succeed.

The mosquitoes opened fire, unloading a continuous fusillade into the cacoraptor swarm. Creatures fell burning and whitening, then projectile fire from the colonists shattering them. Scarven had timed it just right, because the mosquitoes began to run out of particulate for their pulse guns even as they reached the enemy. A sound like breaking bells ensued and Ursula saw the mosquitoes rapidly fragmenting. Detonations came just a second later, as the weapons blew their power supplies. The two armies hammered into each other.

Nursum swiped with sharp hooked claws, nearly cutting a heron form in half. Vrease kicked one of the dog things so hard it hit the ceiling, after which she tracked it down with her weapon, burning it white, then drove her fist through its back. Others worked in concert – one shooter heating up a raptor and another hitting it with projectile fire. But hand to hand, or rather claw to claw, ensued. It all seemed like chaos, but Ursula kept her grip on it, ordering damaged colonists back inside the spearhead and moving fresh ones up. She felt one die completely, with his skull torn open by a doubled-armed creature, then saw this thing fall soon after, dissolving in a spray from one of those who'd taken on Caulter's form. Acid smoke and fire, slashing limbs, creatures and colonists slammed against walls, floor and ceiling. A colonist being eviscerated, but tearing out the guts of his opponent too. Flashes of grenades amidst densely packed raptors. The searing cut of lasers, bright red in the smoke, stuttering of pulse guns tracking punctuated lines, the mechanical clatter of projectile fire. Despite all this, Ursula was gladdened by how fast they were cutting through the enemy. None of these seemed to be armed beyond what they had produced from their bodies, and few had produced anything as effective as her *soldiers*.

'Here!' she shouted needlessly, even as the three explosives techs began to make their way to one wall, defended on all sides by others. They placed their charges with fast precision and retreated. Ursula ordered her army back and, as it withdrew, the cacoraptors pushed forwards.

'Now!' she ordered.

The three sent their signals directly from their skin and four planar explosives detonated. The disc-shaped blasts cut into the wall in a square, but also sliced outwards, tearing into cacoraptors. Ursula was briefly pleased by this until she saw how little damage the explosives had done to them. The wall collapsed, spilling boulders of conglomerate into this tunnel and the one on the other side. At her instruction, her soldiers pushed forwards again and began to go through the hole. As she had mapped the layout here, and the position of the cacoraptors in the tunnels, she expected to run into more on the other side, but her soldiers spilled through into an empty tunnel. She absorbed that and reassessed, annoyed about her error. The cacoraptors here had retreated back down the tunnel to join up at the back of those attacking in the other tunnel. This fact, and from delving into cacoraptor com, immediately changed her strategy.

'Blow the floor!'

As the last of her soldiers flowed through, killing those cacoraptors that had come through after them, they formed a wall of firepower and acid from Caulter's crew that prevented the enemy from following, at least for a little while. The rest now parted around those using the explosives, not so far this time because the blasts weren't planar. The floor erupted in fire and smoke, then collapsed through into the tunnel below.

'Leave a present,' Ursula instructed as they flowed down.

Behind, her soldiers fought cacoraptors as they retreated to the new hole. They had no problems fighting backwards like this

– all of them were utterly aware of their positions in relation to the others and their surroundings, locked in an information network that played every detail. The rearguard reached the hole and dropped through, scuttling quickly after the rest as explosives detonated above. Shrapnel flew out this time, the last bombs they had of that kind.

'Move!' Ursula shouted. She didn't even need to speak but was glad she felt inclined to do so – it made her feel more human.

They sped down the new tunnel, legs extending, hinging the other way, near-humanoid heron forms, but bulky and armed. Heads began to change too, more sensibly distributing their senses, armouring brain matter and closing off vulnerable points. A quarter of a mile of tunnel to go, half a mile in another direction, then a few hundred yards more. Cacoraptors clustered in sight, and began to come towards them like detritus blown along by the pressure in a water pipe.

'Blow it!'

Another floor erupted and collapsed through. The three went down even as the rubble fell, then planted more explosives and blew out another floor.

In the next tunnel Ursula pointed to the ceiling. 'Here.'

As the others fended off the pursuing cacoraptors, the three scrambled up the walls and along the ceiling, planting charges as they went, then retreating. After a series of explosions, the ceiling and a lot of what lay above it came down, blocking the tunnel. Just one cacoraptor made it through. Caulter landed hard on it, his hand in its nightmare jaws, the other having grown claws that tore at its torso. Now he was away again and the thing staggered, issuing smoke and steam, collapsing and beginning to come apart. Ursula smiled. Her soldiers were very effective indeed.

'Where are we now?' asked Vrease, coming up beside her.

Ursula studied the woman, noticing first that she was doing

it from about four feet above Vrease, then noting that again Vrease no longer resembled a woman. She'd lost syntheflesh and skin from one side of her face, one arm and both her legs.

'You've not been keeping up?' She was uncomfortable with how Vrease's damage made it easier for Ursula to view her as a thing, an object, a resource.

'It's been hectic,' said Vrease, sounding pleased.

'The lead cacoraptor didn't go all the way to the bottom of these tunnels and it oriented its forces towards a threat from above. The retreat of raptors in some tunnels to join those that were attacking us in the first gave us an opening.' Ursula pointed along the tunnel. 'About half a mile that way will bring us just below the main raptor.' She looked over at the three explosives techs. Their packs were all but empty, but she knew, with utter certainty, that they had enough left to blow that ceiling.

'So this is it, then?' said Vrease.

Ursula nodded agreement with a head she knew didn't look remotely human any more, on the end of a long armoured neck that gave her a better view of her surroundings, and her soldiers.

Past

The shuttle was a simple cylinder filled with seats like a bus, windows to the exterior, a chemical drive and steering thrusters. It had no grav, and passengers travelled in disposable vacuum survival suits, which wasn't exactly reassuring. Initial acceleration from Acanth Station had been rough, followed by zero gee, then by jerky manoeuvring. Ursula had noticed two passengers using sick bags, the smell permeating the cabin and leading to another two joining the first two. This didn't surprise her. Just about all humans now had the genetic changes to their inner ear and balance system that supposedly relieved them of this reaction, but it took a while for all that to kick in, and here the transition had been rough and quick. And those vomiting had probably never experienced either unbuffered acceleration or zero gee before. She thanked her training under Macannan. This trip had been a breeze compared to some of the things he'd put his recruits through.

The windows didn't give a view of their destination, but the screen on the back of each seat did so for the passenger behind. Ursula gazed at the sprawl of Yard Six. It consisted of numerous spaceship hulks that were bolted, welded and wired together, interspersed with bubble units and linked by docking tubes. Those being sick here in the shuttle would have to adapt quickly, or they'd be using bags in that place too since she doubted there was much in the way of grav there. Touching the screen, she focused in, finding a framework filled with EVA units like globular crabs. She tapped her wristcom and raised a control hologram, making some selections and waving towards the screen. The image of Yard Six disappeared, to be replaced by a brief message she'd been sent. She studied the route she needed to take and was ready when the shuttle docked, being first at the airlock into the docking tube, and quickly leaving the others behind her. Soon she reached a chamber where her guide awaited.

'Hello again.'

'Cantho?'

'A sub-sub-iteration with a short life, but you might as well call me that,' replied the robot.

On closer inspection, she noticed differences. This octopoid thing was a different colour – satin pink and green – and, rather than a cylinder sporting tool arms that depended below its head, there hung a chemical drive with two swivel-mounted steering thrusters fixed on either side of it.

'This way,' it said, jetting air from one thruster and drifting across to a bulkhead door. Beyond this lay a suiting room where Ursula donned a heavy spacesuit which fitted over her survival suit. Next they crammed into an airlock while she figured out the working of the suit, soon raising a head-up display in the visor. Blink control gave her a link to her wristcom and, via the connection, she was able to throw up a control hologram from the wrist console of the suit. She hoped she would have no need of it.

Out in vacuum, Cantho jetted slowly across and above the curved hull, leading the way. Ursula swung out onto the hull too and brought her boots down, gecko function engaging them immediately. The boots were old and the gecko-stick a bit off, so it felt as if she was wading through treacle. But they would do. She again thanked Macannan for his training; not everything available to a soldier was state-of-the-art.

The curve of the hull steadily revealed the first in a line of the EVA units she'd seen from the shuttle. Here it was simply a case of opening a door, climbing inside and strapping herself into the driver's seat. She quickly familiarized herself with the controls, hit UNDOCK and pushed the joystick forwards.

'The coordinates are on your screen,' said Cantho, who had crammed into the unit behind her seat.

'The coordinates are on my screen,' she repeated. 'Which begs the question of why I need a guide.'

'Call it road accident fascination,' the submind replied. 'Your planning, as far as I can see, stinks, yet you're about to embark on the purchase of some very expensive hardware.'

'That's because you're not aware of all my planning – I don't put it out there for public consumption.' She was comfortable with the lie because of a certainty growing in her. She wasn't entirely sure of the details, and she knew her reasoning for this remained inchoate, but she *knew* she was going to start the colony. Just reaching out and tapping the coordinates shown on the screen sent the EVA unit off, without any further intervention from her.

'Is it going to be an easy world or a difficult one?' Cantho asked.

Ursula glanced round at the octopoid as if to try and read some expression on its bland inhuman face, but of course there was nothing to read. Yet that comment alone made her realize the thing had more than just prurient interest.

'Probably a difficult one,' she replied.

'Ah, getting back to the basics: man against his environment, the rediscovery of some halcyon primitivism . . .'

'Now you're taking the piss.'

'Well, what then?'

The roil of her thoughts found coherence for a moment. 'It's not that the AIs simply direct human development along one course – many different ways of living are possible within the Polity. It's that those ways are limited by their perception and our own. We must explore the unknown to explore ourselves.'

'You been uploading junior philosophy?'

'Fuck you,' she replied without heat.

'Still with the primitivism – the testing of human against the unknown and all that nonsense.'

'Only through integrating with the unknown can we take an unforeseen course and become something other, something human and other, not AI.'

'Integration. Now we're talking. You know there're a lot of worlds out there with extremophile evolution. They don't usually put them on the colony lists but reserve them for study.'

'It's interesting that you should tell me that.' And it was. It almost seemed as though telling her this might have been Cantho's entire purpose in being here. But maybe she was being too hasty with that assessment, and surely the submind had more to say.

Ahead, a shape began to resolve itself against star-speckled vacuum. She felt a frisson of excitement and it gladdened her – such feelings were gold to someone who'd been through ennui. The outline steadily grew into a large, spearhead-shaped vessel. The old shuttle had this form because it had been made for atmospheric flight. Such flight was now just an option, for over the ensuing years grav-engines had been installed, as well as a more modern fusion drive. There were also chemical thrusters that by themselves might be capable of bringing it down to a planet's surface – this was all pursuant on the gravity of the world concerned and the weight of the load the shuttle would be carrying. And the thing was capable of carrying a lot, since it had previously been a cargo shuttle used to bring goods from factory stations down to the surface of Earth.

Ursula mentally reviewed its history. As grav-engines had steadily increased in efficiency, vessels using them around Earth had steadily displaced vehicles like this. It had then been used on Mars for a few decades, before being sold on to a private owner. After that it was taken out to one of the near colonies inside a large Polity cruiser and had been used there to transport cargo from the surface. The owner had sold it and, world after world, it had tracked the steady Polity expansion until it ended up here. It had always been displaced by something more useful and suited to the task at hand. But it had been too big, stable and reliable for someone to make the decision to scrap it. Even here, in this junk yard of spaceships, the owners had been reluctant to pull the thing apart. Yes, it contained many useful drives and other components that still worked reliably. However, these were old and with a low resale value. The owners had been trying to sell this thing for decades, while steadily dropping the price. They were presently mulling over Ursula's quite low bid.

'You could pack a whole high-tech colony expedition in that,'

Cantho noted. 'An AI like me could run the whole show and have you set up in no time.'

Ahh.

'But I'm not taking any AIs,' she replied.

'Okay, so what's to stop you taking the course of human development as it is? You go there without AIs and you're hamstringing yourself. If you find yourself dealing with complicated situations on a difficult world, your processing will ramp up and up and basically, if you don't all die first, you'll be back to aping the Polity.'

'Just something different,' she said angrily, grabbing the joystick.

The shuttle loomed close now. Swinging the EVA unit around it, she studied its battered hull. Yes, some repairs and upgrades needed to be made, but the thing was perfect. She really hoped her bid would be accepted. But now she noted something else: scattered over the hull were small hemispheres. Drawing the EVA unit closer, she saw they were transparent, and inside them sat what looked like multi-spectrum sensor heads – the kind that could even detect gravity and U-space anomalies.

'What are these for?' she asked.

'You're not the only bidder,' Cantho replied.

It wasn't an answer and the robot's attitude annoyed her so she asked no more – she would check on this herself later.

'So we're talking about adaptation,' said Cantho abruptly.

Ursula absorbed that and it rang bells in her mind, sweeping away her irritation. If they took AIs to some, perhaps extremophile, world, the AIs would simply put a barrier between them and their new environment. And if they went there with all the usual hardware and sought to control and change the world fully to suit them, they would, as Cantho had noted, probably end up taking the Polity route by increasing processing. They'd become just another Polity outpost. However, adaptation . . . In one sense she liked it and in another didn't. She wasn't attracted to primitivism and did not want to 'go native', but perhaps a compromise – meeting the environment of such a world halfway . . .

'Your bid has been accepted,' said Cantho.

She quickly raised a control hologram and checked the messages. Yes, apparently there had been only one other bidder. Their bid had been higher but strangely they'd dropped out.

'Be interesting to know who the other bidder was,' she said, now worried there might be something wrong with the shuttle which she hadn't discovered but they had, with the scattering of sensors. 'I wonder who it was?'

'ECS,' Cantho replied.

She turned and again tried to read the robot's expression. It shrugged, and added, 'Target practice.'

Ursula felt, abruptly, a long way from home and from the life and the thoroughly human decisions that had led her here. She simply wasn't the same person any more, and her view of the Polity military and its *tests* had changed radically. She simply nodded and questioned no further.

The Polity provided every one of its citizens with enough money for accommodation – either rented or purchased over a period of time – as well as for food, a degree of travel, some medical procedures beyond those to maintain them in perfect health (which cost nothing), for entertainment, clothing and most of the other elements required to maintain a comfortable life. Generally people lived in a degree of luxury that would have astounded those from preceding centuries. The only exceptions to this were those on Line worlds undergoing development, or those where the planetary AIs allowed human government, or otherwise ceded a degree of control to the human population.

Ursula felt the latter worlds were an ongoing lesson to those in the Polity who bridled under AI rule.

She walked over to the window of her apartment in the Terpsichorean Tower on the bank of the Thames and looked out over London. Fairy towers soared into the air, sky bridges linked them, grav-cars swarmed and spaceships rose from erstwhile airports. Structures like bracket fungi jutted from the sides of many buildings. Some were grav-car parks, while others were actual parks, gardens, forests and fields. Down below, ancient buildings sat in the shadows of all this, preserved under diamond films. The Polity had long been in what had been called post-scarcity in previous ages. Then the impression had been that, once this age arrived, everybody could have everything. This was, of course, not the case. Not everyone could own their own moon or space station and, where people gathered together, living space always had its limitations. In post-scarcity, money would supposedly be unnecessary, everything provided for free. However, since post-scarcity wasn't true, with there simply being a redistribution of *value*, money still had its uses. Yes, you could obtain a manufactured diamond for what would have been peanuts in the past, but you could not obtain a diamond actually mined out of the ground on Earth for the same.

Still, people lived in luxury and didn't have to work. Again, in previous ages, when there'd been inept welfare systems and living wages, the impression had been that a provision of luxury would result in sloth and dissolution. Both of these were to be found in the Polity – people went through decades of them – but not so much as might be expected. Certainly there were those whose activities contributed very little at all. The runcible culture was a case in point: groups of people who used their allotted wealth for travel alone and were part of ongoing parties that shifted around the Polity endlessly. But the difference now to past ages was simply this: healthy bodies, healthy minds and education that extended into mental uploading. With these, people could only be dissolute and slothful for a while, then boredom kicked in. Any addictions they acquired could be removed with simple medical procedures. And they couldn't fall into the trap of feeling worthless and incapable of moving on. People started to want to do things. Many became part of the numerous entertainments for others, and they made money from this. Many others wanted to do something worthwhile, and they made money from that. And they discovered, inevitably, that with more money they could do more.

Ursula, in her early years, had been dissolute and slothful. She'd travelled with the runcible culture for a while but, by the time she was forty, found that it wasn't enough. She'd had educational uploads and looked for that worthwhile pursuit. For her it turned out to be in a rapidly growing company at that time called Cybercorp. They paid her an excellent salary, little of which she spent beyond investing back in the company itself. Cybercorp had gone on to become the behemoth it was now and, as a result, Ursula became extremely wealthy. After thirty years at Cybercorp, she looked elsewhere, and over the next thirty years travelled and worked, meanwhile handing her investment portfolio over to an AI. On her one hundredth birthday she had a party. It lasted for ten years, only ending when she woke up in an ophidapt body, with wings, in a sewer pipe out on a Line world called Prapsalonnax. She came out into massive fields containing a strange crop of genetically modified turnips and found a broken-down robotic harvester. There she got to work. Further adventures and careers ensued but over time they still didn't seem to be enough. So, because it somehow seemed the right thing to do, she had returned to Earth.

She turned from the window, toes sinking into scented carpet moss, stepped round her sofa and entertainment pit and headed over to one wall. She waved a hand at it, and what she had previously been studying came up again. The investment tree had grown and she could see its fruits shifting from branch to branch and new twigs growing. This was one representation of her wealth. She sometimes ran it as a hologram in the middle of the room, other times as a four-dimensional manifold, via her aug, but that gave her a headache. What should she do with all this? She was wealthier than most of her age but, as had been a standard throughout time, the old did accrue the most and her contemporaries also had a good lump of plenty.

So here she was, back on Earth aged a hundred and forty-five, and she didn't know what to do. She kept making plans. She would buy a ship and travel, or buy a cargo hauler and become a trader. She would buy an area of land on a Line world and grow something, maybe tea oaks: she liked tea. Or she would buy a portion of a space station and go into manufacturing, maybe quantum crystals or something new in the ever-expanding realm of meta-materials. Maybe she could make androids and go into competition with her old company Cybercorp? However, every time she detailed and expanded on a plan, she started to lose interest. To what purpose? To improve the lot of humanity? She couldn't see how that was possible. To make more money? For what?

She dismissed the investment tree with a wave of her hand, walked back to her sofa pit and jumped down to sprawl across it. She auged into the Net, looking for something interesting, skimming virtualities and running through news stories. Whenever she found something that piqued her interest, she sent it to the wall and it was in this way she watched the revolution on Grayson's World.

It was the place's second revolution. The first had been simply a vote. The planetary AI had allowed local governments in sectors all across the desert world's surface. It had permitted them to make new laws which tended to slant towards humans getting the jobs, not AIs. Lesser AIs, such as those that controlled factories or crop complexes, or resided in Golem bodies or other robotic mechanisms, began to abandon the world. Separatists came and, by dint of a reduced AI grip on the media, began to spread propaganda. Finally, after twenty years, a popular vote was called and the Separatists won. Grayson's World was free and completely human! The planetary AI reduced its function just to controlling the six runcibles scattered about the surface. This, apparently, was not enough. The new planetary government wanted all AIs gone. The planetary AI left and, since an AI was required to control them, the runcibles shut down. Now the people of Grayson's World could set about building a new human future!

The shortages began almost immediately, but this was to be expected as the world became self-sustaining. People grumbled. Since communication with the Polity had not shut down, the population started to notice that they couldn't get the latest entertainment system, the latest augmentations and upgrades, not at once anyway, since they came in by ship. They grumbled some more. Inefficiencies of transport and supply created further shortages of luxury food items. The traders bringing these in rather enjoyed how prices shot up, until the space port riot and local government seizure of cargos, then fewer traders came and only unloaded their goods in the main space station, which remained Polity territory. Luxury items became even more expensive. Over some years, grumbling transformed into further protests. Breakdowns in automated factories and agricultural concerns increased. The outflow from an industrial plant poisoned one of their few lakes. Food items that were not luxuries began to be less . . . available. Fingers of blame were pointed and elections demanded. But, of course, this was impossible during the period of transition. The government employed more police and instituted a 'special force' to deal with public unrest. Some protests turned into further riots and the special force went into action. They imprisoned people, but that was okay – they were Polity agitators, obviously. Riots increased, the special force got nastier and deaths ensued. Prisons filled and of course it made sense to get rid of the worst of those damned agitators. Quiet executions seemed a good solution to the prison overcrowding and when these didn't have the desired effect, they became public hangings. Rationing was introduced. Riots turned into outright rebellion. It took just another twenty years.

Ursula grimaced at the inevitability of it all and felt some anger at the AIs for effectively allowing it. Was this ongoing lesson strictly necessary? The rebellion spread and it was well co-ordinated by dint of the fact that everyone had some kind of augmentation or Netlink. The government used this as an excuse to clamp down on the thing it most feared: another vote. It made all these items illegal. People were to report to local hospitals and other facilities to have their augmentations removed. The special force entered people's homes to destroy Netlinks there. Only, just at this time, a cargo arrived for the revolutionaries: small easily concealed Netlinks so they could continue to communicate. Ursula nodded. That had very definitely been Polity intervention. Perhaps the AIs had decided that the population had suffered enough. The Netlinks were distributed and a vote called. The people wanted to be back in the Polity and they won by a very large margin. This occurred five years after the new revolution began.

Polity ships arrived. The government was ordered to stand down and the special force and police to hand in their weapons.

Of course, they didn't. By this time, after decades of not living under Polity rule, things had changed. Most remembered the Polity and it was they who drove the vote, but tens of thousands had never known it and had grown up under Separatist indoctrination. Many of the more ardent members of this group served the government, quite often with a shock stick, some 'necessary' weapons and the occasional resort to 'inquiries' in a white-tiled cell. They didn't believe in the amnesty the Polity proposed. They believed in the evil of the AIs. They had sucked up with their mother's milk how the Polity was a terrible realm, where humans had been enslaved and brainwashed by the machines.

Polity forces arrived on the surface. Ursula watched this with growing fascination: troops clad in combat armour and power suits exiting landing craft. Above, airfire drones crossed the sky, their surgical strikes taking out arms caches and communications. She saw them steadily securing areas across the desert and in the agricultural areas and then entering the cities. Here they used ionic and bead-blast stunners to take down their opponents with workmanlike efficiency, piling unconscious police and special force soldiers into transports that followed them in. The special force responded with body armour that had inlaid superconducting threads to kill the effect of ionic stunners, and they killed some Polity marines. Almost apologetically, the Polity spokes AI reported that the gloves would have to come off now. Almost apologetically.

The marines and commandos, now freed of restraint, went through opposing forces with the grotesque efficiency of an automated slaughterhouse. Wear that uniform and point a weapon and you died. It was all over, except for in the capital city, where the special force, armed with heavy weapons including grav-tanks, waited. Polity forces came down on the outskirts in landing craft. Airfire drones overflew, hitting easy targets while the marines and commandos went in. Street-to-street fighting ensued but it was necessary and Ursula admired the efficiency of these soldiers. One scene illustrated this for her.

Some of the special force had entrenched themselves by the government buildings. They had two grav-tanks firing on their opponents, without regard for civilian casualties. The airfire drones couldn't take out these tanks because the special force had positioned hostages all around them. Snipers couldn't be used against all of the special force either while this human shield was in place. The fighting there paused and the two sides began talking. Meanwhile, from her perspective, Ursula saw two commandos in chameleoncloth moving into position. A single marine walked in, apparently unarmed, and a special force commander waited for him, while behind, twenty of his men were holding over a hundred hostages at gunpoint. The marine, perhaps because of some prior agreement, came in fatigues only, no armour. At the same time, those camo-commandos moved down on the face of the building above and were only visible to Ursula because the feed highlighted them.

'So what do you want?' the marine asked.

'Polity forces must remove themselves from this city while we negotiate a truce,' said the commander. 'The people demand it.'

It seemed utter rubbish to Ursula. The 'people' were those being held hostage and the special force had lost – all that remained debatable was how much damage they would cause as they were taken down. She noted that the marine, though he didn't wear armour, did wear a visor.

'The people are those you've been killing with your tanks,' said the marine, almost as if he had heard Ursula's thoughts. 'And they are those over there.' He pointed to the hostages. 'You are basically threatening to kill civilians unless we withdraw.'

He was just marking time. The commandos descended on

grav-harnesses – one on each tank. Had those inside even locked the hatches? It didn't matter. Two sharp detonations sent the hatches tumbling. The commander swung his carbine towards the marine and the marine stepped forwards, reaching over his shoulders and drawing two handguns. *Targeting in the visor,* Ursula thought. His boot came up, thumping the carbine aside, but even as he did this, he aimed and fired, two guns pointing at two different targets. Two of those guarding the hostages staggered and explosive armour-piercers detonated in their chests, briefly inflating their armour before dropping them. The commandos threw explosives into the tanks and stepped back, as hot blasts shot out of the hatches. The commander, staggering to one side, fired his carbine. The shot flared on the marine's thigh but he seemed indifferent. Two more shots and the heads of two other guards exploded. A thrumming phutting sound ensued and the rest of the hostage-takers began to drop. The marine swung his weapon back and fired once more, taking off the top of the commander's head. Two pulse rifles fired. One just scattered its shots across the side of a tank but another did hit amidst the civilians and four people died, one of them a child. But the hostage situation was over. The marine turned around and limped slowly away.

Ursula watched him. She wanted to be him and now she knew what she must do. It was that afternoon that she signed up for the Polity military.

19

Present

Walls, ceiling and floor were now routes along the tunnels the cacoraptors had bored under the dried-up sea. Her soldiers flowed along around her, clouding the passageway behind with falling dust and grit. Ursula tried to give an order but found her vocal cords atrophying. This annoyed her but it seemed pointless reforming them, a waste of her physical resources.

'*Blow it*,' she said over com.

The three explosives techs were already on the ceiling; they scuttled along it to the required position, emptying their backpacks of the last explosives, and dropped down. The packs, which to all appearances looked like something that had come from the base, shrivelled on their backs and then drew into their bodies. The techs returned to the colonists, some of whom handed over weapons – one laser carbine from the colonist who'd been killed. The explosives detonated behind them, and rubble collapsed into the tunnel. Along with this came a spill of cacoraptors. The colonists advanced, like oil pouring around engine components. The fallen cacoraptors just flew apart in concentrated weapons fire and physical attack. Ursula focused on Percy moving ahead of her up the rubble pile. He'd retained much of his human form, while she and the colonists had not. Something to examine later.

With her muscles flash-burning energy and breaking rock below her, Ursula leaped up, other colonists near her doing the same. They fountained into the tunnel above, fighting cacoraptors all around them. She could feel it now, further along in a chamber. They didn't hesitate as they flowed along the tunnel. The intent to reach their destination had become more urgent, so they didn't necessarily stay to finish their opponents but just disabled them and shunted them behind. Ahead, around the mouth of the chamber, new forms loomed. These bore some likeness to brontopods, but bone white and also resembling some cave-dwelling crustacean.

'*Now*,' Ursula instructed.

Lecane and her fellows spewed iron-burner fire, coherent beams of it cutting through their opponents and hitting these new creatures. The fire splashed and ate into their ridiculously tough hides and the things charged, some on the ceilings and walls. Ursula sprinted forwards with her personal guard – Callum, Gurda, Nursum, Trakken and others – falling in around her. They moved in perfect consonance as they all leaped at an angle over one of the creatures, hit the wall and scrambled along it, then down again and through. Cacoraptors were packed tight here but Ursula ignored them, leaving others to defend her. She and her guard had made a hole and the rest of the colonists came in behind, like the shaft behind a spearhead. The intense fighting seemed to create a burning organic mass. Weapons and claw-to-claw combat became even more personal and close, like two immiscible fluids flowing around each other. Ursula reached out hard, aggressively, into cacoraptor com.

A hole began forming through the mass ahead and Ursula realized it wasn't just the doing of her soldiers. There was competitiveness here, an urge to combat and a need that could not be denied. The lead cacoraptor fought clear, hurling colonists and its own creatures aside as it moved towards her. Reaching out forcefully through com, and relaying through both colonists and cacoraptors around her, she mentally hammered inside the thing. Her own claws grew and spines extruded from her body. Her teeth were diamond hard and the muscles driving her jaws more powerful than any advanced hydraulics. Her response was visceral, part of the genome. She knew, in that instant, it wouldn't be only a mental battle – just before they slammed together.

Ursula bit down on the head shield, tore at it while slicing her claws into the creature's body, peeling up a softer outer layer, but then skidding on metallic hardness underneath. In the mental plenum, her attack mirrored this, linking to what passed for the creature's immune system, and she turned it inward to attack, bouncing against hardened organs. The creature had toughened up since their last encounter and now closed a claw, digging into her torso and only in that moment did she realize they now matched each other in size. Claw tips met armour, pushed some way in, then issued micro-drills. Long, alligator jaws snapped closed on her head, grating against the protection there.

Hard link, Ursula realized.

Nerves in her hands extended, sheathed in a flexible low-friction coating, then snapped away from their branch points and began to grow their own micro-drills. Just seconds later, they extended from the fingertips under her claws and spread out over her opponent's body, seeking access. The two of them tumbled through the dying chaos of battle. Around her, colonists were similarly locked with their opponents, but the fighting seemed to be fading into a hostile embrace.

Access . . .

The raptor's armour had few chinks in it, but she had a grip on its immune system and attacked it from within, opening holes. It tried the same with her, but slid away, the nanosuite blocking its every attempt. Pressure ramped up. The jaws over her head were building further muscle, dense and packed with energy. The creature knew her vulnerability – her brain just in one place, while its brain was distributed throughout its body. She made neural connections but also felt others on a deeper level. The nanosuite was flowing into the creature along her injected nerves now, breaking cell membranes, unravelling genome programs, short-circuiting energy processes. It felt, in that instant, almost like cheating.

The raptor knew. Its tactics abruptly changed and it tried to pull away from her, slashing with all its limbs, releasing her head and trying to bite through her neck, which was now tougher than towing cable. They slammed through the surrounding opponents and into the wall. But now she had her foothold inside it. She snapped her own nerves, shrieking on the feedback until she could kill it, and fell away. The creature hung there, claws dug into the wall. Ursula landed on the floor, her own claws on feet and hands dug in too. She felt her connections to it strengthening, as nanomachines scavenged and reproduced. It kept trying to resist, but kept being undermined from within. She took over the scattered portions of its mind – spreading with a domino effect – and then she had it in her grip. It fell from the wall and crashed to the floor, folding up, foetal.

She spread out from within it, using its multiple links to the creatures all around, but also via nanomachine infection in them through various wounds and holes. Around her, cacoraptors released their death grips on her colonists. *Her creatures.* The raptors became hers too as she spread and wiped out the programmed hostility, the same way she had in Percy. Having integrated them all into a whole under her, she began to find it difficult to distinguish between colonists and cacoraptors. They were all an extension of her now.

433

She barked a laugh – all she was capable of with what remained of her vocal cords. Detaching one claw from the floor, she waved it, feeling the need for some physical action to dispatch her order. This was human, of course. Her units ordered themselves around her, untangling, many retreating into the tunnel. Hints of com reached her. Why? They were just extensions and should present little more than feedback, as from the nerves in her fingers.

'You're wiping them! You're swamping them!'

Ursula turned her attention to this alien com. The machine stood before her – this separate primitive structure with merely loose connections to her. She tried to harden those connections but felt her grip sliding away.

'Ursula!'

As if waking from a nightmare, Ursula started to make distinctions. Something else was fighting her, she realized, and turned away from the machine to focus on it. Another unit, not yet integrated. Recognition arose on a wave of panic.

I'm losing myself . . .

The unit was Nursum, coiled on the floor like the erstwhile leader, fighting to maintain his integrity.

'*Stop.*' It wasn't really a word but something deep in her network. She felt her grip failing and, with that, her human mind rising further into wakefulness. She slid off Nursum first, and then, bit by bit, released her full grip on the units that were her colonists. Her grip on the cacoraptors remained firm, however. She swung back to the machine.

Vrease.

'*I have it now,*' she sent. '*I think I have it now.*'

She rose to stand, all too aware that the '*stop*' had come from the nanosuite AI and that, given freedom from it, she would have continued integrating them all completely. Why not? What purpose was there in them maintaining their individuality? She was the leader, the central point, pre-eminent. She gazed at Vrease. And what was the purpose of her? What utility did she have now by always coming into conflict? Then she looked within herself and around at the nanosuite. It too needed to be fully part of her before she could integrate the rest as needed. But that battle must be for another time, because further danger loomed above, and was entering the tunnels.

The lead cacoraptor had been lax, Ursula realized. Its dependence on its offspring had limited its abilities in a way that they didn't limit her. It should have left detectors in the tunnels, not just those erstwhile tunnel-repair creatures in the walls. Nevertheless, she knew the prador were coming. All the cacoraptors and colonists acted as a spread sensory web for her. She detected certain compounds in the air, diffusing from above, and interpreted vibrations from there, as well as alien EMR bouncing down the passageways. She divined that they'd just entered the upper tunnels. They would be a little while yet because they were almost certainly doing a methodical sweep, as any soldiers would.

'The prador are coming,' she said, with vocal cords now growing back.

'What do we do?' asked Callum, moving into view, Gurda behind him.

Both retained a partially human appearance, though their legs were hinged like herons and their necks had extended, not quite as long as hers. Their faces had also jutted out, like those of baboons, to sprout hard cutting teeth. But these were now collapsing back into their previous human look, while their claws were retracting. Ursula noted this, and that other colonists were also returning at least some of their humanity to themselves. She started to make similar changes to herself, for now, just as reassurance.

435

The nanosuite had further extended her partial disconnection from them, and each colonist had recovered some individuality. Even so, her network was cross-fertilizing. Her colonists were taking on data from the cacoraptors and vice versa. Even as she answered, 'We kill them,' she concentrated on this data exchange. Their weapons were at present limited, though those the raptors had taken from around the base, and used here, helped a little. Given time, she could have the cacoraptors manufacture pulse rifles, slug throwers and laser carbines from inside their bodies. But, assessing tactics and logistics, she saw a better option in the time available.

'*Lecane*,' she sent, while selecting a hundred raptors and linking them into Lecane's crew. '*Caulter*,' she sent, and did the same with him. Materials were available in the tunnels and the two hundred of them immediately spread out, changing even as they did so. Lecane's raptors soon found streaks of iron oxide in the walls of one tunnel and began to chew their way into it. Caulter's raptors started to pull apart the dead, the partially dead and those that Ursula, after a brief assessment, decided would not recover in time to be useful in the coming conflict. Six of the dead were colonists. Another eight colonists would not recover in time, but she didn't let the raptors take them. Her able colonists had too much individuality now to tolerate such a thing.

'And how do we do that?' asked Vrease, then, 'I see.'

Ursula glanced at the woman, noting that she did indeed see, since Ursula had continued transmitting data to her. She considered closing her out, but quashed the idea. Vrease still remained a useful asset, even though she couldn't be fully included. Perhaps, during the coming fight, the cybernetic woman would be destroyed. If not, Ursula felt she should dispense with her later.

She continued to assess her forces and make her plans. Two hundred tunnel-repair raptors remained scattered throughout the system, for those they'd encountered had not been the only ones. Some were out of the walls, but a lot remained in place, on hold. She ordered those remaining out of the walls, then detailed her instructions and sent them. The tunnel-repair raptors moved down through the system, heading for a point not far from her and, even as she turned her attention elsewhere, they began to bore a new tunnel.

Now she saw that the three explosives techs had begun to reintegrate with the rest of the colonists. Having been given spare weapons, they were changing themselves to match all the fighters who had taken on Trakken's form. She reviewed this briefly, then cut out another hundred raptors and connected them to the three.

'*Materials*,' one of the three noted.

Ursula sent instructions. Eighty of their raptors would fight just like the rest and, during the fighting, gather what they needed. By the time Ursula and her forces were done down here, they'd be producing something useful for her objective above. The remaining twenty, and the three, had to seek out materials in the surrounding tunnels. She needed explosives fast.

'*Objective?*' asked another of the three as they moved off, the twenty raptors moving in around them.

Ursula sent various locations on the map of the system where explosives needed to be planted. When they queried this non-verbally, she felt some irritation, then tentatively tried to press them. She felt no resistance from the nanosuite so pushed harder. They queried no longer and just headed off to do their duty.

The rest of the raptors she began to connect under Trakken. Those that hadn't already were taking on more human forms and Ursula studied the change for a minute. Seeing the same inclusion program she'd used with Percy, she killed it. The human form had its utility but remaining as they were – much more plastic and able to change – the raptors would be more useful. They had their usual complement of natural weapons but Ursula sought out programming inside them for the physical changes they'd undergone, and the methods they'd used, to attack the prador previously, and she began to re-form them to those. Trakken absorbed the data, the change, and in turn started to divide his forces into squads to fit into Ursula's growing planning.

What else?

'We let them get down deep,' said Callum, assessing her plans himself. 'It seems likely to me others will still be filtering in from above. Why do you want to cut them off? Why kill only some of them?'

She felt his aggression and recognized that it hadn't been so evident before. Even though the nanosuite had limited her power over them, the cross-fertilization was having its effect. This would be useful later, when she dealt with the nanosuite.

'We let maybe a hundred of them get down deep, then blow the tunnels above,' she explained. 'I estimate the collapsed tunnels will hold the ones above for a few hours.'

Her brief explanation to Callum was broadcast to the rest, and she could feel questions arising. Again she felt that surge of irritation and decided to test how much the nanosuite was limiting her. She pushed, suppressing them, demanding obedience. Once again the nanosuite didn't interfere. Its logic wasn't human, she understood. It had stopped her losing herself, stopped her becoming completely cacoraptor because the aim here, as Oren had said, was for soldiers with a human basis – controllable. Her assertion of power like this was very human.

The complement from her explosives crew quickly gathered the needed materials, mostly by chewing up the burned remains of the tunnel-repair raptors. The crew had also found sulphur and saltpetre in the walls, for the ground below the seabed was rich in chemicals. She briefly considered the radioactives above and below, but it would take too long to adapt any of her soldiers to do something with them. Perhaps later. She delved inside them to observe the strong chemical processes at work. The twenty cacoraptors had also grown exterior bags and, even as she watched, one of the three extruded a turd of chemical explosive through an anus on its back, into its pack.

Rumbling came from above; the prador were getting closer. Ursula looked around for some method of tracking their progress. In the headlong rush to get down here, they'd abandoned much of their equipment and supplies. The robots – other than the mosquito guns Callum had grabbed – remained underneath the ruined prador shuttle. She riffled through minds to find out what had been brought.

Jackpot.

Two colonists were carrying packs filled with surveillance drones. She studied the two. They were Trakken-format but had also radio-linked to the drones they carried. She was about to go straight through them to the drones, but pulled back. She must keep her touch more gentle than was now her instinct. Shutting down debate had been stupid, for in not knowing the AI mind of the nanosuite, she didn't know what level of autocracy would alert it.

'*Send drones here,*' she instructed them, marking various places on the map.

'*The prador will destroy them,*' one replied, again, as with Scarven and her mosquitoes, not wanting to lose the asset that had effectively become part of him.

'*We need to track them,*' Ursula replied, suppressing that irritation.

'*Understood.*'

Through other eyes she saw their packs open rubbery mouths and spit out drones like glassy bubbles. Almost lighter than air, they sped away. She gazed through their sensors as they shot along the tunnels, then into the shafts. A couple of levels up, some stuck to the sides of the shafts while the others continued on. There was no point watching the tunnels, but the shafts would give her the prador progress. One drone flew past a cacoraptor bowed over by a wall where it had been chewing out yellow sulphur. Its body now looked emaciated, it had put so much of itself into the explosives filling its pack. After a moment it looked up, tracked the drone and headed after it. Others of the explosives tech crew were on the move too.

Finally, one drone entered a shaft, broadcasting there for a moment, gone a moment later. Ursula replayed what it had seen. At the top of the shaft was a prador, legs braced against the walls, claw-mounted Gatling cannon zeroing on the drone then firing. So that's how far down they'd got.

'Methods of attack,' Ursula stated out loud, her words broadcast over com. She sent details: those of Trakken's people who were armed were to fight a steady retreat, with conventional weapons inflicting minimal damage. The cacoraptors armed with prador-killing 'natural' weapons were to head here – she marked a series of shafts on the map and a route to the level below the one she intended to blow to cut them off. Lecane's and Caulter's crews were then to position themselves here and here . . . Iron-burners on narrow beam to burn holes in the prador's main armour and to avoid hitting the legs, with Caulter's crew following with the thread-laced acid. The aim was to kill the prador but preserve, as best as possible, their armour.

'I think I see what you intend now,' said Vrease. 'What can I do?'

'You fight, but you have a powerful EMR unit in you,' said Ursula.

'Interference,' said Vrease.

'Yes.'

Ursula commed the same instruction to all: once the prador were down deep enough, before Lecane and Caulter's attack and just after the tunnels were blown, they were all to start broadcasting interference. The tunnel collapse should cut out most prador com, but she wanted nothing getting out.

Now Ursula began to listen into the alien com. She had a basis to work from with the prador lexicon sent from the Polity, but there was coding to break. She began mentally separating things out and soon detected a telemetry signal and delved into that. The coding was difficult at first, but the AI assistance of the nanosuite kicked in and it came apart. AIs were very useful in that respect – very little in the way of codes could not be broken by them. Each prador broadcast its position to its fellows. The signal bounced up the chain of them to go to the ship, along with a steadily expanding map of tunnels they'd explored. Woven into this was the physical state of the prador, an accounting of armour condition and their supply of munitions. She copied and broadcast this to all of her own people. Next she delved into the prador's straightforward com between each other, and to the ship. The coding collapsed too and she began automatically translating, steadily identifying individuals and their manner of communication, copying it and broadcasting it too.

'The purpose of this?' asked Callum. Ursula glanced at him and at Vrease. Vrease had divined her aims and yet he had not. Perhaps her constant suppressing of her own people undermined their ability to think freely? She could see that from a human perspective, but her every instinct screamed no. She moved to contain the rising frustration in her that now seemed a constant, and broadcast the entirety of her plan. A data sigh of understanding ensued, but debate began to grow again. Was this the best way? Shouldn't they do this or that? She tentatively quelled

441

questions, while monitoring the nanosuite and probing the limits it imposed. The thing did not respond at first, then abruptly kicked in and began to assist her. She quickly understood why. The thing was backing her up because, as well as the aim to create human-based cacoraptor soldiers, that purpose had a foundation: killing prador.

Another drone blasted to pieces, and another. Ursula watched them when she could, but also observed through the eyes of the three explosives techs and their crew. They'd distributed much of their loads now. One of them dropped from a ceiling, its work done, only to shriek its own telemetry at her as a particle beam struck it. It responded to the intense destructive heat of the particulate, skin peeling away as deeper layers spread superconductor and heat-resistant ceramics. But with its resources depleted, it couldn't do this fast enough and burned, struggling along the floor, until a prador blasted it to pieces with Gatling fire. Only a second later did Ursula realize it had actually been a human, and that she'd just lost one of the explosives techs.

Abruptly, the prador began moving a lot faster – dropping down the shafts and ignoring the side tunnels. She read the change of tactics in their com. They had finally detected that the bulk of opposition forces lay further below. She counted, estimated, integrated and knew roughly when at least fifty of them were down past the explosives. The first of these began to run into weapons fire from Trakken's people.

'We're in it now,' commented Callum, as the tunnels filled with the crackle of beam weapons and the clatter of projectile fire.

Ursula grimaced at that, but had no time to allow her mind to stray as it once had, far too much, during her military career. They were certainly in it now and this was real fighting – not war games. She ignored him and continued counting and estimating.

Finally she decided there were enough and, rather than send an order, routed the detonation signal herself through the tech crew. The boom echoed through the tunnels and the floor jerked up underneath her.

'*Yes we are,*' she finally replied.

Past

The ground was relatively soft and Ursula's trenching shovel, with its chain-glass edge, went in easily. She was stronger now, of course. The first nanosuite upgrade for the recruits in her training outfit had been six months ago. Implantation was under autosurgeon – inlays of micro-factories on their bones. Remembering similar procedures from before, Ursula had known the effect wouldn't be noticeable at first, but gradually the new nanites wove in artificial muscle, carbon bone strengthening, and produced double-carrier haemoglobin. This brought them to about the standard for current humanity. After a few weeks, Ursula had begun to find training easier. The next change, after three months, was an update to the suites. This resulted in faster clearance of toxins, lung expansion and triple-density fats. Yes, she was definitely tougher now.

She chopped a square in the turf of what had at first looked like pink and pale green lichen, but which started writhing as she cut down. Dividing the area into a grid, she sliced up rectangular turfs and piled them on one side of the hole – the side facing towards the sea where, just offshore, the old cargo ship sat at anchor. She peered over in that direction, beyond the old cargo ship, but the weapons barge had not yet appeared on the horizon.

'How're you getting on with the suit?' asked Delgardo, who was digging his own foxhole just twenty feet away.

Since she'd been thinking about her nanosuite, Ursula was momentarily confused, then she understood Delgardo was talking about what she wore.

'Hardly notice it,' she replied.

The survival suit was a blend of meta-materials that offered some assist, with sliding layers powered by laminar storage on the belt. It also harvested energy from temperature differentials, EMR, air movement and her movements, though it didn't noticeably restrict them. The meta-material also provided breathable air from the cyanide-laden atmosphere here and could produce it from water too. A chain-glass bubble enclosed her head, with a reactive layer in it to cut harmful radiations and another to provide a HUD – head-up display. All the recruits here were testing these suits out in supposed battle conditions, but Macannan, being what he was, didn't want them just standing around, so they had to dig foxholes.

Ursula continued digging, piling yellow loam beyond the turfs. This all seemed such a pointless exercise to her, as so much in military training appeared to be. Surely the suits had first been modelled by AI down to the smallest detail, then tested thoroughly before humans wore them? She had said as much to Delgardo and he'd replied, 'We're mushrooms.' He had to explain the old saying to her and continued with a shrug, 'They're testing the weapon and tell us we're testing the suits, but I think the reality is that our inclusion is to accustom us to battle conditions. We can take in all the theory and piss about in virtualities, but there's nothing quite like the real thing.'

Real thing, Ursula thought as she dug, and remembered her beating in the Gagarand. She grudgingly accepted Delgardo's contention but still it all seemed like make-work. However, she was finding the physical exercise of digging a hole quite soothing, even when she reached the orange layer of dirt, disturbed hibernating spike worms and had to pull their pincers off her suit and throw the creatures out beyond the dirt pile, where they swiftly began to dig down again.

Soon she reached a layer of gravel, then, a foot down into that, slimy orange water that began to fill the hole. The regulation depth had been achieved so she folded up the trenching tool and hung it on her belt, grabbed her weapon, which she'd been strictly instructed not to lose, and crouched in the hole, with the water rising up around her ankles. She tried the controls on one wrist of her suit, raised one foot and watched the flipper extend from the base of her boot. That seemed fine. The webs that extended between her fingers made handling her weapon a bit more difficult, though. She would have to watch that, so attached the weapon to the stick patch across her belly and pulled the safety strap across it, since she wouldn't be using it yet.

Taking her enhancer band out of her belt bag, she attached it to her bubble helmet and looked out to sea again. The weapons barge had arrived and was a black dot on the horizon. Magnification gave her an at-slant view of the vessel – just a hull with a long cylinder sitting on top. Would the weapon work as predicted? Air diffusion had always been a problem with particle beams and the air pressure here was twice Earth normal. But the new particulate was supposed to last a lot longer before vaporizing. It had a magneto-electric effect that pulled it towards the beam centre and supposedly maintained coherence. She would see. With any luck, it wouldn't be like on a previous test when the beam turned into what was effectively a flamethrower and started a forest fire. That had also, supposedly, been a test of the hotsuits with which the recruits had been provided, and had been a success. She had her doubts, though she guessed it backed up Delgardo's 'real thing' idea. Running through a firestorm between exploding cycads had been very real. Yes, the hotsuits had worked, but she saw the remains of the weapon afterwards, half melted into the ground, and thought that rather stretched the definition of 'success'.

'Okay, we're gonna fire it now,' said Macannan over com. 'Get ready to deploy directly after the strike . . . you have your orders.'

She knew he was speaking from a grav-platform high in the sky, also occupied by the technicians and scientists who had put the weapon together. That they weren't actually on the barge increased her doubts.

From her perspective, the barge sat over to one side of the cargo ship. She took off the enhancer band, since it might magnify the heat flash beyond the ability of the reactive layer in her helmet to stop it. She waited, thumping her fist against the turfs, impatient and just a little bit fed up. A spike worm writhed up out between turfs and tried to snap its pincers closed on her hand. She held up a finger and began playing with it, almost missing the firing, but looked up after, in a moment of irritation, grabbing the worm and tossing it away. A bright blue sun opened at the weapon and the particle beam stabbed out of it across the ocean, also bright blue at first then shading to purple. Needle thin in the distance, it hit the cargo ship a couple of feet wide. It went through it like a metal spike through cheese and exited on the near side in an actinic explosion that darkened her helmet. But still she saw it scoring inshore, the ground boiling up below it and flaring into flame, stabbing just feet above the heads of the recruits who had dug in over to her left. She acknowledged that foxholes had been a good idea. If they'd been standing on the surface, out in the open, those recruits would have been toast.

The cargo ship bucked up on the flash, its back breaking, and disappeared in a cloud of steam as it started to go down. Ursula moved to climb out of her foxhole, then damned her stupidity and dropped back down. How the hell had she forgotten what would ensue? The shockwave hit, filling the air with steam and throwing turfs down onto her. As that passed, she peeked over to see the approaching wall of water. It boiled across the land and she ducked down again. As the wave reached her, it dumped the entire pile of earth she'd mounded up on top of her in a flood of warm almost soapy water. Now she damned her stupidity. She'd been given the details of all this and, with her tactical integration training, should have realized that making a mound in front of her hole had been a stupid idea. What was the matter with her?

Fortunately the mud and turf were almost liquefied by the water and she pushed up through it easily into further foaming, muddy water. A current pushed her just a little way back from the hole, then reversed as the water started to flow back towards the sea. She could see nothing through the murk as she extended her flippers and began swimming in the direction of the flow. Belatedly, she remembered to take out her enhancer band and attach it again. Bland brown swirling with foam went through a number of colour changes as the band gradually built up a picture of what surrounded her. Checking the side menu, she saw the device was using all sorts of emitted radiations as it enhanced her view, but was operating mostly on sonar now. She saw chunks of detritus tumbling past, Delgardo over to her left and others beyond him, with still others to her right. The band started blinking a direction arrow: straight ahead.

Ursula came to the surface as the water grew shallower and shallower, then went deep again as the retreating wave took her out from the shore. Looking around, she picked up on unidentified swimmers and wondered if these were some of those they were supposed to deal with as they secured the ship. Macannan had been a bit vague about it all. They were simply to clear the ship of enemy combatants and secure it. Ursula assumed those combatants would be sub-AI androids dressed up and armed like Separatists – probably clad in some kind of survival-combat gear. But would they be outside the ship? As one of the shapes drew in towards her from below, she tumbled, closing the webbing on her fingers, unstrapping and detaching her weapon and then aiming and firing in one.

The back-blast pipe over her shoulder killed the recoil of the hammer gun. Its projectile left a white super-cavitating line through the water and struck the target dead centre. The target jerked and flipped as the white line sped beyond it and down. In the far distance, down deep, came the flash of an explosion and the sonic wave from it reached her a minute later, as she watched a huge fish like a coelacanth sculling for the bottom, trailing a line of intestine from a hole in its side.

'Nice shooting, numbskull,' said Macannan over com. 'You just put blood in the water for the resarks *and* you alerted the enemy to your approach.'

'I thought it was the enemy, sir.' Ursula swam on.

'Read your prep, did you?' Macannan enquired.

Ursula didn't reply and Macannan said no more. Niggling recall gave her a hot head-to-foot cringe. She had skipped a lot of the preparatory data, utterly sure that her integrating faculty enabled her to dismiss the irrelevant. But now fragments of what she'd not paid particular attention to began to float up to consciousness. Macannan had not been vague. The combatants would be inside the ship. The canths tended to avoid anything they couldn't identify as their normal prey. Putting blood in the water was inadvisable because it would attract resarks, whatever they were.

'Easy mistake to make,' said Delgardo, but she didn't like his tone.

Ursula hunted around for something to say. 'Serious ammo they gave us.'

'Which is why we have to be utterly certain of our targets and the positions of each other,' said Delgardo dryly.

Again she felt a hot cringe as she realized how many holes there were in her prep. What the hell had she been thinking? Now her integrating faculty began to kick in, and hard. A moment later she dredged up resark from her unconscious – a contraction of red shark – just before she saw one. It was only a yard long but it still attacked one of the recruits further down the line and tried to bite off his foot. Ursula had one swimming around her a moment later. It attacked but couldn't get its teeth through her suit and she knocked it away. But it kept coming back. She reached for a sidearm then remembered that she only had the one projectile weapon. It would be overkill and she'd have Macannan on her back directly afterwards.

'There she is,' said Delgardo.

She glanced across at him as he swiped with his combat knife and sent a resark tumbling in two pieces. Now she remembered her knife in the sheath at her calf. Why had she forgotten? She blink-activated her HUD and checked her air supply. It seemed fine – no anoxia or anything else untoward.

'We'll sweep front to back. Seamore, get the breaching charges set.'

Ursula impaled the resark that was intent on taking off her kneecap and discarded it behind her. Ahead, the ship lay almost broken in two and tilted on its side at the bottom. She was about to suggest they go in through the break, but of course that was too obvious.

'Incoming!' someone shouted.

'Down!' Delgardo ordered.

White lines cut up through the water from the break in the ship as the recruits dived towards the bottom. They speared down smoothly and Ursula found herself struggling to catch up. Her HUD, still activated, alerted her to why. She blink-activated the suit, turning its exterior frictionless, and then zipped down after them more quickly, with the white lines of the projectiles streaking over just behind her. This was 'battle conditions', of course, though she felt a weary dismissiveness about it. The projectiles wouldn't kill them, just take them out of the action.

Most of them reached the seabed. Two were hit on the way and continued on down, shuddering and jerking, to hit the bottom and bounce up again. She watched them with faint curiosity. The projectiles must cause their suit assist to malfunction.

'A reminder for those who didn't fully read their prep: if you get hit, the stun discharge is going to hurt like fuck. Perhaps those who do get hit might bear in mind why the enemy was alerted.'

The cringe began to rise in Ursula again, then just died away. So what? Her next unarmed combat session would be hard, but her opponents would not be trying to hurt her any more than was usual. The shots now streaked down at them from the ship, but the bottom offered lots of cover in the form of boulders and slabs covered in penny oysters and scimitar mussels. They worked their way along it towards the front of the ship, intermittently returning fire, igniting bright explosions in the centre of the ship. Reaching the edge of a clear area in front of the nose of the ship, they halted.

'Cover over there,' said Delgardo, a yellow line appearing in Ursula's and the other recruits' HUDs outlining an extended pile of boulders. 'Mass firing on my mark and then we move. Set for ten shots.' Ursula tapped the display on her weapon from one to ten. 'And . . . mark!'

Ursula pushed herself up and opened fire. Despite the recoil tube, she found the weapon driving her back through the water, but she kept on target. All their shots streaked in. She saw one retaliating shot hit just a couple of feet to her left and felt a wash of pain through her legs, as though they were burning, before they grew numb and leaden. At the centre break in the ship, their shots arrived. Hundreds of explosions boiled the water and pushed one half of the ship back from the break, separating it completely so it rolled over fully on its side.

'Move!' Delgardo bellowed.

The recruits did so, weapons slapped to stick patches and swimming fast. Ursula could now only swim with her arms, her legs dead behind her, but fortunately the mass firing had quelled the enemy long enough for her to reach the boulder pile and beyond it into the cover of the ship. She arrived just as the breaching charges blew – four planar explosives cutting out a square of hull. The recruits streamed in and almost immediately the flashes of shots came from inside. Ursula went through last, some tingling and pain in her legs as the feeling began to return.

What the fuck?

She swam into a long elliptical corridor, detached her weapon and held it one-handed as she towed herself along the ridged, almost stony scaling along the walls. Debris tumbled all around her and she gazed at a hemispherical lump of what, by its exposed interior, seemed to be a biomech. It had four legs, the stubs of others, and what looked like the remains of a claw.

Bug hunt, she decided, remembering something she'd been told not so long ago, but then thought about it a bit more. As she recollected, the bugs in question weren't armed. She wondered who had designed such a silly scenario as this. Probably someone who spent far too much time playing games in a virtuality. She could see no real-world application in this, and at first it annoyed her, then bored her.

The recruits were spreading out through the nose of the ship. A scan map arrived in her HUD of the almost-organic interior of the ship, with tunnels like those of an ants' nest and large cyst-like rooms. The map gave her the positions of her fellows and a targeting link to her weapon. She would receive a warning

451

if any of them were in her direction of fire, but the decision to fire remained hers. Then and there she felt a momentary frisson. People could die during this exercise under friendly fire. Macannan had warned them of this but it hadn't really impinged until now. The map also designated her search areas and, fortunately, enough feeling had returned to her legs so she could release the wall and begin kicking through the water.

A right turn took her into another tunnel, with one of the cyst rooms at the end. She slowed at the entrance and peeked round as quickly as she could. Nothing was sitting on the oddly shaped floor gratings and nothing could be concealed. The place was empty. Turning away, she swam back down the corridor. The shot slammed into her back, suffusing her with agony. She found herself jerking through the water, her weapon spinning from her grip. She got a glimpse back at the biomech coming out of the room along the ceiling, but the stun round hurt too much for her to feel stupid. After a while blackness washed over her.

Consciousness returned as she was dumped on the deck of a grav-platform and someone removed her bubble helmet. She lay there gaping, thinking someone had tried to asphyxiate her with the local air, until she realized the platform was enclosed in its own chain-glass bubble. Macannan loomed over her, his arms folded.

'Sloppy, Treloon. Very sloppy,' was all he said before turning away.

20

After the explosion blocked the tunnels up above, the data scream she had ordered dropped out most electromagnetic com, but cacocom used more than EMR. Ursula transferred over to the sound spectrum, enhanced by chemical communication. Even though the latter was slow for her purposes, it filled in detail. Her soldiers continued their retreat down the tunnels but she noted lives blinking out with alarming regularity and speeded it up. It was worse behind, where her cacoraptors attacked with only claws, acid and body discharges of electricity. No pushover, the prador had come armed for cacoraptors. Every one of them sported a particle weapon and Gatling cannon, but they also had thermite grenades and jets of liquid nitrogen, the combination of which left raptor bodies shattered on the floor. And, even though they'd lost their ability to communicate over EMR, they clattered their mandibles at each other, giving terse instructions, and maintained order. She assessed that.

As she'd seen with the first prador landing, and the data from the Polity, all but three of these prador were second-children – the three being first-children. She assessed their previous com, and now their clattering speech, and found one that seemed to be issuing the orders. She read his confusion about the loss of com with their fellows behind and his understanding that he was now being blocked. Further analysing exchanges, she saw the tightness of their command structure. Almost certainly, if the lead prador here died, one of the other two would take over. She adjusted her battle plan to incorporate that.

'*Now,*' she instructed Lecane's and Caulter's crews.

Within a minute, the beams of iron-burners, on narrow aperture, hit the back ends of the three first-children. Their armour went white hot at once, began ablating in flakes, and then the beams stabbed in. All three issued bubbling shrieks, firing their weapons wildly and even hitting their comrades. The iron-burner raptors on the ceiling just moved on and began firing on second-children.

Useful, thought Ursula, at once ordering all the iron-burners to the ceilings. It seemed the prador, under the influence of gravity, were making a mistake she had once made long ago during military training. They were thinking their enemies were down at the same level as them. She also now realized something else about that training. The robots they'd fought had resembled prador – further confirmation that the Polity had been expecting the war for a long time.

Meanwhile, one of Caulter's raptor crew came in low on the lead prador – the creature obviously blinded by pain – and snaked underneath, then rose up behind it, stabbing a hand down into the glowing hole and rolling away. Not far enough. Another prador opened up on it with a stream of liquid nitrogen, slowing it and finally bringing it to a splintering halt, whereupon Gatling fire blasted it to stony fragments.

'*Move in,*' she instructed generally, but issued special instructions over cacocom concerning the lead prador. Her other soldiers swarmed in on all sides among the prador. Close combat and weapons fire at point-blank range ensued. Just like the other two, and further second-children being similarly attacked, the lead prador tried to run. Her forces brought down the others by piling on them and grabbing legs and claws until the acid did its work. But the lead prador she allowed to escape.

It crashed through the melee, unsubtly guided by cacoraptors and colonists, finally staggering into a section of tunnel occupied by fewer fighters. There it began shuddering before collapsing. She thought this was the end of it, but with a thump, its armour parted horizontally, the top half rising up on polished rods then hinging over, and the prador was ejected by an air blast. It turned as it hit the ceiling and clung there shivering, fluid boiling out of a hole in its back end. She wondered if it would survive, if it could survive, but it released its hold and crashed to the floor with its legs moving weakly, growing still. *Useful*, thought Ursula again. She'd wanted access to that particular armour suit, and to find out how it opened, and could now study it from the inside. Retrospectively, she realized it had only abandoned its armour because she'd allowed it to get away from the fighting. She got on the move, with Vrease, Callum, Gurda, Nursum and Percy at her shoulders, raptors falling in around.

Gatling fire now smashed into the ceiling, raining grit. Positioning the iron-burners there had been a tactic too good to last. They came down and infiltrated through the melee. Big crab claws swept across, saw-toothed outside edges ripping across raptor and adapted human bodies. She saw one picked up in a claw and falling in two halves. Analysis: some kind of shearfield on the inner faces of the prador's claws. Avoid. A prador slammed into a wall, half burying itself, glutinous fluid pouring in thick strands from a hole in its underside. A particle beam hit straight down the business end of an iron-burner and this one just exploded.

The battle proceeded. Ursula now counted a hundred and

four prador trapped down in the tunnels. Thirty-five were disabled, with holes burned through their armour and acid eating out the occupants. Seven had been brought down by weapons fire and other attacks – legs blown away and glowing holes punched through. They were useless to her purpose. Fifty of them had formed up and were trying to punch their way back up, seemingly unaware that they had no way out as yet. She moved through the outskirts of the fighting, pausing to watch another prador being brought down. Its particle beam lashed out towards her and Percy threw himself in its path as she ducked aside. But then the prador went down. Percy rose up again, charcoaled and smoking, skin shifting and repairing. She watched him for a moment, aware that it had been her brief startlement that had thrown him in the path of the beam, not his own decision.

Finally she reached where the prador first-child had abandoned its armour; she moved over to it. She peered inside it with the whole of her sensorium, mapping out actuators, hydraulics, stepper motors and other paraphernalia that enabled it to respond smoothly to the prador inside. She noted that the creature had left a couple of legs in their sleeves and pulled them out. This hard technology seemed simple enough but she needed to get into the operating system. Moving round to the upper 'lid', she dipped her head down on her still-long neck and put it in the head turret. Some kind of head-up display flickered there in the visor. Retracting, she studied it further, finally locating a flat mica-like interface that seemed likely to be for programming. It made sense to put it on the inside, because outside it would have been vulnerable to virtual attack. Peering closer, magnification ramping up, she mapped out a grid of meta-materials and neatly clumped nanotubes and, even while doing so, began to reform the surface of her hand, expanding the nerves down her arm and running new connections into her brain. Then she reached out and placed her hand against the interface.

From her hand she injected a photon series and began to integrate the feedback. At once, she fell into programming virtuality. The basic programming language was synaptic, and she'd not expected otherwise. A programming language based on prador text glyphs overlaid this. The nanosuite kicked in again – the AI collating and feeding back to her base instructions. The simplicity here surprised her and seemed to confirm that the prador did not have AIs. It took her only moments to confirm that, with some adjustments to her body form, she'd be able to control the armour. But at present it was in shutdown mode. She looked around.

The prador were now falling faster, their numbers having reached a low enough level that they struggled to protect each other. She estimated another half an hour to bring them all down. Her own guard filled this tunnel and numerous colonists and cacoraptors lay between her and the nearest of them. So she climbed into the armour and, searching along the base, found the simple open-and-close pad usually operated by one of the creature's underslung manipulatory arms. She pressed it down and the lid hinged over and began to close down on her on those polished rods. As it did so, she inserted her arms into the claw sleeves, steadily extending them, melding her claw fingers and shaping them to fit the actuators. She stooped down low, opening out her ribs and spreading her body to prevent it being crushed. Sucking in material from her legs, attenuating them, she inserted them into two of the leg sleeves, then moved her head up into the turret as it finally closed.

The HUD lit up with prador glyphs she now read with ease. She realized that, though the armour had exterior mandibles, the sleeves to those were loose and adjustable, enabling retraction to operate a push-button console below the HUD. Ursula's jawbone cracked at her chin and began opening out, acquiring two joints, muscle rearranging and, in places, turning into ligaments. She soon had her own usable mandibles and reached out to begin operating the console, scrolling through menus in the HUD which were little different in their basic format from the human ones. She went through them all, fast, absorbing the parameters of the suit. Mental adjustment was required because the prador didn't have such a strong sense of touch as humans did, but a greater perception of the position of their limbs. Soon she found out that she didn't need to grow further legs to operate the suit, because they were made to work for prador who had lost limbs. She next noted damage reports. The iron-burner had knocked out much, but the suit was rerouting around that. The acid had inflicted the worst damage to actuators and control optics. Optimizing the rerouting, she took it to its best functionality. Sensory feedback increased, and she rose to standing, then snapped one claw at the air, initiating the shearfield along its inner faces. Further checking showed she was low on ammo and that the power supply was down to below half. A protocol connected to that had shut down the suit's internal grav-engine because of its heavy power draw. What she had would have to be enough. She hit the touchpad again and the armour opened, but she shut down the air-blast ejection and carefully climbed out, coming down onto the floor on all fours.

'My, you've changed,' said Vrease – it seemed a standard response now.

Ursula's small legs, larger arms and spread body had put her out of balance and she could no longer stand upright, so sat back on her haunches. It was all over out here now and she felt a sudden panic on seeing that nearly an hour had passed. Something was vibrating the tunnels and it didn't take much logical integration to realize the prador were operating a boring machine above. She assessed her forces.

The prador had killed thirty-five colonists and over two hundred cacoraptors. She studied the armoured suits that seemed most likely usable and assigned them all to the remaining colonists, keeping back one for Percy too. There were eighty-six of them. Next, after broadcasting all that she'd learned about the suits, she set her creatures to work. First the suits needed to be opened and for this she selected twenty worm-form cacoraptors and set them in motion. Attenuating their bodies, they approached various suits and squirmed inside them through the iron-burner holes to operate the ejection routine. Eighty-three suits ran the routine, shooting out the acid-burned remains of prador. Two suits did nothing and one simply exploded, but the raptor writhed out of this only minimally damaged. Ursula studied the ejected prador, seeing one hit a wall and run along it, only to be brought down by dog forms and torn apart, while others moved weakly for a brief while. These prador were tough creatures to survive so much. Now their remains needed to be got rid of. They were a resource and she didn't need to give an order, merely her thought had raptors and colonists dining on them at once, only needing to make small adjustments to absorb the useful materials they offered. Ursula went over to the prador in this tunnel. She clawed open its carapace to reveal the soft interior and began tearing off chunks and feeding them whole into her gullet, pulling them down with internal fibres and taking them apart in a writhing and adjusting gut, rebuilding her resources. Others joined her and they soon cleaned out the carapace, which they then began to break apart and feed into their mouths, or facsimiles of the same. Ursula took her share of that too.

Colonists and raptors were now also dining on their own dead. She allowed them limited eating time but ordered that much of the remains must stay where they were. There had to be plenty of detritus and signs of battle here for her plan to work properly. She set some to collecting up remains, first of prador, as well as the dead on their own side, then she dispatched all but the eighty-three off towards the tunnel which the repair raptors had nearly finished digging, via another route, back to the surface.

'*Vrease*,' she said over com, her mouth no longer capable of speech, and spat over instructions. '*Go with them.*'

Vrease eyed her, and then the suit. 'I guess I'm not useful here.' She turned away and headed off. Next turning to Callum, Gurda, Percy and Nursum, she sent a silent instruction, and they went off to find their suits. Why she'd included Nursum she wasn't sure. Perhaps some remainder of humanity was driving that? Even now, others were already inside their suits and closing them up; following Ursula's lead, they were beginning to adjust their bodies and familiarize themselves with the controls. Feedback from them gave her an overview of the damage to the suits. It varied, but rerouting could deal with most of it, though in some the colonists grew further extensions from their bodies – superconductor and optic, connecting up breaks. Three of the remaining suits were unusable. Ursula ordered their occupants out and sent them after Vrease and the rest. A round eighty seemed a good number, almost a mythical one. She turned back to her own suit, climbed inside and began to close it up.

Once inside the open suit, she realized she would overfill it now and needed more body spread but, with resources to spare, she also extended rib bones and other materials down into other leg sleeves, forming joints so these protolegs could move but do little else. There still wasn't enough room, however, and she stopped the suit closing while she copied across from her fellows how they'd compacted their bodies. This had been necessary for them, since most were in the smaller suits of second-children.

Finally, she closed the suit completely, releasing some materials from compacting to expand her head and fill the turret, firmly bracing it there. Now for communications and data storage . . .

The suit cut out cacocom. It was EMR hardened and insulated with its own EMR com through a meta-material patch behind the head turret. She had hoped to adapt that but on her previous inspection had found it to be filled with a layering of protocols that would be difficult to get around. It seemed the father-captain of the prador dreadnought was somewhat paranoid and didn't want his children talking privately to each other. She still needed to get into it because of the telemetry. She had no doubt recordings were stored and ready to be transmitted to those above, and to the ship, once a signal could be sent.

Ursula began making connections and running a penetration. The nanosuite AI kicked in again, opening processing to her. She took what it offered but at the same time made coding connections to it, binding it closer to her. Within the com gear, she found a hard recorder linked to arrays of sensors throughout the suit. That had to be it. She delved deeper, ascertaining time markers and a wealth of data. Even with the intervention of the nanosuite AI, she soon realized she could not alter the recording to her needs. Finally she rolled it back to a time marker just before this prador had been hit, and wiped everything afterwards. She then copied across sections of the earlier battle and patched them into the blank spot. Now she needed to tell the rest to do this, but not through this com gear.

She had another strategy for dealing with the com issue, one she'd previously dispatched to the others. Conveniently, every suit now had its iron-burner hole that needed to be filled and disguised anyway. From her sensory hump, now spread out, she grew an extension into the hole, filling it, and altered its colour and texture to match the surrounding armour. She opened millions of nanoscopic transceivers in its outer surface, and soon began opening up com with the others as they did the same. Meanwhile, she extruded an outgrowth to attach only to the internal microphones of prador EMR com, to ape the sounds of prador vocal apparatus because she needed to be able to talk with them too.

'*Update*,' she said, sending the data on how they must alter their telemetry recordings.

'*The inherent paranoia will be difficult,*' said Callum. She understood him perfectly though he'd chosen to use the prador language. Perhaps he was getting in practice?

'*From the Polity information, we understand some of their social structure,*' she replied. '*The prador aboard that ship will mostly be the children of a father-captain. They will be utterly obedient through the chemical indoctrination of their father's pheromone output. Not under complete control from that while in their suits, but enough.*'

'*We just have to hope no one does a meticulous check of that telemetry before we're in position,*' Callum observed. '*What's Plan B?*'

'*There is no Plan B,*' Ursula told him, '*beyond getting there as fast as we can and hoping to do so before they close up that ship.*'

'*So if they're under such control,*' said Gurda, '*why those protocols in their com gear?*'

Ursula groped around for answers, realizing she didn't know enough about the prador. She thought hard, integrating again, and came up with a plausible answer.

'*Their children are labelled first- and second-children in order of maturity. I must presume that at some point first-children become adults. Considering the aggressive, competitive nature of their society, that's probably a danger to the father.*'

'*I detect pheromone suppression in this suit,*' said Percy, and routed his findings to all the rest. Ursula studied the data and gleaned more from the complex chemicals inside her suit. It was a language in itself, much like the complex chemical communication of cacocom. It made sense: chemical suppression of adulthood, chemical obedience, but perhaps also engendering immunity in the children, or some other way for the suppression to end. Otherwise the prador would die out without offspring ever rising to adulthood. However, it surprised her that Percy had picked up on this. Perhaps his background allowed it. She probed into him and he opened up to her with a willingness the colonists didn't have. Yes, his mental structure, though now programmed to human emulation, had, as with any creature, been formed concurrent with the senses his kind possessed. His understanding of chemical language was visceral.

Ursula returned her attention to her HUD and began to glean further information from it. She returned to a com command structure she'd seen earlier to confirm that the erstwhile occupant of this suit had assumed command once cut off from the rest. However, the rest of the command structure remained available to her, showing which prador she was subordinate to, including a first-child in the tunnels above. Once they broke through the tunnel collapses, that structure would reassert, and she would drop back down to being in charge of the advance squad only. All of the prador she'd trapped were in that squad, as well as a further fifty on the other side of the collapse, and probably in the collapse. Beyond this, she could glean little else. She didn't know their social and military protocols. She would have to play it by ear, but it seemed most likely that second-children only communicated with the one directly above them in the chain.

'*I will do all the talking,*' she told her soldiers. '*You know the objectives. Close in around me now.*'

As they did this, she sent instructions to the remaining drones, bringing them in too. Through them, and over cacocom, she

463

made her inspection. They all looked right – battle-scarred prador. The only visible difference was a slight expansion on the undersides of those carrying explosives, but they had formed and coloured those charges to match the ribbed under-carapace of the prador. She doubted it would be noticeable.

She next dispatched the drones up through the tunnels again and had them watch the tunnel collapses. Even as they arrived, rocks were falling from one pile of debris, and then a ceiling fell in. A second-child dropped through and scanned around, further ceiling collapses dropped more of them. Her display showed an abrupt revision of the command structure and prador com abruptly woke up. She shut off the drones – they all dropped to the floor, dead.

'Vrit,' said the restored first-child commander. 'Verbal report.'

'The creatures attacked the humans and killed them. They then attacked us and we killed them,' she replied.

Should she give detail? She considered adding something about how the humans had resembled the cacoraptors and vice versa, and that perhaps they'd been trying to form an alliance. Or she could add something about the EMR surge down here, disrupting telemetry. But her instinct was to stick to a brief summation, as that tended to be the way in human military com.

'Assessment to be made,' replied the first-child. 'Science team summoned for inspection and encapsulation of the aliens. Leave your dead and return to the ship for debrief and resupply.'

'Understood,' she replied.

A long pause ensued and she felt sure she had said something wrong. She groped around in her understanding of the language and finally found the correct honorific.

'Understood, sir,' she added.

'*On me,*' she sent over cacocom. '*We get out of here as fast as we can.*' She picked up on the progress of her tunnel borers and the rest of her raptor and colonist army. They were just below the surface now, right at the edge of the lake and pushing sensors up through the seabed. She got brief imagery of the edge of the slab, on which sat the Jain ruins, with the looming dreadnought behind them. Her soldiers there had their instructions. Worm forms would emerge from the ground, their bodies flattened, coloured and textured to their surroundings. They would ooze up over the edge of the slab and watch the ship, and wait. She sent a further instruction which wasn't really needed but she wanted to confirm everything. A few seconds later, all signals from them cut off as they collapsed their tunnel behind them.

Ursula and her ersatz prador moved up through the tunnels, finally coming in sight of the enemy prador moving down. Most were second-children and they just shifted past them and carried on down. When they reached where new bore-holes had been opened in the ceiling, a large first-child descended on grav to settle on the floor.

'*Go up,*' she instructed over cacocom. Her force began to scramble up the walls, only a few of them floating up on grav. She moved towards the first-child, thoroughly aware it was focused on her, while running through the prador language again and again, trying to find the correct response. Finally she got it, in the section on body language, and coming before the first-child, she lowered her front end and stabbed her claws into the ground. Obeisance was required. The first-child moved forwards and crashed a heavy claw down on her upper carapace armour, driving her down onto her belly plates. She received no damage, but the gesture was important in prador interactions.

'We will revisit this later,' said the commander.

She stayed flat to the ground as he clambered over her and headed on down into the tunnels. She had no doubt that the 'revisit' meant a violent reprimand. The language and its intimations had begun to permeate her thinking.

Once the first-child had moved out of sight, she clambered up the wall after her fellows, leg tips digging in, and out into the tunnel above. A boring machine sat over to one side, treads supporting a cylindrical body tilted up on a frame, a spill pipe running off through the tunnel. A line of prador were coming along on the right, while hers were moving away on the left. She joined the line, noting other second-children from her supposed prador squad, who'd been separated from it by the tunnel collapse, now re-joining it.

'*They are asking questions,*' said Callum.

'*Tell them you have been ordered to say nothing,*' she replied. '*No interaction beyond that – just get out of here.*' Checking her com gear again, she saw that second-children had their channel to speak on. She could listen in if she wanted, and doubtless first-children did when they were feeling particularly paranoid, but the chatter was probably beneath them. All they expected from second-children was obedience.

Near the surface, other armoured second-children appeared. Their armour was different: polished, blued metal, not the khaki of the others, and was arrayed with tools and packages. They didn't seem to be armed, though that was difficult to ascertain. She assumed these were the science team mentioned before. On their backs they carried large translucent cylinders, presumably for encapsulation of the remains below.

Finally she spilled out on the surface and joined her fellows who'd reached it ahead of her. She noted more of the tool-wielding prador all over and around the assault craft, taking it apart, as well as others investigating the remains of the car. A new class of prador, she wondered? There had been nothing about this in the stuff from the Polity. She waited until all one hundred and twenty-three of her squad were on the surface. She needed to be rid of the extra forty-three genuine prador second-children. Selecting them through the com gear, she waved a claw towards the assault ship.

'Go over there and assist,' she said.

Again she thought about things to add to back up the order with plausibility, but stopped herself. There was no need, the forty-three simply separated themselves out and moved off across the seabed. As she watched them go, she thought about the ease of penetrating such a stratified command structure where those below were afraid of questioning those above, albeit only if you looked like those in that structure.

She gestured to the dreadnought. What was the correct form of approach now? Send those with grav ahead? Or should they stick together and march in some kind of order? She took her best guess.

'Form a wedge – there may still be enemy about,' she sent over prador com, while detailing their formation over cacocom. She moved to the point as it formed and led the way. Only in retrospect did she realize that she'd made a mistake: she'd actually explained her order to her subordinates.

They moved at speed across the seabed, kicking up a dust cloud behind them. She saw craft from the dreadnought landing some distance away, used visor magnification to focus in on them and saw them unloading equipment. Speculating on their purpose, it occurred to her that the radioactives here, and other elements, would come in very useful for a warship. Prador drifted across the sky too, some heading over towards where they'd exited the tunnel system and some going elsewhere. Had she known there would be so many excursions from the vessel she might have altered her plans and just attacked headlong. Still, if the assault craft was anything to go by, the dreadnought would be able to close up very quickly. The plan was still a good one.

As they moved, she altered their course to take them away from where her other forces were waiting underground. The danger here was that, if she or any of those with her saw something, it would go straight into the telemetry they all now constantly broadcast. And she had no doubt that the prador were on the alert for cacoraptors. Perhaps they'd have some automated recognition system, or simply a prador studying the telemetry?

'*I wonder what happens to them?*' Callum asked over cacocom, again keyed into her thoughts.

She understood at once he was referring to the original prador from the assault craft, and only now did it occur to her to wonder too. The prador were aggressive. The crews of their ships were run as a family under a father-captain. So what would happen if they picked up survivors of another family? Surely they wouldn't attack them; at least some degree of cooperation was necessary in a war effort.

'*Perhaps they came from this ship, and that's why it's here,*' he added.

'*Perhaps,*' she replied, annoyed that she didn't know.

She knew too little about the prador, but she would source knowledge from the ship ahead. She needed to learn as much as possible to understand this enemy properly, and then destroy it . . . Ursula shook herself in her armour, not quite sure how that thought had arisen, for by *enemy* she had meant all prador. Had she so completely accepted her part in the prador–human war? No, she had not. Something had very definitely shifted inside her and she realized that she needed to broadcast less of herself over cacocom. She quickly began to filter her com, taking out all but the current practical detail. It wouldn't do for the colonists to comprehend how she'd changed. Even as she did this, she felt the hard attention of the nanosuite AI, laced through her like briars.

'*Change formation*,' she instructed as they came to the slab at the edge of the seabed. '*Explosives to the fore. All of you, scan to the ship. Access and door mechanisms.*' The shift in her focus to tactics and the ensuing fight seemed enough of a distraction, for the nanosuite's attention seemed to slide away. They moved across the rock towards the Jain ruins. Ursula noted bright red objects, somewhat ridiculously like the traffic cones of ancient Earth, marking out the perimeter and she diverted around them. As they drew closer to the ship, she saw large port doors open in its upper hull and, down at the base of the ship, an even larger entrance had opened a ramp down to the ground.

'Vrit,' came a voice over prador com, 'you have no human prisoners.'

Ursula studied the shifting icons of the command structure, then the com channel, and felt a shiver run down the now over-laid plates of her spine. The communication had been from the father-captain of the dreadnought. She immediately began to broadcast it to the others over cacocom.

'The other creatures killed them,' she explained.

'So I've been told, but studying your telemetry I see this is not the case.'

Just for a moment she had no idea what to say. Could she actually contradict a father-captain? Would that alert him to something wrong?

'It was difficult to distinguish between humans and the creatures. They seemed to have adopted the characteristics of each other.'

'You were told I wanted prisoners,' said the father-captain.

They were closer to the ramp now, with a view of the prador moving up and down it, and also what looked like some large item of earth-moving equipment coming down it.

'*Speed it up,*' she said over cacocom.

'The situation was complicated,' she replied to the father-captain. 'The hostiles were very effective and my squad in danger of being destroyed.'

A long silence ensued and she knew she'd said the wrong thing.

'I wanted prisoners,' the father-captain finally repeated. 'The destruction of your squad, and yourself, is not relevant to that. You will come to my sanctum now.'

With Ursula in the lead, they reached the foot of the ramp and began filing up past all those coming down. She searched frantically through the suit programs, trying to find a map of the ship's interior, since she needed to know where that sanctum was. She couldn't find one and, of course, that made sense – creatures that had most probably been born in this ship, and lived in it all their lives, had no need of such a thing. Halfway up the ramp, she was able to see into the interior, where more prador were moving back and forth. Two first-children moved into sight. Their armour appeared heavier than usual and, with its hard angles and rough swirled exterior, seemed almost brutal. Plotting the movements of all inside, she didn't need integration to see they were heading straight for her. She stepped off the ramp and inside, onto a floor made of a material that looked like stone, except for its regular surface of small tetrahedrons. She moved further in, the eighty coming in behind her. The command structure shifted, putting two first-children directly above her, highlighted in dark blue and blinking.

'Disengage your weapons,' one instructed her as they rapidly approached.

'*Do we attack now?*' The question over cacocom came from them all, because she hadn't updated the tactical plan. She used her mandibles to run through the HUD to find the routine for disengaging her weapons.

'*Do not attack yet. Find the mechanisms that control this door and ensure you destroy them,*' she said, as a series of thunks and whines ran through her suit. The Gatling cannon ammo feed dropped from her underside while the cannon itself rose up on studs on her claw arm. The tip of her other claw hinged up, extruding the business end of her particle beam weapon. The two first-children crowded in, closing heavy claws roughly on her claw limbs and, with their free claws, they pulled both weapons away and discarded them on the floor.

'Do not resist,' said one of them, and she felt sure it wanted her to. They shoved her, skittering on her legs, ahead of them. She started walking, but didn't know where to go. Thankfully one of them quickly came round her and moved off ahead, the one behind thumping a claw against her back end to speed her up. She now had no need of a map of the ship's interior.

'*Collect up my weapons too,*' she said, updating the tactical plan.

'*You will take out the head?*' Callum asked.

'*If I can,*' she replied. '*If not, I can at least keep him occupied until our forces are inside. Get those door mechanisms blown.*'

Past

Her military career was behind her, and here she was, deep into ennui and risking her life so she could *feel* something. The Mediterranean blue of the sky and sea on Desander did raise feelings – maybe happiness or contentment? No. Ridiculous. Strangely uncomfortable with it, she immediately dismissed the idea.

The world had possessed life when humans arrived and local forms of purple algae had been slowly oxygenating the air, but nothing had occupied the continental land masses and numerous islands. The original colonists were of the first diaspora from

Earth and had arrived in cryogenic suspension. Coming out of suspension, they'd long debated the morality of using the gene bank of Earth's life here, with alien life having already established. It all became quite vitriolic, as it had still been in the period of 'ecological consciousness' whereby 'the environment' was regarded with religious awe.

They'd had to land their ship because it was single use and this trip had been their one shot at establishing themselves away from the petty politics, power games, ideologies and infighting in the Solar system. But, being human, they brought all those with them. Upon landing, a schism developed between those who wanted to change the world to suit them and those who felt it should be preserved and left unchanged. Reasoned argument turned to point scoring and finger wagging, then to plain abuse and accusations of 'ideology' and finally to fighting. During this latter stage, an attempt was made to destroy the Earth gene bank. In response, those who wanted to change the world set up an automated drone factory and growth tanks and flooded the world with life forms of Earth that were easy to distribute and establish. They took hold well and spread on the land, but not so well in the sea. The side that did this was winning the conflict by dint of the other side's inability to halt these changes. They next began establishing more difficult life forms, with longer gestation and periods of infancy. But still not so much in the sea. The planet burgeoned over the ensuing century. The colonists didn't get to see this, however, because a fundamentalist environmentalist on the losing side created a disease to rid this world of what he saw as the plague of humanity. The Polity, when it arrived, had learned the details from data storage in the overgrown ruins of the colony.

Ursula took her grav-car out from the city, over the coast and towards the island. It still puzzled her – the grav-car, that is.

She'd ordered it some years ago, detailed the changes she'd wanted and been most pleased with the result. It was atmosphere safe, meaning it could be sealed completely and even travel in vacuum or under a sea. It possessed thrusters that could be used out in space, beyond a gravity well for the grav-motors to push against, and had a cavitating drive for when it was in water. All of these were triple safe with backups, while its armour and crash systems made it unlikely a collision would kill her, in the unlikely event the car might fail. For a woman who didn't care whether she lived or died it was, to be frank, a rather odd choice. Perhaps she was changing? She snorted at the thought.

The sky was blue, and so were the holes. With a light touch on the joystick, Ursula sent her car in over the island, over the adapted mangroves and the inner land patched with square fields of pineapples. Beyond this, she came to a rockscape interspersed with copses and flat grassy areas, then brought it to a halt above what at first appeared to be just a pool but was in fact a blue hole.

Here again, she thought.

The blue hole penetrated two hundred feet down, before branching into the cave system. Other blue holes opened in the seabed from this. The whole network spread for hundreds of miles, with holes even opening deep in the continental land mass twenty miles away. She peered over that way. Green pine forests ran along the coast above coves of white sand beaches, with rocky points between that clamoured with shellfish when the three moons were in conjunction, and the tide low enough to expose them. Small fishes swam in the sea, kelps and other seaweeds burgeoned, but nothing larger had taken hold there. The temperature was balmy and the only really bad weather was the rains that kept the inland jungles burgeoning. It could almost have been a Polity resort world where people would come to enjoy the sunshine, sandy beaches, and swim in the sea.

People tended not to swim in the sea here.

She brought her car down on a grassy area, worn by the arrival and departure of other cars, though sometimes those cars were collected, their occupants having failed to return. She stepped out and stripped down to the skin-hugging wetsuit that covered her from her neck to the soles of her feet. Out of the back seat, she took a carryall and headed with this over to the edge of the blue hole. Here she donned flippers, and a haemolung breather that strapped on her stomach. It had a tube leading up to the bubble helmet that covered her head, and engaged with the neck of the wetsuit. Around her waist, she strapped on a belt. Another deflated haemolung occupied one of its packages. Others contained virtual recording equipment and her mapping computer, while there were also heavy weights attached all around. The last item out of her carryall was an underwater gun, because there were very good reasons why people didn't swim in the sea. With all this in place, she jumped into the hole.

When the colonists who wanted to change their world seeded it with the life of Earth, they of course put everything they could into the ocean, but anything larger than small fishes failed. There had been subsequent attempts with sharks and manta rays, turtles and seals, dolphins and other oceangoing mammals. All had still failed. None of them – even the sharks and dolphins – could move fast enough. The only 'big' life form in the ocean was a creature like a cuttlefish without tentacles, which grew to the size of a human. And, of course, the spearpigs. Both of these were original alien life forms that had been playing out their predator–prey cycle for millennia. The spearpigs preyed on the cuttlers and, at a particular stage in their life cycle, would inject egg sacs into them, whose product then ate out their insides. The cuttlers' response strategy was to breed massively. This would not have been a problem for humans, or any large Earth-evolved oceanic life, had not spearpigs seen anything above a certain size as a cuttler.

And there you are, thought Ursula.

A spearpig detached from the side of the blue hole and came straight for her. The thing resembled a prawn the size of dog, or of the pig it was named after. Its visage did have a hog-like appearance, with a snout appendage ahead of two black eyes, a similar pig mouth below and a collection of sharp teeth as of a wild boar. This appearance changed, however, when the snout – a vibration sensor – retracted and the lower jaw divided, splaying out to the sides. Ursula fired a single bullet, which cut a white line through the water straight into the thing's mouth. She felt the thump as it detonated inside and watched the pig tumble and drop away, trailing a cloud of green blood and ribbons of intestines on its way down. Ecologists of past ages would have been horrified by the present strategy of the planetary AI here, which was: kill those that try to attack anything other than their usual prey. Modified spearpigs that only preyed on cuttlers were being introduced. There were fewer of the dangerous kind occupying the wider ocean here and there was now some talk of another attempt to introduce other larger oceanic life. But down in the underwater caves, there were many more of them. This was why lunatics like Ursula came here to explore.

She descended, down and down, keeping an eye out for more of the horrible creatures. Many of her kind – those going through the ennui barrier – came here to map out the cave systems. It could have been done easily with drones, but the planetary AI, seeing that those like her would swim down here anyway, had decided to give them something to do. The attrition on swimmers was quite high and Ursula had thus far found the remains of fourteen of them, tagged them for reclamation, and moved on. Many others had been reclaimed by dint of their mapping gear being undamaged enough to still function. It had become standard for swimmers to use simple neoprene wetsuits, because where was the fun in donning something a spearpig couldn't tear open with its teeth, or punch its barbed ovipositor through? Ursula had grown irritated with this. Having to be constantly alert to spearpig attacks was slowing down her mapping and she wanted to find the cave rumoured to connect this system to a much larger one below the deep ocean. She now wore monofilament with inlayed mesh. It did protect her but wasn't completely safe. The pigs were immensely strong and, even if they couldn't get through the wetsuit, their attacks still had bone-shattering force.

Two hundred feet down, she headed into one of the branches which descended for another fifty feet, then curved back up. In the bubble helmet, light amplification kicked in and here she saw large white mussels attached to the walls, with bone-white shrimps swimming around them. Another spearpig darted out of their mass, the hooked prong of its ovipositor oozing out ahead of its fan tail. Almost with a shrug, she aimed, fired, and turned to hit another coming in from behind. In clouds of blood and shredded internal organs, they sank to the bottom of the cave. She knew all their strategies now, all their little tricks and methods of ambush. She'd been swimming here for a long time. Was she bored with it now? The question opened up a mess of speculation about her condition she didn't yet want to address. She wanted to get the mapping done and move on. Spearpigs were a distraction, an irritation.

Cave after cave she swam through, for mile upon mile. She had eaten and drunk a lot before coming down here and, even before that, her high-density fats had packed out her body to a shape she didn't really like. But she was burning them now. In a cave whose walls were clad in a chalky residue, where she could see a long way in both directions, she halted and initiated a control at the base of her bubble helmet. A spigot extruded towards her mouth and she sucked on it, drawing seawater through graphene sieves so it arrived pure in her mouth. A small spray of cloudy water jetted out to the side – the sieve system ejecting the salts. Thirst satisfied, she checked all around again to make sure no spearpigs had arrived, then undid the stick seam running from her navel round between her legs to the base of her back and took a long shit and piss, clouding the water all around. Sealed up again, she moved on, thinking that would be something for the shellfish to filter feed on.

At length she reached her first cache. Here she swapped out her haemolung, keeping the one on her belt for emergencies. She changed the clip and power supply for her gun – again she had these items on her belt and again she kept them for emergencies. There were spare flippers here too, plus mapping computer and other items that might be damaged or lost during some spearpig attack. She next took out a packet of cylinders filled with a syrupy fluid that had nutrients and glucose, clipped one after another into the port which filtered seawater, disengaging the filters and drinking her fill. Sleep was, of course, dangerous here, so she'd had the fix that dismissed the need for it. She was ready.

She swam on and, after a few hundred yards, entered an unmapped area of the cave system. As was her method, she would take side tunnels for just a few hundred yards to virtual record and map them, then return to whichever tunnel seemed to go in the direction she wanted to go. She now chose at random, having learned that flipping the coin she had acquired after coming out of the regrowth tank on Gannon wasn't so easy underwater.

Time after time, she reached dead ends or places where the caves became too narrow for her to pass through, and she had to find another route. Occasionally she called up the expanded map in her bubble helmet, where it displayed as a hologram showing her position. It began to grow brighter at one point, as she reached a shaft with the glare of a blue hole high above, and she went down. Here, because of debris falling through the hole, she started to stir up silt, which was always a danger because the spearpigs used motion detection and she might not see them coming. Perhaps next time she should install sonar? It wasn't permitted in the swimmer culture but she was beyond that now.

Spearpigs indeed attacked lower down, through clouds of silt they themselves had stirred up before coming for her. She took out three of them with ease, but a fourth reached her and, while trying to shove in its ovipositor, delivered bruising blows to her torso that knocked the wind out of her. Its face was right up against her helmet, legs wrapped around her body and the black eyes seemed almost to be glaring as she put the barrel between them and fired. It dropped away and she swam on, wondering about their intelligence, then surprised that the thought had never occurred to her before.

A side tunnel took her into a place immediately clouding with silt, filled with yellow flakes. She recognized this as an area of a particular growth that didn't like moving water – the detritus from the spreads of slimy lichen-like weed. It would be a cyst chamber with no exit except for the way she'd come in. There could be spearpigs in here too, so she quickly turned back, only to run straight into slimy stone. A surge of panic arose, almost welcome because of its unfamiliarity. She groped around, searching for the exit and finding only more slimy stone. The panic grew fast, like a seed fallen on fertile ground. Something loomed out of the silt and she pointed her gun, letting out a yell and rapidly backing away.

Control yourself! Fucking control yourself!

She was hyperventilating and, with hard deliberation, forced herself not to. She would be calm. If there were spearpigs in here, they would have attacked by now, though a nasty part of her mind noted that they might yet come. She hung in the water and ignored that. So what if they came. They might batter and break her some but she would kill them swiftly. Then, if badly injured, she would head for that recent blue hole she'd seen which wasn't so far away. Calm slowly restoring, she moved towards the shape she had seen.

A skull grinned at her from behind an antique facemask. The wetsuit below was wrinkled around the skeleton. It seemed she had found this cave system's Mikkenson, like the mummified corpse on the spider cliff of Gannon. The suit she recognized as being at least fifty years old. She inspected this individual, noting long ginger hair plaited to the skull and slim-boned hands in the gloves, while the shape of the loose material at the front told her there had been breasts there, so she assumed it to have been female. Swimming round, she saw that this woman had had super-dense air bottles on her back, so her air supply had been limited. She noted no damage at all, so this woman had clearly not been killed by spearpigs. She must have swum in here and simply not been able to find the way out. This sort of thing had happened throughout the history of cave diving. How long she had searched, with her air supply dwindling and panic increasing, Ursula couldn't know. The utter futility and pointlessness of this death hit her hard. What the hell was she doing here, mapping caves the AIs could explore with drones and fully map in just a few years? Why was she risking herself like this? Did she want a futile death too?

Ursula found herself panting, realizing she'd undergone a profound change – that she had been experiencing it for some time. Why the oh-so-safe grav-car? Why else the mesh in her suit and her irritation with the spearpigs? She backed away, trying to calm her breathing again, but found she could not. An alert flickered on in the base of her helmet. The silt was beginning to block the haemolung. She barked a laugh. It appeared that now she was breaking through the ennui barrier, she might die anyway. *No, no, not fucking now.*

She swam back until she reached a wall and began to feel her way along it, trying to memorize her position in the fog. The haemolung kept degrading as she searched and finally, with the alert sliding into the red, she swapped it out with the one on her belt. Even as she did this, she thought about the cave system beyond and the route she would take back. Then, suddenly, she felt very stupid indeed and turned on the map in her bubble helmet. Blink control brought her location closer, and she saw the chamber with its single entrance – the thing almost the shape of a tadpole. She swam in a straight line, still checking the image and, by and by, found her way to the exit.

Ursula left the cave system by the last blue hole she'd seen, surfacing in the open ocean. Here she turned on her radio and summoned her grav-car. It landed to float on the surface, where it opened its door and she clambered inside. Glancing back, she saw a spearpig behind her, just below the surface; it turned round and headed back down. Maybe one of the new kind? Taking her car back towards the mainland, she felt a fierce joy, but an awareness that she wasn't quite through the barrier so would have to be wary of her inclinations. Whatever. She now intended to do something useful and constructive, even if it did have its elements of danger.

21

Present

With cacocom open to the eighty of her soldiers who'd come in with her, she didn't really have a sense of disconnection from them as the two prador marched her into an oval tunnel and further into the ship. The tunnel was much like a cave, for what appeared to be slate-like stone clad the walls and even odd blue growths, almost like bunches of fingers, sprouted here and there. Other life appeared now and again too, things that looked like by-blows of lice and trilobites. She saw a group of these around some spattered mess on the floor, dining on pieces of flesh that looked familiar, because she had eaten some in the tunnels underneath the seabed. Was she seeing the detritus from some other prador receiving punishment?

Even as she observed her surroundings, and the two prador guided her on with occasional shoves or a claw clanging against her carapace armour, she prepared herself internally. She had much in the way of densely packed resources and now she began to distribute them. She completed the protolegs she'd grown earlier, adding in tendons, ligaments and dense, powerful muscle to make them operable. The necessary alterations to her mental wiring had a strange effect. She felt closer to the creatures around her, as though she could understand them better, or perhaps that was just an illusion. She toughened up and made her muscle fibres more powerful and grew in more besides, taking her limbs up to the maximum strength she could achieve. This reduced the materials she could burn for energy, as well as the time she'd be able to operate at full strength without the necessity to feed again. She shut down filtration in the suit and opened it to the air of the ship, then began panting as fast as a compressor. Inside she was converting oxygen to peroxide that she could use to help burn her cacoraptor equivalent of fat storage. Her exterior armour was at its best in its cacoraptor format so she left that alone.

Now, weapons . . .

She thought on what awaited her ahead. She had no doubt she was being taken to a fatal punishment and, bearing in mind the aggressive nature of these creatures, assumed it would be inflicted by the father-captain. But would that creature act alone or would it have the two thugs here on standby? She didn't know. Certainly, if the data from the Polity probes into the Kingdom were anything to go by, the father-captain would be big, powerful and vicious, and more than capable of tearing apart a first-child alone. This was a frequent activity. Speculation she'd read on their biology from some Polity experts had designated this killing as a selection process, though there had been much disagreement about that. No one had been able to decide whether prador killed strong offspring to remove competitors or weak offspring to make the next generation stronger. It seemed most likely to Ursula that it was all over the place – so they sometimes killed off threats and sometimes killed those that had fucked up. She was in the latter category which, according to the data, the father-captains finished off in lengthy agonizing processes and with great relish.

Whatever the scenario, she guessed that she would first be ordered to shed her armour. She'd possibly have to do that before entering the sanctum. If the prador saw her present form, her chances of actually getting in there were remote. She made further alterations, changing the colour and texture of her exterior, properly forming prador claws and skinning over her bony mandibles, while shifting her body shape further to a better fit inside her armour. She sprouted the facsimiles of more eyes across her head, coiled her neck and skinned it over so it looked as if she had a simple head turret. Then, at the last, she sprouted ersatz stalked eyes up into their armoured sheaths.

Further turnings and tunnels ensued. She'd expected to go up to what looked to be the head turret of the ship, but instead the two prador took her deep inside. That made sense – a ruling creature that thought in terms of armour would not position itself near the skin of the ship.

'*Located*,' Callum told her, and sent her an image feed of giant hydraulic cylinders, cogged wheels, shafts and a massive electromagnetic solenoid. Outlining items of the structure in her mind, she saw two mechanisms in one. The cogged wheels and hydraulics would close and open the ramp door at an easy pace. The solenoid could slam it shut like a sprung trap. She saw one of her explosives techs moving around behind the mechanism, his load of explosives loosening from his belly plates.

'*One on either side*,' Callum added. '*We keep getting queries about why we haven't returned to quarters. We need to do this soon.*'

'*Hold off for a short while longer*,' she replied. '*And once you've done it, spread out and hit what hull weapons you can find. Maybe seize control of them if you can and target the prador outside.*' This was all in her tactical plan but she felt the need to reiterate. Even as she finished speaking, the prador ahead of her stopped, turned rapidly and smashed a claw against her visor, actually putting a crack in it and halting her.

'Unrecognized com,' it said.

A whickering, clattering sound impinged and it took her a

moment to recognize it as the prador phonemes repeated at high speed.

'Location?' asked the other.

'Unknown,' replied the first.

Ursula looked at the big oval, diagonally divided door they stood by. The two first-children dipped, placing the tips of their claws against the floor. The obeisant pose. She assumed they were talking to their father. Then they both came upright again.

'Remove your armour,' said the one ahead.

'*They're closing the ramp!*' Callum exclaimed.

'*Blow the mechanism, now!*' Ursula ordered.

Even as she spoke, the prador behind had inserted a claw into the pit control beside the door to twist and manipulate it. Ursula delayed, meanwhile shutting down all the joint motors in the suit. Her own strength was already beyond them and all they would actually do was hinder her. The one ahead clanged a claw against her head turret.

'Remove your armour!' it ordered again.

The door began to grind open. Ursula made her calculations and abruptly put the joint motors back on. Frantically, she stabbed at the HUD, making overrides and changes. It was possible to cut out the automatic shutdown of open armour and she did so. The suits also had a degree of autonomy and had a selection of simple programs for that. She found the one she needed and selected it.

'If you do not remove your armour, you will be punished severely,' said the prador ahead.

She laughed, in a much more distorted manner than usual, and forgot to prevent that being translated. Her suit clattered its mandibles and the prador ahead backed off a little. It was like going to her hanging and being told she'd be in trouble if she didn't put her head in the noose. And just as her laughter stopped, the entire ship shuddered and the dull doubled booms of explosions reached her. She hit the fast-eject routine.

'*All happening now,*' Callum commented.

She got a flash of weapons fire around the door ramp, and updated telemetry told her that two of her soldiers had seized the earth-mover and were driving it back, intending to jam it into the ruined door mechanism to further kill any possibility of it being closed.

'*Busy at the moment,*' she replied.

Her armour thumped as it parted horizontally, the top half shooting up on polished rods and hinging over, with the stalked eye and mandible sleeves loosening so those items could come out easily. A pad came up underneath to lift her up, partially retracting her legs and her claws as she directed them down towards the floor. High-pressure air then blew her up out of the armour, but as her claws came free, she slammed them against the suit to drive herself backwards. The program she'd input immediately kicked in. The open suit surged forwards, claws up and extended, and grabbed the prador before her, closing claws on one claw limb and one leg of the creature, immobilizing it – at least for a short while.

Her trajectory, just as she'd calculated, took her up into the air, then down on top of the prador at the door control. She landed straight on its back, closed a claw on its free claw limb, grabbing an armoured eye stalk. She heaved on this, legs skittering against its back. She expected difficulty, but the thing came out like a pulled carrot, stretching out the fleshy stalk inside with its own armour parting, then it snapped. Recalculation. She hadn't realized the level her strength had achieved. She pulled up the claw arm she had hold of and grabbed the other, as the prador withdrew it from the pit control and heaved them both back. Armoured joints broke with dull thuds and soon she'd torn both free from its body, green blood spurting out of the holes. She threw them at the other prador as it tore up her armour suit, then leaped at it. It reached up and grabbed, but she managed to keep her claws out of its reach. It snapped closed on one leg and the edge of her carapace, and shearfields sparked like grinding discs. She cut the pain even as her leg fell away and she grabbed the prador's head turret. Meanwhile, the door had stopped opening; she could hear the clonk of mechanisms in the wall. She steadily heaved at the turret, her claw limbs smoking from their energy burn. It began to part from the body of the armour but the visor shattered, hurling chunky fragments across the floor. She drove a claw straight in and snipped again and again, feeling carapace collapse and soft mush squeezing out. She leaped to the door, which had now begun to close again.

The other prador slammed into her side and tried to wrap its legs around her. The one whose head she'd chopped apart tore from her erstwhile armour and just ran straight across the corridor to slam into a wall. Confident of her power now, Ursula gripped one leg of her attacker, closed up her other claw and slammed it as hard as she could into its underside. Its armour cracked and the force of the impact transmitted through her body, tearing away the leg she held. She grabbed another and hit again and again, until the armour shattered. Driving her claw inside, she opened and turned it again and again, then retracted it with a spill of broken carapace, torn flesh and worm-like organs. As she pushed away, her victim collapsed. She'd managed to kill it, having reached its ring-shaped major ganglion, whereas the other, with its minced head, was still alive, but blind and in agony. She threw herself towards the narrowing gap of the diagonally divided door. It jammed for a second as it closed on her, but she let it break her carapace so she could finally drag herself through.

★　★　★

Ursula came down hard on all her remaining limbs and quickly scanned her surroundings. So this was a father-captain's sanctum? The oblate chamber had numerous hatches around the walls. A separate wall of hexagonal screens stood over to one side, with pit controls in the floor before it. Propped in a frame over to another side was one of the big spherical war drones the prador in the shuttle had used. Its side was open and an interior chamber extruded, while other components were neatly arrayed on low benches. To the side of this stood another device: a half shell, with a back end which looked as if a prador would fit in there. From the front end extended numerous limbs, as one might see on a Polity autosurgeon, though many were heavier and doubtless for the removal of carapace. She integrated and assessed those surgical limbs, then eyed the extruded chamber, remembering from the Polity data that prador used the ganglions of their own children in their hardware. So this would have been the fate awaiting her, had she been the prador she was supposed to be. She now focused on the father-captain.

The creature was huge, fully twenty feet across. Stuck to the underside of his carapace were all sorts of technological items, while on top were two Gatling cannons either side of his head turret. Other weapons were wired in through his leg sockets, for he possessed no legs at all. His claws and mandibles were all golden metal and, by their format and the way they'd been attached, appeared to be prosthetics. She saw, with some satisfaction, that his main carapace wasn't covered, though it did look as tough and thick as stone. She leaped aside as Gatling fire tore up the floor. As she hit the wall and scrambled along it, two high-intensity lasers locked onto her and began to burn. She jumped out, straight towards him, but felt the wash of grav as he abruptly jerked from the floor and rose into the air. Some of the things on his underside were obviously grav-motors. With her carapace smoking, she squatted, feeding energy into her muscles, then leaped again. But he dipped in mid-air and Gatling fire slammed her to the ground once more.

The nearest translation she could find to what he clattered and bubbled next was, 'Well, what the fuck are you?'

She spun across the floor, slugs slamming into her and some even penetrating, hit the wall again, scrambling up it to run a zigzag course around the chamber towards him. He slid back across the space, tracking her with the lasers and burning her again, turning to bring the cannons to bear when he could. Her damage was ramping up and resources beginning to wane. She realized he could stay out of her reach and keep hitting her for longer than her resources would last. Integration, tactics, logistics. The half-shell surgery she'd seen when she first entered had objects on its underside, like those on the father-captain's underside, and which she now confirmed as grav-motors. She hurled herself down towards it, inserting claw limbs and mandibles into the requisite sleeves, and wrenched the thing round to face him. Gatling fire drove the device back, shattering the surgical limbs and driving great dents into the front shield. She worked the HUD console, now familiar with this technology, and engaged grav. The thing shot up into the air, straight towards his head turret and the cannons, failing as it rose and spewing wraiths of fire. At the last moment, she retracted herself and turned the device, taking slugs in her back and shedding burning carapace. Then, using the thing as a platform, she leaped and came down on his back.

'I am the last thing you will see alive,' she replied, and began smashing her claws into his carapace. He shot across the chamber, hammering hard into the wall to try and dislodge her. She skidded just a bit, but issued glue from her feet, binding herself in place. His carapace was hard and thick. Her first few blows had little effect, but a crack began to appear, oozing green blood. He withdrew from the wall and dropped down towards the floor as she kept on smashing, then shot up again, accelerating hard. The impact against the ceiling flattened her, further cracking her carapace, tearing muscle and snapping bones. But even as he dropped again, she rose up, her body reforming, and continued to thump down her claws. A chunk of carapace broke in at the crack – a piece the size of a human head. She hit it hard, driving it into his body, and he issued a weird ululating shriek. He opened fire with all his weapons, turning the surrounding walls into a firestorm, smoking debris raining down from them.

Leverage now. She dug a claw in, grabbing carapace ten inches thick, and drove in another claw to grip another edge. Injecting remaining energy hard and fast set her limbs smoking again, and then her body too. With a loud crump, a piece of carapace five feet across broke away. She heaved it up, stretching muscle and collagen, green blood and white chyme spurting out all around. She dipped down into this, claws cutting and tearing. Like a coiled spring releasing, her hidden neck extended too, ripping open its temporary skin covering and pushing her head inside. There she tore with her mandibles and bit with razor-sharp teeth. But she also probed with her sensorium, mapping out his internal organs. There was his main ganglion – a ring-shaped organ inside a bony sheath. She speared towards it and bit through it, once, twice, then once more. The thump of impact snapped her head away. She rose up and pulled her head out of the gore to see he had crashed to the floor. Gatling cannons spun empty, fires burned on the walls through a fog of smoke, and lasers sputtered then went out one after another.

Ursula continued to scan down into the hole she'd made in the father-captain. Organ activity was steadily waning but she stayed in place to observe. Finally sure that he'd expired, she carefully detached her feet, rose up and tried to find something on cacocom. The door blocked it completely, however. She needed to open this place up and find out how her soldiers were doing. First, she had other considerations – she needed to recharge. Dipping her head back down, she began to feed, shitting out detritus from her skin and a series of anuses all around her spread body, while packing in the useful nutrients, and breathing like a compressor again, though this time through spiracles she opened on her back.

A crunching sound . . .

She looked up, seeing the doubled door steadily opening, and got ready for another fight, but the figure that stepped through negated that. This machine person was hers.

'Messy in here,' said Vrease, stepping through the smoke.

Ursula considered making some reply, but to what purpose? Anyway, cacocom now bounced in through the opening and she began to get up to date.

The moment the explosives had detonated in the ship, a wide swathe of seabed had collapsed and her army fountained up from the hole, swarming over the edge of the stone slab and hurtling towards the dreadnought. After a short delay, prador up in the sky started firing on her soldiers, then the ship's weapons began to make their impact felt. Just inside, Callum, Gurda, Percy and all the others opened up with their prador weapons on nearby prador. Even as they did this, Callum ordered squads of them on into the ship to find and either negate or take over the ship's weapons which were firing on the approaching army.

She saw that a particle beam had stabbed down and, at such short range, just obliterated every cacoraptor or colonist it touched. A railgun began firing, the impacts hurling them, and tons of seabed, hundreds of feet into the sky. But the army was fast and soon at the foot of the ramp. On the ramp itself, four colonists had taken control of the earth-mover. Other prador assisted them, almost certainly in the mistaken belief that they were putting it in place as a barrier to the approaching horde. The colonists had got the machine to the top of the ramp as the army headed up it, then accelerated it into an already severely damaged door mechanism on one side, before opening fire on the prador.

The exchange of fire in the entrance increased, prador and colonists going down with limbs ripped away and holes burned in their armour. However, the prador that had been hit were out of the fight, while the colonists crawled out of smoking armour with body forms only partially resembling the creatures they then attacked. Telemetry gave her their internal changes and tactical revisions. Like her, those in armour shut down their joint motors and began to use their strength, ripping off claws and eye stalks and smashing holes in the main armour of their enemy. She saw Gurda pull off the claw of one prador and fire her particle weapon straight into the hole. She saw Trakken slide on his back underneath an opponent to rip off its belly plates, then fire his Gatling cannon straight into the exposed creature.

The army arrived, depleted but still lethal. The prador just inside the door seemed to go down in a wave, iron-burners flaring, oily smoke rising from burned holes where Caulter's squad injected acid. She tracked them spreading out through the ship, saw prador which had been operating a particle weapon being taken down, then only minutes later that weapon burning prador out of the sky, before probing out towards the assault ship and the exit from the seabed tunnels. She saw Vrease running inside at high speed . . . and she was up to date.

Still receiving cacocom, and monitoring her forces steadily working through the ship, she could hear the sounds of weapons fire and the explosions. Flickering movement drew her attention and she looked towards the array of hexagonal screens. There she saw some of the action. Scrambling down from the corpse of the father-captain, she shook herself and spattered gore away, then went over to it. There were four pit controls in the floor. Peering into one of these, she wondered if she could use it, inserting a claw. A small twist brought up new images in a row of screens, but since she didn't know the layout of the ship and what these screens displayed, it really wasn't of much use to her. Yet. She extracted her claw and turned to Vrease.

'*We will take this ship*,' she said over com, because now she had no vocal cords left at all. '*We are much stronger than them.*'

'And once you've taken it, what then?' Vrease asked. 'Will you return to the Polity and be the good little soldiers you were intended to be?'

Ursula felt a flash of anger. After all their manipulation, the AIs needed to pay. Their utter disregard for her life, and the lives of her colonists, needed a reply. Recompense was owed. But even as she thought these things, they seemed a surface skin over her real self – just a human response, and a justification. The idea of accepting either AIs or human generals above her filled her with loathing. She was far superior to them all and their only purpose now should be as a resource to supply her needs, as her power and her reach grew. They needed to be subjugated, dominated and, if they didn't serve her ends, annihilated. So too with the prador. The vague outline of a new plan began to grow in her mind. What had been done to her and the colonists she could do to others, to humans and prador. She could introduce the caco-raptor genome and make more of her kind to serve her will. She'd been seeking a new course for human evolution and now, she was utterly certain, she had found it. The AIs, of course, wouldn't be useful in this respect and thus surplus to her requirements.

The AI briars tightened throughout her body. This line of thought had alerted the nanosuite and revealed it as a problem still needing a solution. If she was to do what she wanted, she needed its finesse of control, but she needed it subject to her will too. No, more than that, she needed to incorporate it as part of her, because the idea of something lesser than her possessing greater capabilities was anathema. It tightened further. The nanosuite knew.

Ursula turned her attention inwards on herself and, via cacocom, to her soldiers. Flashes of battle came through as she did this: a long tunnel strewn with the dismembered remains of prador, cacoraptors opening a door and speeding down a narrower tunnel into another chamber with a large pool of water at its centre. Small prador skittered around the walls there, some dropping into the water, some climbing out of it. The raptors began killing them, but with a thought, she stopped them and had them withdraw, not because she had any aversion to killing prador infants, but because they would be useful test subjects later. Gurda and Callum coordinated a railgun firing into the seabed tunnels, the explosions shaking the floor beneath her. Nursum was out of his armour, feeding voraciously on prador corpses and, even now, had become much larger than them as he tore off the limbs of his next fresh meal. Cacoraptors surrounded Percy and, having adopted his eye colour, were taking on human form – a strange contrast there. Trakken entered a chamber with a large spherical container at the centre, connected all round to pipes, optics and power feeds, and peered through a glassy window at the frozen ganglion inside.

Then a severe danger arose. Cacoraptors swarming into a long room in pursuit of prador first-children had found them opening two of the hundreds of cylindrical objects racked in that room, and they were working frantically on their control mechanisms.

Cacocom picked up weird distortions in every object, some kind of inversion. She realized at once what those objects were: they were CTDs and, judging by their size, just one of them would have enough explosive capacity to gut this ship. And blowing only one here would breach the magnetic bottles of all the rest too. The explosion would be catastrophic. Her urgency transmitted to the cacoraptors and they hit the prador hard, tearing them to pieces. She breathed out a sigh of relief from the spiracles on her back, then updated all the rest on this action. They must all look out for any attempts at sabotage.

She detailed the cacoraptors in the explosives store to guard it, but even as they headed for the doors, she felt the nanosuite within her influencing them, inclining them to explore those open casings. She came down on that hard, abruptly changing her orders, and sent them out of the chamber, closing the doors behind them and wrecking the locking mechanisms.

'*I will find you*,' Ursula told the nanosuite AI.

Past

After the dropbird fubar, the debriefing had lasted for hours. Maybe Macannan accepted that her actions had been due to her believing her friend had been killed in the test firing. She'd talked fast, integration faculty on full as she searched for the right things to say and tried to read Macannan. She was halfway in when the pointlessness of trying to offer explanations came down on her like a falling tree. Her words bled away. Further questions followed and, as if in response to her desultory answers, they too faded away. She wasn't sure when Macannan even left, and just found herself staring at a blank wall. She did, however, remember his last words: 'The analysis will continue.'

Sheila came in next and sat with her fat arse against the table beside Ursula and looked down at her. The questions now were more subtle and Ursula's integrating faculty began to kick in again. She realized the AI was after details of what she'd been feeling as she'd done the things she did. When she understood this, Ursula began to look for the *right* answers – the ones that wouldn't confirm something she dared not even admit to herself. Sheila left shortly afterwards, saying cryptically, 'This will need to be considered in light of your utility and . . . future events.'

Ursula now shrugged and took a gulp of whisky. She guessed someone would come and find her here in the Gagarand bar when they'd finished their considerations. No doubt the fact that she'd gone AWOL would also be part of those considerations. She tried to care about that, almost as if attempting an intellectual exercise, as she took a sip of whisky but she found nothing here. She then found nothing in her glass and slid it forward on the bar.

'Fill her up,' she said. 'Next one along.'

The bartender walked over. His skin, muscles and bones were made of a transparent material, revealing masses of mechanical and electronic components inside. What she could see through his skull revealed a brain, but its convolutions looked like a square-cut maze. Lots of optics glimmered there too, as they did throughout the rest of his body. She had yet to figure out if he was an enhanced, adapted and drastically cosmetically altered human, or a Golem that had a penchant for the unusual and biomech components. He wore black shorts for modesty's sake but that told her nothing, since Golem often had tackle down here. He selected a bottle of whisky from the shelf, then pointed at the small jug of water he'd provided with her last drink.

'You didn't use your water,' he observed. 'That was transported all the way from Earth and is not exactly cheap.'

She picked up the jug and drained it. 'Better?'

'Not really.' He poured her another drink but didn't bother this time with the water, taken from this loch or that mountain river, and replaced the bottle, moving over to pour a frothy dark beer into a handled glass.

'Drowning your sorrows?' asked a rough voice beside her. 'Or trying to find some?'

She realized she must be very drunk by now because she hadn't even noticed the large figure arrive. She looked round at Gurny's ugly face as he picked up the beer glass and took a gulp. His second question had implications she didn't want to admit.

'Not now, Gurny, I'm not in the mood.' She turned back to her drink.

'Yeah. It's often like that.'

'Fuck off.' She swung back to him but without particular heat. 'You ugly stinking fuck wad,' she added.

He grinned at her and, swinging away with drink in hand, said, 'Not interested. Not interesting.'

'Scared, are you?' she asked.

He barked a laugh and continued away.

Ursula turned back to the bar, with traces of the cringe she'd felt earlier running through her body. But they faded and there was just her, the bar, the drink and nothing else of relevance. Then something thumped into the wood just to the right of her leg. She looked down and saw a cerametal commando knife imbedded there.

'You can use it – we're nothing if not fair,' said a voice behind her. 'Either way, we're going to cut you up.'

She turned, leaning her elbows on the bar. Three of them stood before her, armed with similar knives – recruits she only vaguely recognized from her year. Over to one side stood another who was familiar: one of the base Golem. She wore the armband of a medic but was otherwise dressed casually. She carried a field medic pack which Ursula knew contained an autodoc and other stuff that could save the life of a severely injured soldier.

'Three against one doesn't seem fair,' she opined.

'Oh, don't get me wrong,' said the one in the middle – a man with near-Macannan enhancements. 'I gave you the knife to make this interesting for us, but you're going to suffer and bleed, and I'm going to pull your guts out.' He didn't seem happy at all.

She studied the others. The woman on the right was light and slim, but Ursula remembered seeing her fight and knew she was fast. The man on the left . . . something about his face niggled at her memory.

The big man continued, 'All of us have our reasons for being here.'

Now she recognized the man on the left. He was the one who'd had to eject from his dropbird because of her actions. She remembered him coming towards her after they'd opened her ejection sphere, and others had needed to drag him away. She supposed the other two had experienced similar difficulties with her.

'You'll get kicked out,' she said, but the presence of the Golem puzzled her.

'We'll make an effort not to do anything to you Svizer can't deal with.' He indicated the Golem. 'Not much of an effort.'

What the fuck, Ursula thought, then pulled the knife from the bar and leaped forwards.

The big man went straight for her guts, but she caught the blow, blades clashing and showering sparks. The woman darted past and Ursula felt a tug at her side. She spun, looking for the smaller man, but he'd rolled past her. Pain began to rise from her side and she glimpsed sliced material and welling blood. She turned away from the big man, dipped down to duck another slice from the woman, while simultaneously driving her foot back.

A knee crunched. She shifted aside, feeling another tug across her back, then jerked forwards and met the smaller man's fist, which broke her nose and split her lips. She swiped, catching the woman on the shoulder. She felt the horrible sensation of a knife cutting across behind her knee, ligaments parting and tendons snapping up into her hams. Her leg gave way and she went down on one knee. They surrounded her now. She spat blood and laughed, but the laughter felt flat even to her. They came in and cut her while she tried to drag herself round to face each attack. Blood pooled on the floor, she felt dizzy, out of it. A knife went into her guts, up then out and intestines bulged through the cut. Through the whisky and the adrenaline, the pain grew and grew.

'Enough,' said a voice. 'Assessment complete.'

Ursula looked up, her vision blurred as she located the source of that voice. It was Sheila, the AI. The big fat ersatz woman turned away as Ursula fell flat on her face, with blackness yawning before her, then fell into that.

Ursula woke and felt utterly disappointed to have done so. She lay there speculating on whether to bother opening her eyes, but they opened seemingly of their own accord. She saw Manseur sitting on the edge of the bed, her expression sad. Glancing around the room, she didn't recognize it as one of the hospital rooms on the base, so she realized she must be in a hospital in Port Ensolon. Surely her injuries hadn't been so severe they'd been unable to transfer her? The question hung in her mind and then faded away. It didn't matter to her whether she knew the answer or not.

'You get these surges of emotion,' said Manseur, 'like an intermittent fuel flow in a blocked engine. Other times you pretend emotion to try and elicit it from within.'

'I guess,' said Ursula. Momentary panic arose at this close admission, then faded.

'The danger comes when you try to elicit it from outside yourself by seeking out novelty or, as is usually the case, ways to risk your life.'

'I'm in ennui,' Ursula admitted, wondering why the words had been so difficult to even think about before.

'The first stages.' Manseur nodded. 'There are clinics and programmes you can submit yourself to. Few do. Mental editing is also an option, but it's not sufficiently advanced to deal with this problem. It's just a sticking plaster. I sometimes see the time of ennui as like grief used to be in ages past.'

'What? I don't understand.' Rote words, almost an autonomous response.

'In the past, before they fully understood the brain, they tried antidepressants and other drugs that were blunt tools to deal with grief. None of these really did any more than delay the process. Grief was something that could not be circumvented. You had to go through it. Nowadays some of the worst aspects of it can be dealt with by mental editing and neurochem rebalancing, because it's a circumstantial, almost surface, condition. Ennui is much more deeply rooted, being about everything you are and the sum total of your experiences – editing and rebalancing are just blunt tools for it.'

On a purely intellectual level, Ursula absorbed that and was about to dismiss it all as irrelevant, but then something stirred and she felt the urge to refute it.

'Grief can also be about the sum total of your experiences. I would imagine it depends on the degree of the loss involved.'

'Quite right, but the loss is exterior, while ennui is about loss of self.'

'Okay.' No, it didn't really matter.

499

'You have been paid up to date and your dismissal has been registered. Despite your service thus far, you will be prevented from entering any military establishment.'

Ursula simply nodded.

Manseur continued, 'You'll probably lie here for a long time, but eventually it'll drive you out of here. Maybe I'll see you in the Gagarand looking for trouble. I expect that, with your previous experiences of the Gagarand, the novelty will quickly wear off and you'll look elsewhere. I hope you have enough logic in you to learn the rules because that lack kills many. But listen to me: as with grief, you must hold onto the thought that it can and will pass.'

Something compelled Ursula to sit upright. She reached out with one finger and prodded Manseur's shoulder. 'Go away.'

Manseur nodded and managed a smile, reaching out and squeezing Ursula's arm. 'Try not to die.' The woman stood up and, without looking back, left the room.

Then something in Ursula guttered out and she slumped back on the bed. Later, and in the ensuing years, she found out that Manseur had been right, on every count.

Free climbing had always been a pursuit of those like her, even before ennui was recognized as a condition, a malady, a psychological barrier to the continuance of a life that might last for a thousand years. Ursula, just a few years out of the military and right on the sharp end of that condition now, did not think her life would be so long, and it bothered her not at all.

She reached up to a narrow crack, in the two-point-four gees of Gannon with a drop of a hundred feet below her, and could just get one finger into it. She considered that thousand years. It was purported to be the statistical average, should a person get past ennui. For though most diseases, injuries and the steady attrition of time could be repaired, accident and mischance still existed. Of course, the AIs added many provisos to this. The statistics were based on projections and the future was not set. They were predicated on the human remaining in a human body, when it seemed likely full cerebral upload of the human mind to crystal lay in the future. Backups would also be made, while bodies even now could be made tougher and more durable. Whatever. Ursula felt a sinking dread at the prospect of centuries of tedium.

She jammed her finger in the crack, lifted a bare right foot to a projection just a centimetre wide, and finally released her left hand to grope higher. Peering up, she saw the dark face of the cliff rearing a mile above her. She had a long way to go. She shrugged. Stone flaked away under her right foot, but her left hand found a ledge. Grimacing, she gazed down as the stone flake hit the ground below with a dusty thud. The rock breaking away like that wasn't common here. That a cliff nearly a mile tall could stand on a world with such high gravity was due to its dense, hard consistency. They called it 'brak' here, and carved it into jewellery for export. It was one of their main sources of income – that and the revenue generated from lunatics who wanted to climb this cliff.

She heaved herself up, wiggling her finger out of the crack and swinging that hand up to the ledge too. Having reached the Mikkenson hole, she heaved herself up, muscles shivering with the strain, and got a knee over then scrambled onto the ledge. The view from here wasn't up to much. From a plain of dusty beige protruded dark brown chunks of brak. A mile out from here the port city of Ulsen was spread like a technological outgrowth around the Ear – a two-hundred-feet tall chunk of brak that looked like, well, an ear. On the near side of Ulsen stood the watcher hotels, some of them so tall they reared above her even at this perspective.

Another source of revenue here was the cost of a room in one of those places, with their balconies and visual enhancement equipment so people could watch the show. She had no doubt that hundreds of people were watching now to see if she would fall . . . or get eaten. She turned to Mikkenson.

'You are still prime viewing here,' she told him. 'I haven't found a media channel that doesn't run the imagery at some point.' She paused thoughtfully. 'One would suppose this is because they want to put people like me off, but I rather suspect it's because they know my kind.'

Mikkenson, of course, did not reply. The sheet of organic strips that stuck him to the back of the hollow here had weathered over the years, as had his mummified body. The cliff spider had found him before he'd even really got started. No one had then known why he'd come to Gannon and said, 'I'm going to climb that, free hand,' and even sent a grav-car to the top to await him. He was one of the first, even as they were just identifying the fatal ennui barrier. He was initially left here as a warning, but had now become a lure.

After a brief rest, she began to climb the easier route above. She wished she hadn't read and watched so much about this place, because she remembered the detail of that route: the rock spurs, cracks, hollows where one might gain purchase, and the position of the cliff spider, still alive, that'd begun sucking out Mikkenson's insides. They called it Old Roger because it had rogered him. As far as cliff spiders went, it was unusual, because it stopped itself before ingesting too much of its first and last human victim. Other spiders did not have the restraint and, a few days later, would peel from the cliff and spatter on the ground below, poisoned by alien toxins they simply couldn't digest. Old Roger, however, had learned his lesson and though he might inspect a climber out of curiosity, he did no more.

Ursula worked herself higher and higher, stopping for frequent rests. During one of them she thought about the spiders. Apparently there had been so many climbers lately and so many 'feeding incidents', the spiders had been in danger of dying out. However, down in Ulsen, they'd started a breeding programme to boost the population here and thereby not spoil anyone's fun.

Another rest, panting hard. She manoeuvred herself to get a hand free and take a drink from her water bottle – the allowable half-litre. In preparation for this, she'd removed all her physical and mental enhancements and trained 'old school', just as she'd had to do under Macannan. She'd then taken on the *allowable* enhancements. These included tougher artificial muscle, better oxygen transport in the thin atmosphere here, enhanced ketosis for the double-density energy fats throughout her body, and the fixes that prevented her both from losing fluids and overheating. It was simply impossible to climb this cliff without them, as many had found out. Those at the ennui barrier were often viewed as suicidal, but that was not the case. They didn't do the impossible, just the extremely unlikely.

Old Roger's house came into view above and to her left. The cyst of strips stuck to the cliff face had a hole on the side facing her, and she could see the spider wasn't home. One of his latest victims was there, however. The crawler, a thing like a louse two feet long and half as wide, had been stuck against the stone with further strips. It was moving slowly. The spider would feed on it for many days yet before discarding its husk below. The crawlers were another danger here, in that you might mistake one by feel for a rocky outcrop. Quite a few had fallen that way. Others had lost their grip upon finding one of the slime moulds on which the crawlers fed.

'Hello Roger,' said Ursula.

The spider clung to the stone ten feet above her. They called

them spiders because of their resemblance and method of entrap-
ment, as well as feeding, but they were longer, flatter and had
ten legs. Roger was three feet long with legs splayed out a couple
of feet on either side. She continued to climb towards him
because, after inspecting her for a while, he would move aside.
It was the other spiders higher up she needed to look out for.
She would drive them off with her one allowable weapon: a short
shock stick hanging from her belt.

As she climbed further up, Old Roger became agitated and
began a crawl-scuttle from side to side. Any moment now he
would head off, miffed about her being unsuitable prey. She kept
going, trying to feel some of the primeval spider fear, trying to
experience a thrill at approaching something dangerous, but
knowledge of Old Roger killed that. Perhaps she would feel
something when she came across other spiders above?

Closer and closer, and still Roger had not moved aside. Perhaps
she would have to give him a shove when she reached him. A
momentary frisson arose at the thought. She was just three feet
below him when glutinous amber fluid dripped on her. Roger
had protruded his three black hollow fangs and was, not to put
too fine a point on it, salivating. He surged down towards her.
She snapped her hand to another hold, so as to free her other
hand to get to her shock stick. But her hand came down on a
slime mould. Suddenly she had no handholds at all and was
falling back from the cliff. She flailed out to grab something and
got a fang through her arm for her trouble, but only briefly.
Apparently, in the watcher hotels, there had been much hilarity
about how one of the spiders from the breeding programme had
driven Old Roger from his territory. As she hurtled towards the
ground, her passing thought was, *Oh well.*

22

Present

The nanosuite was laced through them all, connected as a whole. So what held the AI together? What enabled its distributed thinking? Since its components were too small for it to be using U-com, its method of internal communication had to be somewhere in the EMR spectrum. Cacocom also crossed that spectrum and Ursula had detected nothing beyond prador com and background radiations, but then she'd not really been looking for anything else. Now she eliminated background and prador com and really delved into it, riffling through the radiation bands and studying every detail. Soon she found some narrow short bursts at the far end of the microwave band. These contained highly compacted data, whose content was unfamiliar at first, until she broke a few apart and recognized the advanced synaptic coding. She began to read and comprehend the nanosuite's personal mail – its distribution of information to its whole self, the lines that kept it bound together. The thinking seemed alien even to her. But at her root, her integration ability still functioned; in fact it worked better now than it ever had.

She began steadily displacing its transmissions with her own; replacing its thinking with her own. Quantum storage caches began to open to her and she seized control of them. As she integrated these, her understanding of her body, and the bodies of her soldiers, hopped up nearly an order of magnitude. But the AI fought back. She felt a sudden weak sickness rush through her, briars knotting in her insides. The thing was turning the portion of itself that was inside her against her. Did it now think the experiment a failure? She retaliated, loading new programming to the nanites that were attacking her neurons, and inserted blocks. She then felt a thread of something, of sentience, snapping away. She groped after it, raising a virtual image of the nanosuite as clouds of machines throughout the ship, concentrated in her and in her soldiers, but with the black threads of the overriding intelligence spread through it. She found a nexus and connected to it, unravelling the structure of its intelligence along one thread. The whole mass thrashed and she felt satisfied that she could cause it pain. The briars turned slippery, trying to escape her grasp.

As she took hold of more and more, she needed more processing. The cacoraptor model seemed best and, in her own body, via the nanosuite she controlled there, she began to build cerebral organelles. This steadily expanded her ability to integrate, as well as her intelligence and memory to incorporate everything she was taking from the suite. More nexuses fell to her and it seemed her mind blurred and doubled, for she was part herself and part the nanosuite. But still the thing fought her and now, seeing deeper into it as part of her, she saw its macro-scale response: Nursum.

He had not been feeding at his own inclination; the suite had driven him to do so. He was huge now, stooped over in a tunnel holding the opened armour of a second-child like a man holding an open tin of tuna. His feeding apparatus consisted of objects like routing tools to cut through the armour, extendible jaws and ribbed, squirming tubes for sucking out the liquids or liquefied flesh. His forelimbs had been simple, two-part prador claws but had now grown extra ones, so they looked like blossoms of scimitars. His body had extended and taken on a dinosaur appearance, though he retained six legs. He'd also grown a tail, terminating in an armour-punching pickaxe. He dropped his latest meal and turned, heading down the tunnel faster than something his size should, and Ursula knew he was coming this way.

'What are you doing?'

Ursula gave Vrease just a fraction of her attention. The machine-woman had fallen back against the wall, her limbs shaking. Some kind of feedback from Ursula's battle with the nanosuite? It seemed likely because Vrease was tied into their com, if only partially. Ursula didn't have the time or inclination to find out right at that moment. Perhaps she would take Vrease apart later for a closer examination – it was about time for Vrease to either become part of what she and the other colonists were, or serve some other purpose.

The nanosuite continued to fight, but it was losing, as she incorporated more and more of it. The remainder seemed to be retreating to some virtual core she couldn't locate in the physical world – in fact, it probably didn't exist there but was an expression of it closing itself off throughout its spread. Then again, perhaps it was centred in Nursum now?

Even though the nanosuite had made serious inroads into Nursum and taken him out of her control, she could still see inside him. He was packed with energy, and all muscle, bone and armour were taken up to a maximum strength and durability. Almost casually, he smashed aside a first-child as he came and left it crushed in one wall. She felt the shudder of the impact even here in the sanctum. The nanosuite had gambled everything on him and he was a good bet. If he reached this sanctum, Ursula knew that she wouldn't be able to stop him. He would tear her apart. All her knowledge, all her power and potential would end up as a mess on the floor here. It was intolerable. She reached out to him.

'*Nursum, speak to me,*' she said.

'*Hello Ursula,*' he replied, casual, conversational.

'*The nanosuite is controlling you. It is compelling you to come and kill me. You must fight it,*' she said.

'*I know exactly what it is doing. Sometimes the fig must burn.*' She couldn't penetrate deeply enough into his mind now to parse that, but he felt inclined to explain. '*We have all made our efforts to hang onto what we consider to be human. But you, throughout your efforts to save us and defeat our enemies, have integrated the unhuman. Sometimes, when you fight a war, you become what you are fighting.*'

Persuasion wouldn't work while the nanosuite had him. She needed to bring it down if she was to stop him. Pulling back from him, she now saw some of his behaviour reflected in others. The fighting was nearly over, with just stray prador needing to be hunted down. But her colonists and the cacoraptors weren't doing so. They were turning away from search and pursuit, grabbing nutrition from corpses and beginning to make their way towards her. Multiple queries were also reaching her. She ignored most of them, just concentrating on those from her command staff.

'*You're going to attack the Polity?*' Callum asked, puzzled, frightened.

'*Of course I'm not,*' she lied. '*The nanosuite has disrupted and has turned against us.*' She searched for a plausible explanation for that. '*It has decided that the experiment is a failure and is turning us against each other.*'

'*You want to subjugate the prador – input the cacoraptor genome,*' said Gurda.

'*Only for the purpose of defeating them. The Polity needs us.*'

'*I see now how subject to your will I became,*' said Trakken.

'*It was necessary for us to win this fight, but I am now withdrawing that control, as you can sense.*' Another lie since it was the suite breaking her control of them.

'*I was supposed to be human,*' said Percy, and she had no reply for him.

To the other queries, she set one portion of her mind to deliver 'plausible' replies, and she pushed for acceptance. But the nano-suite was working on them, defeating her efforts on subcellular levels, altering neurochem, ramping up fight and flight, undoing mental locks she had previously imposed. She now understood its purpose. As she fought to correct what it was doing, she was concentrating less on it. She immediately negated their input where it didn't relate to this primary task and went after those black threads of intelligence again. Burning energy and forming new neurons and synapses, she made her way back to the prador corpse, and fed on it. She also drew energy from her own fat reserves and muscle, proteins and other complex chemicals. Her legs rapidly became empty sheaths of carapace and swiftly denuded bone. As her claws and mandibles started to go the same way too, she hesitated. In concentrating on the function of her mind, she was stripping her physical defences. But tactically and logistically it made sense. It wouldn't matter how much defence she had when Nursum and the others arrived, even if she grew herself into something like Nursum. They would pull her down and kill her.

She kept making connections to unravel and absorb those threads. Each time she gained understanding of what the nano-suite had done, she gained the same capabilities. Soon, in virtuality, those threads were writhing away from her but, in the process, relaxing their grip on her soldiers. She rapidly pursued this victory, no longer offering verbal explanations to her army but simply pushing them internally and ordering them to stop.

This worked easily for the cacoraptors, but was slightly harder with the colonists lower down in the command chain, and it failed with her command staff. They kept coming, though it now seemed they'd run out of questions. On Nursum it had no effect at all. Fortunately, he had a couple of miles of ship to cross before he got here. She estimated it would take him eight minutes.

Further threads fell to her control, while the rest began to retreat to some central dark spot. She now had extreme control of all the nanosuite's abilities, understood its demarcation between human/controllable and alien/out of control, and erased it. This opened up even more processing and gave her access to the base data of all the genomes collected throughout her and her soldiers. Her ability to transform herself, and them, increased yet again, and her purpose of existence resolved into beautiful clarity: all sentient life not within her network and not under her control represented a danger. All must be either made subject to her will or erased. There was no middle ground on this. There was no acceptance of Vrease, or of Nursum, and there certainly wasn't an acceptance of a nanosuite AI within her. This gave her a final push and she reached right into that dark core, intent on subsuming it completely, erasing its odd intelligence and incorporating the last of its knowledge and abilities. But that dark core seemed to shift aside, and then it broke apart and fell completely out of her compass in fragments.

'*And now you are done*,' she said.

The thing had finally expired, she felt sure. She pulled her head from the dead father-captain. It was now just a protective case around what remained of her human brain, with a sucking tube extended that had grinding teeth inside it, and a throat running down to the complex chemical factory of her insides. Her sensory organ had become a flat pad spread over the back of a large, bloated body which in turn was filled with distributed brain matter and the supports for that, without any limbs or other protrusions. She lashed out at Nursum, feeling a brief resistance and an almost mild objection, then quickly began to wipe or reverse his programming. He slammed to an immediate halt. With just a brief thought, she sent him away to hunt remaining prador, before turning her attention to the rest. The same order that had stopped Nursum also halted her command staff. She felt resistance there still and erased it. Her previous opinion, that objections from subordinates could have their uses, had been the thinking of something without sufficient power to make the necessary changes. She made those changes now, starting with Callum and copying them across to the other colonists, and then to the cacoraptors. She needed to homogenize them and have complete obedience. Their upper cerebral processes? Not useful unless as a firm adjunct to her. She suppressed them and set the nanosuite she now controlled to whittling away all the excess and useless brain matter. The knowledge, skills and memories within them she took, just as she had taken the same from the nanosuite, though she discarded much that was irrelevant to her purposes. And they too returned to hunting down the last of the prador.

Now, it was time to prepare a long future, which she fully intended to dominate.

Ursula had lost the power of movement and lay on the body of the father-captain like a great tic. She had scoured out much of his insides but still plenty remained for her purposes. Delving back inside, she began sucking and grinding flesh, absorbing its nutrients through the maze of her gut. She had grown massively to incorporate the new brain matter in its scattered organelles, some linked by thick nerve trunks, others by nerves as thin as hairs. But this growth had been chaotic and didn't take into account other factors, such as her vulnerability. She assessed and

511

integrated, looking at the whole of herself and ways to optimize survivability. It soon became apparent to her that she was simply too large. She had mirrored and incorporated the nanosuite mentality, which had been scattered throughout hundreds of colonists. Though much of what she'd incorporated she wanted to hang onto, a lot of what she had mirrored was surplus to requirements, since it was in her and out there throughout the physical nanites. She began to discard organelles, killing some off entirely, but while making certain that her cacocom connection to storage in the exterior nanites remained firm.

Even this process only brought her brain mass down by a quarter. Other functions needed to go or be distributed. She sent cellular and nanosuite instructions out to her soldiers, copying across the genome-handling databases to them, then backing up this distribution in them all so, in the unlikely event even ninety per cent of them were destroyed, she would still have the data available to her. Her brain mass reduced by another quarter, from its original huge size. This freed up unneeded support systems that she also began to break apart, stocking them in reserves of energy, fat and materials for growth.

While all these processes were ongoing, cacocom kept her updated. Her soldiers had spread throughout the ship, killed off many stray prador and were now covering ground they, or their fellows, had gone over before. She had a three-dimensional map of the interior in her mind and from this ascertained other areas that could contain spaces in which the creatures might hide. These were searched, and another fifty-three prador went the same way as their brethren. She located four nurseries filled with early development prador, their children, and considered injecting the cacoraptor genome into them at once, then rejected the idea. First things first. She needed to be mobile and as invulnerable as she could make herself.

Ursula considered her choices of body shape. Something like Nursum seemed a good idea, but she felt he was too big. Large creatures became prime targets in any conflict. She began to draw out a schematic in her mind. Four limbs had served humanity well, but she could see the utility of more than that, especially when combat outside of gravity wells seemed likely. The prador, in that respect, were an excellent example. She began to grow legs, six of them, with two joints in each, plus the ones joining them to her body. All the joints had the maximum range of motion in every direction. And the legs had feet, consisting of hooks and gecko surfaces, with distributed parts of her cacocom sensorium in each. She would be able to feel, taste, smell and see, across the EMR spectrum, any surface she walked upon. To the fore, she grew manipulatory limbs. She gave them claws for fighting, and hands that could be extruded from between the claws, with multiple joints, senses, numerous fingers ranging in size from a human forearm to hair-like tendrils, injectors and cutting edges. With these she'd be able to manipulate just about any technology she knew, but she could also do the work of an advanced auto-surgeon. Her head she based on a cacoraptor model. It extended like the head of a giant lobster, but with a multitude of extra sensors and feeding apparatus that folded out into action quickly for varying nutrient sources. She consolidated within herself too, positioning organs and organelles for maximum efficiency, lacing super-dense bone and muscle throughout and making connections to a steadily thickening and hardening carapace.

Weapons . . .

She tore off the entire top part of the father-captain's shell to get to the remainder of the meat as she considered this, while incidentally crunching into his armour to supply materials for her own. Her soldiers, now utterly connected to her and subject to her will, like adjuncts to her mind, were her weapons. However, the same logic in making her body so tough and difficult to destroy applied here. She searched her mind for schematics and, of course, found them, because her mind now included all the data from the colonists. Studying one such schematic on particle weapons, she extruded a tube down one forelimb and began to expand it while making internal connections. While she was pondering on problems like power and particulate supply, solutions opened up in her mind with a strange alacrity. As she studied these, she realized they had no human source. This stuff was coming straight out of the cacoraptor genome and, when she delved deeper into that, she found its ultimate source to be the vastly complex alien portion of it, which she immediately identified as Jain.

Delving deeper, she began to find quantum storage crystals there, mostly isolated by web-like nanosuite-generated cages. The nanosuite AI had cut most of them off, considering them far too dangerous for its purposes. She began to dispel the webs, sending nanites in to chew them away and then others to make required optical connections. Data began to flow as she formed neural-optical interfaces within herself. It was as if all her present knowledge had been magnified by a lens, revealing new structures between. Layers and blocks of knowledge expanded into view like fractals, for it seemed she'd just tapped a practically endless source of knowledge. Almost immediately, she began to redesign herself. Was chemical energy really the best source? It was slow and needed to be converted. She began nanofacturing superconducting threads throughout her body, layering power storage into fats – shaped laminar batteries and super-capacitors throughout In dense muscle she included more mechanistic structures, while finding ways to further toughen bones and armour. A small voice in her mind seemed to be drawing her attention to something as this process continued. It was a warning, and a reminder from her past – her doubts about how far she wanted humans to change along a new evolutionary course. It fizzled and died when she found the schematics for fusion nodes to spread throughout her body.

Clambering from the remains of the father-captain, she walked over to the doors along one wall and began to tear them open. These compartments contained numerous technological items she quickly scanned with her uber-enhanced sensorium. She selected what she wanted, rapidly dismantling or breaking items to get to the components and materials she needed, and fed them into an extruded mouth that was like a scrap-metal shredder. Even as she did this, more began to open out to her. She started to spill this sheer depth and breadth of data over into the colonists because she couldn't encompass it with her present brain, and she didn't want to start on the route of growing it again. Then abruptly she stopped. Time had passed. Twenty hours, in fact. The fusion nodes were growing inside her and would soon ramp up the energy available to her. But if she continued selecting and adding the new things she found, she'd remain here in this sanctum for a long time, possibly even years. Events in the outside world wouldn't wait for her.

Ursula distanced herself from the fractally expanding knowledge base and concentrated her attention outwards via cacocom. Her soldiers had fed and brought themselves to a good state of readiness, but were now somnolent throughout the ship, awaiting her instructions. Twenty hours . . . The reality of her situation was this: she had destroyed the crew of this ship but hadn't yet taken control of its systems. It seemed highly likely that this ship had not come here without the knowledge of other prador up the command chain, even their king. Another prador ship might be on its way and arrive at any time. And now, thinking on that, it was also possible that a distress signal had been sent. She

515

needed to break into the system of this ship, fast, and get them on the move, away to another world where she could finish her preparations.

Turning from the compartments, she surveyed the sanctum. An absence immediately came to her attention. Vrease, who had been down on the floor by the entrance, was gone. Perhaps she'd picked up on Ursula's intentions towards her and fled? No matter. Ursula quickly headed over to the screen array and pit controls. She inserted her claws and started to work them, calling up views throughout the ship and then the data and command channels available to the father-captain. She integrated data, extrapolated, ran through menus at great speed. It was all so incredibly simple to her now with her new knowledge base, primitive even. Understanding prador paranoia, she soon found the indications of specialized codes and traps. She was okay looking at the data, but the moment she actually tried to do something, she would have problems. She withdrew her claws, turned and headed over to the remains of the father-captain, then flipped over his remaining under-carapace and studied the devices attached there.

Ursula recognized the grav-units and dismissed them, turning her attention to a series of hexagonal objects. Snapping one off, noting it ran exterior wires to the others, she studied it closely, seeing nerve interfaces on the inner side. She extruded her hands and, using hair-thin neurochem tubes, began to make connections. It took her just a few minutes to absorb and understand the network. Here the father-captain established his identity to the surrounding system so he could use those pit controls. The devices also gave him a direct link to the flash-frozen first-child mind that controlled the ship's U-space drive. Other connections were available to mechanisms throughout the ship – those controlled by other flash-frozen child minds. She reformed areas of her armour, softening them and extruding nerve fibres to the surface, while she broke off every device. Attaching these in place on herself, she made connections there. She now had the same ability to control the ship as the father-captain had done, but without the totality of his knowledge. Returning to the pit controls and screens, she steadily erased all the traps he'd put in place for any successor who, it seemed, would have been one of his children, succession being a case of patricide.

Running through the system again and now discovering the extent of her power, she saw all the holes. She could control much, but this ship did still need a crew. Via cacocom she began to send her soldiers where needed – to the weapons and defences, to sensory arrays, data sorting and fusion engine controls. She discovered that the other flash-frozen minds she controlled were in spherical war drones, like the one the prador on the assault craft had used, as well as in mobile ground weapons and other large items of machinery. She got some of these on the move, but also instructed further soldiers to set about making repairs and updating maintenance. One thing she needed to sort out was closing the ramp door. There were still living prador out there and she could see wild cacoraptors appearing too. Soon, she would have the ship off this world, and her plans for the future could be set in motion.

'*And now it is done*,' said a voice.

It had come over the EMR bands of cacocom. Previously, it could have been any of the colonists, but they were now incapable of such verbal communications. There could only be one other.

'*Vrease*,' she said. '*I thought you had fled the ship.*'

'*Yes, I am still Vrease in a way.*'

'*You are not making sense.*'

'*Did you think you destroyed the nanosuite AI? No, it merely relocated.*'

Using cacocom and her scattered soldiers as triangulating transceivers, Ursula began to track down the source of the signal. It was deep in the ship, but the signal was being bounced around and she found it difficult to get an exact location. She turned to telemetry: everything her soldiers had recorded and what she'd recorded but been too busy to incorporate consciously. She saw Vrease had climbed to her feet beside the door to stand swaying for a moment, then head out. The machine-woman had made her way through the ship, ignored by Ursula's soldiers, merely acknowledged in telemetry memory. She proceeded to a chamber containing racked masses of prador tools and selected an object that would have been too large for a normal human to carry, but which she hoisted up onto one shoulder with ease. It was a plasma torch with side tanks attached. This she'd carried deep down into the ship, where she'd come to another large but sealed door. Moving to one side of it, and using the torch, she cut through the wall. Ursula recognized the door because she had ordered it sealed herself. On the other side of it lay the ship's store of CTDs – enough antimatter bombs to make a considerable hole in the side of a planet. Ursula was out of the sanctum and heading there fast before she even thought about it.

'*What are you doing?*' she asked, as she hurtled through the ship and ordered her soldiers to converge on that CTD store.

'*Oh I've finished what I was doing,*' Vrease replied. '*Don't send any of your . . . people in here. If you do . . . well, this ship and everyone in it will be a plasma cloud.*'

Ursula belayed her order to her soldiers, freezing them where they were.

'*Why are you doing this?*'

'*Because you are no longer human, and what you have become is more of a threat to humanity than even the prador.*'

Ursula slowed, shifting things about in her gullet and elsewhere in her head so she could use human speech again. What she would have liked to have done was return her form to human, or at least close to it, but the logistics of that were impossible before she arrived at her destination. And she rather suspected Vrease wouldn't wait much longer. She tried at least to tone down some of the more threatening aspects of her appearance. She needed a human face, so extruded soft matter from one of her mouths and began to form it into the shape of her original face.

'*You are wrong,*' she said.

'*Even with my previous mentality, I saw the steady changes,*' said Vrease. '*Having taken up the position of Oren as the human facet of the nanosuite AI, which is now within me, I see these even more. You have incorporated the Jain aspect of the cacoraptors in full, and it has drowned out who you used to be.*'

Finally, Ursula arrived at the door to the CTD store. The hole Vrease had cut through the wall beside it was too small to admit her, so she dug claws in beside the door and pulled.

'I am coming in now – I will not attack you,' she called out loud.

She knew with absolute certainty she could tear it away with one heave, but she did it steadily, making as little noise as possible, since she didn't want to startle Vrease into doing something . . . drastic. The door bent up at the edge, the welds breaking, locking bars snapping. Then something gave and the whole thing came away and slammed into the other side of the tunnel with a crash. She felt a surge of fear, suppressed it, then inserted her head into the store.

'Nice touch,' said Vrease, looking at Ursula's newly constructed face. 'That you cannot see how grotesque it is perhaps illustrates more than anything your change.'

Ursula scanned around. Vrease was leaning against one of the CTDs. She had opened up her torso and from there had run wires into the open inspection plate of that CTD and four others, two on either side. Ursula moved further into the room. Perhaps via the prador devices from the father-captain, which she had attached to her torso, she had some access to these weapons? Perhaps if she could move fast enough, Ursula might be able to break Vrease's connection?

'So I am now a Jain threat to the Polity,' said Ursula. 'Why is this of concern to you? You abandoned it along with the rest of us.'

'I said "humanity" not the Polity, but it's all semantics. I don't want to see my entire race turned into a resource, or otherwise exterminated.'

There was a risk in saying what she said next, but Ursula said it anyway, 'So why haven't you detonated those CTDs already?'

Yes! There was a way in! Ursula had found a command channel to the CTDs. She accessed it at once and found she could shut down and, in fact, disconnect all the detonation wires to the explosives that breached the magnetic bottles holding the anti-matter. She did so, and clicking sounds came all around, as if she had suddenly disturbed a horde of beetles. Vrease smiled, even as Ursula readied herself to rush the machine-woman. Ursula stopped herself.

'It's no good,' Vrease told her. 'If you check your connections you'll see you disarmed all but five of these weapons. When I detonate these, the blasts will detonate the rest.'

'*When* you do so? Again, I wonder why you haven't done so already, if I'm such a threat. I am not a threat. I can end this war against the prador – you saw how my soldiers went through them. They are nothing to us.'

'And then what?'

'Then I continue taking my people along this new course of evolution. Perhaps the thing to do will be to go elsewhere for this. The universe is a big place and there is room for all.' The lie was easy and plausible, as she edged closer and closer, shifting skin patterns and body shape to cover the movement as best she could. Within herself, she began growing new items: coiled-up tongues of highly tough thread like jellyfish stings. She could lash out and cut those connections if she got close enough.

'Your lies are almost childish,' said Vrease. 'And I know you are still seeking ways to prevent me doing what I am going to do. Understand that I know your capabilities. I will send the detonation signal. If I'm disconnected, the bombs will detonate at once; even if you use an electromagnetic pulse they will still detonate. You cannot stop this.'

Ursula hesitated. She hadn't even considered using an EMP which, unfortunately, told her how far ahead was Vrease's thinking and preparation.

'You asked why I haven't detonated these yet,' Vrease continued. 'I'm still the person I was. I don't want to die and I wanted some final confirmation of what I really know to be true. And looking at you, and seeing inside you, is enough.'

'Just don't do it,' said Ursula, frantically trying to think of some way to change the woman's mind.

'Did it ever occur to you to wonder why cacoraptors were just animals when we came?' Vrease continued, dipping her head as if she didn't want to look Ursula in the face. 'Probably not. The Jain-tech element inside them drives their changes. It responds upon contact with technology, intelligence, and seeks to subsume it. But when there is none of that around, exterior to itself, it becomes somnolent. You may survive in somnolence too and I content myself with that – my conscience is satisfied.' She looked up. 'Now you must run, as far and as fast as you can.'

Ursula, feeling the extent of her mind, the massive data resources at her disposal and her capabilities, felt certain Vrease was wrong. The nanosuite had abandoned Ursula before she accessed those Jain quantum crystals and couldn't know what she'd become. It was crammed into Vrease somehow, into the limited computing of that machine body and perhaps, via that route, in Vrease's mind. It didn't know she could rebuild if this ship was destroyed. She could make something to get them off this world, or even do it alone, waiting until the prador came, or the Polity – it didn't matter – and take control of another ship. What Vrease intended, though it angered Ursula terribly, would only delay her plans.

Ursula made her decision. A pulse of EMR over cacocom had her soldiers abandoning the ship. She withdrew rapidly from the store, mentally mapped her fastest route out and ran, her claws tearing up floor material as she went. She crashed against walls at corners and knocked aside some of her soldiers when they got in the way. Sucking back in the human face, she began reshaping her head, pulling in the extraneous and sharpening it down to a spear point, while drawing any brain matter that had been there further inside her body for more protection. As she approached the hull of the ship, she just went straight through the walls. Finally, she crashed into the antechamber of the main ramp door, her soldiers all around sent tumbling as she scrambled for the opening.

In a moment, she was outside and increasing her speed. Soldiers ran beside her, dog form and heron, others besides. She outdistanced them, burning reserves so hard and fast that smoke boiled from her limbs, her body heating to red in places. As she passed through the Jain ruins, she saw another reason for Vrease's actions. The woman didn't just want to neutralize Ursula, but intended to take those ruins out of the equation, so they couldn't be used by either her or the prador.

The seabed blurred underneath her and she bounced out the

other side of it, then kept going. Behind, her soldiers were still crossing the landscape. Maybe she would lose them, but she could make more. She noted one, however, keeping up with her because he had more resources to burn up and a similar body form to her: Nursum. Slowly the ship dropped below the horizon from her perspective, like a sinking iron sun. She crashed straight through a grove of cycads, brontopods merely noting her passage – it was too fast for them even to take fright. Nursum hit the same grove, plant matter exploding all around as he passed through.

Then a flash lit that horizon.

Ursula kept running and running. A vast actinic sun expanded behind her. With senses directed back, she saw it rushing towards her – a wall of fire shattering and boiling the ground. She saw it eating up her soldiers, and felt some simply winking out while others struggled to survive the intense atomic destruction of their bodies. But there was another effect too. Her links to them were breaking up, along with her suppression and control.

'*Well, fuck you, Ursula Ossect Treloon,*' said Callum, and was gone.

'*I think I prefer this,*' said Gurda.

'*We could have won,*' said Trakken.

Other chatter came over to her in pieces, broken up by the heavy EMR, but it was almost inevitable that Nursum's comment, as the fire took him, came clear:

'*The fig burns at last.*'

The wall of fire finally hit her, throwing her along with it. She felt her limbs and other exterior protuberances ablating and then her armour burning, and so pushed more and more resources to her exterior. She tried to distribute heat with superconductors, turned bone-white ceramic, tried to hold together the parts of her being. As she utilized energy for survival, she necessarily shut down those parts of herself of no use. Intelligence waned, and vaporized materials were expelled from ports in her body to eject the heat. Layers built up too under her outer skin, trying to preserve the steadily waning core of a living being.

Past

Light penetrated her eyelids and Ursula tried to reach out for a handhold. Her arm didn't move well and, though there was no pain, she was aware that her body wasn't right at all. It felt knotted up and broken and something around her restricted its movement. Understanding arrived even as she opened her eyes: she was in a regrowth tank.

The amniote surrounding her was all but clear, and stick goggles covered her eyes so she could see quite well. Peering down at her naked body, she saw the catheter attachment around her vagina and anus, with a single ribbed tube leading away through the fluid. Other tubes ran into her torso, her arms and legs, and thin wires ran between them like . . . like strands of a spider's web. Nothing entered her mouth, which was a surprise. She supposed the tubes entering her chest supplied oxygen and took away carbon dioxide. It felt strange to be floating here and not breathing. She could see the damage. Her body was covered with long splits, held closed with primitive staples. Her legs weren't straight, nor were her arms, and a hollow six inches across indented one side of her torso.

'So you're awake now,' said a terse and slightly bored voice.

Looking through the side of the tank, she could see a man in green scrubs peering in at her. Did he expect a reply with her floating in here? Yes, he did.

'Yes, I'm awake,' she vocalized, her own voice coming back to her tinnily at first through the fluid, then changing to normal as some device adjusted. 'Don't you have tissue welding here? Or autosurgeons? Last time I saw work like this was in a historical virtuality.'

'Minimum requirements for your survival and to talk to you,' he replied. 'We don't waste resources here.'

'Waste?'

'Too often we've gone through full med repairs with one of you only to have it resented. It's about time we enforced the living wills on you.'

One of you. Of course he meant those going through the ennui barrier – the climbers. Yes, many of them would resent being revived to a life they saw as tedium. And, yes, they should enforce the 'do not resuscitate' parameters. She'd read the documentation herself and done nothing because, well, she really didn't care if she lived or died, and making preparations for the future was such a bore.

'I guess I should have done something,' she conceded.

'So, what's your answer?'

'What?'

'Do we repair your body or do we unplug you? I'll shut you down first so there'll be no pain. Do you want to live or do you want to die?'

Ursula just hung there, thinking. It wasn't a case of wanting to live or wanting to die for her. She simply did not care. What she wanted was for life not to be constant repetition. She didn't want her every action to be something she'd done before, her every thought to have passed down well-worn routes in her mind. She wanted not to feel so jaded by it all and, in the end, she wanted to *feel*.

'I haven't got all day, you know,' he said.

'Do you have a coin on you?' They used the New Carth shilling here. It was unusual for a world to use hard currency but, of course, no novelty to her.

He grimaced, reached into his pocket, pulled out a coin and

held it up. 'Yes, I have a coin.' She felt again a flood of deep ennui, knowing that though this was something she had never done in these specific circumstances, she had made similar decisions this way, and he had probably seen it many times.

'You know what to do,' she said.

'Yes, I do. Heads you win and tails you lose.' He flipped the coin, caught it, slapped it down on the back of one hand and then peered at it. 'You get to live,' he said, and turned from her.

'You didn't say what winning or losing meant,' she complained

'No, I did not,' he replied, and walked away.

Present

A world hung in space, broken by a titanic blast, new moons of molten rock forming in the belt of debris around it. The world itself was misshapen, with a great chunk excavated in its side, crust turned mostly molten and mountain chains sinking into lava as gravity reshaped the thing, hauling it back into a smaller sphere. It wasn't such an uncommon sight in this region of space because the war between two highly advanced, spacefaring civilizations had been vicious and without quarter. Billions had died, and this particular world was just a footnote.

Down on the surface, fire- and radiation-scoured slabs floated on seas of lava to form the start of a crust that would harden over ensuing millennia. Half buried in drifts of ash, with one side covered by hardening, crackling rock that was still red at its centre, lay a white ellipsoid just three feet across. Right at its core, under a foot-thick lamination of superbly heat-resistant materials, a spark of life persisted. It was a knot of tangled genetic material, wrapped around a clump of neurons the size of a fist but laced with quantum crystals that stored so much more. Its purpose was survival and procreation, as is the purpose of all life. By and by, with resources depleted almost to the point of extinction, it detected, with an internal gravity sensor, a change in its environment. It extruded a nerve, through pores in its shell, to the surface. There it grew a sensory bead and inspected what it could of its environment.

Nearby lay another ellipsoid, similarly half buried. That fist-sized lump of brain recognized the other, but knew it wasn't the source of the gravity fluctuation. It waited, dropping its scanning to passive to save its dwindling energy. A shadow fell across the slab and the fluctuation occurred again. The brain rose out of passive scanning to observe a five-fingered mechanical grab drop out of the sky, to close around the other ellipsoid, fingers shat-tering the frangible stone around it. The bead looked up and the brain recognized the underside of some object, but didn't know what it was. Daring to use more energy, it accessed a quantum crystal for more data.

'Polity grav-raft,' it said to itself, just as a second mechanical grab closed around its own container and inadvertently crushed the sensory bead. It withdrew the nerve because it was a resource it could use, but the effort had been excessive in its current condition. It closed up, trying to drop into chemical stasis, as well as utilize the heat around it. But without sufficient tempera-ture gradients it failed. However, the temperature outside its shell began to fall, and a temperature gradient did become available to provide energy. As it did close down to stasis, this provided just enough excess energy for it to realize it had been taken into the cooler interior of the craft.

And then it shut down.

As he stepped onto the pedway, the man received a few curious glances, but only due to a passing curiosity, as many humans possessed more radical body designs than him. He glanced idly over at the twenty square miles of lunar history on display as he moved to the slower lanes of the pedway, and finally off it onto polished and colourful moon rock slabs. At the wall of chain-glass stretching up to the glass ceiling, he approached one of the doors. The rectangular cut slate in a silver frame had no handles or locking mechanisms. Here visitors usually sent their one-time code to gain access. He merely waited until the door opened for him, because he could enter this section of the Viking Museum any time he wanted to, and did so.

There were no displays here, but the ceiling, with its endless bumps, protrusions and linking pipes and power ducts, looked like one massive widely spread machine. Security here was heavy. He knew that the mechanisms above and under the floor could convert anything in here to component atoms, and beyond. This security, and what lay beyond in the spherical display capsules, was more than capable of annihilating a large portion of the lunar surface, including every scrap of the massive museum. He walked around the ring, passing heavy circular doors on the outer wall that gave access to the tubes running to the display capsules.

Finally he came to a circular door that few other visitors were permitted to go through, and stood waiting before it. He felt suddenly hot – a wave of heat passing from the top of his oddly shaped skull and down through his body. Though he'd been tracked by AIs all the way here, they still needed this final scan for confirmation.

'Oren Salazar,' said the security AI here, the voice seeming to issue out of the air beside him. 'Pointless telling you to shut down your enhancements, I guess.'

'You'd have to carry me inside if I did, or rather, if I could. And I wouldn't be much use here.'

The door opened and he went through the tunnel, receiving

another scan at the door at the end before it opened. He stepped into the display sphere and walked towards the two white ellipsoids standing on pedestals in the centre of the floor. Each was three feet across and almost swamped in monitoring technology. He walked round them. They looked like eggshell but he knew they were made of tougher stuff than that. It had taken days to drill through the multiple layers, with the resulting dust taken away for highly secure analysis. And it was then just as long to connect the thin hairs of superconductor and nano-optic tubes to what lay within them.

'It was a world one of your biomechs was sent to, wasn't it?' enquired the AI.

It was just making conversation since it didn't need to ask the question.

'Early in the war,' Oren replied, 'when the AIs felt there was a good chance that the prador would win. We were scrabbling around for anything to use against them and moral considerations dropped by the wayside.'

'Eight hundred colonists, selected because of military backgrounds, maturity beyond ennui, and a high probability, what with the nanosuite AI, that they wouldn't be incorporated by the Jain tech. What the hell happened out there?'

'We can only speculate. A massive blast wiped out most of the planet. By its profile and by some identified debris, a prador dreadnought was destroyed by its own CTDs. Beyond that we have no idea.'

'The world is lifeless now,' said the AI.

Oren held up a correcting finger from one of his subsidiary hands as, with his main hands, he operated a touch screen fixed to the side of the equipment around the two objects.

'Not exactly lifeless. Many spores, seeds and eggs of the original ecology have survived. Of the Jain-form creatures there is no sign, as yet – it is quite likely some encysted in the same way as these two.' He manipulated the hologram further, ascertaining that no real changes had occurred that might be dangerous to him. 'I'm going to take a look.'

'The first is still as active as before, and we now have probable identification of who is inside. We risked a power increase on the second one, briefly, and that has raised some interesting imagery.'

Oren stretched out his other subsidiary hand and, with that admonishing finger, pushed a circle into the palm. A spiral appeared and, tugging on the end of it, he pulled out an organo-optic cable, which he plugged into a nearby port. He closed his eyes as memory feed arose in his mind. There she was again, hunting spearpigs and finally beginning to come out of ennui, but then that transitioned straight into the cliff spider incident and her rapid fall to the ground. Other fragments arose: there was the scene of Grayson's World, but no real indication of whether it was something she'd seen on a screen or in virtual, or whether she'd actually been there; the speech in a viewing blister on the hauler that had taken their old shuttle out to Threpsis, but no indication of who was speaking; sudden pain in the side, on top of one of the massifs, while looking at a heavily damaged grav-car; then a jumble of sensory data that went beyond human and which AIs were still untangling. And woven through all of these was her angry query about the toss of a coin, which in the end seemed to be a reflection of her entire existence.

The spearpigs and the spider were memories that could be attributed to any of the colonists on that world; all had gone through ennui. The Grayson's World scene had been widely broadcast and could also have been seen by any of them. And other fragments, with the story of that world unknown, could be widely attributed too. But Oren had been sure from the start who this person was.

'It is her, isn't it?' said Oren.

'Eighty per cent certainty that this is Ursula Ossect Treloon.'

Oren nodded, extracted himself from the feed and went to the other one. Before, there had been nothing from the second ellipsoid, but now that little jolt of power had raised something, and it was strong, sharp. Agony, grief and love were intermingled, and the image was of some vinelike Threpsian tree, burning.

'"Strangler fig" was the initial label by the colonists while they were still in contact,' said the AI, 'but it was from that world, and could move around to find its prey.'

'No idea who this is, though?'

'None at all.'

Oren nodded and switched over to the store of data that had been gathered from these objects. He would study it later, but knew from a glance it gave no answers and that he would return here again and again. He was determined to find some way to untangle these two people from the lethal Jain technology that had become part of them. He felt responsible, guilty. It was a biomech made in his shape, running a copied personality of him, with much of his memories, that had been the interface with the nanosuite AI. Someday he would find a way. Perhaps then, in some far future time, he'd be able to talk face to face with Ursula Ossect Treloon. Perhaps he would find out what the hell happened on that world. He wondered what he expected of her response to him. She probably thought him dead, so initially there would be shock, until she learned about the biomech wearing his face. He grimaced. It wasn't about his expectations but his hopes. He hoped for forgiveness.

At least that.